ʌɪy
ɩ0

27·6·17

01

HOOD

EMMA DONOGHUE

HOOD

HAMISH HAMILTON · LONDON

HAMISH HAMILTON LTD

Published by the Penguin Group
Penguin Books Ltd, 27 Wrights Lane, London w8 5tz, England
Penguin Books USA Inc., 375 Hudson Street, New York, New York 10014, USA
Penguin Books Australia Ltd, Ringwood, Victoria, Australia
Penguin Books Canada Ltd, 10 Alcorn Avenue, Toronto, Ontario, Canada m4v 3b2
Penguin Books (NZ) Ltd, 182–190 Wairau Road, Auckland 10, New Zealand

Penguin Books Ltd, Registered Offices: Harmondsworth, Middlesex, England

First published 1995
1 3 5 7 9 10 8 6 4 2

Grateful acknowledgement is made to Yale University Press
for permission to quote from 'Little Red Riding Hood', from
Beginning with O, copyright © 1977 by Olga Broumas

Filmset by Datix International Limited, Bungay, Suffolk
Printed in Great Britain by Clays Ltd, St Ives plc
Set in 11/13¾ Monophoto Baskerville

A CIP catalogue record for this book is available from the British Library

ISBN 0-241-13443-9

Hood was written in Frances's hammock in Dublin, on Denis's couch and by Anne's fan in New York, under Helen's pines in Washington, beside Amy's river and Linda's pool in Vermont, but mostly in my rocking-chair in Cambridge among my second family. Warm thanks to all, as well as to my editors Kate Jones and Terry Karten, and to the best of agents, Caroline Davidson.

'S a chara mo chléibh
tá na sléibhte eadar mé 's tú

I kept
to the road, kept
the hood secret, kept what it sheathed more
secret still. I opened
it only at night, and with other women
who might be walking the same road to their
own
grandma's house, each with her basket of
gifts

Olga Broumas, 'Little Red Riding Hood'

Contents

SUNDAY   I

MONDAY   33

TUESDAY   83

WEDNESDAY   127

THURSDAY   167

FRIDAY   211

SATURDAY   261

SUNDAY

Mayday in 1980, heat sealing my fingers together. Why is it the most ordinary images that fall out, when I shuffle the memories? Two girls in a secondhand bookshop, hands sticky with sampled perfumes from an afternoon's Dublin.

Up these four storeys of shelves, time moves more slowly than outside on the quays of the dirty river. One window cuts a slab of sunlight; dust motes twitch through it. I shut my eyes and breathe in. 'Which did I put on my thumb, Cara, do you remember?'

No answer. I stretch my hand towards her over the Irish poetry shelf, as if hitching a lift. 'All I can smell is old books; you have a go. Was it sandalwood?'

Cara emerges from a cartoon, and dips to my hand. She wrinkles her nose, which has always reminded me of an 'is less than' sign in algebra.

'Not nice?' I ask.

'Dunno, Pen. Something liquorishy.' Her eyes drift back to the page.

'I hate liquorice.' All I can make out now is vile strawberry on the wrist. I offer my thumb for Cara to smell again, but she has edged down a shelf to Theology. My arm moves in her wake and topples a pyramid of *Surprising Summer Salads*.

I'm sure to have torn one. I have only ninety-two pence in my drawstring purse, and my belly is cramping. It occurs to me to simply shift my weight on to the ball of my foot and take off like a crazed rhinoceros through the door. Then, being a responsible citizen, even at seventeen, I put my mother's spare handbag down beside the sprawl of books, and kneel. The princess who sorted seeds from sand at least had eloquent ants to help her. All I get are Cara's eyes

3

rolling from the safe distance of the Marxism shelf, and a snigger from some art students over by the window. Luckily the black-lipsticked Goth at the till is engrossed in finding a paper bag for an old atlas; in any other bookshop a saleswoman would be pursing her lips and planting her stiletto heel six inches from my fingers. The tomb of *Surprising Summer Salads* I build is better ventilated than the original, almost Japanese. I have been neat, no one can make me buy a copy. If it were *Astonishing Autumn Appetizers*, now, I might consider it.

I'm blithering, amn't I?

Cara is over by Aviation pretending not to know me, so I set off downstairs, trying to soften the slap of my feet on the wood. Ragged posters for gigs and therapies paper the winding stairwell; their sellotape fingers flap in my breeze. Between the third and second floors the blood wells and I think I may be going to topple. Familiar clogs hit the steps behind me.

'Cup of coffee?'

Cara doesn't seem to hear, as her shoulders poke past, but when we have come out of the bookshop on to the dazzling quay she says, 'I'm off caffeine, Pen, I thought I told you.'

'Since when?' I shout into a surge of traffic.

'This morning.'

I let out my sigh as a yawn. 'A glass of water and a doughnut?'

'As you wish.'

I pause for a second halfway along the Ha'penny Bridge, to feel it bounce under the weight of feet. I refuse the first and second cafés we pass, as rip-offs. Cara wipes a dark red strand off her eyebrow. 'Pen, you know I've got plenty.'

'I'd choke on a bun that cost thirty-five pee.' It sounds like a point of principle, but is based on the ninety-two pence remaining in my purse.

We thread our way through the crowd on College Green in what I hope is a companionable silence. Town is full of twelve-year-olds in limp minis and pedal-pushers; their shoul-

4

ders are peanut-red, scored with strapmarks. I have often wondered if the Irish consider it ungrateful to use sun block. As we head up Grafton Street the light is like a splash of lemon juice in my face. I turn my stiff neck to find Cara, but she is ahead of me. Five yards ahead, in fact, sprinting. How odd. I scan the mass of shoppers for a familiar face, but then I realize that she is not running up to anyone, just running. Her head is down. Her fringed purse is smacking from rib to rib. I stand still and lose her.

When I catch sight of her narrow body hurtling past the flower barrows, a great weariness comes over me. It occurs to me, by no means for the first time, to let Cara go. But while that thought is worming its way down the nerves, through the labyrinths of flesh, to reach my feet, they are already flailing a path up the street. When I get past the cluster of tourists around the mandolin player, I grip my handbag under my elbow and gather speed. Cara is nowhere in sight, but I trust that even lanky footballers run out of energy when they've eaten nothing all day and their clogs are heavy.

Exercise is good for cramps, I tell myself, ho ho. It is not so much the pain that worries me as the possibility that I may take a leap too far and leave my reproductive system, steaming gently, on the pavement outside Bewleys Café. What was the name of that woman in labour, who, forced to race against a horse for the men of Ulster, gave birth at the winning post and cursed them to suffer the same pains every year?

At the top of Grafton Street I begin to doubt my lung capacity. Motivation falters too; Cara could be halfway to Belfast now for all I care. Then I catch sight of a moving dot halfway along Stephen's Green. I heave a sticky breath and launch myself forward again, swerving round a lamp-post.

My little gold boat is swinging on its chain, its points pricking my throat. Slow down, Cara. 'Caaaahra! Cha-cha-cha!' as the girls at school bawl when we play rounders out the back field. You've made your point, my beloved. I am

5

following, the puppet is still attached to its string. If you slowed to a walk we could process with more dignity, a hundred yards apart, blinking in the sun. Slow down, damn you.

When Cara reaches the church she pulls up. Touched by one of their pink billboards, perhaps: 'Repent' or 'Come to Me'. She slopes on to a bollard, her hands in her lap. I pound down the last stretch of pavement, feeling like a right eejit. Should I slow to a walk, or fall in a gory heap by her feet, or (this might surprise her) canter right by? I could catch that revving doubledecker before it leaves the bus stop.

Twenty feet before her I come to a halt. I had thought she might be crying, or at least sweating. Instead she is watching the traffic, her gaze neutral. The colour of thin typing paper, as ever. Her ribs are not heaving like a deck in a storm. Only a string of burgundy hair, dangling from her widow's peak, shows she's been running.

I don't expect her to look at me. She doesn't. 'You can't be very comfortable there,' I wheeze.

Cara gets up from her bollard and falls into line. I loosen the thin gold chain from where it is stuck to my collarbone. We plod along two sides of the Green. It occurs to me to suggest cutting through, but what with sparrows and roses and all, it might seem inappropriately romantic. They are gutting some Georgian tenement; the bulldozers cover our silence. I stare up at the yellow crane, seeing myself fluttering from it like a snagged kite.

'Mind.'

Her long arm has tugged me out of the way of a truck. 'Sorry,' I say, absurdly grateful.

The cramps begin again now, throbbing in my thighs. To distract myself from self-pity, I marshal my pity for Cara. 'Are you all right, love? Did you suddenly feel sick? Is it the exams? I know you mightn't feel like talking about it, but I need to know so as I can help.'

Not a word.

I finger my sailboat, my thumb fitting into the slight concavity in its back. 'Was it something I said?'

Her mouth twists, a smile or disgust, I can't tell from this angle.

'Please, pet, tell me.'

In the shop on the corner I buy us choc-ices for something to do with our mouths on the long walk home.

A hint from Mr Wall's elbow, and I shut down on the memory of that peculiar afternoon and slipped to my knees. If it wasn't for him I knew I'd daze right through the consecration, and I couldn't blame it on the exceptional circumstances because I always daydreamed in mass. There was something so hypnotic about the pattern of antiphons and coughs and acclamations. Six o'clock mass in particular, the day having rubbed out the lines of thought until I could slip into a memory at the drop of a hymn book.

Right up to the responsorial psalm tonight I had focused on the appropriate pieties, especially about the funeral, which was likely, I decided, scanning the vast beige walls, to be grim, as grim as it gets. So I aimed my gaze at the tabernacle and asked to be uplifted. If not all the way up then at least a couple of inches. For the first minutes of mass I had concentrated fairly holily, then, even muttered along with 'let your face shine on us and we shall be saved', but of course didn't that start me off on Cara's white, unshining face charging through the crowds on Grafton Street. Not a good choice, as memories went, not at all uplifting. Not even educational, since I had never worked out what the hell had got into her that day.

Gotten, Kate would say; Americans said gotten, that much I knew. And sidewalk for footpath, of course, and jello for jelly and jelly for jam. None of which we had in the house since Mr Wall preferred marmalade, and personally I could kill for chocolate almond spread, right now in fact, on toast. How I wished the Pope would do away with the hour's fast before communion; not even the saints could have concentrated through fantasies of chocolate almond spread. And there might be a scraping of Cara's leatherwood honey left but she probably used that up before going on holiday. Find out what Kate eats, I wrote at the top of a mental list, and buy it tomorrow morning after Immac. Also catfood for Grace; he's resisting those rabbit chunks.

My eyes dawdled across the missalette. I had never noticed before that the official title of the 'Lord have mercy' prayer was the gracious phrase 'Invitation to Sorrow'. Hey there, Sorrow, how've you been keeping? Come on in. If your bike doesn't have lights you can always crash on our sofa tonight. Oh, so you'll be staying a while, Sorrow? Planning to get to know me better? Grand, so. There's tea in the pot.

All at once I was very glad, staring at Mr Wall's worn corduroys on the kneeler, that he had decided against a traditional funeral with cold ham and aunts trying to make the best of things. 'No flowers', I had put in the newspaper notice when I was drafting it at the kitchen table this afternoon – only a matter of hours ago – and 'donations to Women's Aid'. I had picked that charity almost at random, but now I seemed to remember Cara saying that everybody should have somewhere to run to. (Or was it just the kind of thing she would say? Was I her ghost writer now, putting words in her mouth?) I had to explain what Women's Aid was to Mr Wall, who seemed rather shocked that such things were needed.

'Take this all of you and drink it', Canon O'Flaherty was suggesting through the microphone, 'this is the cup of my blood.' Kate would be delayed at Logan Airport, I decided, adding it to my list. Winona too, of course, but I couldn't visualize her. Kate I could see, at least in outline, with her Wall kneecaps set against the back of the seat in front. I could imagine the apologetic drone over the speakers: ladies and gentle captain speaking unfavourable weather traffic controllers considerable period on behalf cabin crew opportunity to complimentary beverage. She'd be sparing a thought for her sleek leather luggage, moving her watch five hours to

Irish time (impatient, wasn't she? wouldn't she be?), and deciding not to bother with the in-flight film, a heartwarming saga of this that or th'other. Movie, she'd say, not film. I would have to refrain from sniggering when she came out with an Americanism. I couldn't expect a Dublin grin from someone who went over to the other side the year she turned sixteen.

The Canon was speeding up, probably aiming to be home for the repeat of *Glenroe* at seven. Or maybe he just knew the words so well that they slid together like raindrops on a window. 'Welcome into your kingdom our departed brothers and sisters and all who have left this world in your friendship,' he said conversationally. It had the ring of a holiday brochure: Fly Aer Lingus to Kingdom Come – passengers in Eternal Rest Class get a free pair of travel slippers.

I'm rabbiting, I thought. It's the shock. Must calm down, wise up, and so forth. Margarine, or some kind of low-fat dairy spread, that would be best; Americans were known to be paranoid about cholesterol.

Was Kate a smoker? Maybe the minute the captain switched off the no-smoking lights she'd be reaching into her holdall for one of those brands that are aimed at executive men and smoked by women who don't like being patronized. No boiled sweet for the take-off, thank you. She would have accepted a paper and pursued the economic scandals by now; perhaps she would already have launched into the crossword, her carved lips twisting at the worst of the puns. Black rain might roll over the wings, but she wouldn't be looking out her porthole. What was I talking about, she wouldn't even be in the plane yet; she'd probably still be packing, back at the smart apartment.

'Let us offer each other the sign of peace', and Mr Wall's cool hand was taking mine before I woke from my daze. No need to meet his eyes. Receiving my clammy fingers back into my lap, I returned to wondering about his elder daughter. Tense, Kate would undoubtedly be, but which tensions would lie topmost, out of all she had to choose from? If she hadn't been home in what, '92 take away '78, just over fourteen years, then chances were she despised this dog-shaped island and all of us foolish enough to cling to its wet ridges. Perhaps she was one of those people who couldn't stand the rain, though I never remembered her complaining on drizzly days at Immac. But then there was so much I couldn't remember, or never knew in the first place; I had only shared a classroom with her for nine months. It was just that I could imagine her as someone whom the rain would irk wildly. She would crack three black umbrellas into it every winter and shove them in bins with the lids blown off.

The good thing about all this frantic thinking was that I would sleep tonight. It might take a hot bath and cocoa and a cry but I would definitely be too tired to stay awake listening out for the phone, rehearsing the words of the call that would tell me it was all some Monty Pythonesque mistake and everything was grand, see you soon pet.

Stop. Stop it this minute, Pen, don't get sentimental on me now. The ushers will have to carry you out on a pile of collection plates, you great blubbering Cleopatra. Mr Wall was straightening his blue silk tie as he stood up and bent towards me. Come on now, I barked at myself, get into the queue.

It had all been most businesslike on the phone at lunch-time. I tried Winona in Texas first, but couldn't bring myself to leave such a message about her daughter on an answer-phone. Whereas Kate picked her phone up on the second ring; her bed had to be right beside it. The line was crackly, with a barely noticeable time lag. I said who I was and why I was ringing – calling, they said, never ringing, remember – and that the funeral would be delayed until Wednesday to give her and her mother time to get here. For a minute I thought we'd been cut off. I was shivering in the hall with my head against the mirror, a draught slipping under the front door. I bellowed 'Hello? Hello?'

Then Kate's voice came back, and said she'd be there.

'Do let us know your flight number and I'll pick you up

from the airport,' I told her, erring on the formal side rather than the maudlin, because that was Cara's favourite insult for me any time I showed sentiment she wasn't in the mood for. When I challenged her on what it meant, all she could come up with was the qualities she associated with the name Maud.

Anyway, the sister said that she'd see about a few days off, and would ring from the airport on arrival in the morning. (Ring, she said, not call, which threw me a little.) 'Which morning?' I asked, adding that I could never quite remember which way the hours went.

'Monday morning,' Kate told me, and clicked off.

This communion queue wasn't moving. What were they doing up there, baking the host from scratch? My mind kept lurching between memories. The last time Cara and I had exchanged more than two lines about Kate, that I could remember, was during the big snow. We were in Cara's bedroom overlooking the back garden; it must have been after I moved into the big house. Schools were shut, Mr Wall happened to be staying with his aunt in Cork, Cara's eco-socialist-feminist-whatsit newsletter was skipping an issue, and the buses were off. We made a snowlady down behind the pear tree and reddened her nipples with wine, then went to bed for a three-day breakfast. If I closed my eyes now – only for a moment, as the sluggish queue of communicants came to a halt – there, framed in the small window, was the garden muted with snow, the pear tree dozing under its load, and Cara's hot flank against mine.

'I had the weirdest dream last night,' I tell her, making my voice sleepy. The end of the quilt has a seizure; Grace is worming his way in.

'Mmm?'

'I'm out in the Wicklow Hills, right, walking up a steep bit, I think it's the heathery patch above Lough Dan, and there's a few stragglers coming down, Germans with ruck-sacks and such.'

'Nothing weird about that,' yawns Cara.

'Well but, just as I've turned sideways against a granite boulder to let the last walker go by, I glance up and it's your sister.'

'Kate?'

'Have you another sister I don't know about?'

'Not that I remember.' Cara reaches down for the cat and lifts his clenched orange limbs on to her knees. 'Though I suppose they could have smuggled one or two away before I was born.'

I lean up on one elbow and keep my voice airy. 'In the dream her hair's blowing across her eyes, and when she pulls it back the face is all dark, like those leathery bodies they found in the bog.'

'Uuurgh.' Cara sits up in bed and puts her crumpet down. Grace springs on to my thighs, clawing at the quilt.

'No, in the dream it isn't frightening,' I tell her. 'Or only a bit. Otherwise she's normal. She's got this black leather jacket and a cigarette in her hand.'

'Kate doesn't smoke.'

'She might by now.' I am concentrating on the cat, scratching the triangle of skull till his eyes narrow with pleasure.

'Nah, she's a control freak, she'd hate to need it.'

'It's just the dark brown face that's so strange.'

'You wouldn't recognize her if you did meet her, you know.' Cara tweaks the tip of Grace's tail. 'Big sis is probably in a twinset and pearls by now.'

'I would so. I was in her class.'

'That was decades ago.' The crumpet pauses, halfway to her mouth. 'Listen to me. I used to say that when I just meant a while. But now it's true. I've been on this planet for practically three decades.'

I laugh and take a bite out of her crumpet.

Cara pulls it away, getting butter on my cheek; her face is thoughtful as she bends to lick it off. 'Honestly, you wouldn't recognize Kate now, even I mightn't.'

'When did you see her last?'

'Must have been that awful weekend we all spent in the cockroach motel in Cape Cod, in '84. After that we stopped pretending we were a family.'

'You must miss her, though,' I say.

'Really? Why must I?' Cara sounds as haughty as her sister used to.

'Well, you know, blood being thicker than water and all that.'

'Bullshit's thicker than either.'

I recoil. 'I was only saying . . .'

'Everybody's always been only saying,' she snarls. 'Pitying me for my "broken home", assuming all my problems can be attributed to my being a motherless waif.' Slowing down, she adds, 'One guy at college asked could that be why I turned out, ahem, the way I did.'

I groaned. 'He didn't! Freud lives.'

Cara rests her nose in the dip of my collar-bone. 'Didn't mean to bite your head off, by the way.'

'Craven apology accepted.'

She puts her buttery tongue in my ear for a moment, as if taking a reading. 'I do remember missing Kate for a while, actually.'

'What about your mother?'

'Missed her a lot more. Kept waiting for her to come back. The visits just upset me. But at that age you change so much in a year. You get used to anything. You forget your life was ever different.'

I nodded, not believing her.

'In the long run I did fine with Dad. It was him I always used to run to if anything went wrong, anyway. He didn't think I was feeble the way Mum did.'

'Surely –'

'And the year after they left I got you, didn't I?' she interrupted, leaning to rub her nose along my wider one. 'Kate and Mum are more like distant relatives now.'

'That's a bit sad,' I told her.

'It's pretty normal. How often do you see your brother, who lives in the same city?'

'Fair enough.' I go back to stroking the cat, who is writhing in the valley of duvet between us. 'Her face would still be the same, you know.'

'Kate's?'

'I bet she still looks just like her photo.'

'Which?'

'The one of her on rollerskates, in the dungarees.'

'I don't know any photos of her on rollerskates,' says Cara puzzledly.

'Don't you?'

'You mean those blue dungarees she never let me try on?'

Almost too late, I remember which photo I mean. The one I stole, all those years ago, on my first visit to the big house. I was a sweaty teenager in a red uniform, irked to be stuck watching television with the little sister when what I wanted was a walk in the woods with the big one. 'Must be confusing it with some other picture,' I tell Cara, and swipe the end of her crumpet.

My stomach was rumbling as I came back to the present, and to the top of the queue. A gleaming nun deposited the white circle on my tongue. It had taken me years to learn how to dissolve the sweet papery wafer off the ridges of my mouth. Processing down from communion now, head dipped in what my employer Sister Dominic still called the modesty of the eyes, I tried to realize that this was God, sliding down my throat. It was good practice, believing improbable things.

Believing was easier than bowing to his will, anyway. Once I began questioning his motives, I got so angry I wanted to hawk him up again. Why did you do it, you bastard? You couldn't have needed Cara more than I did. If times are all one in eternity, why couldn't you have waited a while longer for her?

Like me, Mr Wall must have dreaded the after-mass

jollity of neighbours who hadn't heard the news yet. Better to have them come across it in tomorrow's paper. So instead of sitting down for the final prayers we slipped out the heavy door into the dripping twilight. We got to my dark green Mini just as the rain turned heavier. While we fastened our seat-belts in unison it spattered on the windscreen. 'Kate's due in tomorrow morning,' I told him.

'Who's that?'

Was he losing his mind on me now? 'Kate,' I told him warily. 'And Mrs Wall.'

'Oh, forgive me, I still think of her as Cáit, must get out of the habit. Is her mother still calling herself that, Mrs Wall? Sounds a bit old hat.'

'I believe so. It goes well with Winona.'

'Yes, Win always had a weakness for alliteration.' He blew his nose into a large cotton handkerchief.

'So I'll pick them up at the airport, will I?'

'Would you mind, dear, that would be wonderful.'

As I drove through the deserted suburb Mr Wall looked out the window, head bobbing like a child on a trip. He glanced over once to say, 'About Wednesday.'

'I have that all in hand, don't worry your head. I left the ad on the newspaper's answerphone, and the Monsignor's booked.'

'You're very good.'

'And as far as I know all the friends are in the address book so I'll do some ringing round tomorrow.'

'Ah, yes. Won't they see it in the paper?'

'They're not all *Irish Times* readers,' I explained, sliding the car on to the kerb outside the big house.

'Of course not,' said Mr Wall guiltily.

The honeysuckle hung around the front door, gemmed with rain. I held my breath so as not to smell it. The breeze caught the wind chime made of forks that Cara sent back from her Californian trip a couple of years ago. Such a honeyed tinkle they made; I stilled them with my hand.

We stood in the kitchen with nothing to do. The cat-flap

crashed; Grace was off on his evening rambles. I had put my handbag on the sideboard and now my arms hung down, fingers tingling. The kitchen was full of that fuzzy grey light which builds up when a house is left empty round teatime. I was afraid to move and disturb a cloud of it.

'Have you eaten, Pen?' asked Mr Wall. 'I suppose one ought to.'

I bent to click on the electric fire; its bottom coil bloomed from rust to orange. 'I had some cheese before mass, but you know me. I could fancy one of your soufflé omelettes.'

'Yes, you're partial to them.' I could hear his face brighten. 'Very good, give me ten minutes.' And he set off like a dog loosed from its chain, snapping on the light and rummaging in the larder.

I checked Grace's water. I heard the sound of an egg smashing on the parquet, but pretended not to notice as Mr Wall mopped it up. I leaned my bulk against the mahogany sideboard, soothed by the sound of fork whipping egg-white. My eyes began to shut.

'I wonder, dear, could you do me a favour and run me in later on?'

'Run you in?'

'Pay my respects.'

My head was still fogged up. 'Oh of course. I just, yeah, sure, whenever.'

I cleared my throat in a roar and strode off. Though the living-room was dark, the sky was still blue gauze in the windows. The first thing I did was to draw the velvet curtains and shut it out. Then I snapped on the reading light by the fireplace. There was a torn envelope sticking out of the shelf between *Encyclopaedia of World Knowledge* and *Asterix the Gaul*. 'Cara', it said in an unfamiliar scrawl. A birthday card from last June? It was empty. I found a dusty biro on the hearth and began to make a list on the back of the envelope.

'To Do', it began confidently. 'Notify Registrar of Births and Deaths'; the nurse on the phone had assured me it was urgent. I wondered had I spelled the word Registrar right; I kept visualizing him as God's recording angel. 'Funeral home will arrange chapel of rest and do med. certs', I scribbled to reassure myself. 'Ring relatives', that was unless Mr Wall showed any signs of initiative. And while I was at the phone, 'Ring friends'. Cara's Snoopy address book was down the back of the leather armchair, I remembered spotting it the other day. I walked over now and dug in for it; my back ached. I riffled its three-by-three pages; whose were all these first names, I wondered, all these Sues and Mels and Jays, and how many of them had she slept with? Moving on, moving on, best not to get bogged down in details. 'Send back ID cards and passport', I added to my list; I had read in some novel that you had to do that.

It exhausted me even to think of doing all these things. I folded up the envelope and put it in the pocket of my trousers. To kill time, I read the spines of all the books in the fireside case, left to right, top shelf to bottom. Nineteenth-century titles were the most comforting. When I had watched the last five minutes of Biddy and Miley's thoughts on the weather in *Glenroe*, Mr Wall carried in the airy omelette on a tray, and we switched over to a documentary on otters.

I was calm, I was doing fine. He passed me the unopened Bourbon Creams. It was only at the bottom of my second cup of tea that I realized I had eaten halfway down the packet without a pause. I tucked the cellophane over the top and put it back on the tray.

Mr Wall had left his biscuit on the saucer. 'Perhaps a quick round?' At a time like this, the man wanted to play Scrabble.

He cleared his throat. I could see his lips tightening over his teeth.

'Good idea,' I told him.

The odd thing was, he played better than ever. He seemed gripped by the need not to think, not to daydream, not to let a word slip by. He put 'seize' on a double word square and countered my 'zebra' with a nest of the kind of two-letter words that are used only in Scrabble. I watched his face light up with achievement.

At eight exactly Mr Wall stared at the hands of his watch. 'Perhaps we should be thinking about making a move.'

'Yes indeed,' I said, too hearty.

I stood on the doorstep, waiting for him to get his raincoat. I would drive him there, I decided, but I would not make myself go in. Not that I was particularly squeamish, or would have been repelled by a battered face; Cara's face had often looked battered from the inside. I just felt no need to see it, the thing they would call the remains. I knew it was more true to say that she was still wandering round the Aegean, buying postcards but no stamps. Not getting around to coming home, but not to be thought of as any less real than she ever was.

Mr Wall was double-locking the front door. The honeysuckle dangled near my face, but I breathed through my mouth.

Minnie's ignition moaned into life as soon as I turned the key; no excuse there. The damp streets were deserted, the last courting couple having dawdled home with a steaming bag of chips between them. I always got this fantasy, driving through Dublin on a Sunday evening, that they had dropped that bomb which leaves buildings untouched but turns people to dust. I alone, through some whim of fate, had survived, full-fleshed, and was crossing town in a dirty green Mini. Where would I be heading, if I was literally alone in the world? I could raid the gourmet delicatessen, I supposed; shame to let it all spoil. Or perhaps a library, to hide under a table in the children's section. The bomb couldn't kill Cinderella.

'Next left we turn at, isn't it?'

'Oh yes,' I said, glad of his tactful reminder. Then I admitted, 'I was heading on in to Immac, on auto-pilot.'

'I never quite understood,' replied Mr Wall, 'why you girls called it that.'

'What, Immac?'

'Of course I can understand that abbreviations are irreverent and therefore amusing, but why the change in stress? I would have expected not *Imm*ac but Imm*ac*, for Imm*ac*ulate Conception Convent.'

'Oh, but did nobody tell you in all these years?' I stared at him. 'Immac's a brand-name for, what's the word, a depilatory cream. You must have heard of it.'

'My wife preferred an electric razor.' Then, embarrassed by this confidence, he murmured, 'At least, as long as I knew her. I believe the police often set up a speed trap at this corner, perhaps . . .'

I went down to forty.

After a minute Mr Wall began again. 'Immac, I get it now. The link must be the taming of adolescent females.'

'I don't remember the original reason, it just seemed funny at the time. When I was a pupil I thought they were trying to tame us, but since I've been teaching there, I realize what an impossible task that would be.'

For the rest of the journey through the increasingly seedy streets of the old city we talked about our jobs: my zealous nuns, his vague cataloguing assistants, my pre-pubertal brats, his precious books.

Sitting at the traffic lights, I watched the other drivers. They looked sober and careful but you never could tell. We were all potential killers nowadays.

I had never been to that hospital before, and never to a morgue. Or no, mortuary, that was the polite word. When my father died I was eighteen. I spent the day before the funeral cleaning the house so as not to disgrace us in front of the neighbours. My mother was hit much harder than I was. He had been a nice man, but not a very memorable one. I felt very low, of course, but not so low that I wanted to go to the mortuary and kiss his glassy forehead.

And since my father there had been no occasion. Remarkable, really, that death hadn't laid a bony finger on me or mine for more than a decade. If it had, I would be practised in such matters, would know what to think when, would have some experience of the opening and shutting of the gates. As it was, I felt such an amateur. About to embark on the biggest loss I could imagine, with no practice at mourning a mother or even a pop star, and never having so much as stepped inside a hospital mortuary.

I wheeled in the gate and parked near the entrance for a speedy getaway. I mouthed a quickie: 'Eternal rest grant unto them and may perpetual light shine upon them.' The vision conjured up was of a neon-lit meat safe.

'You go on in,' I told Mr Wall as he picked at his seat-belt.

His face was grey, with a bar of orange streetlight across it. 'Ah. You're not –'

'I'll stay in the car.'

'Right so.'

It didn't seem to have rained in this part of town. I watched him straighten his tie as he walked across to the light spilling from the main door, an unaccustomed slowness to his pace. I wondered was he getting a touch of arthritis, then realized that he was trying to be reverent.

The radio kept me going for five minutes of a play about Queen Medhb and Cúchulainn, but then I snapped it off and the silence closed in. Not that a car was ever entirely silent, especially not an old banger like this. As the engine cooled a series of gentle clicks filled the air. 'Hey, Minnie Mouse,' I whispered, 'what say you 'n' me go take a ride in the hills, see ourselves some stars and cut ourselves some turf for a bonfire by the light of the silvery moooooon.' But no, we were waiting for the good gentleman in whose house (and garage, respectively) we lived rent-free, owing to our illicit amorous connection with the aforementioned's younger daughter, the late Cara Máire Fionnuala Wall.

At that the silly voices slid away and my face shut down. The cheeks sank heavy as leather; the bones around the eyes fused into a helmet of pain. It was the word 'late' that did it. Such a stupid word to use of the dead, implying that they would be with us today if they hadn't happened to be delayed in traffic somewhere and phoned ahead to say 'Might be late, don't wait up, pet'.

My fingers were locked around the steering-wheel. I made them tap out 'Knocking on Heaven's Door', which by some perverse association was the first tune that came into my head. After the second verse I had myself in hand again. I could let the fresh memory through the valve, inch by inch.

It was just gone midnight last night; I remembered it because I had been glancing at the kitchen clock, just beginning to let myself worry that Cara's plane had been delayed in Athens. It was a short call but a good one. Between echoing yawns she said that her tote hadn't turned up on the conveyor belt yet, so she had told the others from the Attic to go ahead on the last bus to town. She said she'd come home in a taxi as soon as the bag emerged from whatever cavern they hid them in. Little bourgeoise, I called her, joking about the taxi fare. I hoped she knew I was joking, all the times I was. Actually I was glad to think of her laying her head back in the comfort of a taxi and speeding through the night to our hot pillows. When I had put down the phone I climbed upstairs, pulled the duvet over my head and slept like a trusting spaniel. In my dream a bare-breasted Amazon sat on a motorbike under my window, playing the bagpipes.

When I woke, even before the bagpipes turned themselves into the sound of the phone ringing, I knew it was later than it should have been. The flowery curtain was filling up with light.

The nurse had to ring twice. When she told me first, I thought, what poor taste, they say the best thing to do with hoaxers is to put the phone down on them straight away. But when she rang back I believed her, because she sounded so embarrassed. I apologized over and over for having slammed down the phone, and she kept telling me it was understandable. But there was nothing understandable about any of it.

Even as I sat here in the darkening car park of the

hospital, I could make no sense of the story. I remembered the order of events, but that was all. My forehead pressed on the wrinkled leather of the steering-wheel.

Once the nurse had got it through to me that there was no point dashing in to the hospital, I started asking for details. I supposed I was afraid to stop talking, cut the umbilicus of the phone-line. I made her tell me all she knew, which wasn't much. 'Some kind of crash on the dual carriageway; sorry I don't know any more', she kept repeating. I got her to admit that the crash had happened round one in the morning, and the surgeons were finished by three. She said I wasn't rung till six because I'd need all the sleep I could get. I expected to be angry with her, but I found myself touched at her concern for such a small thing as sleep.

After I had put down the phone, I stood there, telling myself 'Be brave', over and over. Then I got dressed, pausing for quite a long time to decide between a blue and a grey cardigan. I went about all my immediate duties, including telling Mr Wall, though now I came to think of it I could not for the life of me remember what ghastly words I had chosen, and I would never dream of asking him. All I could remember was standing in his doorway, the hall light spilling in as far as the bump his knees made in the blanket. Not a sound came from his face, lifted off the pillow. I could tell he'd heard me.

Then, I remembered, I'd looked at the kitchen clock and it was still only a quarter past six. The best thing, the nurse had insisted, would be to visit the mortuary in the evening. So there was the whole of Sunday to fill. I was sitting at the kitchen table, considering whether or not to have breakfast; I was hungry, but under the circumstances it seemed vulgar to do anything about it.

And then it hit. It was as if I was crushed in a giant hand, like the tiny people in the fairytale illustrations. I was dangling by my hair one minute, my ribs popping between the giant's thumb and finger the next. A scream too wide to let out bulged behind my teeth.

I ran out the front door, as far as the gate. It was such a pretty morning. Hacking drily, I ran up the hill towards the woods; I must have had some notion of finding a space big enough for such a scream. I stumbled, jogged faster. Past the hair salon, pet shop and bridal boutique with all their metal shutters down. Past the inaccurate wrought-iron house names: Three Wishes, Four Willows, Seven Oaks, Avalon. As always when I passed the wall with its ancient white graffito that said 'the cure', I wondered what would be cured, and when, and how. My lungs failed; my steps slowed and faltered. I was no longer running to get anywhere, just running.

When I got to the woods there was no more room than in the big house, and I had no breath left. I opened my mouth and the wind pushed in and sealed it up.

A woman and her golden labrador emerged from the cluster of horse chestnut trees. I waited till they were gone; I didn't want to frighten her, or have to give embarrassing explanations. When she was out of sight I opened my jaw again but only managed to produce a little gasp, a sort of yawn of pain. I realized that I was such a tame conditioned creature that I couldn't scream, even under circumstances that should have allowed for anything.

And it seemed that even here, hours later, soundproofed in my own vehicle in a deserted car park, I couldn't let out a sound. Mr Wall was taking a long time in there. Glancing at the old-fashioned dial set into Minnie's dashboard I saw that only ten minutes had passed. Was every hour from here on in going to be played in slow motion? Was each of these new days going to feel like a week?

I wondered why Mr Wall wanted to see his daughter's body. It was not something he and I would ever bring ourselves to talk about. We would each be far more afraid of upsetting the other.

He really was taking ages in there. Maybe I should go in and see if he was all right. Maybe I should stop being such a chicken and go and get it over with, this being the last chance to see what was left of Cara. They said it made it real, seeing the body. Not that I particularly wanted to make it real, I was much more comfortable with unreality, thank you very much. But if it was likely to become real on its own behalf one of these days – in a traffic jam, say, or while lifting a dish out of the oven – then I supposed I would prefer it to be now, with her in the flesh, or rather, the flesh but not her in it.

I got out, stretching my stiff knees. I'd parked beside an electricity generator; it was humming like some alien space-craft. 'Dang', said the notice, above half a lightning zigzag; the rest of the message had been ripped away. As I was locking Minnie's door, a horrible thought occurred to me: they might have made Cara up. She had always been intimidated by women who wore makeup, because they looked dramatic, and equally intimidated by those who wore none, because they scored higher on politics and self-confidence, so she compromised by putting on eyeliner, then wiping it off till you couldn't be sure she was wearing any. If they had got some mortician beautician type to do a full job on her, she might look grotesque.

Get on with you, PenDulous, stop procrastinating.

A knot of people emerged from the mortuary entrance. The only face turned up was that of a small girl sucking on the end of her plait, her eyes raised to the bulging moon. Couldn't be more than eight, and she was coping. I slammed the car door, goading myself into action. As I strode past the family the child gave me a thoughtful stare, with – bless her – no pity in it.

The corridor was white. The last of their group, an emaci-ated grandmother, was coming out of a door which she held open for me. I headed blindly through. No sign of Mr Wall; he must have gone out another way. The coffin was on a sort of marble plinth, with a sheet up to the chin. Otherwise the room was empty. I was glad not to be observed.

Leave the face till last. Begin on the creamy cotton of the sheet. How small a body was, laid out this way; how little even Cara's long limbs came to in a standard box. The hands were waxy, knotted together in the clasp of prayer; I had expected that. Come on now, I hissed at myself, one look at the face and you can go back to the car. Get on with you. I turned my head and looked.

My first wild thought was that death had drained Cara's blood-red hair to a muddy blonde. Then the face below me was that of a young girl, twelve or so, and I ran, lungeing through the swing-doors and out into the cool air. Seat-belt on, door locked, radio filling the car with seventies rock, I coughed and sobbed and coughed again. My cheeks stayed dry as paper. The tears were dammed up in my head, scorching me from the inside. They were not for Cara. They were for the girl on the wrong slab, with shiny knuckles and a nose pointed at the ceiling. It occurred to me that she must have been sister to the child I saw at the door, the one who had seemed more interested in the moon.

I could, of course, have gone in again and found the right slab this time, but I came to the swift conclusion that no slab would be the right one. By the time Mr Wall tapped on the window I was calm again, and before I let him in I remembered to turn off the radio, which was playing something unsuitable about holiday, drive away, babe-ayyy.

Crossing the city, the only sound was the rain returning to spit at the windscreen. Mr Wall sat upright, his hands clasped in his lap. I offered him not a single opening to tell me how it was, how she looked, what the small mercies were. Instead, I planned how to fill in each half-hour: *The Living Planet*, cocoa, *Cagney and Lacey*, a game of chess if Mr Wall and I got desperate, and half a sleeping tablet just in case.

I was so worn out I fell asleep before I even took the tablet.

I dreamed of the big house, of chasing someone who was Cara but also a nun. We danced through the rooms, falling on soft carpets, sporting on the stairs. It was dark but we knew our way around. Halfway through we got the munchies and she, this nun who was Cara but also not Cara, went out to get twenty packets of crisps. I lay in a doze of content, the dusty fibres of the carpet under my cheek. At one point I heard the chimes tinkling madly outside, but I thought it was the wind. Surely if it was Cara she would use her own key or ring the doorbell? I did think of throwing the front door open, but was afraid all of a sudden in case it was an intruder. I curled up on the carpet and fell back asleep.

But when at last I seemed to wake, still in the dream, it was morning, and I was cold. Then I found Cara's key, forgotten beside the teapot, and I knew she was lost out there. I ran on to the road then, and hurtled down to the traffic lights. There was an unexpected opening in the tall hedge. I heard laughter, light and metallic. When I climbed through the glossy branches, I found a garden. There were hedges in the shape of letters I couldn't read from that angle, and fruit trees pruned into elegant poses. There was a summer-house painted white, with lanterns that trailed ribbons. I glimpsed Cara disappearing round a corner in knicker-bockers and a frock-coat, her hair powdered high, her cheeks whitened above a beauty spot and a startlingly red cupid's bow. When she reappeared from a nearer corner of the maze, she laughed and glanced back over her shoulder at her pursuer. I could hear the swish of skirts along the hedge, louder than the wind in the trees. I turned away in terror of seeing the face of the one who was taking her away from me.

I woke up for real then, and found myself shivering under the heavy duvet. I was flat on my back, stretched out like washing on a line. The minutes passed, one by one. No more sleep for me tonight. Cara had this irritating habit of asking life's biggest questions in the dark just before falling asleep herself, leaving me flat on my back in existential turmoil. Or sometimes we'd lie together in a post-erotic daze, and just as I'd be slipping away from consciousness, she would turn with a great heave of the quilt and announce 'I'm wide awake, are you?' Other nights she was convinced she heard burglars, and even if I knew it was the wind against the larder's broken window, I had to pull on my dressing-gown and go see. I was not sure what I was meant to say to any burglars I might meet: 'My girlfriend's upstairs and she's taller than I am, though thinner'?

At least we did sleep compatibly together once we managed to stop talking. One couple I knew at college just couldn't do it. He got snoozy after sex, she got wired; he liked heavy blankets, she threw them off; he fancied sleeping all squashed together like tiger cubs, whereas she needed to turn her back and get him out of her head. They tried single beds, then they broke up.

The only other person I'd ever slept beside was my mother. Not at night – Dr Spock's child-rearing manual would never have allowed that – but sometimes on Sunday mornings when I was small she'd let me into her bed and we'd snooze till we had to leap up and go to mass. It was like being in a bird's nest; all sharp bones and warm curves. Her skin was infinitely softer than mine, starred with tiny creases, and it hung slightly loose on her bones so it moved when you squeezed her. Skin like that was what I still looked forward to about getting old. As we lay there, we'd play a game where Mammy would name the parts of my body, her firm palm descending in turn on Timothy Toe, Edgar Ear, Nelly Knee.

I wondered did she sleep well these nights, my mother. I remembered her saying once that you couldn't expect to sleep as long or as deeply when you were getting older, so it was best to keep a book by the bed. I didn't like to think of her propped up on her narrow headboard, reading Stephen King late into the night; how could someone so gentle relish such horror, and how on earth did she get to sleep afterwards?

Over on my back. I reached for my headphones, and turned on the *Goldberg Variations*. I was all right for the first few minutes, letting the trustworthy rhythm row me along, but then came a series of minor chords that pulled at my heart. I fumbled for the stop switch. At first the unemotive silence was a relief, then it began to sound just as loud as the music.

I turned on my side. Then on the other side. This was ridiculous. I couldn't be expected to get through the days if I didn't sleep through the nights. I fumbled for the two halves of the sleeping tablet on the dressing-table, and swallowed them down. The edge of the pillow wrapped round my eyes, I reached for an image of something warm and real, to clear the shreds of that costume-drama nightmare out of my head. A memory of our beginning, maybe, to ward off our end.

Sun and skin were the things that brought us together in the first place. Not a Greek island but our own island of concrete and iron, floating above Dublin. This was a film so old and re-run I couldn't tell fact from fiction. It was a memory I saved for when I really needed it, in case I wore it out.

Light spills across my desk, bleaching inky scrawls off the page. I know I won't mess the exams up again, because this year I have a friend. Cara thinks she will. She is taut and baking whiter in the hottest June in years. She grabs the elbow patch of my jumper when the bell rings for lunch. 'Come with me, little girl.'

'There's something I want to look up . . .'

'Shut your face and come with me.' She stands imperious, balancing pencils and rubbers on her sketchpad.

I leave my jumper sprawled on the back of my chair and follow her upstairs past the assembly hall, past the sixth-year common room, upstairs again past the art room, up once more past the bedridden nuns, up to the dead end where a small diamond of window looks on to the roof.

'This door's never open.'

'Never say never.' Cara is fiddling with the lock, her hands shaking. I take the key from her, and after a minute the door does shudder open. Blue comes to meet us. Breeze snatches at our long skirts.

'But do you know the best thing?'

'No, my lanky miracle-worker,' I say, 'tell me the best thing.'

Cara cranes upwards. 'The best thing is, it was her who gave me the key.'

'Which her?' I ask, knowing the answer.

'Mrs Mew.' She is hushed. 'I told her I'd love to see what everything looked like to the birds. She just slipped it off her bundle of keys and said, "Then you must go up on the roof at lunchtime and draw".'

'She never. You nicked it.'

'I wouldn't.' Cara's voice is stern.

'I know.'

We lock the door behind us. Over the baked black roof we pick our way, half-expecting a foot to rip through into reality again. Our steps get bolder. Cara does a twirl, her red pleats lifting like cramped wings.

'Want me to pose?' I ask, spreading my arms.

'Nah, it has to be the environment.' She chooses the longest pencil. For a while we sit against the warmth of the wall, peering over our elbows at the world we have escaped from. Black-habited ants inch along the front drive; red jumpers loll and chase across the back lawn. Cara draws and rips, draws and scribbles out, showing me nothing. I shut my eyes, and everything disappears but the sun, scarlet through my lids.

'I can breathe up here, Pen.'

'Mmm.'

'No, seriously, the air is different. Down there, I dunno, I can't be doing with it.'

I sit up and remember my lines. 'What's up with you today? Is it the exams?'

'Only partly.' Cara shades in a curve, her mouth pursed. 'It's the bloody summer. I won't see Mrs Mew for sixty-seven days, minimum.'

'Don't think about that yet. We'll work something out.' My eyes are full of light, I can't come up with any practical suggestions. Why can this girl not just sit in the sun? 'Maybe –'

'No but you're not listening to me.' Cara slaps down her pencil on the concrete and turns her angry eyes, almost colourless in this glare. 'It's like I'm carrying a stone urn on my head across a desert, right, only no one can see it but me. The voices are all going "Caaaa-rah! come play tennis, come to a disco, come down to breakfast, come on" – when any minute now the urn's about to topple.'

'And what if it does?' I surprise myself by the question.

The corners of her mouth sag. Her breath hisses out. 'Everything will soak into the ground, and there'll be nothing left.'

'Nothing to carry either.' I cannot prevent the breeze from lifting my voice.

'You don't understand,' Cara tells me. 'If I didn't love Mrs Mew I'd be nothing. I'm just a haze of iron filings round her magnet.'

How can such a tall girl look so small, as if she is being dragged backwards through a tunnel? 'I wish I could help.'

Her look is gracious. 'You do.'

'I wish I could carry your damn urn for you.'

Cara takes my hand, shyly. It's not something we tend to do. 'You have the second-nicest eyes in the world.'

'Why, thank you kindly, ma'am.'

'I wish, Pen, I dunno, I'd like to smile at you. I haven't given you a real smile in ages.'

The faint lips are opening as if to go on explaining, and I kiss them. They are so much softer and less frightening than I expected. I kiss them again, because she hasn't said no.

Then Cara does the most extraordinary thing. She opens the top three buttons of her blouse, picks up my hand and puts it in. She has always claimed to be flat, but under the hot sheen of fabric something is pointing into my palm. I have no idea what to do.

Her eyes are white with surprise.

Experimentally, I curve one finger down, and her eyes

30

narrow, and her mouth slides as if to say something. I kiss the dry lips again. The bell for end of lunch goes, ten times in all. This is the signal for breaking the spell, gathering our possessions and wits, going back to the real world. Neither of us moves.

I suck soft air into my mouth. This rooftop is no longer attached; it has become our flying carpet, nine miles above the convent, sailing nearer to the sun. Cara is pulling up her hem. She is so near I can hear her breathe. She is cradled in my hot skirt. I would do anything for this girl. I will make her smile, make merry, make up for it all.

MONDAY

I woke wet, my body straining to her ghostly wrist.

Three full seconds of lull after I slapped off the alarm clock, before a great fist punched me in the guts.

I lay still for a moment under the shock of it. Then my soles thumped the carpeted boards, my hand lunged for the hairbrush. September sun was blazing through the window. Snap the bra shut with practised fingers, eight strides to the bathroom, face, teeth, underarms, eight strides back.

The phone rang twice, but Mr Wall got it. I could hear his subdued vowels in the hall.

I had certain techniques for rationing emotion and making the hours click by. I was fairly sure I could do it, having got through other days which were each the first day after something unspeakable. If you put all those previous losses together they might add up to something approaching this one, and similarly, I reasoned, pulling on a loose skirt and shirt and my baggiest grey cardigan, my strengths would add up and be sufficient. Else what? the remaining third of a broken button asked me, but I ignored it and reached for my shoes. Eyes low, averted from everything that might remind me, which would have to include most things. Knotting my laces in a double bow, I focused on the blank wall, and saw the grey smear where Cara dabbed correction fluid on a scuff mark the day before she went to Greece. I shut my eyes and concentrated on my laces.

Straightening the pockets of yesterday's trousers, I found my 'To Do' list and used a seashell pin to stick it to the cork board over the desk, between a rumpled sticker that said *Cork Women's Weekend is Fun in '91* and a photo of Grace dangling resentfully from the hammock a couple of summers

35

ago. It was blurred, but then Grace was often blurred.

When I reached the kitchen, the windows were foggy and the kettle had boiled dry. There was an evil-smelling black patch on its base. I wrapped it in a paper bag and pushed it deep into the bin, then boiled a cupful of water in a saucepan. The tea tasted faintly of garlic.

Grace was up on his hind paws scratching at the back door, his outraged orange face pressed against the glass. Though there was a cat-flap cut for him, he sometimes disdained to use it. I let him in and crouched to stroke him, but his spine shrank under my touch. He headbutted the fridge. He had eaten already, but who was I to stint him at a time of trouble?

Watching the anonymous meat glisten, I couldn't face breakfast. Mr Wall was nowhere to be seen; he must have put the kettle on to boil then forgotten all about it, something as foreign to his usual careful behaviour as if he had gone to work with no trousers on. I left a scrawl on the phone pad: 'If Kate rings from airport I'll be back by nine – Pen.' Handbag on one wrist, money, tissues, car keys, more tissues in case of hysteria, then run. Grace tried to follow me out the door, but I held him back with the side of my shoe.

At the red light I braked and removed the tiny black triangle from my lobe with shaky fingers. Not that the nuns would be contemporary enough to interpret it, even if I forgot, but if you were going to live in a closet you might as well make it draught-proof.

The little light above Sister Dominic's office was green, so it was safe to knock. As always, this door reduced me to twelve years old. Though there had been a decent interval of five years between my leaving the senior school and coming back to teach in the junior, where I had never been a pupil myself, sometimes it seemed that I had been a prisoner of Immac all my life, and this woman my gracious warder.

'Come in, come in!' The Dominatrix had her inspiring Monday smile on, and a camel-coloured week-at-a-glance diary open in front of her.

I cleared my throat, to give my voice some authority. 'I'm afraid I'll be needing a few days off, Sister.'

The pale brown mouth began to furl.

'I know it's dreadful to give you no notice but I only heard yesterday.' This scene was going to be harder than I thought.

'This will cause some hiccups in our schedule. A crisis of some sort, Penelope? A bereavement perhaps?'

I nodded. Which word, out of all the wrong words? 'My friend's dead.' A glossy walnut cross hung on Sister Dominic's linen chest, holding my eyes. Concentrate, Pen, sound convincing, you've years of lying behind you. 'My housemate. In a crash.'

Her eyes grew owlish. 'My poor dear girl. Would you like to sit down and have a cup of tea?'

I was alarmed to find myself lacking the energy even to want to scrape my ring into Sister Dominic's windpipe. I shook my head. How I wished I could make up a story, a complete and safe fiction. Maybe a fiancé in a private plane, call him Séamas, say, and let him plummet out of the blue in the Australian outback, and let me cross the world with a black mantilla over my eyes, and don't ask me any more questions, Sister. But nuns had long memories, and some geriatric at the convent's unseen dinner table would be bound to connect me with the death notice about that poor skinny Wall girl, the redhead with the broken home. That was their term for such things, as if when a wife walked out of her house the walls rent themselves in protest and the children were left coughing in the debris.

Sister Dominic waited a few judicious seconds for the tears. I looked her in the eye. 'Maybe, I was wondering, if I could have up to Wednesday – that's the funeral – I have to make arrangements, there are family visiting – and be back on Thursday.' Grammar fell apart in her presence.

The nun consulted her book; the turning leaves sighed. 'Rather a pity you didn't think to ring the convent last night. I suppose we could bring in that nice Dundalk girl if it's no more than three days; she's always grateful for the work. We don't want your class to be falling behind, so early in the term.' Sister Dominic looked over her bifocals with the eyes of a Baroque martyr. 'I don't suppose you could go to them now and keep them occupied until I can get hold of the girl? Just till lunchtime?'

Thirty faces rose in front of me, squealing their requests. 'No, Sister, I'm afraid not, sorry. I have to pick up some visitors from the airport.'

'Can't be helped.' Sister Dominic shut her book with a weighty snap. 'I'll have to send Sister Barbara to sit with them if she's feeling up to it. Now I would love to say a little prayer with you for consolation, but I'm in too much of a hurry; as you know, I don't like to begin Assembly much past 9.03. You may be sure I'll have all the children pray for the repose of the soul of ... what did you say your friend's name was?'

'Cara.' My throat locked on the word.

'Of poor Tara.'

I wanted to claw the name back out of her mouth. She didn't even remember her, after six years of merciless teasing about redheads.

'Well, Penelope, God grant us all such a swift end.'

Any minute now she'd inform me that the good died young. 'See you on Thursday, Sister,' I muttered, backing out of her office as if away from a throne.

I walked downstairs like a zombie. Robbie was staple-gunning his children's pictures to the noticeboard; he looked relieved to see anyone out of pigtails. I tried to get by with a limp smile, but he called me back. 'Where you off to at nine in the morning, hen?'

'Going home.'

'Lucky bastard,' he said in a careful whisper.

'Something's come up,' I told him; such an awful euphemism. And then a sudden need for company seized me. 'If you've a free now, could you come for a coffee?'

Robbie pushed his fringe out of his eyes. 'When have I

ever got a free? After getting this lot of potato prints on to the wall I've thirty-six infants to club to death.'

I glanced at the rows of printed hearts, clowns' faces, and something that looked like a purple mushroom, repeated over and over, getting fainter towards the bottom of the paper. How good it would be to be five again, with nothing to do but cut slices out of potatoes.

'Monday morning, and I'm panting for the weekend already,' he yawned. 'You ever going to come walking with me and Sheila and the pups?'

'Some Sunday, definitely. Give me a ring later, maybe?' I asked him, my voice getting a little vibrato. 'Only if you're not busy,' I called, and crashed out through the swing doors into the warm air.

Down in the loose gravel of the car park, squashed damsons from an overhanging tree sent up a whiff of ferment. Scrabbling in my handbag for Minnie's keys, I let my eyes rest on the grass. Across the back lawn a red uniform came loping. Whoever she was, she was going to be late for Assembly. Carroty hair, clashing with the jumper. Shorter, too; a much more ordinary body than the one it had reminded me of.

If I shut my eyes I could see Cara in uniform still, though I had watched her rip it up with relish on the day of the sixth-year party. The red hood she hated in particular; once, bored at the bus stop, she buttoned it on the wrong way round, over her face, and tried to get me to lead her on to the bus, with her repeating, 'I am noth a monsther. I am the elephanth woman.'

Seventeen and a half, she looked, as long as I knew her. It came flooding at me now, as I stared over the car door at the redhead pounding towards the side entrance, the distillation of god knew how many wintry afternoons.

Ten minutes after the bell I stride out of the school gate with my gaberdine hood up and shielding my face, just in case the day is considering another dash of rain. My mind is full of algebra and whether Mum will have bought any bread. I am always hungry in winter. Halfway to the bus stop, I hear feet flapping behind me on the pavement.

Cara, who was supposed to be out sick. I have to hug her, she looks so Snow White with the cold.

'Get your hands off me.' She recoils.

'Sorry.'

'You could get us both expelled.'

'Friends hug,' I tell her forlornly.

'Not in uniform.'

I fall into step beside her. 'I don't see why you're giving out to me, I'm not the one who's been skiving off.'

'I amn't skiving exactly.' When I scan Cara's pale face, her eyes dip to the ground. 'I did come in today,' she says, 'but when I got off the bus I couldn't face it, with it being Thursday and all.'

'What have you got against Thursdays?'

She gives me a pained look. 'No Art.'

'Sorry, I forgot.'

'I knew I wouldn't get a glimpse of her all day unless I could contrive to be hanging round the noticeboards at the exact second when she'd be coming out of the staff-room.'

'Ah, Cara, there's more to life.' I cannot stop the exasperation from welling out.

She stops in her tracks, suddenly witch-faced. 'No there isn't. What's with you, are you turning jealous on me? If you can't accept –'

'I've always accepted it.' Careful now, Pen, soften the voice again. 'You know that your, what you feel for Mrs Mew, is the thing I admire most about you.'

Cara nods reverently, and we fall into step again. 'You see why I couldn't face today. It made more sense to stay away from school and dream of her. I knew I'd do her more good that way.'

We stop at the oak on the corner, and I glance at the bus stop too briefly for her to notice. Probably missed it already. 'So what did you do all day?'

'Hung around the Proddie cemetery mostly; they've got such funny double-barrelled names. Sheltered in the hardware shop when it was raining.'

'Did you have your pack lunch at least?' I know I sound like a mother but I need to ask.

'Cheese sandwiches, but I left them at home; couldn't have faced them anyway.'

My face sinks. 'Ah petal, you need your protein. So what did you eat all day?'

'I must have overdosed on sherbet because I was sick behind a tomb statue of a little girl with wings. I hope she didn't mind.'

'You can't go on like this.' My voice snaps harder than I meant.

Cara stares down at me as if I have stabbed her under the arm. The plump lower lip juts. 'But that's what I said to you on the phone last night, and you said yes I could, if I thought positive thoughts and had lots of comforting hot baths.'

I take a heavy breath. 'No, what I meant was you could go on with life, with coping – but this isn't coping.'

'I cope,' she says in surprise, wiping her fringe out of her eyes. 'I haven't run away to sea or anything. Bet you wish I would, though,' she adds.

'No I don't.' I find it hardest to sound convincing when I am telling the truth.

'Bet you do sometimes. Didn't realize you'd be letting yourself in for all this when we became sort-of-girlfriends, did you?'

'It has its compensations,' I tell her, and she grins wider than a slice of melon. 'So. How long have you been lurking out here?'

'Couple of hours, I think. Left my watch at home so I had to guess by the sun. I thought you might come out early,' Cara adds wistfully; 'hadn't you got a double free after Maths?'

I lean back against the hedge, then feel the wet and

straighten up. 'No, sorry, I stayed in the library, it's easier to work there than at home.'

'You're a swot. You prefer books to me.'

'No I don't. Listen, petal, I'm really sorry I didn't come out earlier, but you mustn't stand round in the cold.'

'Yes, boss.' Cara is perking up, twisting her cow's lick between her fingers. 'Can I come home with you now?'

'Ah, you know you can't.'

She opens her grey eyes till she is Deirdre of the Sorrows. She knows I'm a sucker for that look. 'I wouldn't be any bother.'

'It wouldn't be fair to surprise Mammy with a visitor on a Thursday.'

'Why, does she hate Thursdays too?' asks Cara.

'No, you eejit. Daddy's payday's Friday.'

'So?'

I am ridiculously awkward. 'So Mammy won't have been shopping yet, and we might have nothing but baked beans in the house, and Gavin will be mouthing off.'

'Ah,' she says, her forehead still furrowed. 'My dad shops every two days, I think. But I like baked beans,' she smiles.

'Oh, stop it.'

Cara can change tactics faster than anyone I know. 'Tell your mother I'm not hungry, I'll wait in your room.'

'And that's another thing, the walls are paper-thin.'

'Ah da pur wee gurlie, is she ashamed?' She skips around me.

'It's not about shame, it's about getting thrown out into the street without a spare sock.'

'You've got me, I'm your old s.o.g. But your parents wouldn't throw you out.'

'I wouldn't bet money on it. Anyway, it would be worse if they let me stay but had thrown me out inside, if you know what I mean.'

Cara takes pity on my incoherence, and puts her chilly hand deep into my gaberdine pocket to find my thumb. 'I only meant, they're not likely to guess; we look like all the other pairs of best friends. Let me come over, and I promise I won't squeak this time.'

My head shakes, heavy as a marionette.

'Ah, please please please. I'll twiddle your nipples.'

'Stop it, they can hear you.' I allow a smile to bubble up. 'Why can't you go home to your own house?'

Her face is sullen. 'It spooks me.'

'But it's so roomy, and all that lovely furniture, and your father's so nice.'

Cara pulls her fingers out of my pocket. 'He's not on this planet most of the time. He comes in for tea from the library with his fingers grey from those mouldy old books. It's a ghost house since the others went to the States. If I go into the middle bedroom I always feel Kate watching me in case I touch her trophies or try on her clothes.'

I restrain my head from turning towards the bus stop. 'Look, love, if you go home now I'll ring you at eight.'

'Seven.'

'If I have my Biology done. And I'll come over tomorrow afternoon and we'll go to the woods and I'll make you smile.'

Without changing colour, Cara can give the impression of going pink. 'If you really want to.'

I am winning. 'And no following me on the next bus and hanging round outside the kitchen window; you scared Mum witless last time.'

'I said all right. But what'll I do tonight?'

Not wanting to trip at the last hurdle, I scan my memory. '*Top of the Pops* is on; that gorgeous Mexican woman might have made it into the top ten. And you could have a long scorcher of a bath.'

'Borrrring.' My sort-of-girlfriend smiles, showing her canines.

'I'll ring you at eight.'

'Seven. Pen?' Her face slipping again.

'What?'

'Tell me nice things.'

I turn back, weakened by compassion. 'We could go to the mountains on Saturday.'

'No, but about her, Mrs Mew. I won't see her all weekend.'

An inspiration: 'The photos of the school concert will be ready; you'll have your own picture of her.'

Cara's face lights up then fades in one wave. 'It's hopeless. Be honest with me, amn't I pathetic?'

'No you're not. More nice things, let's see. Not long to Christmas.'

'You're scraping the bottom of the barrel there.' She plucks a tiny leaf from the hedge and sets it in my palm; it holds a platinum drop of rain.

'Bye now, love.'

'Pen?'

Her voice melts my exasperation, and I walk back one more time. 'Yeah.'

'Do you, I was wondering, do you still love me when I'm not here?'

'When are you not here?'

'When I'm not with you.'

'Oh yes,' I tell her. 'Probably more so.'

'That's because I'm a gobby little toe-rag.' Cara's face is joyful. She waves behind her head as she canters down to the traffic lights.

My mind crawled back to the present, to the hot car seat stuck to my thighs. I had so much to do today, so many surreal little tasks; I had no time to waste daydreaming about schooldays.

Parked outside the post office, I turned straight to the back page of the newspaper for the first time. Babies and engagements and . . . yes, they'd got my message and fitted it in. I supposed they kept the columns empty until just before going to print. But how did they know how much space to leave for each category? Perhaps there was some sort of equation that gave you the average number of *Irish Times* readers' deaths for each day of the year, adjusted for seasonal variations such as office parties.

WALL, it began, like a children's spelling book. *WALL, suddenly, Cara, beloved daughter of Ian and Winona.* How she would have liked that name; how she would have pranced round introducing herself with 'Hi, I'm Wall Suddenly Cara'. *House private*, it went on; what a discreet way of telling relatives not to waddle round with cheesecakes. *Deeply regretted*, the notice concluded, *by her family circle.* That was my phrase, one that could include me by some stretch of the imagination; 'circle' sounded too symmetrical, but it would have to do. I read the words right through twice more, trying to believe them, but they sounded more fictional every time.

I folded the newspaper in half and laid it on the other seat. Sun drizzled through my thick lashes. I waited to start crying, but nothing happened. I generally thought of myself as someone quite easily brought to tears, and not just by *Little House on the Prairie.* Whenever Cara and I had one of our trial breakups, I used to spend awful afternoons meeting her 'to talk it through' in city-centre cafés, tears plopping into cups of Earl Grey tea. But now I was sitting here on my own it was not safe to cry, because there would be no one to hear, no one to mop me up, no way to stop except to cough my way to a halt and feel the water crust into salt on my jaw. So I drove home instead.

Though I didn't get back till half nine, there was no message from the airport. Damn it, I had known something would go wrong. Walking into the kitchen with my finger skimming the woodchip wallpaper, I wondered whether they would look American. Winona would, of course; according to Mr Wall, she looked American when she was Winnie Mulhuddart fresh from County Limerick. But Kate I was not sure about. Vigorous dark hair, I remembered, curlier than mine; the curls cropped by now, no doubt. A strong jaw; I remembered it one afternoon in French, grinding a honey-filled cough lozenge in slow motion, hypnotizing my eyes. She'd say 'Pehhn' – no, more like 'Pain, ahll cahl yah'. No, you eejit, that was Deep South. What was a Boston accent? 'Pen, al cawl yew'. Why would she be calling you anyway, you daft egg, when she'd be staying at your house? Her house, I meant. Or was it a little of each now? Got to get a grip.

On no account must I try to impress Kate Wall, I reminded myself, filling the saucepan from the spitting tap. No ironed cotton napkins at dinner, no medium-expensive wine. She would have no need of a hug or a tampon or anything else a gracious hostess could provide. Neither should I cook anything ambitious; this was a woman who probably served sushi at dinner parties. Cara used to reminisce about the way her sister made brandy snaps, curved over the handle of a wooden spoon. She once mimed it for me on a biro, reverent.

I brought a cup of coffee in to Mr Wall, but his study was empty; he must have walked to his walnut-panelled office in the Wotherby library at twenty to nine, like any ordinary day. And after all, if you wanted it to be an ordinary day, it was probably best to pretend that it was. Then for a few seconds at a time you might forget your personal headlines and escape into wonderful mundanity. I left the cup to cool on a pile of *Rare Book Digest* while I browsed through his tape collection of composers whose names all seemed to begin with B.

On top of the stereo was the message pad we kept beside the downstairs phone. 'Garda O'Connor', it said at the top, followed by 'one ten or thereabouts, taxi hit behind, lone driv., poss. alcohol. Both drivers crit. inj.'. There was a space, and then, at the bottom, 'C. no belt, head impact window, prob. instantaneous'. I stared at the words as if at hieroglyphs that gradually deciphered themselves. That must have been the police who rang this morning. I wondered why Mr Wall had made these reporterly notes. Could he not trust his ears to retain such grotesqueries? As the clock hand moved to five past ten with a tiny scrape I drank his coffee myself, in three gulps.

Phone calls, shopping, clean sheets, I muttered over and over, like a list of demands on a march. Dust sparkled past me on the stairs. I leaned against the hall mirror and turned the overwritten pages of Cara's Snoopy address book. I began with Amazon Attic, which was top of the list in several senses.

Of course it would have to be Sherry who picked up the phone; I recognized her husky giggle. 'Who? Oh, Cara's Pen, sorry. Listen, could you tell her I want my toothbrush back? I've just remembered, we found it at the last minute and she put it in the side pocket of her bag.'

'I don't think –'

'It's a yellow one. Listen, how are you, Pen? We had the *best* holiday, has Cara been telling you? Spent the last day on the beach having a contest to see who could put their nipples in their own mouths.'

I opened my lips against the mouthpiece, but nothing came out.

'So, how are you yourself?' she rolled on. 'Did the measly Irish sun shine on you at all while we were away?'

'On and off.'

'It's glorious today, though, I have to say. The roses are gone all crumpled, it's wild. You must come round and sunbathe nude in our clover patch.'

'I don't think I can.' The conversation was becoming impossible. 'Could I possibly, is Jo there? I have to –'

'Sure, hang on, she's making yoghurt.' A violent crack in my ear; Sherry must have let the receiver slide off the counter and dangle in a fern. I felt a momentary urge to put the phone down and steal away to the kitchen for something to fill my hollow belly. But Jo would be sure to ring me right back.

'Howarya.' Her voice patted my ear.

'I hope you've wiped your hands,' I told her, 'or your phone will be breeding its own culture.'

'That's what "lesbian subculture" means, you know, it's a kind of yoghurt.'

I had thrown back my head and laughed, before I remembered. Could I sober the conversation down in gradual stages now, or would it have to be wrenched into the mode of mourning?

'Seriously, now, what can I do you for?' Jo's vowels were very Dublin, very easy on the ear. 'Did Cara forget anything?'

'No. At least she might have.' Don't be silly, take a breath, your lungs are not sealed up. 'But she, I can't actually say this so why don't I ring you back later.'

'Whatever you like.'

Jo's gentleness gave me something to rest on, so I told her. My voice was curiously steady; I heard the sentence from a great distance. She went quiet for a long minute. She didn't say she was sorry. At last she cleared her throat in a great roar and said, 'I haven't taken this in at all yet.'

'Me neither.'

There was a pause. I thought I heard Jo swear, in an abstracted undertone, but couldn't be sure. Then in her practical voice she told me that she was sure they'd all be there on Wednesday, except Sherry, because she had sworn never to darken the door of a Catholic church again, but she'd probably come to the cemetery.

'Right.'

'Oh and by the way, are you, were you out to her family?'

I leaned my temple against the cool mirror and examined the little red tracks across my eyeballs. 'Not in so many words. I mean, some of us have homes and jobs we could lose, you know, we can't all just up and . . .'

'Don't get your knickers in a twist,' said Jo. 'I was just wondering should we go easy on the T-shirts.'

'Which T-shirts?'

'Well, Mairéad's latest full-time garment says "Fit for a Clit"; I thought I should warn you.'

'Oh god no, make her wear a plain black one.'

'Trust me.' Another long pause. 'Listen, I'm surprised you're holding together at all. Are you?'

'Far as I can tell.'

Jo wanted to know what she could do, people to contact and so on; she rode over my polite refusals. I read her any names and numbers I recognized from the address book; it gave me such relief to surrender them. I supposed that Jo, being the wiser side of forty, must have done this before. I wondered what formula she would find to leave on answerphones all round Dublin: 'Hi, this is Jo Butler ringing on behalf of Cara Wall. She can't speak to you herself right now because . . .'

As soon as Jo had finished talking, I promised myself, I could go out in the garden to let the sun bake my brain to powder. The light blinded my left eye as I leaned back against the banisters. That small window over the stairs was streaky and cobwebbed; I'd have to see to it. Couldn't have the homecoming Walls thinking I'd let their house go to pot.

'. . . and I can't even claim to have known her that well.' Jo seemed to be winding down. 'It was only the summer really. This is completely unreal.'

I shut my ears to her. The last rainfall had left long fingerprints on the glass.

'And you two had something really special going there, Pen. I could tell how much she cared about you. I've always thought, you know, it's not whether a relationship is monogamous or open or whatever, it's the quality of it.'

'Sorry?'

There was a hesitation on the line. 'Well, with you two, the issue wasn't like being a one-to-one exclusive coupley-type couple, was it?' Jo was asking. 'The way Cara described it, it sounded like you two had a strong bond, but also room to breathe, you know? Which I happen to know from experience you don't get if you're doing the monogamy thing.'

'I was.'

'Sorry?'

I kept the stream of words gentle and blistering. 'I've been faithful to Cara for thirteen years. I've never been to bed with anyone else. What do you think, Jo, does that make me monogamous?'

Silence on the line.

'Though of course I was well aware that she had a little current something on the side, or in the Attic, rather. Didn't know she was telling the world we had an open relationship, though. You'd be the one to ask, actually, I've been wondering: was it Sherry?'

Jo's voice sounded tiny. 'I don't think this is the best time to talk. I'm sorry I've upset you.'

'No, no, I'm fine. See you Wednesday,' I finished, almost jovial, and put down the phone, very careful not to let it slam.

Big breaths until the helmet over my brain started to lift off. There was no harm in Jo. She wasn't to know. There was no need to take things out on her. My face met me in the mirror. So near, it looked chalky and monstrous. There was fog on the glass from my breath, and my nose had smudged it. I went to rummage in the cupboard under the stairs for a fistful of rags.

By lunchtime I had done every mirror and window in the house except the one in the back bedroom. I sat on the rust-sprinkled sill with my feet tucked under Cara's bed for anchorage, leaning out backwards to try to smack a cobweb off the outside of the pane. The last time the outsides had been done was the spring, I remembered. Cara had gone up on a ladder while I scrubbed at the insides. I was kneeling painfully on the radiator in the back bedroom when her manic grin appeared from the ivy. I jumped, but she was safe enough. We leaned on the window for a kiss, half a centimetre of cold glass between us. Her eyes shut and her tongue escaped from her lips, but when she tasted grit and cobwebs she made a face and reached for her cleaning fluid, spraying a circle to white out our faces.

'Ah, hi there?'

I woke from my daydream, and peered down past my shoulder. My headscarf was slipping over one eye. 'Yes?' I called.

'I'm looking for Mr Wall. Or Ms O'Grady. I rang the bell.'

It could be, except there was no luggage. 'Are you, is it Kate? Be right down,' I bawled, and wrenched myself off the sill. A glance in the mirror showed that there was nothing I could do except pull off the scarf and practise a bedraggled smile.

When I opened the front door, breathing hard, I thought there was no one there. Then she stepped out from the overhanging honeysuckle. 'So, is my father home?'

Such a restrained voice, after all my expectations. Darker skin than I remembered, darker everything. The curls remained, but lay back more slickly. 'Not right now but come in, come in,' I gabbled. Kate wiped her heels on the mat. My hands were sticky with window-cleaner; I couldn't offer one to shake. 'Well. Welcome home.'

'Thank you, but it's not my home.' She stepped past me into the hall. Not as tall as I remembered, or maybe it was I who had grown. I seemed to be looming over her.

'Is your mother in the taxi?'

'Afraid not. I called her yesterday morning. She was committed to giving the keynote address at a conference in Detroit. It just couldn't be cancelled at such short notice.'

I sucked on the inside of my lip.

Kate turned. 'And you are?'

I looked at her blankly, digging my fists into the pockets of my cardigan. 'Oh, but I'm Pen, I spoke to you on the phone.'

Her face opened into a guilty smile; all the bones shifted under the skin. 'I do apologize. I thought – well, it was the headscarf.'

A wave of shame began at my neck. I turned away and answered, 'No, I'm afraid we don't have any cleaning ladies, it's just me and a bottle of window-cleaner twice a year. Come on in, let me make you a cup of tea. Or coffee, if you . . . have you no bags?'

We discussed the criminal negligence of luggage-handlers as I hung up her trench-coat in the bulging cupboard. I said I would have been happy to have come and get her from the airport; she said it seemed simpler to take a cab. Then she was staring past me. 'My god,' she whispered, 'he never threw away my duffel coat.' I stood out of the way. Its stiff hood ducked and its sleeves bobbed as she lifted it down by the neck.

To fill the silence, I let out a little breath of amusement. 'Haven't seen toggles like those for a while. We've got a box of old clothes for Oxfam . . .'

'It would seem cruel to make a nineties child wear this.'

'No, no, they love them.'

Kate gave the coat a disdainful shake. 'Filthy with dust. And look, the bottom toggle's missing.'

Complicit, I tugged open the back door, and Kate stepped into the yard. She pushed the grey duffel well into the bin. Then in the middle of our first grin I remembered that we were virtual strangers, and busied myself with the saucepan. When I caught her looking over my shoulder, I explained that we'd had a little accident with the kettle.

The clinking of teaspoons filled the chinks between sentences about how unusual this weather was for Ireland. I was going to offer to lend her some clothes until her bag was recovered from its detour to Zurich, but a glimpse of her suede shoes cost me my nerve. Once the coffee had been poured I asked, too bluntly, 'Do you want to know about the accident?'

Kate's eyelids flickered. 'Sure.'

I found it helped if I kept the sentences short and pretended I was reading the news. 'It was just after one on Saturday night. Cara was in a taxi coming back from the airport. She'd been away in Greece with some friends.'

'How many were in the taxi?'

'No, just her, they'd gone ahead, she'd had to wait for her bag.'

Kate nodded, businesslike.

'Well apparently,' I resumed, 'a car stove into the taxi from behind. They think he might have been drunk.'

'Did he –'

'Both the drivers got hurt. But they had seat-belts on. Cara was in the back, you see, because it was a taxi. If it was a private car she'd probably have been in the front where they have seat-belts. But only new cars have to have them in the back. The taxi must have been an old car. I don't know what the law's like in America, but that's how it is over here.'

She was nodding still.

'So that's all I know,' I finished, almost brightly. 'The funeral is on Wednesday; I'm sure your bags will have turned up by then.'

'I could always wear this,' Kate said, casting her eyes down at her dark brown trouser-suit, 'but it might scandalize the relatives. I presume they've been told?'

'Mr Wall said he'd do them tonight,' I said.

That was clearly all we were going to say about the main event. I chattered on: 'I've never understood why we still wear black to' – suddenly I couldn't manage the word – 'these ceremonies.' I took a slug of tea and went on. 'Black is glamorous nowadays, it's no privation to wear it. Beige, now, that'd be a true mortification of the worldly mourner.'

'I think black was always glamorous,' said Kate with a yawn behind short smooth nails. 'You know, the grieving widow look.'

That's me, I thought, disconcerted: the grieving widow. I was suddenly ravenous, remembering I had eaten nothing all morning. 'Cheese?' I hauled the plate of odds and ends out of the fridge, and showed it to her.

'I'm too tired right now, but thank you.'

I laid into the leaking wedge of Brie. I didn't care if she thought me insensitive.

'My mother used to wear a lace mantilla to nuns' funerals,' Kate went on. 'They dropped like flies in the cold season.'

'They have to live longer now; the stream of new vocations is almost dried up. But Sister Dom will live for ever.'

Kate's bushy eyebrows drew together in a look the pit of my stomach remembered. 'Excuse me?'

I felt rather foolish to be rabbiting on about the nuns. 'Where would we be without them, eh?' I asked.

'Book about them a few years back, very big in the States,' she went on, her bony fingers snapping a water biscuit.

The cat-flap slammed open, and there was Grace, scratching at my chair leg; I pushed him down.

'Most of them went into the convent because they had the hots for some choir nun and thought it was platonic.'

I tapped my knee, and Grace leaped up, knocking his head on the table and pretending it hadn't happened. He licked up a splinter of cracker. 'Never knew a choir nun who'd lead anyone's thoughts to God,' I said lightly, scratching behind the cat's toast-brown ears. 'Remember Sister Luke? Tone-deaf but still loves music. She used to burst in through the swing-doors halfway through "Jesu Joy of Man's Desiring", shouting "Sing up, girls! Sing up!"'

Kate's eyebrows contracted again. 'How would I know your choir nun?'

'She wasn't the choir nun, she was just passing by,' I said. 'You were there. Immac.'

'Immac? Oh, Immaculate Conception, I'm sorry, my brains are addled with jet-lag. What, did you go there too?'

Grace clung to my trousers as I stood up, then heaved himself away. I went over to the larder for some mustard to stimulate my disappearing appetite. 'I was in your class, Cáit Máire Fionnuala Wall,' I said over my shoulder.

'You weren't! God almighty, I had no idea.' Kate's voice was slipping into Irish intonation. 'I'm not Cáit any more, though.'

'I know.'

'I never let them call me that, past the age of reason.'

'I remember.'

'That's such a coincidence. Small world, Dublin.'

'It's not a coincidence.' I nibbled on a hard rind of cheese. 'It's how I know Cara. Didn't she tell you who I was?'

'Look, all I got for the past few years were Christmas cards from my father, with a big C scrawled on the bottom.'

Well, there was me in my place. Hot-faced, I focused on the last corner of cracker. To be expected, really, I mean, Cara had no call to mention me.

Kate's mahogany eyes were sizing me up. 'You weren't the hockey captain, were you?'

'That was Penelope Pearse.'

'So which one were you?' she asked, combing her hair back with her fingers.

'I wasn't anyone in particular,' I said. My cup was leaving a wet circle on the wood; I wiped it away with my hand. 'I only came to Immac in fourth year, when my family moved to the southside. And then after I ballsed up the Inter I got moved down into Cara's class to repeat it.'

'Hang on, I think I'm getting there. Were you –' Kate paused. I could tell she was straining for tact. 'The girl I'm thinking of was much smaller. With hair held back in clips.'

'That's me,' I said excitedly. 'I was a real skinnymalinks in those days; it didn't suit me. Nor did the clips.'

We grinned at each other. 'We all looked such geeks in that uniform,' she commented.

'Except Cara. Her hair was the exact shade of the gaberdine.' The words trailed off. I sipped the last of my coffee.

I left Kate yawning over her cup, and ran upstairs in search of clean bedclothes. Five 'Our Fathers', as I tucked the sheets under the mattress in the middle room. This bed hadn't been slept in for years, not since Mr Wall's last visiting archivist. I left the window a little ajar. The heady smell of cut grass floated up from next door's garden where the dentist with the sunburnt bald spot was mowing.

Coming through the hall, I paused outside the glass door.

Kate and the cat were watching each other. She took a crumb of cheddar and held it at ankle level; Grace ignored it. His tail spiralled in the air as he walked away.

'Don't mind him, he has personality problems.'

Kate looked up, then put the cheese back on the edge of the chopping board. 'I never know how to behave around animals.'

'Ah, Grace is a particular bugger.'

'Why is he called something so . . .'

'Girlish?' I slid the cheese plate back into the fridge. 'Well, at the time Cara rescued him from a bankrupt wholefood co-op, she was going through a liberal phase where she thought patriarchy could be gently dismantled by educating boys to be more like girls. He was the only young male she had to experiment on.'

Kate absorbed this. I could tell that the very vocabulary of her sister's life was alien to her. 'But why Grace?'

'Look at his one white paw. Isn't it just a little bit like a Grace Kelly above-the-elbow glove?'

The cat, always loth to comply, skulked in the pantry.

'Come on out of there.' I pulled him out by the scruff and sat him on my chest. 'He liked to sleep in there among the onions when he was very small. He was always knocking containers over, and that's another reason we called him Grace, because he hasn't got any.'

Kate's hand was covering a yawn. Why would she be interested in the details of our ménage, anyway? She was only passing through. Grace dug his claws into my cardiganed breast; I plucked him loose.

'I do remember you, you know,' she said as she followed me upstairs.

I made a non-committal grunt.

'It's starting to come back to me. We used to kid around in choir, right?'

'The odd time.'

'Funny how moving somewhere new can wipe the slate clean. I haven't thought about Immac or this place for years. But as soon as the plane touched down at Dublin Airport it all started opening up in my head.'

'Can of worms?'

'More like a can of soup. Just tiny things, all blurred together.'

I held the door of the middle bedroom for Kate to go ahead of me. She glanced around as if something was missing.

'I don't think much has been changed, except the wallpaper.'

'I never could stand that floral stuff anyway,' she said, folding her jacket over the desk chair. She ran her finger along the inscription below a silver statuette of a javelin-thrower; it came away grey at the tip. I felt a stab of guilt. For god's sake, she could hardly have expected me to stay up late dusting her school trophies.

'So, were there any sports you didn't win prizes for?' I asked.

'I wasn't all that good. These are just kids' stuff.' Her voice closed like a box.

I offered to bring her an alarm clock; she didn't need one. A glass of water? No, she was fine. An ashtray, if she was a smoker? Not any more. I backed out, wondering how someone could go from chatty to taciturn in half a minute.

'Doing good, Pen,' I chanted under my breath on the stairs. A highly creditable morning, clean windows and all. The next thing to do was to find something to fill the afternoon. Pity it wasn't a home funeral, come to think of it, because then I would have to spend today and Tuesday making little savouries and ironing tablecloths. As it was, I could hardly start cooking dinner before half five. Two and a half hours, that wasn't long at all; wash up the cups, see to the compost heap. I wouldn't take the hammock down from the pear tree yet, it was still summery enough, Cara would want it. I meant, she always hated to see it taken down. Like the Christmas tree, which in the big house was always exquisite in white lights and snow webs, not like my mother's gaudy edifice. Cara made me leave the tree up till the fourteenth of January once, and it shed needles all over the carpet.

Between the bottom stair and the kitchen door all my energy drained away. It seemed too great an effort to keep on taking breaths, one after another after another, let alone do a productive afternoon's housework. I pulled a shiny magazine from the hall bookshelf, one so old that I would have forgotten the contents and it would seem new again. I shoved it into the pocket of my cardigan, found my house key, and set off for the woods.

The big house actually backed on to the bottom of the park, making Mr Wall nervous of gangs of cider louts, but the wall was too high to get over. I had to walk up to the main gate, past a bungalow that had a vicious Jack Russell who always waited till you went daydreaming by his wooden door before shrieking at your feet and giving you heart failure. The little mutant wouldn't stop me today; I'd kick him as soon as look at him.

A benediction of sun fell on my half-closed eyes as I headed up the empty avenue. Past the bungalow, no sign of the beast. My steps slowed as sweat began to cool the backs of my knees. I went to the woods every day I had a spare hour, which was most days. It was one of the only places left in Dublin with a bit of wilderness about it, even if they did pare a couple more trees away every year.

Long before I knew the Walls I used to get the bus out here once a week. Mum would have liked me to stay on in the Girl Guides and win badges for Punctuality or Needle-craft, but I preferred to spend my Saturdays wandering. Then later on when Cara and I became sort-of-girlfriends, we used to come here all the time, to chase each other with handfuls of leaves and kiss in the chinks between the rocks. She hadn't been coming with me so often the last few years; said it was a wee bit boring and would I mind if she read *Spare Rib* instead. Cara's idea of a walk, I used to tease her, came complete with a torn map and wizened villagers and the thrilling possibility that fog might come down on the mountain-top. I didn't mind, really. I liked leaving her folded up in the sagbag with her pint-glass of jasmine tea while I went walking. But I never understood what she meant by boring. How could trees be boring?

The gate was hanging open today, its varnish peeling in the heat. Not as many people here as I expected for this weather; maybe they were all attempting to go topless in their back patios, seizing their last chance for a September tan. All I could see as I made my way over to the rock pile was a cocker spaniel and her slow-moving nuclear family. They had gone by the time I reached the summit of the rocks and fitted my hips into a warm crevice.

Five minutes, Pen old chap, I told myself, then read your magazine or you'll be blubbering, and that's just too exhausting in this heat. But oddly enough I felt in no danger of tears. My skin was parched, that little dry spot on my right eyelid beginning to itch again. The trick seemed to be to remember only the irritating times. The good times were dangerous. Last night, for instance, that was a mistake, letting myself remember the sweetness of her on the convent roof. The hours after that particular memory had been bitches. But the endless discussions (as we used to call our rows), they were easier to remember unmoved, perhaps because every line of them was so hackneyed.

After the first year together, it occurred to me now, I could have left Cara at home in the sagbag every time and strolled into the woods to have our discussions on my own. You see, I was better at them. I was more concerned for the logic of each accusation, the assignment of points, whereas at a certain stage Cara just couldn't give a shit and her grey eyes would wander towards the horizon. This arrangement could have saved a lot of time, I realized now, because on a half-hour's walk between the trees I could have presented the week's complaints with more brevity, reached the penultimate insults more rapidly, swung to a reconciliation and still been home in time for tea.

Jo had a theory – I had heard this at second-hand through Cara – Jo claimed that the reason people survived breakups was that within days of the amputation, Mother Nature started reminding you of what you had been doing without, what could have been better, all the small discontents you had been filing away. And Jo, having survived twenty-odd years of serial and overlapping relationships, should know. It sounded a plausible enough theory, and quite comforting in the case of such a breakup, but not applicable to my situation. Since Cara came back to me after the last time, half a decade ago, we had never given a serious thought to breaking up. And never would now, it occurred to me. How odd; wedded for life, because one of us had died.

On that word I paused, watching for a seizure in the throat, an iron bolt behind the eyes. My hand reached for my magazine just in case. But no, I seemed perfectly numb this afternoon. Kate being so ordinary, in her smart way, so much less evocative than she might have been. Besides, I needed all my energy for coping with this weather which was growing heavier by the minute, the hot air thickening on my cheeks, my thighs, the backs of my fingers.

I could see all the way across the southside from this knob of rock. The books Cara brought back from England and America were mostly about urban dykes in trench-coats solving capitalist mysteries, or rural bare-breasted ones tending wounded deer. But most of the real ones I'd ever come across were quietly rebellious products of the suburbs, wearing waistcoats over ladylike shirts at dinner-parties. I grinned to think of them all going about their business down there, all the dykes I didn't know. Nowadays 'invisibility' was supposed to be the big problem, but the way I saw it was, all that mattered was to be visible to yourself. I didn't watch telly to see anyone remotely like me, anyway. Though it was fun to catch sight of the odd out-and-proud lipstick leather lesbian on a Channel 4 documentary, it thrilled me far more to think of a mother-of-three reaching out to touch another woman's breast for the first time. I looked down on the miles of grey roofs, now, imagining the spread of the quiet epidemic.

The towers on Sandymount Strand were belching idle smoke. What a messy structure a city was, each street echoing its neighbour before trailing off into a crescent or a cul-de-sac. Rather like our discussions, Cara's and mine, which were variations on one basic pattern. Certain key phrases got repeated endlessly: mine were 'Ah, come on, pet' or 'You know you're exaggerating', and hers were much more dramatic, 'I make myself sick' or 'What's the point?' Sometimes, just for an experiment, I would sneak in one of her despairing phrases; for a moment she would look at me in puzzlement, and then rush to offer reassurance. If that's my role, I used to think, watching the words flow out of her tender mouth, what a bore I must be.

But the trees were never boring, as I wound my way between them; tall as Rapunzel's tower, wrapped in their own hair. I didn't know all the right names, since my Biology class had finished trees by the time I got back from having mumps. But I was intimate with their skins. There was the peeling one with orange bark behind flaking grey; the gnarled, ever-pregnant one; and the tallest and smoothest, on which some thug had carved a swastika with their penknife. I liked to stroke that one with my fingertips; I imagined the scar pained it. They would look their best by October. Already the leaves were baking into lemon and caramel.

The very best thing about these woods was the suspension of time. Compared to these topless towers I was no taller now, in my long cardigan, than the teenaged Pen who had spent her Saturdays here. Apart from the distant thumps and calls of the tennis court, and the odd discarded condom, nothing had changed since the seventies. In the thickest part of the woods, where the trees were only ten feet apart, it could be any date I chose, and sometimes it seemed to me that all the years were one, a handful of seasons repeating themselves, the conversations like snakes swallowing their own tails.

'That day in town in the summer,' I begin, walking in the woods with Cara.

'Which summer?'

'Last summer. The day you ran. Why was it that you ran?'

'Away.'

'From what?'

'Away.' Cara's skin is bone-white behind the freckles.

I try again, my voice as friendly as a talk-show host. 'You must remember what you were feeling.'

'Afraid.'

At last. 'Afraid of what?'

'The people.'

'So it was a sort of an agoraphobic feeling?'

'Oh, don't ism and obia me,' snaps Cara.

'Well, was it a panic, then?'

'And you.'

I speak slowly to make the words sound less defensive. 'What had I done or said to make you afraid of me?'

'Nothing.' Cara's voice is weary.

I must get to the bottom of it before she runs out of momentum. 'Maybe it was basically the crowd that spooked you; it was a hot day and a terrible crush.'

Her gaze is cool. 'No, it was mostly you.' She winds a dark strand of hair around her finger.

'I hadn't done a thing.' My voice cracks with annoyance. 'You just upped and ran away from me like a madwoman.'

'Forget it, so. Momma knows best.'

Calm the tone again. 'No, I'm not blaming you' – (lies, lies) – 'I'd just be interested to know why you did it.'

'Don't remember.' She yawns.

'You must. Think back; it was that really sunny day, we were on the top floor of that bookshop and I'd just knocked over a pile of –'

'I know it was a sunny day, for fuck's sake.' Her eyes are gun-metal. 'I'm telling you why and you're not listening to me, you're swallowing me up again. I didn't want to be on the same street as you, that's all.'

I glance down at my hands; they are folded in their Mother Superior position, bouncing slightly on my belly as we walk. 'Why did you stop running, then? Just because you ran out of breath?'

She lets her eyes unfocus; the pupils are webbed with grey, like stagnant ponds.

The rock was crushing my hip, so I tugged myself up and headed for the gate. My legs were aching and my head was hammering. I lowered my eyelids but the sun still came through, diffracted into a spectrum on each lash. I rubbed at my right eye, then told myself to stop.

We used to go on arguing like that for hours, Cara and I. Solving nothing, changing nothing, simply exchanging words by role, by rote, until the day was filled up and we could run a hot bath and lie peaceful together, the water lapping all language away. And it did me no good to recall particular conversations (if indeed these were particular conversations I was remembering so vividly, rather than inventions of my uneasy brain). Remembering clarified nothing. There were few things more pointless, I told myself as I shut the gate with a clatter, than arguing with a dead person, and that, though I didn't believe it myself, was what she officially was.

It was ten past five by the time I got back to the big house, but the day had got no cooler. Sweat had sewn an invisible scarf around my throat. I leaned against the kitchen counter, its tiles deliciously cold across my waist. I drank half a pint of raspberry cordial, then headed for the hammock, but it was full.

I was not half so angry to see Jo as I thought I would be. My outburst on the phone this morning seemed rather silly; she had been quite right in her facts. Besides, I liked Jo. Mostly, I had to admit, because she was fat like me. We were not exactly friends – I only knew her through Cara, and from bumping into her in bookshops and at women's dances – but whenever she and I found ourselves sitting side by side, we grinned, and all the others looked so insubstantial.

Today Jo was the colour of buttered toast. She hauled herself up and made room for me on the edge of the hammock. Doubting it would take the pair of us, I leaned against it, watching Grace stalk invisible insects through the lettuce bed.

'Nice tan,' I remarked.

'You should have come with us.'

I gave the politest explanation. 'Term started weeks ago.'

'Right, I forgot. Oh, I brought some copies of my photos from the trip,' she added. 'Left them in the kitchen.'

And then, for the first time in weeks, I saw Cara's face whole, white in the sun, with the sharp widow's peak and the uneven, laughing lips. It was usually impossible to visualize someone you lived with, I knew, because you had seen so many of their faces that they overlayered and cancelled out. But just then Cara's came to me, sharper than a photograph.

'You don't have to look today,' said Jo, her hot palm hovering on my elbow. 'I just thought you'd like to have them, but you should put them away in a drawer till you need them.'

I nodded slowly. 'Yeah. Would you . . .'

And down the garden path, in a brown satin dressing-gown, with bare feet that disappeared between the chrysanthemums, Kate picked her way. I hadn't even begun working out how to tell her about her sister and me, and now she found me practically lying in a hammock with a woman whose old blue T-shirt read 'Like a Fish Needs a Bicycle'.

'Ah, hi, Kate, this is –'

'We've met,' she said, passing a mug of coffee to Jo.

I sat down on the baked grass. 'Where d'you find the dressing-gown?'

'In the closet in my bedroom. It's my mother's; too Katharine Hepburn for me.'

'I thought you were sleeping,' I commented, too accusingly.

'The kids playing ball in the street kept waking me up. This kind soul has been giving me an update on Irish politics for the last fifteen years.'

'Bet that didn't take long.'

'Well, I have to admit,' said Jo, slurping her scalding coffee, 'that I just ranted a bit about gerrymandering in the North, then hopped straight to the abortion referenda.'

'Why does that not surprise me?'

'Ah, Pen, you're only a young thing; you can't help being pig-ignorant about your country's history.'

I watched Kate arrange herself on the wrought-iron seat, its white curlicues dragon-scaled from twenty years' painting and rusting. She folded the satin round her knees and took a careful sip of coffee. My eyes took the measure of her: all the same features, but some blurred, some hardened, as if I had glanced away for a second in which she had aged fourteen years. Grace hurtled by; Kate jumped, then settled back against the uncomfortable bars of the seat. How ridiculously genteel the setting was; ladies paying calls on a summer afternoon. The copper beech beside the bench was pale yellow still, only the top few leaves on each branch having aged into brown.

'Cara tried to claim the dole once,' I said aloud. The other two glanced up, as if embarrassed by the name. I carried on: 'She told them how hard up she was, how her father was an elderly widower who couldn't help, how they lived in this rotting bungalow with no hot water. So the dole office sent an inspector round here and found Mr Wall deadheading the roses. He was most embarrassed.'

Kate exhaled scornfully.

'I suppose Cara's argument,' said Jo lazily, 'would have been that she spent most of her days doing crucial voluntary work that the state should have paid for, so why not get them to fund her directly?'

'Still sounds rather parasitical to me,' said Kate, adjusting her dressing-gown.

Rage bubbled behind my forehead. I kept my mouth clamped shut until I could trust myself not to respond. Then I turned towards Jo. 'Tell me what I missed in the way of my country's history, so,' I instructed her, shutting my eyes and breathing in a waft of new-mown grass from next door.

'Well, the Pill train, for starters. I was there.'

'Ah go on. That was centuries back.'

'I was on it, I'm telling you. Belfast to Dublin with my knapsack full of pills and condoms.' Jo shook back her sandy layers of hair. 'And then the invasion of the Forty Foot gentleman-only bathing place by land, sea, and air. I've no head for heights or waves so I ran across the cliff and slapped my towel at an old fella who was covering his knick-knacks with one hand and making a fist at us with the other. Sarah, she was my' — a flicker of the eyes — 'friend at the time, she got a great photo for the *Irish Women's Liberation Newsletter*.'

Kate was smiling, with appreciation or disdain, I couldn't tell. I was suddenly uncomfortable under this stranger's half-lidded gaze. Faking a yawn, I straightened up. 'I've potatoes to put on; how are you at peeling, Jo?'

'Famed in the four provinces.'

'Don't be expecting anything gourmet,' I told Kate over my shoulder. We left her on the bench. I knew it was rude, but I couldn't bring myself to care. I dumped the ham in the biggest pot to boil and started scrubbing the carrots, while Jo stooped over the potatoes, cutting out the sprouting bits.

Her voice went soft so I knew she was going to talk about it. 'Everyone at the Attic was shattered when they heard.'

'I'm sure.' Did I sound appropriately grateful?

'We all got so depressed last night we had to have a toast party.'

'What's that?'

'Have you never been to one?' Jo glanced up through her faded fringe. 'You must come over to the Attic more often.'

'My job keeps me very busy,' I said. I was damned if I was going to accept a sympathy pass to their touch-feely commune.

Jo returned her gaze to the potatoes. 'Well, you buy two white sliced pan loaves – you need at least one per three people. Then you put the toaster in the middle of the table, sit very close around it, and eat hot buttered toast all evening, with tea to wash it down.'

'Not herbal?'

'Caffeine, tannin, milk and sugar. You have some funny ideas about us, don't you?'

I evaded her eyes. 'It sounds rather comforting.'

'I'll give you a ring next time. There's nothing like group bingeing to make you forget your own problems.'

'And remember everyone else's.'

Jo's mouth twitched into a momentary grin. 'So what's the sister like?' she went on.

'You tell me. I only talked to her for half an hour this morning. She didn't even recognize me.'

'Should she have?'

'We were in the same class at school. The mists of time, I suppose . . .'

'Ah, go on.' Jo studied me in concern. 'If they ever had a reunion at Sacred Heart, Drumsharry, I bet I'd be able to spot the gang from my year at least.'

I offered her a baby carrot to chew on. 'So how many girls in gymslips did you corrupt in your time, then?'

'Not a one, more's the pity. I was into boys at the time, or trying to be. I even married one.'

'You're having me on.'

The fair head was still bent over the chopping-board. 'Shrove Tuesday, 1971. We had pancakes at the reception.'

'I was only nine, and you were getting married? God help us. So where've you been hiding hubby all these years?'

'It's a long and nasty story,' said Jo. The sunlight was fading to grey on the wall of the garage. Her light blue eyes

67

swivelled towards me. 'I've got the wedding ring to prove it. I'll show you next time you're over in the Attic.'

'I won't be, most likely,' I said. 'You were always Cara's people.'

Jo put the peeling knife down on the gritty draining-board. 'You're being very hard on yourself, woman.'

'What am I doing?' The air in the kitchen was damp and stifling.

'Well, for one thing, cutting yourself off from all of us just because you think —'

'Jo,' I told her, 'you needn't worry, I'm not going to ask who it was, I'm not blaming anyone. But whatever about how I coped with it under other circumstances, I can't right now. I don't need to ask, I happen to know it was Sherry, but if you want to protect your housemate that's very honourable.'

'Ah, shut up with your honourables.' Her bottom lip was wet. 'You're missing the point.'

I bent to lean my elbows on the stainless-steel rim of the sink. My head weighed like a cannon-ball; I pictured it hurtling through the air, ready to explode. 'So tell me the point. What exactly is the point of all this, Jo?'

She said nothing.

My eyes were still dry. I leaned them on my knuckles, trying to break the seal that kept back the waters. I saw black sand, stabbed with green stars.

A hand on my shoulder. 'Are you —'

'I'm fine.' I stepped back out of reach. My hands lined the carrots up on the board. I bit into a sliver of one; its indifferent taste calmed my tongue.

Jo was watching. 'Hey, I've remembered what the point is.'

'Yeah?' I offered her a small smile. If I was going to turn into a bitch overnight, there truly was no point to anything.

'Well,' she began carefully, 'even if Cara might have had the odd fling over the years, didn't she always come back to

68

you? I remember her saying that you'd tried breaking up quite a few times, for a couple of years once –'

'Four.'

'Right.' Jo had lost her rhythm; she flailed for the words. 'But she kept coming back, didn't she? The woman couldn't have got away from you, even if she'd wanted to. Which she didn't,' she added hastily.

'She made a good shot at it,' I commented. 'Got as far as Denmark. And what about Ben, she nearly had a baby by him.'

'But she didn't. She couldn't actually leave you for good.'

'That might say more about her incapacities than my attractions.'

'Ah, bullshit. Stop waving the big words around, Teacher.'

I glanced over, startled by her rudeness. And then my own anger surged back. 'You know, Cara once told me that my kind of love was like a feeding tube forced up a hunger-striker's nostrils.'

Jo's throat wavered as she swallowed. 'She was just being melodramatic.'

'She meant it.'

'Maybe that particular minute she meant it. But the girl invited you into her family home, for god's sake,' Jo ploughed on. 'She chose you over and over again since she was a teenager. Doesn't that prove something?'

'What? What exactly does it prove?'

The door was thrust open, and in came Kate, rain spots on her mother's dressing-gown. 'Did you hear the thunder?'

Jo and I didn't look at each other. I leaned over the sink and stared into the yard. 'I didn't notice the sun had gone in, even. It is looking awful dark.'

Kate smacked a few drops from the curls over her forehead. 'I'd better get some clothes on; I seem to remember that my father scandalizes easily.'

She made it to the hall before the key turned in the front door; she paused to wrap the satin robe around her more tightly. I left her and Mr Wall to their shrill greetings, and shut the kitchen door on them.

Jo was rinsing the mud off the potatoes in a colander. Outside the rain grew heavier. The squeal of the cat-flap broke the silence; Grace's tail smeared the back of my ankles. Jo set the colander on the draining-board with a clank. I kept my head down, cutting the last section of carrot into transparent slips. 'Listen, Pen, you're digging yourself into a hole.'

I slapped down my knife. 'Just because you're in your fucking forties doesn't mean you know the first thing –'

'Shush, shush.'

The cat was watching us disapprovingly.

Jo scratched her cheek, leaving a smear of mud from the potatoes. She went on more gently. 'I know you have to grieve for the woman, but you don't have to go round doubting everything you two had. Don't you know you were the beginning and end for her?'

'Never suspected you were such a romantic.'

'It's not my language, it's hers. She talked about you all the time, we were sick to the teeth of hearing about her wonder-lover.' Jo tried a chuckle.

The rain was hammering on to the roof of the garage now, and slashing at the windows.

'That's what she called you, didn't you know?'

The hammock would be sopping by now. 'Yeah, that was one of the names.' The rumble of thunder drowned my words.

'Pen?' Jo peered into my face. 'Do you hear what I'm saying?'

'You're probably right,' I said, to shut her up. 'Was that lightning? I thought it went bright for a minute.'

'Didn't see.' Jo bent over the sink to look into the yard. 'I don't want to alarm you, but you're four inches under out there.'

'I'm what?'

'Your drains must be choked.'

I hauled open the kitchen door. 'Oh buggery, it's coming over the doorstep. I didn't give the drains a thought all summer.'

Jo's laugh was a little cracked. 'If you can lend me some wellies . . .'

'No, I'll do it.' I wrenched off my shoes and began to tuck the hem of my skirt into the waistband.

'Crazy woman –'

But I was in the yard already, my ankles numbed by the swirling water. If it caught me off balance I'd be swept down the crazy-paving steps and into the garden. The rain crashed in my face as I waded across the yard. I had my fist in the first drain, wrenching out handfuls of grass and leaves, by the time the window opened.

'Here, you great otter,' Jo called, 'would you do it with a wooden spoon at least.'

'Hands is best,' I shouted through the downpour. I pointed to the whirlpool already forming round the first drain. 'Shut that window, the rain'll saturate my tea-towels.'

By the time I staggered in, sniffing, Jo had brought a towel from the cloakroom to wrap my head in. She wouldn't stay for dinner, she said; I had enough on my plate.

I lent her my crow-headed umbrella in case she didn't find a parking space near the Attic. At the door, there was one of those moments when two people realize that they like each other more than they know each other. This is nicer than the opposite situation, but more awkward. You try to remember the protocol for touching. You hate to gush, or presume too much, yet you are unwilling to let the moment pass without some gesture. Jo was standing on the step below, staring into the rain; she looked back up at me. I put out my hand towards her, not for a shake but in a low wave. But she put her hand out too and they met tentatively, fingers sliding over palms, the tips of the fingers resting together for a fraction of a second, then dropping away.

Then she was trudging through the garden to her purple Volkswagen Beetle, not looking back, and I was momentarily

71

warmed. Apart from the sign of peace at mass, Jo had been the first person to touch me since it happened, to lay hands on the new Pen.

When I'd changed into dry clothes I went back to my chopping-board, listening to the small sounds of the house. Cara used to read poetry aloud while I was cooking; mostly right-on women's anthologies, but sometimes Wordsworth, for whom she had a secret yen. She got louder at the bits she liked best; I used to wonder what Mr Wall made of all this muffled oratory booming through the walls. Being read to was lovely, but somehow Cara expected me to notice metaphors and irony while I was chopping mushrooms. I always had to apologize before turning on the noisy blender, and even then if I failed in concentration she might flounce out with 'Never mind, I'll read in the garden.'

Dinner was muted tonight. The potatoes were firm but the carrots were mushy. I gave Grace a sliver of ham; was that a flicker of disapproval I caught on Kate's face? Her chocolate-brown suit still looked freshly ironed. I felt an irrational surge of resentment which had something to do with her being so well groomed, and something to do with her air of detachment, but was not justified by either.

She and her father passed each other dishes. She had brought him an express-mail letter from his wife; he folded it away in his breast-pocket to read later. It was painful to watch them; sometimes civil as strangers, then a flash of an old disagreement. With questions like 'So how is the library?' or 'I hear terrible things about the American school system', they tried to reconstruct the missing years.

He was too polite to ask her any of the really interesting questions. At sixteen, in cotton bell-bottoms, could she really have volunteered to give up the mossy woods for a country of shrieking sirens? I had never been to the States and never wanted to. Watching *Cagney and Lacey* was stressful enough, and I only did that to ogle Sharon Gless, who wasn't my type anyway, too blonde. Cara had always insisted that going was Kate's choice entirely, but I just bet her mother bribed her with boot-skates and summer camp. Cara got seagulls. The summer the others left, Mr Wall took her to West Cork and she drew endless seagulls. She had kept all the pictures and showed them to me when she was spring-cleaning last year. They were not like any seagulls I had ever seen.

I was considering these questions and forking down some apple pie when the doorbell startled us into silence. It was a puny boy whose feet were rapidly outgrowing him; he rested a black leather suitcase on the upturned toe of one boot. 'Wall?' he asked me, indecently cheerful for someone employed by a hospital to deliver those possessions no longer needed by their owners. I took the case from him without making myself smile.

If I brought it into the kitchen, Mr Wall might ask what it was, and suddenly I didn't trust my voice. I hauled it upstairs. I resisted the urge to hide it under my bed; who would I be hiding it from? It would only delay things. Besides, I had to find Sherry's damn toothbrush; I wanted nothing of hers in the house. So I lifted the case, hissing with effort, and placed it centrally on the bed, like a great carcass on a sacrificial altar.

A call from down below; I walked to the top of the stairs.

'Coffee?' Mr Wall's voice was oddly hopeful, a sort of elderly Oliver Twist.

'No thanks,' I said automatically.

'Sorry?'

Then I couldn't bear to disappoint him in anything. 'That'd be great,' I called, too enthusiastically. She would think I was a callous hedonist, an empress stuffing my face with pie and coffee as Rome fell around me. Why did I care what this stranger thought? Just a habit, left over from the year I was fifteen in red gaberdine and thought the world spun around the girl who used to be Kate Wall.

Back in my bedroom, the suitcase opened with a prompt click. Folded autumnal clothes, none of them familiar at first glance; Cara must have gone on a spending spree around the Isles. How could she have afforded all this? Mr Wall must have slipped her some particularly lavish handout for her holiday. Under a layer of cotton I found a cream satin camisole. I fingered its milky folds; for a moment I imagined its pencil straps on Cara's freckled shoulders, and smiled in anticipation, my mouth watering. Then I remembered, like a great hand closing around my throat. How many times would I have to remember and make myself believe it, before remembering once and for all?

I covered the camisole with a black jumper I thought I remembered. Then something struck me: what had Cara done with her old stuff, her tie-dyes and political T-shirts? What kind of weird transformation had she undergone on this holiday? If I was going to lose her, at least I wanted to be sure how to remember her. In a clear plastic toilet bag there was a yellow toothbrush, which I pocketed for return to the Attic. There was also a box of pills, marked with the days of the month and arrows. My stomach contracted. I could handle most changes, but not this. Not a change, even, but a slide back to the old world, the old boring story, fucking men.

I stuffed the pills back into the bag, zipped it, then slammed the case shut. Why did I feel such a voyeur, when there was no one alive to have her privacy respected? I hauled the case on to the landing, not wanting to share a room with it. Mr Wall was calling; I went downstairs and took a cup of coffee from Kate. The glass chattered on its saucer.

'Did my bag turn up at last?' she asked.

I stared.

'From the airport. They said they'd send it on.'

My mouth caught up with my brain. 'Oh yes.' She was looking puzzled. 'I left it on the landing,' I told her, and bent to my coffee, cheeks scalding. Not caring whether her eyes were on me, I dipped the spoon into the sugar for a third time.

Mr Wall cleared the plates away, smooth as a robot butler.

I left them exchanging comments on world news and tugged the kitchen door shut behind me as I stepped into the yard. Jet-lag would force Kate to bed soon, I thought, and Mr Wall would ring round the relatives. Was it rude to stay out here in the steaming garden, checking the drains and righting fallen plant-pots? Everything looked not newly washed, but battered. Smeary as a woman after an afternoon in bed. The slabs were patterned with snail-tracks of mud, and the gutters on the garage roof were still dripping. I leaned my face into a yellow rose but could smell nothing; a cold drip ran down my nose. The white ropes of the hammock were dark with rain. On the grass lay a cushion I made years ago of dirty yellow brocade from an old jacket of my mother's. I knew I should take it inside and wash it, but it looked so well against the grass that I left it there.

I remembered that cushion from a few summers back. Cara and I in the hammock after mass, limbs entwined under a shifting blanket of Sunday supplements. I had stuck a row of buttercups between her toes. My hand was a daredevil mouse, scrabbling between layers of newsprint, creeping under her hem of Indian gauze. Cara's hiss of protest trailed off, and her head sagged back on the yellow cushion. 'Lie still,' I whispered, 'you've got a touch of the sun.' The huge scent of her clouded around us, filling the garden. I remembered the swallowing up of my thumb, and that look of hers, like fury, like astonishment.

The grating echoed behind me; Kate's step, firmer than her father's. Damn the woman, could she not go to bed like any normal highflyer? 'Hey there,' I said, not turning my head. I busied myself with pulling some withered leaves off the lemon balm.

'Hey.'

'Dinner all right?'

'Great; I haven't tasted real home cooking in a long time.'

I felt patronized, but shoved the feeling away. 'Good thing your bag turned up; I don't think I could have found you anything of mine that you'd care to wear.'

'Oh, those morons are always misdirecting my baggage.' She yawned behind her pale brown hand. 'Someone had obviously gone through it in a hurry. Do you know what they stole, of all things?'

My stomach churned. I hadn't, I wouldn't.

'My toothbrush.'

I gave the obedient giggle of breath and kept my head down, contemplating the plants. The yellow toothbrush was suddenly stiff in the pocket of my trousers; I was sure it was outlined down my thigh. 'There'll be a spare in the cupboard beside the sink,' I told her.

I headed down to the compost heap, picking up a dead leaf or two along the way. The sky over the wall was the slate-blue of my mother's all-purpose eyeshadow. Any minute now it would be dark.

'This her?'

I turned and peered through the twilight.

Kate held up a packet of photos. 'Found them beside the phone.'

'They're Jo's.' I turned back.

'Is this one her?'

I kept busy at the compost heap. 'What's it of?'

'A crowd of women on a beach. The one I'm looking at has practically no hair, but it seems red. Sitting on a motorbike.'

'Nah, that's Sherry. Cara's terrified of motorbikes. Look for the tallest of them, with hair to her chin.'

Kate was silent for a while. Part of my brain wondered how indiscreet the photos were; which graphic T-shirts, which casual embraces, had been caught by the camera. I walked up as far as the pear tree. 'Found her?'

'Yeah, there's quite a few. I saw her in the first one, actually, but she looked so young I thought it couldn't be.'

Kate tapped the pile on her knee to straighten it, and put it back in the envelope. 'You want a look?'

'No need.' I picked up the sodden cushion and tossed it into the hammock.

I could hear Kate's voice deepen as if the power had been switched on. 'I hope you don't mind my saying so, but you seem a little hostile.'

'Hostile? Really?' I held her gaze for a second, to show I could.

'I know it's probably just the shock. I wondered if I'd done anything . . .'

'No, no, sure what could you have done, you've only been here a day. I'm not quite myself this week. But you're not to feel . . . I mean, you're welcome to this house.'

'Thank you,' murmured Kate, equally formal. After a minute, 'I'm not really coherent, I should probably hit the sack.'

'Do.'

'Have you got a bus schedule? I have to go into the city tomorrow and fax a report to the office.'

'So they don't let you off work even for a sister's funeral?'

She cleared her throat tiredly. 'We're always expected to stay in touch. They want me back Thursday morning.'

I relented. 'The buses are impossible. I'll drive you into town tomorrow, if you can stoop to a Mini.'

'Oh no, I wouldn't put you to the trouble —'

'I've nothing else to do, I'm off school till Thursday. Honestly, I'd be glad to.'

'That's kind of you,' Kate said uneasily.

I caught her eye and we were suddenly laughing, a short burst each. 'See,' I told her, 'I can be nice. Get a good night's sleep.'

'You too.'

I watched her walk up the garden path, and suddenly I recognized her. Not just the similarities to the girl she was at sixteen but the sameness, the two Kates blending together as she walked away from me, their angles merging. I supposed

I knew her best from behind. There was a Yeats line I used to mouth in my head, watching her from three rows in a sleepy classroom: 'high, and solitary, and most stern'. And now I found myself as angry with her as I ever felt, as I was the day I sat the Inter Cert for the first time.

It is five minutes before the Maths exam and I am being calm. '6 June 1978' I have printed unnecessarily at the top of the pink answer book, and a minuscule K in every corner for good luck. Some girl – I remember a plait, no name – leans over for a last gossip. 'D'you hear about the Walls?'

'What walls?'

'Kate 'n' Cara. Their parents are getting a separation, isn't that awful? Lucy says Kate claims the mother's got this hightech architecture contract out in Ohio, they're going in July, but it sounds to me like the mother's got a boyfriend.'

An echo of her sentence strikes me. 'Who's they who's going?'

The invigilator rapped on his desk and a hush falls as the papers are handed out. 'Kate,' the girl's chapped lips form. It is unmistakable; the lips widen to let out the sharp vowel. If it was the younger sister, Cara, the girl's mouth would only have dipped a little.

After a minute I remind myself to breathe. I will not scan the line of heads before me for Kate's brown curls, the determined dip of her Roman nose towards the first question. I look down at the fresh page and think I will be sick on it, thus breaking some examination rule they never thought to make. I lay down my biro. There is nothing it would make any sense to write. My fantasies have been truncated; the story has been ripped up. My plans for the choreographed winning of Kate Wall over several years have been crushed into two weeks.

I will not ring her. I will not say something every schoolfriend will say, like 'Sorry you're going.' How dare she do this to my life and not even notice?

They don't let you leave for the first fifteen minutes in case you hand the exam paper over to a confederate in the toilet. I keep busy, writing K over and over and darker and deeper scored into the paper, covering the inches, because when the page is full then I can go.

I was standing in the wet garden now, and it was night. Best time for remembering, I supposed, the sky being a black retina on to which the mind could project any image. Though what possible good it could do me to remember being mad about Kate Wall I did not know. What had it amounted to but a riot of adolescent hormones that cost me my exams? The only useful thing about remembering her was that it distracted me from her sister. It almost convinced me that I had an independent self, a Pen who pre-existed (and so might even survive) Cara. A younger self who knew nothing of the compromises and endurances of a long-term partnership, who knew only the basics: longing and hiding, a lust so distilled it felt almost platonic.

I felt my way down to the end of the garden. The dump was filled with ash from last month's bonfire; its whiteness caught the light from the kitchen. I fished in my pocket for the toothbrush, and pushed it well in.

I shut the kitchen door behind me, brushing the last dab of ash from my fingers. They ached a little, as if I had been carrying heavy bags. No sign of either of the Walls; my castle was my own again. Robbie hadn't rung, it occurred to me, which was just as well really. Our connection, over this past year since he had somehow got himself hired by the nuns, was a matter of matching raised eyebrows in the staff-room and the odd gorge at the nearby Pâtisserie; what would I have to say to him tonight?

I made myself a cup of cocoa, very milky, hoping the associations of comfort and sleep would outweigh the caffeine. I shut off the light and sat down at the table. The dark was balm to my eyes. Grace leaped from nowhere on to my knee. When my heart had stopped hammering I reached to scratch his head, but he winced as if I had hit him. A leap, and

79

there he was, stalking along the counter, nosing a chopping-board. A dislodged envelope caught the light as it floated down on to the tiles. Then the cat-flap smashed open and he was gone on his night prowls.

My elbows slid a little on the smooth plane of the table. I leaned my full weight on them, holding the steaming mug close to my face. There was a girl in our class who had spilt a pot of cocoa on her arm as a toddler; the flesh there was red and rippled. On the hockey pitch one day, someone made a crack about it. My eyes were on Kate as usual, and when her mouth opened to laugh I laughed too, and when hers shut, so did mine, and only then was I ashamed.

Of course I might have laughed on my own initiative anyway, being as cruel as any other schoolgirl. There was no need for me to go blaming Kate Wall for everything. She was not to know the effects her slightest actions had on me the year I turned sixteen, and the earthquake it set off in my head when she moved to Ohio. As for the Inter Cert, I might have mucked it up anyway, what with period pains and panic-stricken nights listening to the whisper of Radio Luxembourg under the blankets.

Just as well I failed the exams that time around, really, since otherwise I would never have stayed back a year and found Cara. But I didn't want to think about her now. She took too much out of me. Another swallow of cocoa scalded my tongue; I poured the rest down the sink and climbed the stairs to bed.

What I needed was someone to tell me a story. Once, during a particularly stressful summer term at Immac, I borrowed one of those relaxation tapes from the library, and was amazed by how well it worked, with what relief my mind handed over my body's reins to the firm voice of some stranger. It was such bliss to be told what to do, muscle by muscle. It reminded me of being read to by my mother, before I was able to read for myself. I used to curl up around her hips like a prawn. She read with her eyes on the page, looking down every few pages with a slightly stern smile to ask was I sleepy yet. The best was that book about the princess and the goblin; when it got to the bit about the silver-grey thread that she had to follow all the way back through the mines and up to her grandmother's room in the moonlit tower, I used to squeeze my eyes shut and concentrate till I could feel the thread between my fingers.

This was ridiculous; thirty years old, and my head was cluttered up with the detritus of childhood. I rolled over on one side, pressed half my face into the pillow, and resorted to the original mantra:

Now I lay me down to sleep I pray to God my soul to keep
If I should die before I wake I pray to God my soul to take

It was working; the iambic octameter was hypnotizing me towards sleep. I began to stumble over the rhymes, playing with them exhaustedly.

Now I lay me down to wake I pray to God my fear to take
If I should cry before I sleep I pray to God my fear to keep
Now I lay me down and die I pray to God my soul to try
If I should sleep before I wake I pray to God my wake to keep

Some hours later I woke thirsty, my tongue raw. I rolled on to my back, lifting my knees to ease the stiffness. Usually when I stirred in the night, Cara would wake too, and make some enigmatic comment – 'Pen, Pen, I've just realized that three full stops make a dot dot dot' – before sinking back to sleep.

I padded off for a glass of water. Halfway down I jolted in fright. Mr Wall was standing at the foot of the stairs. I had never seen him in his pyjamas before; they seemed to be beige, with long sleeves almost covering his knuckles. He was looking up, his eyes dark below a patch of streetlight that illumined the carvings in his forehead. He filled the stairwell like a daddy-long-legs about to be smashed between dictionary and wall. I waited for him to explain what he was looking for, but he said nothing. I couldn't bring myself to touch him, or brush by.

'I'm just getting a glass of water, would you like one?' I said inanely.

Mr Wall blinked several times. Perhaps he was losing his mind. He never usually came upstairs; that was our place, mine and Cara's. He seemed to be nailed to the ground, his mouth hanging slightly open.

A crash; no, just the warped door of the middle bedroom opening. Kate's decisive steps went by above us, and the bathroom lock squeaked shut. I realized that I had been holding my breath. The man below me had turned his face; he seemed to be watching something on the front lawn. All at once I felt immensely heavy, my King Kong limbs swelling to fill and crack the stairwell. I had to lean against the smooth wallpaper until I was convinced of my human proportions.

The bathroom door opened, and I followed the diminishing sound of her steps. I looked at her father. His mouth was shut and his eyes were down. 'Goodnight now,' he said, almost normally, and turned away.

TUESDAY

I woke to the phone, with the sense that it had been tolling in my ears all night. Groggy from the tablets, I pulled my orange robe around me and stumbled downstairs. Taking the receiver from Kate – she had a triangle of dark toast in her other hand – I held a brief and mutually hostile conversation with the plumber who was meant to come the previous Friday. Then I straightened the frayed towelling round my neck and climbed back to bed.

I dug my face into the crease I had left in the pillow. The world should go away and let me sleep. Too many mornings I had been woken by the sobs of the phone. The one in the small terraced house I grew up in, the house my mother inherited from her mother, had a rich old-fashioned sound to it. But when my father's job gardening at the university brought us to the southside in my teens, the new phone turned out to be a whiner. I had taught myself to leap out of bed on the first ring, saving Mammy's temper, because Cara always seemed to phone at the most unsuitable times of day. The time she rang with her big news, it couldn't have been later than seven on a Saturday morning, a matter of weeks after she'd left me for the second time.

I lift the receiver and for a second the silence scares me, but then I can hear her stifled air. 'Is that you? Come on, Cara, breathe.'

'Can't.'

'Yes you can, you couldn't speak if you weren't.'

She hates logic.

'Talk to me. Is it the Leaving Cert results, are they out yet?'

Cara wails.

'Come on, lovey.'

'Can't, it's so, I didn't know how, wish I, you wouldn't understand.'

'You could get the bus over if you'd find it easier to talk here.'

Her breath shudders like an old engine. 'Can't. Leave the house.'

'Have you tried?'

'Far as the gate.'

'Why don't you tell me what's the matter.'

'Lost . . .'

'What have you lost? I'm sure we'll find it. What's really the matter?'

'Virginity.'

'What?'

'I've lost it.'

The words slap me in the face, welding my bones together. Put an ad in the evening paper, I want to spit, but do not, but hold it in, but hold my breath until I have control. Until I am kind enough to say, 'I'm sorry. If you are. I mean if you didn't want to lose it.'

'I wanted to but now I' – Cara's voice rising to a keen again – 'wish I hadn't.'

I summon all that remains of my liking for this girl. I am too tired; the words drip out as if from a rusty pipe. 'Did it hurt?'

Between gulps, she tells me. 'Yes, but that's not why. I just didn't realize it would be such a big deal until it suddenly was. You wouldn't understand unless you'd done it. We, Roderick and me, the minute we did it we both knew it felt wrong and something irreplaceable was gone . . .'

I wish I could laugh, it would relieve the feeling that my head is made of tight rubber. 'Jesus, Cara,' I say – too loud, is my mother awake? – 'it's only a wee flap of skin.'

'It's not the skin, it's the symbolism.'

'Bollocks to that, if it's the symbolism you lost it two years ago on the convent roof.'

Silence from her end. A snuffle.

Fury is hitting the arches of my skull from the inside with ungloved fists. 'But of course, I was forgetting, as a born-again het you wouldn't count fingers.'

'It's not the same thing.'

'Thank god for that,' I say.

'Don't be horrible.'

'I'm sorry.' Then I hear myself, and the words are false. 'Actually, no, I'm not sorry at all.' A weight lifts off; I don't care if my mother can hear me. 'You are the most insensitive little gobshite I've ever met.'

A hoarse giggle down the line.

'I don't believe this. You're ringing me, me of all people, for congratulations on your defloration, and sniggering –'

'It's not like that,' says Cara. 'I'm still upset. I just, you always did know how to make me laugh.'

'Stop flirting. This is not how ex-lovers are meant to behave.'

A pause. 'Well, we weren't exactly lovers were we, strictly speaking?'

'I beg your pardon?'

'I read on some problem page that lots of girls, you know, do things with each other when they're teenagers. It's not unusual.'

Which would give her less satisfaction, for me to slam down the phone or not to?

Another peal from the phone in the big house hoisted my head off the pillow; this time I leaped down two stairs at a time and got to it first. A wrong number, wouldn't you know.

Kate's mood was no better than mine, I could tell at a glance as I walked into the kitchen. Her linen suit was one of those colours with a pretentious name, ash or bone or some-thing. She held the coffee cup an inch below her lip. 'I suppose you'll have made arrangements with my father about the move, Pen?'

I tightened the threadbare belt of my dressing-gown. 'I didn't know he was moving.'

One thick eyebrow lifted, a trick I had always wanted to learn. 'Well, he can hardly rattle round here all on his own.'

I shut my mouth without letting more than a breath escape.

Kate set down her cup with a clink and stared at the walnut cabinet. 'He'll have no space for a great monster like that.'

And all of a sudden I was furious on behalf of the cabinet, its burnished grin. 'I'm sure he would have told me if he was planning to move. He's very fond of all this.'

'I remember. He bought it all with my mother's salary, you know; more fool her for having a joint account.' She licked the cool coffee out of the bowl of her spoon. 'Probably in shock,' she added.

'Who, Mr Wall?'

Kate's lip curled up at the corner. 'That's a rather formal title, isn't it, if you've been part of the furniture for years?'

I ignored my flush. 'He hasn't asked me to call him Ian.'

'I'd nearly forgotten that was his name. How grey can you get.'

A wheeze from the handle, and the door jumped open. 'Good morning, girls,' said Mr Wall, halfway to the sink.

I didn't meet Kate's eye. 'Morning. Are you not at the library today?'

'Slight little bit of a headache,' he admitted, rinsing his cup. 'I should go in this afternoon.'

'How's that coffee I brought?' Kate asked.

'Fine, just fine. Though I may in fact' – picking up the jar and rubbing at the label with his thumb – 'it might be the case that I used the instant. Had it to hand.' Mr Wall gave an apologetic glance over his reading glasses.

'I like instant better sometimes,' I assured him idiotically.

'Indeed. Requires less appreciation when one's in the

middle of something.' He looked down and removed a yellow sticky label from the edge of his cardigan. 'Though I will,' he added, giving us each a brief smile, 'I will definitely try the gourmet brew after lunch.'

'Do that.' For a moment I wanted to cry, but it passed.

Kate asked for another coffee if he was making it. He wasn't but it would be a pleasure. His pace quickened; he seemed glad to know what his daughter wanted and have it in his hand, smoking and jittering in the saucer.

'So, Dad,' she began; it had the ring of a line in a play read through by an understudy. 'I was just asking Pen what your plans were. Vis-à-vis the house.'

His eyes did a cautious circuit. 'Is anything the matter with it?'

'It's much too big,' she said, as if to a small boy. 'Now, what might suit you is one of those new flats down by the river, there was an article on them in yesterday's paper. They've got a security porter and a laundry service.'

'And an automated bath-chair, no doubt, in the fullness of time.'

I snorted before I could stop myself. Mr Wall looked down for the duration of his smile. 'Excuse my flippancy, Cáit. I do appreciate your concern. I shall give the matter thought.'

'And don't worry about all this clutter,' Kate drove on. 'We can put it in storage or something.'

I expected his head to snap up, but he continued drying the handle of his coffee cup. 'I shall give it thought,' he repeated, shutting the door behind him.

'He and Mom weren't even Irish-speakers, you know,' murmured Kate. 'Totally false nostalgia, this Celtic Revival shit. Cara, Cáit, Cáity, coochy-coo; it's always bugged me.'

'He knows,' I said.

She gave me a wary glance. 'Will we make a move?'

'Sure.' I was picking up her nasty Bostonian accent already. 'Just let me get some clothes on.'

I took a good fifteen minutes, just to make her wait. I

could tell it was going to be another scorcher, so I lingered in the shower, turning down the hot tap until the water was cool enough to raise goose-pimples along my upper arms. I shut my eyes, letting the stream cover my face. The delicate brown pores around my nipples reminded me of a rubber plant after the rain.

Last year my soaping fingers found a pea-shaped lump. I told myself it was hormonal, but walked around for days with the whiff of death in my nostrils. My conversation turned enigmatic and sentimental by turns; I stroked Grace a lot and left sentences unfinished. Then I went to the doctor and came home crowing, 'It's a cyst, I've got a cyst, that's all.' Cara was furious with me for not having told her before, but I couldn't see the point of having both of us fretting over something that might not be anything. She said I was a stupid woman, and I was to promise to tell her anything like that in future. I stuck out my tongue and she closed her teeth over it.

When I emerged at last, Kate showed no signs of impatience. She sat into Minnie as if she was used to being chauffeured, tucking her leather portfolio between her ankles. So that we wouldn't have to make conversation, I turned on the radio, and the earnest discords of a debate on emigration kept us going all the way into town. It was another ridiculously sunny day; what was the Irish climate playing at? Just when I could have done with a bit of pathetic fallacy, a sober rain or cruel wind, the sun was insisting on dazzling Dublin.

After dropping Kate off at the print bureau, I picked up the paper and read it over a polystyrene cup of coffee in the car. The rush of caffeine made my palms damp. I bit into the snow-topped Danish and read the ads for end-of-summer sales; it felt like a holiday. On the fifth page of the paper was a small headline: 'Road Accidents Claim Six Over Weekend'. Claim, what an odd verb, as if the roads had a certain toll they were entitled to collect in pounds of flesh.

Listed in the second paragraph was 'Ciara Wall'. All I

could feel was irritation that the journalist hadn't bothered to check the spelling. The report added that the driver of the car that had hit the taxi had died in intensive care on Sunday evening. On balance, I was glad. This way, I wouldn't have to track him down and kill him. Really, it would have been worse of me to wish him to live with that on his conscience. For a moment I wondered whether the driver was counted in the weekend's six as claimant or claimed, dragon or virgin. None of this was real, not a bit of it. These names, even this *doppelgänger* 'Ciara Wall', were strangers to me. I could feel the appropriate things but only at a distance, as if reading a book which, however moving and engrossing, would be put aside as soon as there was a knock at the door.

Driving home through spacious streets of terracotta brick I passed the Alternative Bookshop. I paused on the kerb outside to blow my nose, looking up at the hand-painted sign on the third-floor window. It had only been an alternative for a couple of years. I had tried it out not long after it opened; I remembered it as a spring day, or maybe it just felt that way.

The air smells green that afternoon. Unwilling to spend another lunchtime in the staff-room listening to the stress symptoms of women with lines around their mouths, I have gone walking halfway into town. I decide to try this new lefty bookshop on the corner by the synagogue; three flights up and very poky, but nearly empty at this time of day.

I am browsing through a history of quilting when I stagger over this girl who is crouched at the bottom of Women's Studies. But she turns round before I have a chance to be mortified; swivels on her heels, like a squirrel, and gives me a devastating grin.

'Really sorry,' I add for what sounds like the tenth time, and edge my swollen feet away.

The bookshop has its own miniature café. I have squeezed in behind the corner table and almost finished a slice of mushroom quiche before the woman comes over to the next table, which is only a foot away. Out the corner of my eye I have spotted her badge and am going light pink. It's not even one of those joined women symbols or a discreet labrys. It's a yellow badge with 'BY THE WAY, I'M A DYKE' emblazoned across it.

In order to dissociate myself from this lunatic I take a vast mouthful of pastry crust.

She leans over and says, 'That's quite a waistcoat.'

I open my lips to answer, then remember the quiche. My eyes bulge slightly as I begin to cough. I hack and choke and generally behave like one of the Junior Infants down the hall at Immac. More than half the laughter is coming from this stranger; she passes me her glass of water.

When I have recovered, we discuss the waistcoat. How I made it from an old curtain of my mother's one night when I couldn't get to sleep after watching that film about the woman with multiple personalities; how I like to make my own clothes when I can find the time, because the shops have always mysteriously run out of anything in my size; how the quiche is not bad at all, considering. She seems quite ordinary, apart from the badge which I hope the waitress can't see from over there. She's got a North of England accent. But how did she spot me? It's a very flowery waistcoat I'm wearing, nothing Radclyffe Hall about it.

'Would you make me one?' she asks, leaning back till her wooden chair rests against the wall.

I smile wanly.

'A green one. It wouldn't take much, a couple of scraps; I'm only small. I'd pay, of course.'

'Oh, it's not that, it's just a question of . . .'

And she is leaning over, plucking a biro out of her jacket pocket. No paper, no napkin. I must look a right egg, sitting here letting a strange woman write on the back of my hand. I just hope I won't get the tickles as her ballpoint moves towards the wrist.

'Well, it depends on whether I have any green,' I tell her hoarsely, and add, 'You didn't give me your name.'

She pulls open her denim collar, and angles towards the light, showing the curve where her neck becomes her shoulder. 'Day,' it says, the olive letters deformed into the silhouette of a leaf. 'That's me. Short for Dymphna, wouldn't you know.' And picks up her wallet and goes, grinning over her shoulder.

When the door has clattered shut I realize that she doesn't know my name, but I can hardly chase her down the stairs bawling it out. Besides, it's ten minutes to the bell; if I'm late back those hyperactive bowsies in Fourth Class will be throwing milk cartons at each other again.

In a whirl of occupation the afternoon goes by. I don't let myself think of Day again until I'm washing chalk off my hands in the staff toilet at ten past three. Suddenly I am bone-tired, longing for the big house and its sofa, kettle, crocuses. I could ring Day's number tonight, I suppose, if there's any of that pea-green velvet left in the back of my sewing drawer. I could ring just to say 'Hey'. Cara's taken her roll-up banner to a Right to Choose march in Leeds, and anyway, after that last workshop on Polyfidelity she dragged me along to, didn't I decide to consider myself a free agent? So I can ring who I like, cut my life to my own fit, kiss whose shoulders I please.

I stare at myself in the mirror. Rather pale, my hair closing to a Cleopatra silhouette round my face. I could be just about anything, and the nuns and brats wouldn't notice. Spanish Armada somewhere in my ancestry, Cara remarked when she hung the gold boat on the chain around my neck on our first anniversary. Under my collar against the metal my skin is slippery and sweet.

I glance down at the bits of me I have always liked – my long, plump hands, drying themselves automatically on the towel. And too late, about a minute and a half too late, I see the tail of a green digit across a vein. No, two digits: a six, then a scrubbed pink patch of skin, then what could be a seven or a two. I lean my forehead on the icy mirror. How many six-digit numbers are there that start with six and end with seven (or, of course, two)? It doesn't bear thinking of. It must be a sign, a judgment on me for trying to be something I'm not. Go on, get your folder and car keys, move.

A shrill voice lifts my face off the sweaty glass. I follow it to the door where a girl from Junior Infants is standing with her legs entwined like snakes. 'Please, Miss, can't do my zip.'

I have her tiny dungarees undone and around her ankles just in time; she shuffles across the corridor to the kids' toilet. How I love being necessary.

Pulling my mind back from that peculiar afternoon when I had seriously considered seizing for myself the freedom Cara held always in her hand, I looked out my window and up at the sign. 'Radical Books for All the Families,' it said in bubble letters. 'The Only Alternative.'

The door at the bottom swung open: of all the people in the world I did not want to see, Sherry. With a freshly shaved head and a small boy for accessories. I started up the engine and was edging off the kerb by the time she patted the window. I rolled it down halfway.

'Pen, what are you doing here? I'm so sorry, I was up all night crying, Jo told us after dinner, I just can't believe it yet.' Sherry shoved up the sleeves of her ragged crochet shirt and leaned her elbows on the window edge. Freckles stood out across her creamy cheek-bones. 'How are you coping, I mean how's it all going? I'm just unbelievably shook up. Came back from Greece on such a high but this has brought us all way down, it's like death is just around the corner for any of us, you know? Cara was just so . . .'

I couldn't stand much more. 'Who's the wee sprog?'

'Oh, he's my ex-before-last's nephew.' She hauled him up between her delicate wrists. 'Say hi, Jonathan. His parents are bringing him up without, like, any gender stereotypes.'

The boy gave me a dubious glance and kicked the door. I started up the engine again.

Sherry put her bud of a mouth against his sticky cheek, then let him down on the kerb. 'Well, listen, Pen, I suppose we'll see you at the cemetery tomorrow. But also, we were thinking we might do some kind of wake thing at the Attic this weekend. A barbecue in the garden, if the weather holds, with maybe a circle dance and stuff. So if you can think of any poems Cara was into – it'd have to be women's stuff, obviously – or any special songs we could learn . . .'

'I'll keep it in mind,' I told her, barely civil. 'Now I really have to hurry, there's so much to do.'

'I'm sure.' And Sherry leaned her fuzzy copper head in the window to give me the compulsory kiss on the hairline. She smelt of milk and incense. 'You take it easy, now. Go with the flow. Jonathan, you want to say bye-bye?'

But Minnie was rumbling off along the main road. My girlfriend, I decided, as I sped through an amber light, had no taste. What she had seen in that bald hippy I would never know. Cara was skinny enough herself; they must have struck sparks when their hips touched. If they touched. When. If. Don't dwell on it, Pen, watch the traffic. I had nothing but a hunch that it was Sherry, I reminded myself; it could have been anyone or no one. Besides, hadn't I sorted out my attitude to all that years back?

From the very beginning it was never going to be me Cara was infatuated with, not my mouth she watched for minutes on end. I got so much from her, more than enough, plenty. It would have been greedy to want more, that continuous full-face look. What bothered me, I decided as I slid Minnie on to the dual carriageway, was Cara's declining standards. Not the fact that she fell for other people, always and over and over, but the slippage in what she felt for them – from religious devotion to Mrs Mew, in our schooldays when I used to help her pace out giant M's on football pitches, down to this mundane lust.

When I got to the shopping centre, I couldn't face the midday crowds yet. I allowed myself a choc-ice, sitting on the wall outside the supermarket, blinking in the sun. The

taste of white ice-cream dripping down the side of my wrist brought back the day I first told Cara, and she me. This was one I kept to run past my eyes when I needed it, for comfort and absurdity.

We haven't known each other long; only since October, when I was moved down into her class to repeat every tedious part of the Inter Cert course. On the first day of term I said, 'How's your sister doing in Ohio?' and Cara said, 'Fine,' and then we talked about something else.

Nowadays we get each other's jokes when no one else does. I can't go another year without putting words to what's on my mind.

We've known each other long enough. If she is my friend then she will not hate me.

'I want to tell you something,' I begin, as we stroll the circuit of the athletics field.

Cara stares up from her choc-ice. 'If it's about what I said before Maths I'm really sorry, I knew it was a bitchy . . .'

'No, that was nothing.'

She licks chocolate off her lips doubtfully. 'Is it something I won't like then?'

'Probably.'

'Go ahead, so.'

I am disconcerted to meet with so little resistance. I pause to collect the words memorized in the small hours of the night before. 'I've been fretting over whether or not to tell you for ages. I know you'll try and understand but you won't be able to, but I don't mean that as an insult.'

'Go on.'

'No, actually I don't think I can, I think I better just leave it there.'

Her grey eyes are small. 'Would you rather a kick in the bladder?'

'I really can't say it.'

Deep in her throat she squawks and begins to flap her long elbows.

'It's all very well for you, you're not the one who has to.'

Now Cara makes like a chicken on acid, tripping across the hummocky grass.

I cannot break my sulk to laugh. 'Look, do you want to hear or not?'

'Not particularly.'

Before I am halfway across the stretch of green she scurries up and falls into line at my heels. I slow down. 'I'm in love with another woman.'

Cara's pause is brief. 'Who was the first?'

'First to what?'

'First one you were in love with.'

'This is the first.'

'Then why d'you say another woman?'

'I just, it means a woman, it's what you say. I'm a woman so she's another woman.'

'We're girls really,' Cara comments after a minute. 'Who is she, then?'

'It's,' and my throat closes on the hard K, so I veer into, 'I can't tell you the name, I barely know her and it's all pretty bloody stupid but I can't help it. But she's not even around any more, she's gone away.' Hot-faced, I look down and see the remains of my ice-cream sliding into the grass. A blob of white dances on the point of a stalk. 'Look, if you're scandalized, just say so and be done with it.'

'Did you expect me to be?' she asks.

'Don't know. Are you?'

'Don't know.'

I begin to despair. In TV movies when you tell people hard things they go wide-eyed and say, 'Oh, honey, it'll be all right, and I'm so proud of you for telling me.'

'No, actually' – Cara's voice is very soft – 'I think I'm the same, only different.'

I am licking chocolate off the naked ice-cream stick at this point, and I can taste the wood on my tongue. I give her a suspicious glare but she meets my eyes and suddenly it makes sense, this feeling of correspondence. 'What, you mean you too?' Carefully, 'I don't think you mean what I mean.'

'Do so.'

'Is there someone you actually fancy?'

'If you're going to drag it down in the mud,' she snaps, 'let's drop the subject.'

I contract.

'Fancy sounds like pigeons.' Cara curls her lower lip. 'It's higher than that. You know Mrs Mew?'

'The Art teacher? Just to see.'

'Well, it's her.' She stares at her black patent shoes. 'It's a sort of obsession.'

'I know exactly,' I assure her. 'It feels sort of platonic, doesn't it?'

'Mmm.'

The pause fills up with embarrassment.

'But it doesn't make me one of those people,' Cara adds.

'Which?'

'Not gay or bisexual or any of those horrible words.'

'Do you know any of those people?'

'No, but I know I'm not one of them.'

'Me neither,' I confirm hastily.

'I just feel ordinary,' Cara insists, clearing her throat. 'I think it's all very silly. They should just let us get on with it.'

'Mmm,' I say, then, 'The bell went ages ago; we're in for it if it's Big Dom.' And we lope across the grass.

Cara begins again as soon as Sister Dominic has given us a section of eighteenth-century history to read through. She points with a surreptitious finger to a neat note on the margin of the book we are sharing. It says, *About what we were talking about. Platon. Obsess. etc. Explain more re: you.*

My answer is warily pencilled. *I put it a bit too strongly. Seem to be getting it under control these days, since she's gone.*

Give hint who?

Nope.

I told you.

Well, I can't, sorry.

Cara considers, her hand curled round the minuscule writing.

My shoulder leans against hers, the heat leaking through our blouses as my pencil skids along the margin. *Listen, I need to know what you honestly think, because I couldn't bear it if you were just doing the sophisticated liberal act and saying you knew how I felt just to make me feel better . . .*

Cara tugs the pencil from my fingers. *I do have some emotions of my own, you know,* she scribbles down the side margin, *it just happens that we happen to be in more or less the same dilemma.*

Glumly, I add a daisy to the last letter. I draw a zigzag line under *more or less* and add *well to be honest for me it's a bit more rather than less* across a faint portrait of Marie-Antoinette.

Her question mark is huge.

Not exactly platonic, I admit in tiny letters across the diamond necklace. *And lots of them. What I said about the one whose name I couldn't tell you, well that's the most important but I've had dreams about others.*

With a lunge of the hand Cara moves on to the next page, which has a blank space in the chronology of social reforms. *But you can't be truly in love with lots of women,* she scrawls, ignoring my shoe crushing her little toe. Her hand finally freezes under the nun's stare.

'Would you two girls care to entertain the class with your correspondence?' asks the Dominator.

'No, Sister, I'm sorry,' the rubber on the end of my pencil already grinding the words away, 'it was just about home-work.' I will rip out the pages if she comes any closer. I'll swallow them and die like a double agent.

Cara won't catch my eye for the rest of the afternoon.

I blinked, focusing on a pyramid of pineapples. It was too hot to shop. We thought we were so important, when we were sixteen. We visualized our lives as a series of significant emotional tasks, from Platonic Obsession to Coming to Terms with Death. It didn't occur to us that most of our existence

99

would be spent in mindless activities like trailing round the supermarket.

It took me ages to find even half the strange foods Kate had admitted to liking. The girl in the dust-striped apron had never heard of fat-free tortilla chips or felafel powder, but I did manage to track down some bio-yoghurt. Beef chunks for Grace – macho enough for his tastes, surely? – and instant coffee for Mr Wall, as well as a hunk of stilton in case my appetite returned.

By the time I got back to the big house, my shirt was stuck to my shoulder-blades. I had left the pineapple behind, probably under a plastic bag at the till, nor could I be bothered to drive back for it. Cara hated pineapples. She said they lured you in with promises of sweet tender flesh, then stuck spines between your teeth and roughened the roof of your mouth with acid. Maybe her spirit wouldn't allow a pineapple in the house? I was often haunted by Cara when she was away on trips. The radio tended to play the songs she hummed in the bath, and somehow she always guessed when I had given in to exhaustion and watched something embarrassing like *Emmerdale Farm*. In the front bedroom – the one I had to remember at all times to call 'mine' and never 'ours', not as a point of principle but in case Mr Wall would hear – whenever I was vacuuming I found scrunched-up tissues under the bed on her side.

Having dumped my grocery bags in the larder, I went out and sat on the edge of the hammock. It would leave a wet mark on my trousers, but I couldn't bring myself to care. Only ten minutes before I'd have to think about lunch. At some point I should probably get around to crying. If it was cold and rainy I could weep, nose against a window-pane like an ingénue in a film. As it was, I bounced on the edge of the hammock, tanning my toes in my slippery sandals, thinking about pineapples. If I did manage to cry it would feel like just another undignified symptom of sun, a sweat of the eyes. Besides, the merry bawl of the birds would drown me out.

I surveyed the overgrown herb bed. Hadn't weeded it in too long; over the summer my pace always slowed, and since I'd been back at Immac I hadn't been able to summon the energy. The kids took it out of me, what was left of it after living with Cara. Everyone I ever mentioned my job to said, 'You must love children.' But I thought it impossible to love children, in general, any more than you could love the human race. In fact I had gone into primary-school teaching with a vague sense that I was not much good with kids, but at least I could save them from worse, from the kind of teachers who scare you into silence or make you feel guilty for life. My policy with children was what I liked to think of as non-interventionist, which meant leaving them alone as much as was legal. If I saw a girl peacefully lost in her own head, wandering down who knew what paths of fantasy, I let her be, and turned to a more eager volunteer for whatever two-plus-two answer was required. Such inane things I had to teach them, anyway, especially the Irish dialogues, which had not changed much since my day.

'*Cá bhfuil an cat?* Come on now, Sharon, you know what that means. Where do you think the cat might be? The word for table is . . . *bord. Tá an cat ar an mbord*, say it. That's right, good girl yourself.'

'Please, Miss, Miss.'

'Miss, can I go to you know where?'

'Miss O'Grady, my mother won't let the cat on the table she says it's not hygienic. What's Irish for hygienic?'

I had no idea. 'The table is only an example, Aisling. What about the cat is on the floor, who knows how to say that?'

And so on, and on, peacefully enough, the greatest part of my mornings. Could be worse, as I always reminded myself, could be gutting chickens.

What was I doing anyway, daydreaming of work on my precious days off? I should get around to weeding the herbs before cooking lunch. Shame to, in a way; the garden looked so plump and plentiful, I didn't want to start ripping out handfuls and leaving brown holes. Oh, this ludicrous heat. I kicked at the grass too hard, and the hammock went into a twist.

The familiar sound of a footstep on the grating in the yard: how many afternoons, how many years of home-comings? Not her. The sister. A leggy figure standing at the top of the garden, her suit off-white against the Virginia creeper that was just beginning to darken to red. 'What in the name of god are you wearing your jacket for?'

'Puts me in business mode,' said Kate, her voice carrying as she walked down the garden. 'How do you feel about anchovies?'

'Some of my best friends.'

'Excuse me?'

'Some of my best friends are anchovies. I'm being flippant, sorry.' This woman must think me so crass, wisecracking on the eve of her sister's funeral.

Kate's mouth wavered into a half-smile. 'Right. Well, they're on a pizza I picked up at the mall; I couldn't imagine you wanting to cook.'

'Shopping centre, shopping centre,' I tutted, 'you can't say "mall" over here. Surely you remember how you used to talk?'

She was folding her jacket over one arm; I was struck by the curve of muscle. 'Bet you don't talk like you did at fifteen either,' she said. 'Besides, Ireland has nothing but a past tense. Did you know there are more Irish living in America than in Ireland?'

'Not real ones.'

She smiled guardedly.

'Come on,' I told her, hauling myself off the hammock, 'the pizza will be getting cold. We forgotten primitives don't know how to insulate a cardboard box. What are you doing buying fast food, anyway? I remember you upstaging us all in cookery class.'

'Did I?' Kate said wonderingly. 'Too busy to eat in

nowadays. I do Thanksgiving for my mother, but that's about it.'

'That's a shame. I'll get plates if you call your father,' I added, bumping the kitchen door open with my hip.

'Call him where?'

'Call him down from his study, you know, shout.'

To the best of my knowledge, Mr Wall had never tasted a pizza; he would have had no reason to. But he rose to this occasion, and gave his slice the most urbane of glances: 'Anchovies, how nice,' he repeated.

When she had finished Kate got up, wiping her fingers, and pulled an electric kettle out of a box: 'Tah dah,' she said, as if announcing a mediocre circus act.

Mr Wall stared at it. 'There was no need,' he said. 'Our old kettle must be in the garage still. I was planning to look it out this evening.'

'Yeah, but this one shuts itself off automatically by thermostat,' Kate assured him. 'It's foolproof.'

I winced at the word.

'Very clever,' said Mr Wall, and refused a cup of coffee.

Embarrassed by the tension in the air, I said I'd love one, and that it was really thoughtful of her to remember the kettle.

After lunch Mr Wall set off to the library, his shirt neck open; I could see the edge of the white cotton vest he always wore, even in this weather. I brought my stack of books downstairs and prepared end-of-month tests at the kitchen table. I couldn't seem to remember what nine-year-olds would be likely to know about the French Revolution, apart from who was said to have said the thing about the cake.

Kate came down halfway through the afternoon in a crisp shirt and long shorts. She watched the kettle as it wheezed towards the boil. 'Am I in your way?'

'Not at all, I needed distraction. Rigor mortis was setting in.' I flinched as soon as I heard myself say it, and didn't meet her eye. There was a long pause while she filled the cafetière.

'Is that decaff?'

'It should be,' she said wryly.

'Nice to see Americans aren't quite perfect yet.'

Kate didn't rise to it; she was staring at a photograph of her grandparents on the mantelpiece. I went back to the Reign of Terror.

'I was thinking of taking a walk,' she mentioned.

'The woods?'

'Where else?'

'Did you used to like them too?'

'Well, there wasn't really anywhere else to go after a row with my mother,' said Kate.

'What did you fight about?'

'Just stupid things like what time to be in by, or having to give Cara my hand-me-downs.'

I put the cap on my pen. 'I might join you, if you're not planning a long hike.'

'Sure, why not.'

I pulled the kitchen door shut behind us. The sun was hazed over but still bewildering to my eyes.

Kate's were hidden behind prescription shades. 'God, it's hot. We're not going all the way round by the road, are we? Let's hop over the wall.'

I looked her up and down. 'My body doesn't do that sort of thing.'

'But there were footholds,' she protested. 'Or at least some bricks to stand on.' I waited in the yard while Kate jogged down to the back wall to investigate. Her steps were slower on the way back. There were drops of sweat on her hairline already. 'Can't find the breeze-blocks; my father must have moved them.'

'Come on, it's only five minutes by the road.'

But a damp had fallen on our spirits. As we walked up the hill, Kate commented on the lack of children around, our own boom generation having spilled across every avenue and cul-de-sac. 'When did they shut off that field with bollards?' she asked, pointing.

'Dunno. Some time in the eighties.'

'The itinerants used to camp there,' she said. 'Wonder where they are now.'

I confirmed that the Fitzwilliam Inn used to be called Moroneys, that there weren't any American-style twenty-four-hour garages when we were young, and that the woods had indeed got smaller as the upmarket housing estates squeezed in on two sides. I was beginning to feel like a tour guide. It took all my energy to keep walking into the grey glare; sweat traced the line of my jaw. 'It said in the paper it would reach thirty degrees today,' I said.

'What's that in Fahrenheit?'

'No idea, sorry.'

When we reached the wall around the woods, searching for something to say, I pointed to the daub of faded white and said, 'I've always wondered what that means: "the cure" for what?'

Kate's hand paused in the act of wiping her forehead. 'Are you serious?'

'What?'

'The Cure is a band, Pen. Didn't you know, for real?'

'What, like a rock band?'

'Yeah. The lead singer has all this backcombed hair . . .'

I stared at the letters. 'And all these years I've been reading such profundity into it.'

Her laughter was throaty, much lower than her sister's. 'You're a little out of touch. What do you play on that old ghetto-blaster of yours?'

'Bach,' I told her. 'Sometimes Pachelbel, Handel, people like that.'

She was walking ahead into the trees. I couldn't make out the phrase she threw back.

'No, they're the business,' I insisted. 'They'd resign you to anything.'

It was a curious sensation, following her through my familiar places. Above the cluster of beeches, yesterday's rainstorm had muddied the ground. Sun on the back of my neck made me suddenly bend down to undo my laces. Kate watched as I stepped out and felt the mud squelch between my toes. It felt cool and sweet, slightly obscene. She made no comment, but I could almost hear her thinking that it would be hell to clean the muddy toe-marks off the insides of my runners. If Cara had been beside me she would not have thought that, or warned me against broken glass, twigs, caterpillars or foot and mouth disease. She would not have made me feel foolish and theatrical, wanting to put my shoes on again but resisting the impulse out of pride.

See how nostalgia was addling my brains already? Cara wouldn't have smiled at my toes, she would have been too busy with her own. She'd have rushed to get there before me, to be the spontaneous one, kneeling and rolling and being one with mother earth, making muddy handprints up a silver birch, while I stood by, holding her shoes. If I ever got around to loving anyone else, I thought suddenly, it would have to be someone who would neither muffle my thunder nor steal it.

The earth was delicious on the worn pads of my heels. 'You ever been spat at, Kate?' I asked to break the silence as we emerged into a clearing.

'Not that I ever noticed,' she said amusedly. 'Why, have you?'

'Just the once. It was Cara and me –'

'Wasn't it always?'

'It's just the place that reminds me,' I went on after a few seconds. 'We were sitting on that blue bench over there one Sunday morning, minding our own business – I think Cara was reading out Nell McCafferty's column from the paper – and up comes this little old lady.'

'How old?'

I paused to remember. 'In her seventies, maybe; not senile, as far as I could tell. And not a bag-lady either; she was a typical Dublin 4 granny. She had one of those expensive beige raincoats buttoned up to her neck, in spite of the sun.'

'Sinister.'

'Ah, you're slagging me now, but wait for it. So I spotted her walking towards us with this little fluffy dog on a leash, right, one of those ridiculous Lapsong Souchong things, and I grinned at them, and the next thing I knew, this great gob of spit was sailing through the air at us.'

Kate laughed under her breath. 'Are you sure it wasn't an accident? Maybe she was trying to say hello and her dentures slipped?'

'No, it was quite deliberate. It landed on Cara's shoe, but she never noticed, just kept on reading out bits from the paper.'

'And what outrage did she perpetrate next?'

'You don't believe me,' I said.

'I believe that the lady spat at you,' said Kate diplomatically, 'but there must be a reasonable explanation.'

'We hadn't done a thing to her.'

Her steps were picking up speed. 'Then she was just a weirdo. We've plenty of them in Boston. They talk to themselves on street corners.'

The back of my hand stroked the moss that furred a sycamore. 'You can't just write someone off that way. We're all weirdos in one way or another.'

'Not me,' said Kate. 'I'm boringly normal.'

'Are you?'

She gave me a dazzling smile over one shoulder. 'All except for my dreams. They could get me locked up.'

'Really?' After a few seconds I went on, 'I suppose the difference is, most of us confine our weirdness to the privacy of our own homes or nightmares, and don't go round expectorating at strangers.'

'So what happened next?'

'Well, I was expecting her to offer some justification or insult, but she just took a folded tissue out of her cuff, wiped her mouth with it and walked off.'

'And how did Cara react?'

'She wouldn't believe me till I showed her the gob of spit

on her shoe. She still claims, I mean she always used to claim that it was a pigeon dropping, and I was hallucinating the rest.'

'My sister sounds like a pain in the butt,' observed Kate under her breath. 'I'm rather glad we lived in different countries.'

We had emerged on to the top of the hill. Rain lingered in a puddled stretch of grass; a couple of seagulls steeped across, shuffling blue sky through their toes. 'Ah, Cara was all right,' I said softly. Too softly. Who was I kidding, with my edited stories and flippant references? This East Coast sophisticate could probably see right through me. 'I doubt you two would have had much in common, though,' I said. 'I don't suppose you've ever adopted a whale.'

Kate groaned, wiping the sweat out of her eyes.

'She called it Samantha,' I added enjoyably. Then I heard the cheap satire in my voice, and my mouth went sour. 'Actually,' I said, 'she wasn't some bleeding-heart hippy, she did a lot of good work.'

No comment from her sister.

'I mean, I know she sort of sponged off your father in the big house, but that let her do lots of crisis helplines and stuff, when others just couldn't afford the time.'

'Why do you call it that?' asked Kate, surveying the smoky horizon. 'The house isn't very big at all.'

'I think it came from me taking the piss out of Cara for being rich, like, the gentryfolk up in the Big House. Besides, it was bigger than I was used to.'

'I guess when they bought it Mom and Dad were expecting more of a family.'

'Would you have liked other siblings?'

'No,' said Kate, considering. 'I'd have preferred to be an only child.'

I let the silence lengthen, waiting for her to qualify the remark. Then I said, 'Anyway, the house seemed huge to me when I first saw it. Do you remember that day?'

'Which?'

I wiped the sweat off my throat with the back of my hand. 'What were you on, all through fourth year?'

Kate pursed her lips. 'Had we been shopping?'

'No, swimming. Stop pretending to remember.'

Her teeth flashed in a grin, very white and strong. 'OK. You're the storyteller.'

'We'd bumped into each other after school at the pool,' I explained, 'and there wasn't another bus for an hour, and my hair was dripping into my collar, so you invited me home for tea.'

'What a nice girl I must have been.'

'You took the last slice of chocolate gâteau and ran yourself a hot bath, leaving me to watch *Top of the Pops* with your little sister.'

Kate's mouth twisted in amusement. 'Turned out Cara was more useful to you in the end, though.'

My fingers were following a crack in the bark of a horse-chestnut tree. 'Still, I'd have liked some gâteau.'

'I'll buy you one tomorrow, all right?'

'Too late,' I said with a theatrical sigh. 'But I was so impressed by your house,' I went on, picking my way across the slope.

'Why?'

'Well, for a start it was detached; I'd never been in more than a semi before. It seemed so grandiose, and your parents were so civilized, with their long words and glass coffee cups, and you had a hammock in your garden.'

'You were easily impressed.'

'Well, for someone from my background –'

'Hang on, something's coming back to me: didn't your father work at the university?'

For a moment I felt the old shame behind my eyes. I produced a snigger, as I wiped my muddy feet on the grass before tugging on my runners. 'I used to say that, while I was at school. What I meant was, he was one of the college gardeners.'

'Ah.'

'And of course as soon as I got to college myself, after he died, my snobbery inverted, and I told people, "My father used to dig here".'

Kate's voice expanded in a laugh.

'It was a sort of running joke. Sometimes when I'd come over to the big house and Cara'd open the door, I'd say, "Beggin' yer pardon, yer honour", or "Top o' the mornin' to you, young mistress, and would there be any little thing I could be doin' for you today?" Just stupid stuff like that,' I trailed off, feeling pink.

'But we're not Anglo at all,' Kate insisted. 'Catholic peasant stock on both sides.'

The warm paint splintered under my fingers as I pushed the gate open. 'Nobody's a peasant with money and a hammock.'

'Who are you to talk?' Kate added playfully. 'You live here now.'

'Yeah, but I'm only the window cleaner.'

Her hands were dug deep into her ironed cotton pockets. 'I'm really sorry about that. I was jet-lagged, and the headscarf confused me.'

'No worries,' I told her magnanimously.

By the time we got home the sky was beginning to cloud over. Kate looked in the kitchen window while I struggled with the lock. There was a muffled crash from the tool-shed. 'That'll be Grace,' I told her, and sure enough there he was, edging along the whitewashed window-sill. I got the door open at last, and paused on the step, wiping my runners on the mat. Kate hadn't moved.

'You all right?'

'Something else is coming back to me,' she said, following me in.

I busied myself with the kettle's strange new switch, leaving a silence for her to fill, but she didn't. 'You've probably had more than an earful of Wall family history over the years,' she said at last.

Fishing for an invitation, was she? Would the words not

come without the asking? I smiled at the floor. 'No, actually, Cara said very little about it. And all Mr Wall's stories are of you two as small children.'

'Really? What kind of stories?'

'Like when you were fighting in the back of the car, and your mother stopped on the roadside and made the pair of you get out, and threatened to drive away unless you promised to be civil.'

'Did she do that? Good for her,' Kate added uncertainly. 'If I ever have children, I'm going to buy an old cab with one of those sound-proof screens between front and back.'

'So what was it you were remembering?' I sat with my elbows on the table and waited.

'Just, why I went with Mom, back in '78,' she said. 'It was the evening they told us they were splitting up. I hadn't noticed a thing.'

'Mmm?' I said after a few seconds, to bring her back.

She jolted slightly. 'Anyway. Can't remember the euphemism they used, something like "Mum's going to take a job in America for a while and Dad's going to look after you two here till we decide where we'll all live."'

'That what they said?'

'They probably meant it at the time. But I should have known Dad would never have the guts to emigrate.'

Considering a retort, but knowing it would slow the story down, I reached up for two mugs.

'So anyway, much later that evening, round bedtime, I was coming past this window – probably on my way back from mooching round the woods, which I wasn't supposed to do after dark – and I looked in and saw Dad and Cara.'

'Doing what?'

'He was on his own by the sideboard, polishing the forks. I couldn't hear a thing but it looked like he was crying, from the way he was bent over. I didn't think crying was something he did.'

'So where was Cara?' I followed Kate's gaze, taking in the sideboard, the white lightshade, summoning up the scene.

'She walked in with an empty mug and saw him. Now if it had been me, and I'd known that Dad had seen me seeing him cry, I'd have been so mortified I'd probably have gotten the hell out of there. But Cara went right over and put her arms around him. She was taller than him, even then.'

'Yeah?' I said, to keep her going.

'They stood there for ages,' said Kate, staring at the sideboard. 'His head was on her shoulder and she still had the mug hanging from her little finger.'

The kettle was starting to pant. 'I still don't see why that made you demand to go to Ohio.'

'It just seemed . . . appropriate.' A hint of irony undercut the word. 'I knew Cara was Daddy's pet; when she was small she was always knocking things over and cutting her knees and needing them to be kissed better. But it was never so real to me till I saw the two of them standing there, and I thought, yes, that fits.'

The skin was shadowy below her mud-brown eyes. 'Couldn't you have fitted too?' I asked.

'Nah, I wasn't in that picture. But it all worked out,' she added after a minute.

I watched steam ribbon up from the neat mouth of the kettle. 'Did it?'

'Sure. I knew the States would suit me better; I was always getting impatient with Ireland.'

'At least you got to keep your mother.'

'Oh, Cara did all right out of the bargain,' said Kate briskly. 'I suspect my father was the better mother.'

I made tea for two, without thinking, then poured out one mug and made her coffee. Apparently drained of words, Kate opened the newspaper and leaned into it, her eyes intent on the page.

I stood for a second, my arms hanging by my sides, then went off for a shower. The mud clung to my toes; I had to lean against the side and scrub them hard. After standing in the water for ten minutes I was no cooler. My skin crisped up but the heat stayed in my head and stomach.

Cooking seemed far too much effort, so when Mr Wall plodded into the yard at five to six I simply arrayed cold ham and pâté and a cucumber across the tablecloth. I asked Kate something about her mother's job, but she had retreated into monosyllables. I put out three plates, my ears comforted by the familiar clang as each hit the cloth. Kate lifted her paper out of my way without looking up.

Mr Wall was in form at dinner, chatting away about the Wotherby library's more peculiar users. He was looking rather dashing today, his Adam's apple firm against his wine silk tie. I wondered whether, if Irish law had allowed it, he would have married again. He might still, I supposed, if divorce came to Ireland in the nineties; unless he considered himself to have outgrown that sort of thing.

Kate sat across the table from me. When her long knee brushed against mine, I shifted away imperceptibly. I decided, as I reached for the bottle of white wine, that Mr Wall's daughters had little in common except their mother's height. He seemed a gentle Joseph who had contributed nothing to their features. I passed dishes, commented on weather and politics, and kept on watching Kate. Only the odd gesture gave an unnerving reminder of their sisterhood. Funny word, that; why did 'hood' added to nouns make them into states of being? Perhaps sisterhood was a hood that sisters had to wear, or rather, two hoods. Wide brims framing the eyes, I imagined, rather Florence Nightingale; perhaps harmonizing tones of the same colour, azure and midnight blue, with ribbons to match. Then what about maidenhood? Definitely the hoods off our old Immac uniforms, stiff red gaberdine to shade us from rain and male glances. They were detachable, too, I remembered, and the bad girls used to unbutton theirs and lose them in the first week: how very suitable! And under the maidenhood was the maidenhead, and girls lost their heads just as easily.

I took the bottle from Mr Wall's outstretched hand and poured myself a toast to my enduring maidenhead. After

Cara gave up men she stopped mocking me for it; in fact I suspect that, with her taste for extremes, she rather envied my being what Jo called a cradle-dyke. (The phrase conjured up an image of a baby lolling in a cradle, one blurry eye on the breast, deciding that nothing else would do.) Cara brought me back a badly printed red badge from Manchester once that said 'Technically a Virgin'. I had never worn it, but every time I glimpsed it on the inside of my wardrobe door I grinned.

At a certain stage, it occurred to me now, chewing on a strand of ham, even the most technical of virgins becomes an old maid. Twenty-eight it was in Jane Austen's day, so being thirty last May I was well past it. The spinsterhood, I decided, would be tall and crooked, in dark grey felt; not the prettiest, but I'd prefer it to the flapping gingham mother-hood, or (god forbid) the wifehood drowned in off-white lace. Dykehood was definitely a baseball cap. There wasn't a lesbianhood that I knew of, only an ism, sounding like a digestive disease. Someone would have to invent something better.

In the cool of the early evening Kate insisted on doing the washing up. I filled up the kettle for yet another boost of caffeine, and sat on the high stool by the counter, reading the crossword clues without bothering to reach for a biro to fill them in.

Mr Wall padded in. He was wearing his best grey suit. 'Twenty to seven now, girls.'

We stared at him.

'The removal's at seven. Is that what they call it? Reception of Remains?' The words were slipping around in his throat.

'Right,' said Kate, all business.

'I don't think,' I began, and the two of them stopped in their tracks. 'Actually, I can't manage it.' They waited. 'I could ring you a taxi . . .'

'Why don't you give me your keys.' Kate's voice, solid as a church bench. 'I'm insured for any car.'

'But you're used to . . .'

'I've driven plenty of manual cars on the left when I've been in London on business trips.'

'Couldn't spare a day to stop off in Dublin and see your sister on any of these trips, no?' The words spat themselves out like bullets.

We were all equally startled. Kate's mouth opened as if to answer, mine as if to apologize, but nothing came out of either. Mr Wall's face was uncooked dough. I fumbled for the keyring in my littered handbag. 'Mind the clutch,' I told her, 'it's a bit touchy.'

I turned away as they hurried to the door. The kettle was growling; its lid gave a jerk, and then it sighed to a halt. It made me nervous; I pulled out its plug and leaned against the sink. Not only was I irritable to the point of being a complete bitch today, but I was a coward as well. If I couldn't handle a brief ceremony, just accompanying the body from the hospital's chapel to the parish church, then how was I planning to cope tomorrow when they started shovelling earth on top of her? My throat contracted. I folded myself over the sink but nothing came, only a delicate necklace of spit.

Hush, ba, shush now. It was all right. It was understandable not to want to go look at what was left of her in the chapel of rest – what a ghastly euphemism, as if the bodies had dropped by voluntarily for a little siesta. I knew they'd leave the lid off, and I couldn't bear that. I wanted to remember Cara live and exasperating, not floppy in a box. Whereas Mr Wall seemed to take comfort in doing this mourning thing according to the letter. I could just see him now, stooping over the coffin on its brass trolley, lips puckered as if approaching an irreplaceable manuscript. What about Kate, was she going along just to be polite? I wondered whether she would kiss the papery forehead she had last brushed with her lips at Logan Airport in 1984 after the family reunion. How much did she really care whether this flickering memory of a sister lived or died?

The sink was scummed grey. I tipped in some boiling water from the kettle and scrubbed at its sides. I knew I would have to get myself psyched up for the funeral, but this stupid removal ritual was more than I could take right now. If I broke down, blubbing on to the wooden rim of the box, there would be no one to look after me. Cara wouldn't slip her cold hand surreptitiously into mine; she would be lying there all blithe and callous. As on the odd night when I couldn't get to sleep and used to curl up on my side, watching her mouth move in the gibberish of sleep, those wholly private conversations.

I reached under the sink for the disinfectant and filled up the sink with water hot enough to hurt my hands. Time to get a grip, get to work, batten down the hatches. I thought it best to clean all the surfaces I could reach, in case any day now I lost whatever was keeping me in one piece, and sat in the corner for a month with unwashed hair, clutching a biscuit tin while the whole house went to seed around me.

When my sponge had swabbed its way as far as the bookcase above the sideboard, it caught the edge of a pamphlet. I tugged it out from behind a stack of *Bibliopegy Quarterly*. On the front was a drawing of a crystal ball with hearts and stars rising off it like steam from a freshly baked loaf. Inside, the blurred print asked, 'Would you like me to tell you all you need to know?' and, undeterred by the lack of response, explained that 'through using her exceptional gifts of clairvoyancy since childhood, direct descendant of the Romanies Miss Dora Moon will answer stressful questions and up-tie the tensions in your life, with the use of psychometry and holding a sentimental item.' God yes, I remembered it now; our private catchphrase for a month or so had been 'Ooh, hold my sentimental item, big girl'. Cara had brought this back from a Psychic Fair in Edinburgh, amused by the grammar but attracted by the promises. I never knew whether her healthy cynicism or wide-eyed belief would win out; I could never tell when it was safe to laugh. The back of this dust-stained booklet offered a course called 'How to Attract and Keep the Partner of Your Dreams, in 7 audio cassettes for only £55'.

I folded it in quarters and put it in the compost bin, so it could take part in the great psychometrical cycle of rebirth, as Miss Dora Moon would probably describe it. I balanced the chairs upside-down on the table. Only when I had swept the floor and mopped all of it except the corner I was standing in did I realize that I was listening out for the phone.

Once during a breakup Cara rings me at my mother's. 'Will we ever get back to being just friends?' she whispers.

I sit on the kitchen counter in the very centre of the small empty house, hugging my knees. 'We were never just friends,' I tell her. 'We were always sort-of-girlfriends.'

'Old s.o.g.s,' she murmurs, savouring the resurrected phrase. 'But we get on OK nowadays, don't we? Considering?'

'I suppose.'

'I really enjoyed that last phone call,' Cara says, like a child at a birthday party.

I breathe out between my teeth, focusing on the hiss of air. 'It's not so bad when you ring, but whenever we actually meet, in those rare half-hours when you manage to tear yourself away from reassuring Roderick about his masculinity, those times are bizarre.'

A heavy pause.

'I sit beside you in a coffee shop and feel like there's an electric fence between us, like your shape is broken up by all these horizontal force lines. I look at your hand holding a cup,' I rush on, 'and it's foreign to me. I distinctly remember that I used to kiss that hand and tell you that I'd know it anywhere, if I ever needed to identify your body in a morgue, say, but it's just not true any more. I sit there thinking, how could I have loved this stranger?' The words hang on in the air, hollow and theatrical.

Cara's voice is almost too low to hear. 'Am I suddenly so unlovable?'

'No,' I tell her tiredly. 'But it's like you've emigrated.'

Another time during another breakup, Cara rings me at my mother's. 'So what's new?'

'Nothing much.' I smile at Mammy as I grip the receiver between shoulder and jaw and carry the phone into the hall.

'Do you still hate me like you said?'

'No,' as I pull the door shut, 'I hate you in different ways.'

Cara's voice is a hoarse whisper. 'All the time?'

'No,' I say civilly. 'When I wake up in the morning it's lying on me like that lead apron they make you wear at the dentist's, but then I shove it off and pull on my jeans and I'm free.'

'Bully for you.'

'Ah come on now, love, don't be petulant. If anyone's entitled to be petulant it's me.'

In the pause I can hear the characteristic jagged rhythm of her breathing. 'Do you hate Kevin too?' she asks. 'Because really he wasn't the reason.'

'I couldn't care less about Kevin,' I tell Cara, hoping it rings true. But I cannot sound careless when I ask, 'Have you gone on the Pill yet?'

A stagey sigh. 'I keep telling you, Pen, I know when I'm fertile. I'm in phase with the moon.'

'So that's what "lunatic" means.'

'Huh?'

'You could get pregnant, you stupid little fucker.'

'Ah stop,' she says in surprise, 'I'm all right.'

'Don't I even have the right to worry about you any more?'

Another time, during another breakup, I ring her at her father's.

'Hey, Cara,' I begin. 'The reason I missed lunch with you on Friday wasn't that I was upset but because I spent the day in bed with a woman from my pottery class. She's called –'

'I don't think I want to know,' Cara cuts in.

'Suit yourself,' I carol. 'I suppose I should be flattered that you're jealous, though you've no right to be.'

'I'm not jealous,' she says painedly, 'I'm actually really glad for you.' After a second, 'What's her name?'

'Bella.'

'Right.'

'What do you mean, "right", in that tone?'

'Well, you must admit it's a bit naff, as names go.'

'This,' I say in amusement, 'from a woman who claims not to be jealous?'

Then Cara's voice goes low and wispy. 'I miss you,' she says. 'Why was it we parted?'

Parted? That's such a nineteenth-century word, you can't use words like that any more. And she has the gall to ask why, as if it wasn't her who gave me a ten-page letter of reasons why, being bad for each other, bringing out as we did each other's worst contrasting attributes, we had to part. The pause this time is long. Anger is bubbling like oxygen in my veins, so I hardly notice she has put the phone down.

I write her a note on the back of a Picasso blue woman. *Cara,* it begins – *dear Cara* would be too great a concession – *you are fucking me up big time. How dare you get all nostalgic now? I wouldn't mind so much if you meant it but you don't. Don't humiliate me by even suggesting you might come back when you know I'd take you back anytime even though I know right well you never will.* I find it difficult to hold on to grammar around Cara.

By return of post comes a sunset with writing tiny enough so that no one but me would have patience enough to decipher it. *You misunderstood me,* it begins, *I was just slightly shocked by your news about B. Communication is too sore right now. We have entered separate folds and if we turn back our wool might snag on the wire as it were.*

Cara, I snap in reply on a postcard of the Eiffel Tower, *I'm not asking you to turn back. The way I see it is, we're in this mess together. Think of it as a lab experiment, not sheep but rats; I am*

Control and you are A, exposed to the male virus. I look forward to seeing how you turn out.

Dear Pen, says her next card (a cruciform stained glass), *I can do without that sort of condescending crap. Have fun humping Bella.*

The irony of the situation being that Bella is a lie, a fairy tale, the first name that came into my head. But Cara's hurt makes it almost real. I walk round all week in the arms of my invisible lover.

As I put the mop and bucket away in the cupboard under the stairs, I remembered with a quiver of satisfaction that I'd never let on about Bella. Cara used to ask the occasional question about her, which I answered only in the vaguest terms. She became a sort of running joke between us, after we got back together and I moved into the big house.

'Gimme the last slice or else,' I'd say over a mince tart.

'Or else what?'

'Or else I'll feck off back to Bella.'

Somehow I could never bear to reveal – not even in our closest moments, when stories bubbled up for the offering – that the whole Bella thing had been a lie. Not that it would bother me to be caught out in a dishonesty; no, what I winced from was the prospect of Cara knowing that, all those times she left me, I sat at home and watched television. I thought it might go to her head if she discovered that, sometimes unwanted but more often unwanting, I had never gone to bed with anyone but her.

I replaced the chairs on either side of the table and sat down. A patch of lino, still wet from the mop, glistened by my sandal. To be fair to Cara, the asymmetry did bother her. Once she was lying behind me, her long body cloaking me from draughts, and she said, 'I can't believe I've been the only one for you, apart from Bella.'

I grunted sleepily.

'No, but I mean, how boring. If I was my only lover, I'd go demented.'

I chuckled under my breath.

'Surely it got a bit raunchy between you and that substitute teacher last year?'

'I know you'd like to think so,' I yawned, 'but I never bothered. She was only a bit kissable.'

'How'd you know till you try?'

'I just didn't fancy her enough to try.'

Cara tutted, shifting position in the bed. 'What about that long-haired woman whose B&B you stayed at in Cornwall?'

'Mmm,' I said reminiscently.

'Did you fancy her enough?'

'Plenty.'

'Well then?'

'She had a really classy come-on line, too; I was queueing outside the bathroom in nothing but a towel at midnight, and she walked up, took hold of the edge of the towel, and said, "What a nice sight."'

Cara wriggled round excitedly. 'So why didn't you fall to the floor with her?'

'It would have felt wrong.'

A weighty sigh from Cara.

'Look, I've told you before: my head doesn't have room for two women in it and me as well.'

She gave a gentle snort. 'Why does your head have to come into it?'

'Heads always come into it, you know that.'

'Suppose.'

'Besides, sex doesn't interest me just for itself; it has to stand for something.'

'You're such a Catholic. Couldn't it stand for fun?'

'Sweetheart, I'm sorry, but I'm not going to rush out and sleep with someone else just to salve your conscience.'

'My conscience is doing fine.' Cara pulled back, and cold air slipped a blade between our bodies.

'If you say so.'

'Don't start guilt-tripping me again. Monogamy's not natural.'

'No, it's just not easy.'

'None of it's *easy*,' said Cara with a groan as she sat up. The bedclothes heaved with her, letting in a whirlpool of draughts.

I tucked myself in up to the ears. 'Tell you what's easy: make me a cup of tea.'

Oh, I was always good at the soft words to end a difficult discussion. But now it occurred to me, she was right. How very foolish I had been, in this age of pic-'n'-mix consumerism, to have slept with only one woman in the thirteen years since I discovered the whole business. Now I was left high and dry and loverless. Though I knew theoretically that there were other people in the world who could heat up a bed for me, I didn't believe in them as anything more than fantasies. Bed was Cara, and without her, without at least the possibility of her return, I felt infibulated.

I revved up the vacuum cleaner and ploughed it through the house, veering round corners, plunging under coffee tables. The snarl filled up my ears so I didn't have to think. I hauled it upstairs, its heavy head bouncing on the carpeted steps. Bathroom, hall, my room at the front, Cara's bombsite at the back . . . not Kate's room, I didn't want to disturb any of her things. I carried the vacuum back downstairs and wound the cord into place before stowing it in the cupboard.

I stood in the hall. My hands were scaly; I was sweaty, cold, and almost satisfied. It occurred to me that I had not seen Grace for hours. I went through the rooms, calling to him, then tried upstairs in the wardrobes. He was such a clumsy animal, there was no limit to where he might have got himself stuck. I wondered whether he had picked it up from Cara, who bounded and jerked as if used to the gravity of a heavier planet. All the carpets in this house were watermarked from her setting down a glass beside her chair, then kicking it over as she crossed her legs. We didn't let her wash dishes, Mr Wall and I; it was too hard on the nerves. She had less chance of breaking anything if she swept the floor and emptied the bins.

I watched her playing football with a crowd from college once, and she wasn't clumsy at all. At high speed there seemed to be enough room for all her limbs. Oh, and Cara was never clumsy when making love to me. The stress was not on the *me* there – no doubt she was equally graceful when in bed with other people – but the *to*. As long as Cara was running the show, moving, teasing, adjusting, parting, lifting her knees over me, she was as graceful as an acrobat. But as soon as she was being made love to – keeping with these crude distinctions for a minute – she lost all control. Bliss dissolved her brain. She might throw out an arm and smash an alarm clock off a table, or hit her head off the headboard, and she was so anaesthetized by pleasure that she didn't care. I learned to clear a little space around us if I had intentions. I told her she might brain herself entirely one of these times, and she laughed lopsidedly, and said, 'What a way to go.'

No sign of Grace anywhere upstairs. There was nothing else for him to get trapped in. Then I told myself to stop being paranoid, and went back down.

By the time the key turned in the front door, I was watching a documentary on pollution. I had sat through five minutes of a sitcom before feeling ashamed at the prospect of being caught laughing by the Walls on their return from the chapel of rest. I turned the TV off, then thought that if they found me staring at the blank screen they would worry about my sanity; finally I flicked through the channels till I found something sober.

I got to my feet and turned off the television. Mr Wall nodded a few inches to the side of my eyes, and went straight into his bedroom. Kate dropped Minnie's keys into my palm.

'Did she give you any trouble?' I asked, trying to convey warmth and apology.

'Not once I'd got used to the clutch.' She yawned, stretching her arms over her head and knocking against the paper lightshade, which swung crazily. She stilled it with one hand. Silence filled up the room in drifts. I wanted to say something nice, but nothing occurred to me. 'I'd better get another early night,' she remarked. 'My body clock's not right yet.'

'Do that.'

'Get lots of sleep yourself,' Kate added over her shoulder. 'It's Cara's big day tomorrow.'

Our eyes met, startled by the remark. 'Night,' I said, and watched till the curve of the banisters took her.

A hot bath would be the best thing for me, I knew, but I was too tired to wait for it to fill. I went straight upstairs, took all my clothes off and slid into the wide bed. I lay still on the outside edge until it began to warm under my body. I stretched one foot into the void of the other side; the sheet lifted reluctantly, like skin coming away.

When Cara was off on holidays or work jaunts I used to take to sleeping in the middle, but then when she came home again she'd complain that my body had become accustomed to the whole bed and was squeezing her against the wall. Apparently in sleep I used to turn my back and bend like an arrow head, taking up the whole square of bed. 'Bottom from hell,' she would mutter, shoving against my inert flesh; if I was fast asleep I wouldn't notice until a particularly sharp poke produced an outraged 'Ow' and I shrugged over a little.

Tonight I clung to the edge of the mattress. It seemed unfair to steal any of her space now. I squeezed my eyes shut until I saw stars on black.

I am leaning back against the enamel, my flesh a wet padding for the bath. My left hand is skewed under the weight of a book; the fingers strain to keep the pages open and the hard corner off Cara's freckled shoulder. She is lying back against my breasts, her head weighing on the skin below my neck which is beginning to soften as I near my thirties. Her hair, its ends darkened to peat by the water, lies in chilly strands across the dip of my collarbone. She is drifting, snoozing, rising and falling as I breathe. Every now and then I reach for a bigger breath and she rises an inch through the steaming water. My right elbow is propped up on the side of the bath, the hand hovering over a saucer which bears the remains of a crumbled chocolate bar. My eyes shift from the page occasionally to supervise my fingers as they brush the flakes of chocolate into a little heap without toppling the saucer, press it between the tips, raise it slowly to give the crumbs a chance to fall on the saucer rather than the water, then lift it to my mouth. Every second time I bring my hand round to where I can feel Cara's drying lips; at my touch she opens them a little and receives the fragment of sweetness. She sucks on my fingers, whether to please them or to get all the chocolate or both, I am past telling.

She gives a little shiver and rears up with a splash, leaning forward to turn on the hot tap. I take advantage of this pause to shift my position, lifting a bit of skin that was stuck to the back of the bath. I slide down a little lower in the water. The tap runs cold under Cara's fingers at first – she hisses disapprovingly – then it starts to steam and she lies back, her head on my expanse of belly, water covering her ears. Tentacles of hair stream out behind her.

When it is becoming uncomfortably hot round my calves I give a heave to swirl the hot water upwards. Cara opens her eyes and reaches down with one long foot to twist the tap off. I watch her prehensile toes with admiration, remembering all the things she can do with them. Cara settles back between my breasts. She shakes her head to loose the water from her ears. As she turns her face, her mouth dips to my right nipple, gives it a brief kiss, squeaky with water. I go back to my book.

Later I put it down, take up the white soap and start to lather it, covering in foam Cara's narrow shoulders and secretive armpits. I can see her eyelashes flutter open for a moment, then she shuts them and sinks back into her dream. I circle her small breasts with the tips of my fingers, first a large circle round the outside, then spiralling to smaller ones, honing in on the nipple. No bumps this month; I say a silent thanks. We are told to do this ourselves, but as Cara says, I know her breasts better than she does, and have more motivation for feeling them.

I reach behind me for the glass jug, scoop up warm water and rinse her with it. The suds flee to cling to where the water edges our bodies. I raise the jug and dowse her from a height, the water falling harder, its stream twisting like that waterfall in Wicklow we climbed once. I focus its fall on her left nipple, which hardens under the pressure, until Cara's mouth twists up at one corner and she reaches above her head to slap at my nose till I stop.

Later I haul my dripping bulk up and step round her to sit by the taps and wash my hair. Cara steals some shampoo to make a moustache for herself. I lie back between her endless legs; she hooks her heel round to anchor in my fuzz.

Later still, when our lower bodies are prune-like and our upper bodies cold and shiny, Cara stands up. The water runs off her like crystal covering a statue. Diamonds hang on the ringlets between her legs; I reach up with my mouth to catch a drop.

In the early days, perhaps in our first few hundred baths, we used to talk. Nowadays there's no need.

WEDNESDAY

I was Superwoman the morning of the funeral. In the shower, sheets of water armoured my body.

Still no sign of Grace, but his food dish was empty. I tucked a black silk button-down shirt into black linen trousers; no one was going to guilt-trip me into wearing a skirt today. I strode round the kitchen stacking place-mats and sweeping crumbs into my hand, asking Mr Wall his opinions on the general election and the chance of rain. He was impeccable in his charcoal suit and tie. The sides of his hair had more streaks of silver than I had ever noticed; I realized that I had no idea how old he was. Was he going to fade to grey before my eyes? I made strong coffee all round, to keep us awake through the service. I was a great black walrus, commanding her herd with each toss of the tusks.

At the last minute I remembered that my maggoty dirty car, bearing the nearest blood relatives, would be expected to lead the cavalcade. I rushed out and turned the garden hose on her. The day was warm and grey, sun hovering behind a veil of cloud. The jet of the hose lashed dust from Minnie's headlights and blasted her wheels till they gleamed like open mouths. Spray lit on my shirt, moulding it to the curves of elastic. While I was at it I hosed down the black paint of the garage door, and directed the wand of water along the yard which was still streaked with mud from Monday's flooding. When I was small, and we lived in my gran's house with no garden but a flower barrel behind the bins, Mammy used to cure our tempers on hot days by taking out the hose and making a fountain for us to run through in our knickers. As we yelped under the spray, the sun split into a flock of rainbows, and the bin lids were transformed into the shining shields of Saladin's army.

Kate was on the step. I turned off the hose; it dribbled beside my feet. 'So are you still a regular mass-goer?' I asked, for something to say.

'No, only weddings and funerals. Though they're getting to be regular enough.' She was crisp in a business suit of pale grey and a cream shirt.

I was a mess. The shirt clung to the slopes of my breasts; I pulled it out of the waistband, flapped it in the humid air, and let it hang. My sensible lace-up shoes, I realized, were both stereotypically dykey and spattered with water. Aunts and family friends would ask who that rather large girl was. No, worse, they would read the signals of clothes and grief, draw their disdainful conclusions, and I would have outed Cara posthumously to her entire clan. At this rate I might as well rear up at her graveside singing 'Lavender Jane Loves Women'.

Graveside; I tried out the word again, said it several times in my head until I was sure it wouldn't break me. Water streamed from Minnie's side as I opened the passenger door for Kate. Then I remembered my handbag – surely that would win me points for respectability? – and went back inside.

I leaned round Mr Wall to get it. He was standing beside the teapot with an expression of unease. Surely he wasn't going to crumble right here, before we even got to the church where there was room for such demonstrations? His suit was too big for him; the padded shoulders projected an inch beyond his own, giving a Harlequin tinge to the outfit. He turned with an automated smile. 'We right, so?'

'Just have to check I have my keys.' They were in my pocket, but sometimes I faked an inefficiency to make other people feel better.

The driver's seat was too far back; Kate must have adjusted it last night. Beside me, her knees were bony against the sheen of overpriced tights. Mr Wall tucked himself into the back seat. I reached to turn on the radio, then thought better of it. I began backing out, but found a van blocking the way. A man in white overalls leaned in my window: 'Sign for bags from the hospital?' he asked.

I scribbled a curt 'P. O'Grady' on his clipboard, sweated my way out of the car seat, and picked the black leather suitcase, cracked tote and several plastic bags off the gravel. My brain stayed switched off. I dragged Cara's luggage along the flagstones half-buried in the lawn, unlocked the front door, carried it upstairs to the back bedroom and shoved it all out of sight under her bed.

I squared my shoulders against the car seat. Just before the church, Mr Wall cleared his throat and asked, 'Are your family coming, Pen?'

'They have to work,' I said, too quickly.

As I parked near the entrance, the bell began calling the faithful. Kate's head jerked up at the campanile. 'I don't remember them playing little tunes,' she said.

'Oh, we went electronic back in the late eighties. It's all done with time switches.'

'Nasty.'

We exchanged a grimace in the rear-view mirror. Then I thought Mr Wall might object to our flippancy. I watched him covertly as we walked up the car park; he seemed to be thinking about something else.

Quite a crowd, edging in the side door of the parish church of St Cecilia. Few of them could have known Cara; it must have been respect for Mr Wall that brought them, as well as pity for his broken home. A strange kind of neighbour-liness, in this suburb of detached hedged-off residences; they wouldn't pass the time of day with you, but once you died they'd don heavy jackets in a heatwave to nod to your coffin.

Speaking of which, there it was up near the altar on the brass trolley. Weighted down with circles of roses and crosses of gladioli, despite the notice in the paper. Perhaps people forgot; perhaps trekking off to buy wreaths for that poor Wall girl relieved their feelings more than obeying her wishes would. Cara never could bear the idea of cut flowers; if you thought something was beautiful, she asked me once, why would you want to pay for its execution? Discussing our hypothetical deaths, that evening when we sat up giggling over a baking tray of ginger snaps, I seemed to remember suggesting pot-plants instead of wreaths, so that mourners could take them home afterwards and tend them in one's memory. Cara had liked that idea, but fretted over just how many pot-plants you could fit on the top of a coffin before one might slip off, scattering soil and brown plastic all over the altar carpet.

As we neared the coffin – Kate walking at, but not on, her father's elbow, myself a few feet behind – I thanked the Lord that the top had not been left off. Here was nothing to wrench at the eyes. Rich red-brown wood and, beyond the massed flowers, a tiny plaque just as I had ordered, with the vital statistics: *Cara Wall, 1963–1992*. Such a tiny span of years, from mini-skirts through to the revival of flared trousers, from Kennedy to Clinton.

I looked away, scanning the crowd for a familiar face. Like a theatre audience at a doom-laden preview, the mourners were sitting as far from each other as possible. Elderly neighbours were sprinkled in the back aisles, and the black jackets near the front had to be relations because some of them were nodding soberly to Mr Wall as he led us into the third pew. When these people looked at me they could have no idea that I was anything to their missing relative; that I had let her dip her biscuits in my tea, on and off, for thirteen years; that sometimes, in the middle of a conversation on inflation or groceries, she would look down at my hand in sudden wonder and would tell me, her voice hushed as if in church, 'Oh, I want your hand inside me.'

My mind was hurdling memories, jumping high so as not to trip. My shirt was sticking to the straps on my back. Strange how it was more respectable to show the distinct outline of a bra than the smooth surface of a back. Presumably true feminists all had small breasts and so could afford to burn them. The bras, I meant, not the breasts. That theory about 'Amazon' meaning one-breasted, the burning off of one breast in case it would impede archery, being an etymological red herring meant to convince us that along with obedience we would also have to cast off the sweet unnecessary flesh. Last summer when Cara went to the Michigan Womyn's Music Festival – I was invited to go along, but didn't think it my kind of thing – she came back singing the praises of breasts. The sheer difference of them: the nipples that simply shaded in, the ones like raspberries perched on top, the fiercely pointy ones, on all the long and flat and globelike bosoms. Watching thousands of women walk round naked in the woods, what had struck her was not the naturalness of breasts in the human body shape, but the opposite; how, after the logical lines of hips and ribcages and limbs, breasts seemed completely gratuitous.

Cara's breasts – I saw them for a moment, pale birds startled from sleep – were nesting now behind wood and brass and dying flowers. I bent my neck to the side for a look, quickly, so that no one would see me staring at the coffin and pity me. Most of the flowers were white. Traditional, I supposed, for a young woman, who is still presumed to be somehow innocent and virginal, no matter how she spent her cluster of decades.

I knotted my hands and leaned them on the back of the pew in front. No one was sitting in the first row, though whether from a reluctance to claim the status of primary mourners or the need for a kneeler I was not sure. The organ was persuading the choir into a particularly bleating rendition of 'Jesus Remember Me'. As soon as the Monsignor began to call us to attention, I allowed my forehead to sink down on to my hands, the thumb knuckles denting my skin. I always liked to pray in this position; it was both uncomfortable and unbecoming, forcing humility.

It was not private enough in this church to have a really good conversation with the Lord – or rather, one of my satisfying monologues – but I did thank him for certain things, the lack of certain expected agonies, and I did ask for some of the strengths I thought I would need to get me to the end of the week. This unreal week, not part of the weave of my life, this set of days in which I was running round thinking and feeling and remembering with all the vivacity of a headless chicken, the bloom of a cut flower. What I dreaded and demanded help with was not so much this week – which had a certain adrenalin, an Amn't I Doing Well air to it – as the following weeks, months, years, the causeway of low times. I decided not to think about those times. I leaned my head on my hands until the thumb knuckles were digging two neat pits of pain.

A sniff to my right; I glanced at Mr Wall but he was only wiping his nose with his voluminous handkerchief. I sat back, letting the bar of coat-shined mahogany take the weight of my hot flesh. The bench plaque was to my left, its brass corner under Kate's elbow. *Pray for the parents, relatives and friends of,* it began. It was as if we were sitting on the bones of the dead, and this whole building a memorial. If I were to put up a seat to Cara it would not be a pew. (What would the plaque say – best wishes to my beloved housemate, friend, schoolmate, pal? Which words would I be allowed?) Nor would it be one of those rustic benches by a canal on which old folk rest their bones in the spring evenings. I decided it would be a plank across two forks of a tree, so high that only leggy dryads like Cara could climb it. The earthbound, like myself, could stand at the bottom, craning through broken sunlight, ready to catch any fruit thrown down.

A particularly fast group gabble of the liturgy brought me back to my body. I decided that I did not want to be here. Of course mourning rituals were psychologically useful, I remembered that from the first year of teacher training. But I could not see the relevance of mass to Cara, who, in the middle of a sermon on sexual morality back in the early eighties, had got up from her seat – I thought at first that she was just adjusting her tight jeans – and strode down the aisle, her runners squeaking in outrage. It had occurred to me to join her. We had roughly the same opinions. But by the time the thought reached my feet, Cara had burst through the doors into merciful silence, and I could not bear to start up the noise again. Besides, I would not have left Mr Wall alone there. I seemed to remember that we had bent our heads over the pew, avoiding the stares, and said nothing about it to each other, then or ever. So here was Cara, back in this very church a decade later, because it had not occurred to me or Mr Wall that there was any other option. And this, after all, was the place where the whole business had begun, water from the granite font streaming over her shock of red hair and screaming new face in the summer of '63.

The Monsignor was sermonizing now. Little he knew about Cara Wall. He was making her sound like the most respectable of young women, and even if he didn't know the important fact of her being what in lighter moments she called a pussyeater, someone should have told him about her walking out of mass all those years ago.

I think she missed the church; she was always keeping an eye out for a replacement. I remembered her running home after a New Age Fair to say she was thinking of becoming a Bahá'í. (When I challenged her to spell it, she got the accents wrong, and I felt mean.) She said they promised lack of dogma, the equality of the sexes, world harmony and peace through unity in diversity. I took a quick browse through the leaflet and read aloud the bit about being 'completely chaste before marriage and totally faithful within it'.

'Bugger that,' said Cara disappointedly, and went off to grill some rashers.

The priest's clichés were turning my stomach; listen out for it, yes, 'cut off in the bloom of her youth'. Under cover of the heavy drape of hair, I buried my chin in my palms and crammed my fingers into my ears. I used to spend the greater part of each mass in this pious position when I was a youngster, face closed over the most lurid of sexual fantasies.

Mass brought out the worst in me that way, especially when I used to try giving up masturbation for Lent, or at least Lenten Sundays. Somehow the attempt always threw me into a frenzy of eroticism, as when someone tells you not to think of a certain word, 'pineapple' for instance, and your sentences become haunted by that word, and all you can see for hours is that fruit, prickling across your retinas. Not that I tried those givings-up in order to enhance my solitary sex life; the attempt to quash my lust was genuine, if hopeless. It was just that the church was the perfect environment for what they still called impure thoughts in those days. Perhaps because the body was so limited in its movements, so dulled and contained, that the mind ran riot. Besides, I had always found the most effective fantasy was not to imagine one thing and do something similar, but to imagine one thing while doing something totally different. This did require some mental gymnastics; I had to practise quite a bit before I was able to lie on my back in bed and imagine I was standing against a wall in a dark nightclub, or face-down in a field of daisies. But the effects were wonderful. The body was bewildered, tricked into letting go. On my own or with Cara, I found that a demanding hand could metamorphose into an angelic tongue, or vice versa, and I could float free of the literal. Though always at the last minute Cara managed to hook me back, anchoring my swell to the here and now.

The Monsignor's regretful homily was over at last, praise be. We all struggled to our feet and chanted our way through the creed. I used to take this very seriously indeed, trying to comprehend and wholly believe each item on the list in the second or two it took to say it. I had them all in hand by the time of my confirmation at the age of eleven, I remembered, except for the resurrection of the body, which was just too silly to believe. At least, until I discovered the big O a few years later. Such rapture made me believe anything of the human body, even that it could rot away to nothing and then be revived in the playing-fields of heaven.

When it came to the sign of peace, the man in front of me

with the roll of shaved red neck turned and took my hand in both of his, very gently. I gave him a startled smile. Mr Wall's papery fingers were next. I hesitated before reaching out to Kate, as did she; then we shook hands too heartily, to compensate. Her palm was startlingly warm. I tried to remember if I had ever touched her skin before.

'He Is Lord', the choir were moaning. Of course God wasn't really a he; I couldn't imagine that there were testicles in heaven. But pronouns were handy things, and that was the one I had been brought up with; 'it' was horribly inanimate, and 'she' a nice idea, but too self-conscious for me. I had to work with what I'd got, the childhood patterns of helpless prayer. It should be said that I had little interest in God the Father; he seemed to be the chief executive, rarely glimpsed in the corridors, with his own fan club of those Christians who could really only respect a middle-aged man. No, the one I worshipped, in my low-key chatty way, was Jesus, because though I called him Lord as I had been taught, he was not by any stretch of the imagination a patriarch. I saw him as a nice young guy with five o'clock shadow, the kind who might turn up on your doorstep, clearing his throat deferentially, and you would say, hey, come in, there's spaghetti in the pot. To be really fair, I supposed, I should have worshipped the widely neglected Holy Spirit, but I only know it as a flame or a dove, and doves were basically pigeons, and pigeons outside museums were irritating to the point of deserving a kick. Once I tried to imagine the HS as a woman, but the result kept flapping her Victorian lace sleeves and coughing and saying 'Don't mind me'. So I talked to the Lord instead. He was a better listener than most men I knew; he never butted in with 'I think what you're trying to say is . . .'

Mr Wall was plucking at my sleeve; I followed him into the queue for communion. Kate sat with her eyes set forward, one of the outsiders. Though, paradoxically enough, as a lapsed member, she was actually more worthy of the sacred host than was I, a practising Catholic wading through mortal sin with – how the catechism phrases rang on in my head – 'clear knowledge and full consent'. But then again, I was not alone; all the smug married women on the Pill in this queue were as guilty as I was. Besides, what I was taking into my mouth was not the church but the Lord, nourishing as bread, and he had never judged me harshly.

Despite all the contradictions and annoyances of this church, it still gave me such relief: wood, brass, the calm disc melting on the roof of my mouth. Coming down from the altar, I saw Kate staring forward, her nose and lips sculpted like the figurehead of a ship. I wondered whether she missed him, the Lord in her mouth. What did she take in that gave her equivalent relief? I knew so little about this woman whose half-grown image had haunted the margins of my thoughts for fifteen years, and I had the weary sensation that if she stayed here another year I would not know her much better.

I slid into the pew. Kate's leg was warm against mine for a fraction of a second till I balanced myself and moved away. I studied the prayer leaflet for inspiration. All I recognized was that old heroic one we used to chant at Girl Guide meetings while we practised our knots and polished our brass badges. 'Dearest Jesus teach me to be generous,' we chorused:

> to love and serve you as you deserve
> to give and not to count the cost
> to fight and not to heed the wounds
> to toil and not to seek for rest
> to labour and to look for no reward
> save that of knowing that I do your holy will.

What stirring iambic metre, and what dangerously masochistic sentiments. Reading it again, hunched in my seat as the communion queue thinned to a trickle, I smiled to remember how much I used to like this prayer. In the early days with Cara my strongest motive had been to help, to keep her alive and halfway sane.

What a big barrack of a building this was. The stations of the cross seemed to have been painted in watery coffee, egg, and blackberry jam; these drab humiliations of the Lord's life and times would not be likely to prompt the congregation to repentance so much as to embarrassment. Of course, it was hard to encapsulate any life in fourteen pictures. I tried to visualize my own in a set of snapshots. How many should I save for the rest of my life, which might turn out to be action-packed or entirely uneventful? Definite choices so far were: (1) that picture of me at three days old, upright in my father's hand like an outraged ice-cream cone; (2) at six, waltzing with Zizzy, my rag doll, who was taller than me by several inches; and (3) the one of Cara and me leaning against some brick wall, laughing ourselves sick.

Well, at least I was used to doing without her at mass; I hadn't shared a roll of the eyes with Cara during a sermon since that day she walked out. The first time I came to this church was for midnight mass the Christmas of our first year together. It had to be carefully set up; I dragged my mother and brother all the way over here on the pretext of having heard there was a great choir. Cara caught my eye at the door and waved us over to introduce us to her father. I stood beside her, shaking with the excitement of having got away with it, so that we could stand together, our first Christmas Eve, and carol our thanks for this body magic we had discovered between us. The choir that year turned out to be appalling, from the saccharine hush of 'Away in a Manger' to the cracked descants of 'Hark the Herald Angels Sing'. Gavin was forthright, and on the way home – we had to walk, there were no late buses in those days – I said rather feebly that it must have been the other choir, the folk one, that had such a good reputation. Mammy made no comment, but squeezed my fingers and said, 'Look at the stars.' The back of my hand was still burning from brushing against Cara's as our voices peaked in the final hosanna.

I looked up now at the wooden box under the flowers, and told myself that Cara was inside. But I didn't believe a bit of it. I could grant credence to the story up to the point where the front of the car behind smashed into the bumper of the taxi in front. I could see Cara thrown by the impact, flying free, but not beyond that. Not the landing. She wouldn't dare. Last time she came back she promised she'd never go away for good without asking or at least warning me, giving me something to hold on to. And she'd always said she wouldn't be seen dead in a church again, those were her exact words, I remembered with an awful gulp of laughter that I turned into a cough.

Instead of a final hymn, the Monsignor asked us to join in reading 'St Patrick's Breastplate', which I always thought of as the 'Christ be'. I began obediently, my voice blending into the muted clamour of voices, but found I had slipped into 'Cara be with me'. If I said the first word of the phrase low, I discovered, no one would notice.

> Cara within me
> Cara behind me
> Cara before me

And in a sense it was true and not blasphemous, I thought frantically between the lines, because if God was in us then all the titles meant the same thing.

> Cara beside me
> Cara to win me
> Cara to comfort
>   and restore me

And even if I was being blasphemous, I was sure he wouldn't mind. The Lord had so many millions chanting his multiple names, surely he wouldn't resent my clinging to the name I knew best?

> Cara beneath me

(I could see her now, her face crushed into the pillow, the long notched bow of her spine under my thighs)

> Cara above me

Instead of a final hymn, the Monsignor asked us to join in (her ever-young nipples dancing over my eyelids)

Cara in quiet
Cara in danger
Cara in hearts of all that love me
Cara in mouths of friend and stranger

But my voice faded at that line, paralysed by my imagination. I wanted her to be in nobody's mouth but mine.

Six men I had never seen before carried the coffin on their shoulders down the long aisle to the back doors. It balanced lightly between them, dipping a little at the front because one of them was shorter. I set my mind to thinking of weights and pendulums in Physics class, of finding some fixed point from which you could use a lever to shift the world. I thought of reeds bending and trees breaking and cog puzzles in spatial reasoning texts. I tried to calculate how many bearers it would take to carry my coffin at threescore and ten, if I continued to put on five pounds a year. I wondered whether it was the dwarfs who carried Snow White along at the level of the prince's knotted thighs, and why they hadn't stumbled at once, on a knot of root or just in the awkwardness of grief, so that the bite of apple would be jerked from her throat without delay and she could sit up, pale but laughing, and dance at her own funeral. Why the time lag, the metaphorical coma, the years of watching her through the dusty glass, waiting and hoping and despairing and knowing that by the time she woke up again you might be too tired to care? I also thought of the chance of rain, and the hundred and five or so minutes till lunch, and all this passed through my mind by the time the six men made it to the church porch. I would have thought of anything to keep myself from thinking of what was really in the box lying on those strange shoulders, the few inches of wood and velvet that divided them from Cara's cool flesh.

Why wasn't it me carrying her? I hadn't thought to ask. How stiff she would be by now, how very awkward if she tried to sit up from the pious position they had locked her in. I imagined her tittering through her paralysis, fingers knotted, gasping 'God help us, Pen, I can't move a muscle, would you scratch my nose for me?'

What seemed like hundreds of strangers were clustered by the door to commiserate with Mr Wall as we struggled out. He was introducing Kate to many who would remember her only as the dark girl, the one who went off to the States with her mother and never came back. I held back, not wanting to hear him fumble for a title for me.

Beside me was a nun I thought I recognized from Immac; her thin lips widened as she tucked a leaflet into my hand. It bore a cartoon of a bubble-headed person going through a pair of pillars that reminded me of the gate to that swanky new housing development down by the sea. 'The Bereavement Support Project', it announced in one of those curvilinear typefaces meant to give the impression of handwriting, 'is offering a Weekend Retreat for the Newly Bereaved.' I supposed newly-bereaveds were like newly-weds, only less prone to waterbeds and champagne. I wondered what the BSP (that was their simple logo, BSP in a teardrop shape) would have to offer. Were there specific skills someone like me could learn for getting through this? I suspected the Retreat might consist of exactly the same confidentiality ground-rules, getting-to-know-you exercises, and vague expressions of confusion and goodwill, as every other damn workshop Cara had led me into by the coat-sleeves.

I left the leaflet on the porch table just before the crowd inched me through the door. A curtain of warm air slapped against my face. I couldn't see the sun, but one patch of grey sky was burning whiter than the rest. I was borne along with the restless mass-goers as they clattered towards their Toyotas and Volvos on narrow heels. I found myself standing at the top of the steps, holding on to the rail, the pads of my fingers registering a faint rash of rust.

In the far corner of the car park I recognized Jo's purple Bug with the labrys painted on the side. There was Mairéad's heavy plait, and a straw hat on, what was the quiet one's name, Sinéad, that was it. I watched for a few seconds as they all crawled in through the front door. None of them waved. Maybe they didn't see me; maybe they were being discreet.

Glasnevin cemetery was a good forty minutes away. Minnie chugged along behind the hearse – a grossly shiny thing, reminding me of the bootleggers' cars in *Bugsy Malone* – while aunts and uncles purred behind. We sat in traffic, my elbows on the steering-wheel, Kate with her hands tucked between her knees, Mr Wall in the back with his greying head occasionally bobbing into view in the mirror. Everything that it occurred to me to say was too heavy or too light, too big or too small. To keep myself from gabbling I held my breath.

It felt better as soon as we parked the car and went in on foot, escaping from the twentieth century. The three of us led the straggling procession down a corridor of yews that opened out into a lattice of gravel paths, dividing the grass as far as the eye could follow. I busied myself with keeping an eye out for section L. Mr Wall said something too hoarsely for me to hear.

'Sorry?'

'So many.' When I didn't answer, he cleared his throat with a deafening bray. 'I had not thought death had undone so many.'

I waited.

'It's a line from something,' he apologized, and bent to pick a weathered ice-cream wrapper off the verge and put it in his trouser pocket.

Just as Mr Wall stopped at the plot half-full of Wall doctors and lawyers, just when the sky should rightly have let down tears of acid rain, didn't the sun come out. Not the glare we had had all morning, but full honest-to-god radiance through a patch of blue sky, making a pool of light that caught white headstones and angels for hundreds of yards around. This was weather for the last trip of the year to Brittas Bay, or a picnic in the heather above Lough Dan.

Instead we were standing round a rectangle of earth, watching a box being lowered on ropes. Some woman was sobbing already, and strangers were fumbling for their balls of tissue. I couldn't see Kate. Mr Wall was standing beside me, his face as private as a wardrobe.

The priest began to talk again but I shut my ears to him. The lettered slab at the head of this plot was dabbed with lichen; there had been no new guests at this party for twenty-two years, it seemed, since the paternal grandparents had gone within six months of each other. Cara, ever impatient, had skipped her turn, burrowing under this quilt of earth before any of her father's generation. There were ten in the bed and the little one said ROLL OVER.

I shut my eyes now – swaying slightly, as balance became harder – and told myself that this was the right moment to cry. I squeezed my eyes together till they stung; surely something would emerge? My right eye itched again; I rubbed at it furiously. In my mind I recited some trigger words: *grave, death, gone, funeral, Cara*. None of them worked. I felt the sun between my shoulder-blades, burning on the black silk, and I longed for a fresh grapefruit, grilled brown with sugar and a glacé cherry on top.

There was Kate at my right elbow. She was not doing the tears thing either. I watched the lean lines of her face. She was scanning the crowd like a store detective. I looked away as soon as she caught my eye; I wanted no sorority with her over the grave of her sister.

I waited for the men to start scattering earth – or perhaps to invite Mr Wall to begin with the first gritty handful – but instead they lifted a panel of fake grass piled high with wreaths, and set it over the grave. What a cheat. I had been counting on seeing it done now, the filling in. I was prepared to feel the earth, damp and real between my loosening fingers. Instead we were going to be fobbed off with this green plastic lid, and the priest's voice rising and falling over it like some lethargic seagull.

Mr Wall had disappeared. I peered around until I recog-

144

nized the back of his dark suit, his arm propping him against a tree.

When I looked back at the crowd, the sunlight caught a bronze head: some girl with her face buried on her mother's shoulder, a cousin perhaps, crying presumably not for love of Cara (who never had any idea how many cousins she had) but in outrage that such things should happen. What was making those slight shoulders heave was the possibility of her own death, the knowledge that the big D was not always busy stalking the old folk but could slice down the brightest of red hairs.

I only learned that myself at fifteen. A girl in the year below got a brain tumour and died quite suddenly, and for a week or so the school was filled not so much with mourning as with tremendous embarrassment, as each of us realized (without saying a word of it) how blind to our own danger we had been. We forgot again soon enough, of course. You can't go on bearing such things in mind.

The girl was sobbing louder into her mother's lipsticked tissue. Her face was choked behind curls. I wanted to take her into my arms, kiss her better, make her mouth part with such astonishment that she would not worry about death any more, would not even believe in it, would laugh it to scorn as girls can. I wanted her hair to be straight and redder, and her face to be Cara's, and when she died in her turn I would find another, and another, an endless supply of sixteen-year-old virgins to feed my dragon smile.

I felt tired at the thought. People near me were walking away now, but my hot feet were rooted where I stood. Cara would be yawning after all this fuss, and inquiring after a cup of tea, or the nearest metaphysical equivalent. Cara was most herself when she was asleep with a half-drained cup of tea beside her. The lines of her face loosened, and she looked, not childlike as we were supposed to look in sleep, but older, calmed into her age.

As the last stragglers turned away from the grave, I stared at the wreaths, topped with a heavy circle of white lilies.

'Her mother.'

'Sorry?' I turned my head to Mr Wall.

He was picking at some wax on his sleeve. His voice sounded like it was electronically generated. 'Mrs Wall sent those white ones.'

I strained to look right through the flowers that pathetic woman sent instead of being here, past the fake grass panel, down the rabbit hole, past the wooden lid to where Cara was sleeping. I wanted her to stay asleep all afternoon, pale and arrogant, and not wake to burden me with her crises. I wanted her to find comfort and have no further damage done to her, to let all the marks of life be rotted away, down to the clean bone.

I walked through the maze of gravel towards the car park. A tap on my shoulder. It was Jo, almost unrecognizable in a black dress with a shawl collar. I looked her up and down. 'Wow. Josephine Butler, I presume.'

'Ah, don't talk to me. It was the only respectable garment I could lay hands on that was long enough so I wouldn't have to shave my legs. With the sunburn on my nose I must look like a Liquorice Allsort.'

'No, it's nice, in an odd way.' I saw Kate approaching, head bent among a cluster of relatives, so I pulled Jo along the path.

She looked back over her shoulder. 'Are your family here?'

'My father died when I was eighteen.'

'And your mother?'

I watched the pebbles disappearing under the scuffed tips of my shoes. 'Haven't got around to ringing her.' Jo was rolling up her flimsy sleeves. Because she said nothing, I wanted to go on. 'Mammy only knows of Cara as my housemate. They met a couple of times and I don't think they liked each other.'

'Did you ever try telling her?'

'No. Once when I was home for the weekend I thought Mammy was going to bring it up herself. The air went all prickly, so eventually I asked was she worried about something, and she said, "Well, I've been thinking, Pen, I don't suppose you're" – and then the phone rang. Afterwards it was too late to take up the conversation again.'

Jo pursed her lips. 'Did she say "I don't suppose your", as in "your brother", or was it "you're" as in "you're a raving loony lesbian"?'

'I couldn't tell. If she was more middle-class she'd have pronounced the vowels differently.'

'Would you like her to be?'

'Not really. I get my fill of gentility with Mr Wall.' We walked in silence for a few steps. 'I did think of ringing Mammy last night, but I couldn't bear to tell her about this' – my wave took in the hedge and a marble cherub – 'till I'm ready to tell her everything.'

'And when will that be, say the bells of Stepney?'

I watched the gravel subside under my shoes. 'I don't see her very often.'

'Then you've nothing to lose, have you?'

'Yes I do. I know she's there. She approves of me, generally. I ring her every couple of weeks, and she sounds glad to hear my voice.'

I did not realize how loud and fast the words were coming until Jo interrupted with a whisper of 'OK, shush, it's all right.'

We were almost at her empty Volks. I couldn't face accepting sympathy from the whole gang of them. I patted her briefly on the upper arm and said, 'Thanks for coming. See you soon, yeah?'

'Saturday?'

I ignored that.

I was the first back to Minnie. I wanted so much to jump in like a bank robber, foot to the floor and screeching away across the tarmac, slamming through amber lights and . . . ending up in a coffin beside Cara? Was that what I wanted, to lie there comparing rainbow bruises in the sun-warmed earth?

I put my key in the lock and found it was already open.

Getting careless, or maybe my subconscious had thought nobody would rob a car from a funeral. I slid on to the seat, my thighs sticking to my trousers. The windscreen was smeary; its glisten irritated my eyes. I felt behind the gear-stick for the cloth. Across its grimy yellow surface was laid a single hair. About ten inches long, a tiny shred of root at one end, the other just beginning to feather. As I rotated it in the sunlight it caught fire, then faded to brown.

My head was suddenly too heavy to support. I would have leaned it against the steering-wheel except that the passing file of chatting mourners might have seen and – god forbid – tapped on the window to offer succour. Instead, I let my skull sag back against the top of the headrest. I found that I had dropped the cloth; the hair was stretched between my fingers. Apart from a little dust which I blew off, it was clean, sparkling in the sun. When I pulled it between finger and thumb, it made a rich squeak, decreasing in pitch like a passing ambulance. I tried this note various ways, until I could hear nothing else. Could you string a lute with hair? I pulled it taut, then a little bit farther, testing its elasticity. Cara's hair always hung straight and fine, spraying in the wind, not like my thick shutters. This single strand was beginning to curl from my pullings. Put it away now love before you break it, as my mother used to say.

I looked at the white root, where the cells had begun building their painstaking chain from Cara's scalp. I imag-ined her leaning over one day to struggle with Minnie's old-fashioned seat-belt or find a fifty-pee coin for the tollbridge, her bob sliding against her face, one particular hair already hanging loose in the curtain that her hand was now lifting to brush back. It must have clung to her knuckles for a moment before falling in slow motion down the gap between the seats to land on the yellow cloth. It must have lain still for weeks before I found it. Months, now I came to think of it, because Cara had got a shorter cut some weeks before she went on holiday. None of the hairs on the body they had buried was as long as this one.

I wanted to laugh; Cara was playing tricks. We thought we'd seen the last of her today, but here she was shedding over everything as usual. I folded the hair around my finger and tucked it in my breast-pocket for safety.

The engine started on the first try. There were Kate and Mr Wall at the passenger side, the door opening and letting in their voices halfway through some sentence about the Boston climate.

On the way home the atmosphere was limp, like a school bus coming back from a long day's outing. We stopped for Mr Wall to buy bread and the paper, just like any other lunchtime, except that we hadn't a word to say between the three of us. While we were waiting for him, I looked back over my seat-belt and told Kate I'd give her a lift to the airport for her four o'clock plane. She thanked me absent-mindedly. I stared forward again.

None of us was hungry, I suspected, but each felt it would be attention-seeking behaviour to refuse to eat. Mr Wall scrambled three eggs and walked down the garden for some aged parsley to sprinkle on top. I buttered and bit into two slices of Vienna roll until I felt bandaged from the inside out. The tea tasted metallic. That was how my mother knew she was pregnant, the second time; it was the only thing that made her go off the taste of tea.

A rest would be a good idea. Take the day in stages. As I climbed up to my room, I could hear Kate dialling a long number. She sounded more East Coast the minute she began talking; evidently it didn't take her half an hour to click back into business mode.

I lay down on the duvet. After a minute I used my toes to push at my heels, straining at the laces, until my shoes squeezed off one by one and dropped heavily on the carpet. It took more effort than unlacing them would have, but it satisfied me more. Finally I sat up, pulled the silk shirt over my head, wriggled my trousers off, and draped them across the desk chair. When I crawled under the sheets, they were wonderfully cold against my calves and shoulders.

I was falling into a daze when there was a tap at the door. 'Come in,' I called, my irritation much too loud.

Kate's face blended into the dull paintwork of the door; only her dark halo stood out. 'Sorry, I didn't realize you were in bed.'

Why had I not noticed the heavy shadows under her eyes? 'Are you all right?' I asked.

'Just tired,' she said with a faint grin. 'I've had one of those mystery viruses recently.'

'Yuppie flu?' I suggested, without much malice.

'Whatever.'

I leaned up on one elbow, folding my other arm around the duvet. It looked dreadfully naked, this river of flesh bridged by a beige strap at the crest of the shoulder.

Kate's eyes returned from the window-sill. 'Anyway, what I came to say was, I've managed to beg a few more days from my boss so I could get a proper rest, and I've changed my flight. So I'll be staying till Saturday morning – unless that'll put you out too much?'

'No, no,' I said, and was surprised to find that I meant it.

There was a long pause; I kept expecting her to go. Her gaze angled and drifted around the room like a paper plane. Her eyes seemed to be focused on the mules stuck in the pockets of my dressing-gown when she said, 'You were a couple, weren't you?'

'What, me and Cara, you mean?'

She nodded warily.

'Yes,' I said, 'of course we were.'

Kate rested on the very end of the bed and crossed her legs. I was heartened to see that her skirt, like anyone's, got creased from sitting. 'I kind of wondered, when I realized you'd been living here for years,' she said. 'But I wasn't absolutely sure till I saw you at the grave, looking sort of weighty.'

'I always look weighty,' I told her with a diva's smile.

She shook her head slightly, like a horse bothered by flies. 'No, I mean responsible. Like, widowed.' The word created a little pool of silence round it. 'I should have picked up on it before . . .' Kate's voice trailed off. She recrossed her legs and anchored her hands around her knees. 'My job keeps me so busy. I never really wondered about Cara's life; she was just the kid sister back in Ireland, you know? We talked on the phone couple times a year, Christmas Day, but her voice always sounded just the same.'

'It doesn't affect the vocal cords, you know.'

'What doesn't?'

I let the consonants roll. 'Lesbianism.'

Kate looked me in the eyes and tried to laugh. 'Guess not.' When the pause was growing too long, she added, 'I can see that it must have been good for Cara to have you around.'

'Thank you,' I said. I tugged the duvet a little higher, but her weight was holding it down. I longed for a shawl.

'Does Dad have any idea?'

'I don't think so. We thought he'd prefer not to.'

She considered it with pursed lips. 'Probably right.' After a minute, 'So when did you two first . . .'

I let her wriggle on the hook for a few seconds, then relented. 'We got together the year after you left.'

'At school? Jesus.'

'And we've been actually living together for the last four years.'

Kate nodded soberly. 'That must have been great.'

'It has its moments.'

'I mean, to be sure enough to move in together,' she stumbled on. 'I've never met a guy yet I'd want to share my apartment with.'

My mouth twitched slightly. Cara and I had a running joke about straight women: any time you came out to one she'd managed to register heterosexuality by mentioning boyfriends within the first five minutes.

But Kate's eyes were unguarded. 'So,' she asked, 'did you, did you love her a lot?'

What an unlikely question, from this grey-suited executive. And where was the yardstick? I sat up and leaned against

151

the chilly wallpaper, tucking the quilt around me. 'Mmm,' I said.

She nodded, and made a little movement as if to get up.

'I wasn't obsessive about Cara,' I added, to keep her there. 'I never wrote out her signature over and over, or sank to the pits of identifying with Beatles lyrics.'

That won a small smile.

'It was all very ordinary,' I told her, hugging my knees. 'I liked to do stuff like brushing the fluff off her jacket, but that's not what you call a grand passion, is it?'

'Don't ask me,' said Kate. 'I wouldn't know what a grand passion was if I found it in my french fries.' She stared at her knees as if she had only just noticed them.

'So,' I said after a minute, my voice lifting, 'it's nice that you've got a few days more here. Are you wanting to sightsee at all?'

Her face was blank. 'What sights are there I didn't see when I lived here?'

Damn the woman, no sooner had she seduced me into conversation than she always had to shut down. She yawned as she stood up, and shut the door tightly behind her. I let myself slide down the wall until I was curled up halfway along the bed, the duvet arching over my face.

In my dream I am face-down on this bed, leaning up on my elbows. My white chest is bright with sweat, scattered with hairs and crumbs and bits of red thread from my shirt. Cara's mouth comes angling round my neck to reach my mouth; she kisses, bites my lips, pauses to take a bit of fluff out of her mouth and laughs throatily. Then her face disappears, and she is at my back again, tracing my spine with a rasping tongue till I flinch over and over, chewing on my shoulders to make them squirm.

I try to roll over but Cara won't let me; the whole weight of her is pressed down on my back. Her fuzz brushes the cleft at the base of my spine, then shoves me deep into the mattress. It surprises me that such a skinny girl can weigh down so heavily, can ride me until the pleasure begins to knife its way through the bed. I arch back like a boat about to splinter. Cara is clasping my curves between her legs, wearing my thighs and back like a saddle in this trickling rodeo. She jolts against me and I wonder if my back will break. She grinds my hips into the fine dust of pleasure.

'I can't come this way,' I hiss. And then of course I roar like a woman in labour (into three pillows, so the sound won't carry down to Mr Wall's room) and I do, I do, I do.

Afterwards Cara lies flat and heavy, growing into me like a sod of grass. 'Sometimes I fancy others more,' she whispers to the back of my ear, 'but you take me farther.'

I bend my arm and reach behind to find her hip, her fuzz, the folds I have so often frisked for secrets. She leans up on her knees to make room for me. This is what I imagine parachuting to be like: as the white silk of her skin rushes through my fingers, she flaps open and we are saved.

I woke and found that my feet had gone to sleep. Though my dream body was wet and spasmodic, my waking body lay dull and dry. I reached out for Cara, searching the sheets with my hand.

Then I remembered and felt sick to my stomach. How dared I lie here feeling, thinking, desiring, when she was in a box underground? What made me want to be alive more than I wanted to be with her? Always when I had been laid waste by pleasure, when I felt helpless as a beached whale, I restored myself by reaching out to Cara. It was a matter of finding the balance of power, riding the seesaw between dignity and abandon. I could only hand it all over because I knew that ten minutes or three days later she would trust herself equally to me. If sometimes I felt like nothing but a creature of pleasure, a poem made flesh, then at other times I was all creator.

That was another loss, it occurred to me now. The skills I had honed over the years for making love to her body had become redundant. No doubt I could use the basic techniques on someone else, but not all the little nuances, not my inch-by-inch knowledge of what Cara liked. It was as if I had spent thirteen years specializing in a certain language, only to discover that all its speakers had scattered and renounced their native tongue. No, worse than that, because at least dead languages could be studied. This was as if I had spent my life learning to play a certain unique instrument, only to see some crazed vandal smash it to pieces.

Not an image I wanted to dwell on. I hauled myself out of bed.

Standing by the kitchen window, blowing dimples on my coffee, I caught sight of Kate disappearing behind the garage. The cat-flap opened and Grace wriggled in, pinching his tail on the plastic. 'Hey, pusscat, where've you been?' I murmured, going down on my hunkers and holding out my hands. But he didn't want to lick them today. He glanced at his replenished bowl and slunk into the hall.

I went outside, not caring how shabby my orange dressing-gown looked to any neighbours peering over the trellis littered with yellow roses. Kate didn't notice me as I looked into the passage between garage and hedge. Her hand was on the elephantine trunk of the sycamore that blocked the end. I picked a late nasturtium and nibbled on it. 'What are you doing?'

She spun around, her face more enlivened than I had ever seen it. 'I planted this.'

'You did?' The flower was hot and peppery. One afternoon years ago, Cara had tucked nasturtiums under my arms, between my knees, in every crevice she could find, then ate them all off me. How had her tongue stood it? I struggled now to bring my attention back to her sister.

'I've just remembered digging a hole for a sycamore key behind the garage, when I was a kid,' she said.

I waited.

'It's grown so tall,' said Kate, her voice muffled as she turned her gaze up into its branches.

'Too tall,' I told her, dropping the rest of the nasturtium.

And then I embroidered: 'It's for the chop, one of these days. If it fell it could smash the roof.'

'Really?' A pointed leaf came off in her hand; she put it in the pocket of her jacket. When she turned, her face had set back into its accustomed lines.

I went back inside, and tried to flush away the taste of the flower with my cooling coffee. It was Cara who planted that tree, she told me so. She loved to catch sight of it tossing and head-banging in the breeze above the garage roof. She would never let it be cut down. I drained the coffee to the dregs, then rinsed my mouth with cold water. No matter who had planted the sycamore, there was no excuse for venting my miscellaneous rage on a woman who had never knowingly done me any harm.

After getting back into the same clothes, I came downstairs and switched on *Children's Newsround*. It had always been my last resort for getting out of a sulk after bad days at school, killing time while waiting for Mammy to come home with the bread. Somehow *Newsround*'s alternating stories of world crises and clever pets put my own problems in perspective. Once Cara and I were watching it together, and the Zee-brugge ferry disaster came on. The tears ran on to her cheese on toast. I went on eating mine. She looked at me, and looked away again.

'What?' I asked.

'Nothing,' said Cara.

'Look,' I said gruffly, 'what good will tears do them? They're wet enough.'

'It's not to do them any good,' she said, 'it's because I can't help it.'

I put down my toast. 'I'm rationing.'

She glanced at my plate.

'Tears,' I explained. 'I'm saving them all for when I need them. What if it was you in that ferry? I'd need reserves.'

Cara leaned her eyes on the heels of her hands. 'You're morbid,' she snuffled.

'Doesn't everyone imagine these things?' I asked. 'When

you hear a siren go by, don't you wonder for a second if it might be the one you love?'

'Well actually,' said Cara, 'I did used to look at every passing ambulance and think Mrs Mew might be in it.'

I had learnt to wince so slightly that she didn't notice it. 'Exactly,' I told her. 'Fantasies ward off the evil day.'

But here I was with the evil day come upon me, and I couldn't feel it. I stared at the newsreader as he chatted his way through a child-sized version of global warming. Right this minute I couldn't care less, not about the planet, not about Cara. When would I start to produce all those tears I'd saved from ferry, motorway and plane disasters, from stories of infant heart transplants and letters to Gorbachev? My barrelfuls had obviously been mislaid in the back of some emotional warehouse. Maybe if I started I'd never stop till I filled the big house and drowned all who came in the door. 'Cry it all out,' we were told, as if grief was a simple toxin that could be converted into liquid and drained out of the body. Maybe I was saving the tears for some safer time, waiting for some delayed reaction that would bring them on as water spills in glittering strings from the roof of a bus shelter, ten minutes after the rain.

At five past five, halfway through a two-inch wedge of madeira cake and a cup of tea (Kate refused one), I decided to get around to ringing my mother. It was her afternoon off; I could have gone to see her, but I had conveniently forgotten till now. I couldn't face one of those cosy, irritable afternoons over a pot of black tea. Cara came with me one time, and my mother handed her the wrong bowl by accident, so Cara put salt in her tea. She took one sip, then drank a whole glass of water, but never said a word about it till we got home.

I polished the back of the receiver with my sleeve. When did it break, the connection I once had with my mother? No, not broken exactly, a much more gradual attenuation. Not that I was ever the type who ran home and disgorged every detail of the day at school – we both liked our privacies –

but we used to be close. As a child I sat for hours on end at the scuffed kitchen table, reading or drawing ballerinas or just staring at the whorls on my fingers, while my mother hurried in and out. Sometimes we wouldn't say a word for hours, wouldn't need to.

No doubt Jo was right that I should get around to coming out to my mother, as I crawled into my fourth decade, but I couldn't bear to try it right now. I could just imagine picking up the phone: 'Hey, Mammy, how's tricks? What have I been up to? Oh, nothing much, just the funeral of that lover of mine I never got around to talking to you about. Ah, you know her, my housemate, you met her a couple of times, remember. Yeah, lover, that's the word, or one of them. Yes, I know you thought I wasn't that kind of girl but that's one of the things you thought wrong about.'

I took three deep breaths, holding them for a count of ten each, and dialled. I intended to say the bare minimum about the funeral. But I didn't even manage that. From the moment my mother picked up the phone, my voice slipped automatically into the usual gear. A little work, a little weather, a little gossip about Gavin's new posh girlfriend, a little more weather. After the usual apology for not having rung over the last few weeks, I offered to drive over to her shop tomorrow after Immac and take her out for coffee and meringues. Lies of omission, lies of blandness, lies of not bothering, what difference did a few more make?

She'd been watching the wildlife, she said, something about red pandas. I listened not to what the words meant but to the sound of them, the comforting pattern of hisses and vibrations. But all at once I needed to know something about this woman before she disappeared too. 'Mammy,' I broke in, 'I was just wondering, what were you doing when you went into labour with me?'

Her voice trailed off. 'What sort of a question is that?'

'I've always been meaning to ask.' Grace came down the stairs in a gallop, then froze on the bottom.

'Let's see now,' she said. 'I think I was taking the car in

for a service, the mechanic was giving me cheek . . . No, that was the other time, with your brother.'

I waited for a few seconds, reaching over to scratch the cat's skull, then asked, 'And how long were you in labour?'

My mother gave a little sigh. 'Couldn't tell you, pet. Not too long.'

'No?'

'But quite a while.'

I held in my exasperation as I watched Grace toe his way upstairs again. 'What was the worst moment, then?'

'I don't remember.' Her voice was beginning to stiffen. 'Why would you want to dwell on such things?'

'How could you not remember the worst moment?'

'I had other things on my mind,' she told me, 'like pushing a great lump of a baby out of myself. I had no time to keep notes.'

I could tell I was annoying her but something drove me on. 'What was it like, though? Is it true the pain's like passing a whole melon through your bowels?'

'I wouldn't know, Pen,' she said. 'On the rare occasions when I can afford melon, I cut it in slices.'

I laughed under my breath. 'Fair enough.'

'You have a terrible negative attitude. Just wait till it happens to you, then you won't be so interested in remembering.'

'That'll be the day.'

There was a pause. Was Mammy going to fall into maternal stereotype and start nagging me about reproduction, now of all times? But her voice was soft, like a chamois leather rubbing the phone line. 'You don't sound like yourself.'

'So who do I sound like?'

'Ah, if you're going to start acting the maggot now I'll go back to the pandas.'

'Do that thing.' I said goodbye gently and put down the phone.

But what I couldn't tell was, was my mother reluctant to

tell me about the birth because I was the baby, because I was what had hurt her? Or had she honestly forgotten?

I knew that normal people did not remember much, except in indexed summaries, with the odd spotlit detail. Whereas I was cursed with a good memory, or rather a big one. At points of crisis I tended to live in many times at once. The pictures rushed at me like anxious pets, especially when I was tired. Cara used to hate it when I'd quote her; she never could remember conversations in enough detail for her to tell if I had got it right. She often begged me to learn to forget, to let things flow. But the way I saw it, what use was it to run towards the future if your purse was slit and everything you gathered fell out on the road?

My hand, I noticed, was still clutching the phone. I released my grip and walked into the kitchen. I couldn't decide where to sit. The problem with living so long in one house was that every corner of it was silted up with memories.

Cara also claimed that I must have made things up, because it was not possible to remember entire conversations in such detail. On that point she may have been right. But the lines that came into my head did have their own authenticity; they were things that she or I would have been likely to say in a given situation, or perhaps did say in another conversation. It did not offend me that my stories might not be exactly true, so long as they rang true. Once when I was small my mother asked what I'd been up to all morning. 'Dressing up,' I said. When she found that the dressing-up trunk was locked, she was troubled. I was never able to explain that the dressing-up I would have liked to do, if the trunk had been open, was in its own way more real than whatever I happened to have been really doing, which I was hard put to remember anyway since it was much less interesting. Sometimes I thought the truth could only be got at like the hill on the other side of the looking-glass, by walking in the opposite direction and talking aloud to distract yourself.

Cara and I knew too much about each other, after a few

years, to tell the perfect truth all the time; you couldn't go naked for so long without itching for some clothes. She asked me once, did I trust her? I gave her the most precise answer I could think of: that I didn't trust her not to lie or do me harm, because she had done both before, but that I did keep choosing to trust myself in her hands.

I meandered around the kitchen with nothing to do. The slice of madeira I had been eating when I decided to ring my mother had my bite marks in it; I threw it away. Grace's bowl looked rather nasty in this heat; I breathed through my mouth as I scraped it out, washed it under the hot tap, and added half a can of fresh catfood. I listened out for the faraway squeaks and crashes of his progress through the house, but heard nothing.

Who could I talk to? I stood by the phone, hoisting my shoulders then letting them drop. It only made me more aware of their stiffness. I was removing a hair from the back of the receiver when the phone convulsed under my hand. I jolted in fright, then lifted it.

Under pressure Robbie sounded very Glasgow. He didn't recognize my grunt. 'I wonder could I speak to, to Penelope?'

On any other week I would have faked a BBC housekeeper-style voice and asked him to hold the line while I fetched young Miss O'Grady. Instead I said, 'Hey, Robbie. It's always Pen. Do you let anyone call you Robert?'

'Only my grandmother.' His voice trailed off.

Robbie was one of those workmates that you think of as a friend but can't call by that name in case they only think of you as a workmate.

'I'm really sorry, hen.' He left tiny pauses between the traditional words, as if trying to find their elasticity again.

'Did Sister Dominic make a general announcement?'

'Just to staff, on Monday.' Robbie cleared his throat. 'I don't mean I'm sorry about that, but. I mean yes of course I'm sorry about . . . Ciara, wasn't it?'

We could both hear the past tense swallow the verb.

'Cara.'

'Cara, sorry. No, but what I'm really sorry about is that I haven't rung till now.'

'Oh well. Doesn't matter.'

'It does. To me. See, I'm a bit squeamish that way; I just never know what to say in these situations.'

'It's OK.'

'I can't believe you asked me to ring you on Monday and I've left it till now. I mentioned it to Sheila, and she said to get on the phone this minute.'

'Really,' I told him wearily, 'it's fine.'

'No, but, it was the same with my uncle last year. His second wife died of cancer and I couldn't bring myself to send so much as a Christmas card.'

'I doubt he noticed one missing card.'

'Still.' After a long minute, Robbie asked, 'So what was it like, today?' almost brightly.

'Suppose I've had worse.'

'Like?'

'Time I stubbed my toe on the wall in a ballet exam.'

Robbie made an uncomfortable grunt of sympathy. I realized that we had no way of getting through a conversation without wisecracking; it was our common dialect. I hadn't stubbed my toe, anyway, that was an invention; I'd actually got my first period in the ballet exam, but that was a word I'd been brought up not to say in front of men.

The strained politeness came back into his vowels. 'Were you and your housemate close? Was she, like, an old friend?'

'Mmm.' I didn't trust my mouth to open.

'Can't think of anything to say that isn't totally trite,' added Robbie after a minute.

'There isn't anything.'

'Well listen, I'm afraid I have to go now.' His voice coiled up again. 'I can hear Sheila revving the car, and I have to ask her to get some toilet paper. So when are you back to the grindstone?'

'Tomorrow. Meet me for coffee after, at the Pâtisserie?'

'Sure, any excuse for a bun. Bye now, hen, take care.'

In the next few minutes I got a lot done. I trimmed chicken breasts, washed and chopped courgettes and peppers. I was upstairs giving my bedroom a bit of a tidy when it happened. As I was straightening out the quilt, the back of my hand brushed against something soft coiled behind the bed leg like a hibernating animal. Cara's white knickers, half the size of mine. I sat on the edge of the bed and uncurled them. A faint smile of yellow marked the tired cotton. I couched the cloth to my face, and breathed it in, the faint unmistakable smell of the live woman who must have dropped her clothes beside this bed (as she tiptoed her way through the doorway, in hushed laughter or lust or fatigue, I couldn't remember which) not three weeks ago. The tiny scent mocked the box, the funeral, the official story. It felt rather like the time I was standing on a chair to change a light-bulb when an electric shock stopped my breath and slammed me on to the floor.

I could hear hysteria gathering now, like a storm outside the window. I put the milky cotton between my lips and bit down on it. I pushed in another fold of cotton and another and another till I was fully gagged. I breathed through my nose, with difficulty. The quilt came up to meet my cheek as I slumped over.

It seemed days later when I sat up and pulled out the cotton; it tugged at the insides of my cheeks. I straightened the duvet again and tucked the crumpled knickers under the pillow. My eye fell on the jar of sleeping pills; I walked straight downstairs and put it back in Mr Wall's bathroom cupboard. I didn't want to have to keep making the decision not to up-end the whole jar into my mouth. As I passed the kitchen door I could see yellow and red and orange peppers curling on the chopping-board, but there was no time for them now. Back in the bedroom I was cold as mud. I put my dressing-gown on over my clothes, then girded on Cara's outsized blue velvet one which she had left over my wardrobe door. I waited for hysteria to overwhelm me, but nothing happened.

I sat on the edge of the bed and shivered. Shivering keeps you warm, I remembered. Then I realized that it didn't matter, so I loosened my muscles and relaxed into being cold. When I shut my eyes, the grey swallowed my head.

It was a couple of hours later – or so I guessed – when I heard a step outside my door. My body cringed. One foot leaped out as if to jam the door shut, but nobody tried to open it. Nobody even knocked. I could have been dead in my bed for all the Walls knew or cared. I listened out, ready to bawl 'Leave me alone,' but nobody came. I supposed they wanted to be tactful and not intrude on my grief. At that particular cliché my mouth curled up at one end. Egocentric as ever, PenInsula; doesn't it occur to you that her sister and father have enough on their plates without worrying about you? Another pair of feet went by. I wondered who had made dinner. I was surprised no one had knocked on the door to offer me the traditional cup of tea. Not that I wanted tea; what I wanted was to call 'No thanks' in such a cracked tone that they would blush to have thought tea would be any help.

Then all these theatricals fell away and I was hit by a sense of loss so sharp that I doubled up under it and pressed my face into the duvet. If this was grief, it felt more like acute appendicitis than anything else in my experience.

Much later, when the light from the window had slid down the wallpaper and faded out, I found my hand between my legs. It was simply pressing down, willing me to sleep. It occurred to me that it would only ever be my hand, now. How dull; never again the pale elongated hand with the freckles on the back of the knuckles, clumsiness dissolving in certainty. Oh, Cara, what long fingers you've got! All the better to fill you with, my dear. What bothered me now was the thought of those fingers beginning to putrefy in the cemetery. Dead fingers inside me, so cold I couldn't heat them up. ('Let's find somewhere cosy to put them,' I used to

163

joke on winter nights, 'I guarantee they'll get warm.') The image took away any lust my body might have mustered, so I pulled away my hand and slid it under the pillow.

After another hour or so, when it was fully dark, I dragged my legs inside the duvet. I thought I heard Grace scratching at the door, but I might have been dozing already. I was hungry, but the warmth overcame it, and I slept.

My dream started as the comforting fantasy I invented to get me to sleep when I was small. I had added the details one by one over the years, so although I had not thought about it for a long time, the images came easily to my mind.

I begin about thirty feet from the gingerbread house, walking towards it through the dark glade. Its walls are padded, the crusts at the corners shining. The window-frames and leading are of dark toffee; the glass is barley sugar. The roof is made of brandy snaps, dripping occasionally on to the grass. The door, made of a single sheet of thick black chocolate with ornamental knob and letterbox in white – they didn't have white chocolate in medieval times but my subconscious has obviously caught up with the nineties – is a little ajar. I pause outside. I don't eat anything, but I stroke the wall and taste the trace of treacle on my finger.

I push the door wide enough to let me in. It is almost dark; the only light from outside is coloured by the barley sugar and further dimmed by curtains of soft swinging caramel. I am not sure what to expect. Will she come in from the wood as a wrinkled hag or a young apprentice with pink cheeks? Will she reappear in animal form on the liquorice hearthrug? I pull back a chair – nut crackle, polished to a woody sheen, only slightly sticky. On the table I find a tiny box, chocolate with mint edging, precise and virginal as the first chocolate on Easter Sunday. In it there is a match made of burnt toffee; when I strike it, it turns blue. Its light reveals a candle made of glistening nougat, white with cherries embedded. I light and lift it.

I start to notice webs in the corner: spun sugar? No, just

164

cobwebs. Some of the window leading is cracked and dented. A nut in the brittle I am sitting on is crumbling to dust. I nibble the corner of the chocolate box, but it has a whiff of mould. How long has this cottage been standing empty? Maybe she hasn't been here in years. Maybe one day she never came back from the woods. How am I to be fought, taught, held in thrall, if the cottage is empty?

I reach out to bang on the wall, but my hand goes right through gingerbread softened to slime. Horror comes soundless from my mouth. I claw my way out, the roof caving in behind me. The wood is utterly dark.

I didn't think I made any noise, but I must have done, because Kate was behind the door, her soft knocks alternating with 'Pen? Are you all right?'

'Yes,' I said hoarsely.

There was a long pause. 'Did you get anything to eat?'

'I'm fine.'

Kate's voice, when it returned, was muffled by the door.

'What?' I called.

'Do you want me to come in?'

Such a small thing should have been easily answered. I could have said no, I could have said yes. I lay there wrestling with the decision so long, my mind slipping in and out of a doze, that eventually she must have gone away.

THURSDAY

When I woke up next morning I couldn't remember Cara's face. I lay still for several minutes, calling up my store of images, but they had been robbed in the night. I could visualize her shape curled up on the sofa, or plucking a saucepan from a high shelf, or running down a road, but the face was wavering as if digitized, like footage of criminals.

The first thing I did was to run downstairs, my pulse twanging in my shoulders. Grace was curled up on the third stair; I took a double step to avoid him, but he somehow inserted himself under my slipper, and yowled in complaint. The Greek photos weren't on the sideboard, or on the mantelpiece in the living-room; where could the sister have put them? I finally found them in the top drawer with the scissors and string.

I didn't spare a glance for the cliffs and sunsets, the action shots on motorbikes. What I was tracking was Cara, hidden in every third or fourth picture. I studied these centimetres of plastic, recognizing the familiar elements of winey hair, faint eyebrows and blanched skin, but somehow they did not add up to her face. None of them looked very human either; she seemed like a creature from another planet who was trying to blend into the crowd of tourists.

We certainly didn't live on the same elements. Once, I remembered, she had buried her face in the front of my grey mohair jumper. After a minute I became alarmed, and asked, 'Can you breathe down there?'

Whatever she said was muffled by the wool.

'What?'

She turned her face a little sideways, leaning her eyelashes

169

on my breast. I could hear the smile in her words: 'There are better things to breathe than air.'

None of these photos looked quite like the woman I knew. I brought them upstairs and put them on top of the pile in my photo box. Then I slid my fingers underneath, and flicked through the sparse schooldays photos till I found what I was looking for. The sheer audacity of me, to nick it from the Wall family album the first day I visited the big house. Kate was in the bath, I remembered, and the little redhaired sister was pestering me to admire pictures of their late basset hound. She ran off for a minute, to check the starting time of *Top of the Pops* in the TV guide, and I turned the pages of the album. There were not many of Kate – clearly she resisted cameras – and in most of them she was smiling boredly to order. But when I turned the loaded page, one picture caught my eye. Kate, on rollerskates in a deserted car park, hunched forward, giving the photographer one of those stern looks that used to stop my breath. She was in blue denim dungarees, the legs a little too short for her, one of the shoulder straps undone. Behind her, the little sister in a gypsy shirt scrambled to keep up, laughing through a faceful of hair. Glancing up to make sure no one was about to come into the room, I tugged the photo out from under its clear cellophane. The tape left four square brown marks on the paper. I shoved the picture deep in the pocket of my school skirt. By the time I got it home, it had three big creases, but they didn't touch Kate's face.

And now here it was back in its own house where it belonged. And the strange thing was that over the years it had transformed itself into a photo of Cara, with her big sister scowling in the foreground. As if people were invisible ink until the warm iron of love ripened their lines into something we could see.

I shut the box. I could tell I was hungry now; my stomach was complaining to itself. In the kitchen I filled a big bowl with cereal and milk, then couldn't begin to eat it. Not that it seemed repellent, not that I felt sick, just that I no longer had the hang of how to open my mouth and swallow. It was like forgetting how to ride a bike, having lost the thread that connects each movement of muscle to the next. I emptied the bowl into the sink tidy, then decanted that into the compost bin so that Mr Wall wouldn't see it and worry.

A frayed end of one of last night's dreams came back to me. We were walking in the woods, Cara and I, and suddenly we heard Mr Wall's voice through a megaphone, ordering us to come out from behind those trees. He was saying how he had known about us two for twenty years now, how it was primitive, repulsive, and totally unacceptable. 'I'm afraid I feel it incumbent upon me to inform the police,' he kept repeating. I shook my head now, to break the dream's hold.

His presentation letter-opener with the gold feather on it (thirty years of service to the scholars at the Wotherby library) lay on the kitchen counter beside several neatly slit envelopes and the first batch of mass cards. I counted two Blessed are They Who Mourns, two Deepest Sympathies, one whose sympathy was Sincere, and even one Heartfelt – the last a little over the top, I thought, considering that it was from an almost indecipherable relative never mentioned by Cara in all the years I knew her. The pictures were rudimentary: chalices in paper relief or outlined in silver, the occasional tastefully meagre spray of blossoms. The statements on the inside were rather official, with the names added in spidery writing. *As an Expression of Sympathy from: scribble scribble, The Holy Sacrifice of the Mass will be Offered by: scrawl scrawl, For the Repose of the Soul of: Cara Wall.* If they didn't know how little repose mass ever gave to her soul, why were they bothering to send a card at all? Oh, PenItentiary, stop being so critical. Whatever made them feel a little better.

What would a non-religious lesbian sympathy card be like, I wondered? A postcard with a cartoon on it, no doubt. I tried to come up with a suitable slogan. 'A woman without a body is like a kite without a string'? 'Death = Life'?

Half past eight already, and no sign of Kate. I'd have to

grab a cup of tea in the staff-room. I pulled off my dressing-gown as I pounded up the stairs to find some respectable clothes. Everything seemed to be crumpled or unwashed, except for a polka-dot blouse which was far too merry. I settled for a loose purple shirt over a grey skirt, the Victorian colours of light mourning.

Five long rattling coughs from the engine, then nothing. Ah, come on now, Min, of all days to go dead on me. Ah, be nice. Good wee car. I tried again, three times in a row, then realized I had flooded the engine. Damn you anyway, rotten little banger. I slammed the car door so hard I thought it might drop off its rust-gnawed hinges. Evidently my entire life was about to fall apart. I wanted to kick the wheel, but that would be just too *Fawlty Towers*. I considered getting Kate up to help me push Minnie down the hill, but I couldn't haul her out of bed if she was convalescing.

I peered under the bonnet: everything looked all right. Machines and mechanics made me feel so powerless. Why hadn't I ever listened when my father talked to himself as he fiddled around with our third-hand Fiat's engine on Saturday afternoons? I should probably sign up at the community college this autumn to learn about car innards. There, that was a future plan, that was healthy. No lover, no life, but a possible course in car maintenance.

Giving up on Minnie, I went back inside and rang for a taxi, then made a shamed call to the school secretary to ask if someone could keep an eye on my class till I turned up. Leaning against the gate, peering up and down for anything that said SpeediCars, I could feel my stomach growl. The day was heating up already. What ludicrous weather, calling for garden parties and walks along Sandymount Strand, but who with? Somehow over the years I had slipped into being unsociable. Between the straight schoolfriends I had inched away from, and the dykes I met only through and with Cara, I found myself on a kind of island. As long as Cara was around it seemed full of voices; living with a Gemini, one was never short of company. But now I had no idea how to go about filling the evenings. Living in a couple made you so comfortably lazy. Of course I had spent many satisfying days alone while Cara was out or away, but they were framed by her presence; now they had nothing to contrast with, and stretched out like prison terms.

That eggs-in-one-basket cliché was inescapable. We all knew we should store our eggs one by one, tuck each in moss and hide it in the roots of a different tree. But was that what we did? No, of course not, that would be much too sensible. It was all very well to swing your laden basket through the woods if you knew there was someone waiting for you with the door open and the kettle whistling, but what if there wasn't? Suddenly you found yourself alone in a circle of trees, with the branches snatching at a basket too heavy for your hand, and the flies buzzing at the tail-end of summer.

'O'Grady?'

My eyes focused at last on the man leaning out of the taxi window. When I climbed in, I found that he was not only smoking, but also playing his radio. I thought if I complained about either, my voice might crack. We were passing the miniature Eiffel Tower of the television station when, to my horror, I found myself identifying with a pop song that rhymed 'missing you' with 'kissing you'. Luckily the driver twiddled the knob at that point and settled for a discussion about Catholic majorities on school boards.

We wheeled in Immac's double gates at a quarter past nine. I paid the man, then stood on the drive, watching the taxi disappear along the double row of slowly dying elms. The gravel shifted under my feet as I scrunched my way up to the main door. I was suddenly unconvinced of my ability to do this: the day, the job, the whole thing. Panic seized my hand as it reached to push the door handle, and it occurred to me to turn back, but that would be Cara's kind of carry-on, not mine.

As I hurried along the corridor, an old nun nodded at me and a sixth-classer running in late gave me an apologetic smile. I must have looked normal. I was walking round with snake-bite in my veins, a bomb ticking in my skull, but evidently no one could tell. I took the stairs two at a time, swinging where the banisters turned and almost headbutting Sister Dominic in the stomach. I reeled backwards. Her veil hooded her glasses. 'I'm so sorry, Sister. I know I'm horribly late, the car wouldn't start, it's most unlike it. I did ring and leave a message . . .'

'Calm yourself, Penelope.' Her hand perched on my shoulder for a moment, then returned to hang on the cross.

'Yes, Sister.'

'Since your class has PE first thing on Thursdays, they won't be in till nine forty-five.'

My breath slithered out. 'I forgot.'

'Though of course you may wish to go to your classroom straight away and begin collecting your thoughts.'

'Of course.' How many years of my life was I going to spend hating this woman?

Big Dom's eyes shone behind her thick glasses. 'How was the funeral?'

'Fine,' I told her brightly, and carried on up the stairs.

'I've been remembering your friend in my prayers, Penelope,' she said without raising her voice.

'I'm sure she's grateful,' I called back, and then, afraid that my sarcasm was audible, hurried on.

Everyone else in the world managed to get their tongue round 'Pen', even Mr Wall; Sister Dominic used my full name simply to remind me that she set the terms. And why had my mother given me such a wifey name anyway? The original Penelope should have run off to an island with the wittiest suitor, or woven a fabulous tapestry that would spread her fame, or just taken the dog and run along the shore. Why sit home for years in one long nightmare house-party waiting for your true love, who is probably changed, grizzled, faded, and even if they are the same, how dare they expect you to have waited that long? And as soon as they come home, they're off on their travels again. I've never

174

woven anything, but if I did, I wouldn't rip it up; I'd wrap it round me to keep warm.

By the time the girls had all straggled into class with their bagfuls of runners and damp T-shirts, it was ten o'clock. The hour before break slid by in a blur. I was relieved to find that I had lost none of my competence. Ruler in hand, I conducted all thirty-one mouths through the *comhrá*, pointing to each of fuzzy-felt Seán and Caitríona's activities to elicit the set phrase.

As soon as the bell went, I trudged off to the staff-room. Always before my hand touched the door I felt a thrill of taboo, as if I were still a pupil, forbidden to enter. It was smoky and warm, except for a cool channel of air from the window that new nun who taught music was holding open. I found an armchair with its guts spilling through a lattice of threads, and sat back in it. I could not face food. I had nothing to read. I composed my features into a pleasant tired mask so that nobody would ask me what the matter was, or remember about the funeral. I did not want to disown Cara by diluting her into my 'housemate'. Of course I had done that very thing over and over while she was alive, but it seemed wrong now that there was no longer any possibility of calling off the lie, now that there was no chance that I would ever bring her on my arm to a staff Christmas party and say, this is my beloved, in whom I am well pleased.

I tried listening to the lethargic argument taking place to my left between Mrs Bayle (Home Economics) and Mr O'Leary (Physics) about the length of school holidays. Soon the talk shifted to flight prices to the Canaries in the New Year which after all was a bare four months away. I did try to interest myself in the conversation; once or twice I thought of something to say and took a breath but it died away in my mouth, as I was struck by the complete pointlessness of all such chat. What did it matter how many pence, how many days, how many inches? Surely what mattered was whether we were living or dying, half-empty or half-full? Not that I was usually a particularly cosmic person, but this week it seemed to me that all our thinking was on too petty a scale. I shut my eyes and lay back in the armchair, hoping my body language would be read as ordinary first-fortnight burnout.

After break I filled the blackboard with long division; since maths was my weakest point, I liked to get it over with early. The girls moaned contentedly and started taking the figures down in their copybooks, the hum fading to an occasional whisper of 'Is that a 5 or a 6?'. This won me fifteen minutes. I bent over a stack of homework, and let my eyes unfocus.

Immac was hardly the ideal environment for escaping from thoughts of Cara, since, just as much as the big house, every dusty corner reeked of her. Not that she had been back through the door since our maudlin sixth-year concert in 1981 – she said the place gave her the shivers, and that I was a perv to take a job there – but her younger self still haunted its corridors for me. Because I'd come late to the school, I never met her in the junior part of it, but now I was teaching here I could visualize her on a smaller scale in the years before I knew her, with dark red plaits caught in her collar, and the expression of a suspicious elf.

Not the best years of our lives, far from it. When Cara left me the first time it was for Lent. She said she was dirty but she was going to go to eight o'clock mass every morning and get clean. Couldn't we still love each other even if we couldn't do the holding and stuff, I pleaded, and she said just friends, all right, just friends. So I spent the mornings clearing my throat, and the breaks leaning against the cold wall of a toilet stall, letting tears stripe my face. They ran plentifully back then. Doing my homework at the kitchen table before tea, I used to reach under and press my knuckles between my legs to keep me still. That was 1980, the year Gay Byrne interviewed a lesbian on *The Late Late Show*, but I missed it because I was upstairs writing an essay on *Great Expectations*. At night I held on to the gold boat on a chain

Cara had given me, and dreamed of a crack in the timbers, of water rising and washing across the deck, sucking at the sailors' feet.

Next thing was, Cara stopped going to mass every morning. She slammed her way out of the confession box, and wouldn't tell me what the priest said. She left a primrose on my desk, and because I didn't want anyone to see it, or it to fade or get crushed, I ate it. Then I had to rush to the school library to check that primroses weren't poisonous. I only half fancied dying for love.

One lunchtime Cara found me lying on my back out in the long-jump sand-pit. My eyes had filled up with water that the sun was drying into fresh salt. The sun seemed to go out; I looked up and there was Cara's face, ringed with fire. 'Come back,' she said. 'I was such an eejit.' That was one of the best days, the day she came back after the first time. If she hadn't left, it occurred to me now, there would not have been the sweetness of her coming back.

My class were beginning to stir. Correcting the hard sums the substitute teacher had set them filled the time till the lunch bell. The smell of the nuns' sausages had put me off the idea of food again, nor could I face the staff-room. Instead I stretched my legs by walking the whole circuit of the school grounds. At the corner of the hockey pitch I crossed paths with Sister Luke; she looked up from her tiny laced shoes and nodded, her smile bobbing. I didn't say anything, in case she was busy praying. Did she not eat dinner these days? She was considered old as the dinosaurs when I first came to Immac, so god alone knew how old she was now. Whenever I bitched about the nuns, sooner or later the thought of Sister Luke occurred to me and shut me up. I was surprised to see her out here; the nuns generally avoided the back of the school, so they would not have to see the girls speed-smoking behind the hockey pavilion, and take official notice of the crime. Maybe Sister Luke would turn her white head to the clouds as she walked by, or smile beatifically at the girls and confound them. Or she might offer them one of her more gruesome anecdotes about the effects of smoking, from her days as a Biology teacher. I still remembered her hunched over a microscope, peering up in the occasional blaze of excitement to tell us what to look for in our pieces of onion skin.

In the senior yard the girls were languid on window-sills and bike racks. Nowadays they wore skirts that gave them the wide-hipped silhouette of bored office women, whereas the tunics we used to wear pretended we were pure and rectangular, like playing cards. I caught a bawdy snatch of 'Summer Loving' from one knot of girls, and was suddenly struck by the oddity of 1990s girls performing a 1970s pastiche of a 1950s song that was one of the few points of continuity between my own schooldays and theirs.

The tennis courts looked dry and dusty; the nets were sagging in the middle. Outside the junior school one small girl I didn't know pointed me out to two others, who exchanged a giggle. I passed near a group of skippers whose feet landed heavily over and over just after the rope slapped the tarmac. Only a couple of breathless voices kept up the chant:

> I'll tell my ma when I go home
> The boys won't leave the girls alone

Oh, but you won't, you know, I wanted to say to them. You won't say a word to your ma, because what good would it do to tell her about the boys? Wouldn't you rather protect her from knowing how little she can protect you from the boys, the weather, or anything else?

I set my class to tracing maps of Italy ('Rivers in blue pencil, girls, and brown zigzags for the mountains') while I corrected last week's essays. I usually got through the mound of English copybooks on Sunday evening, but obviously this weekend I hadn't got the chance. It would hardly have given me peace of mind, after the phone call from the hospital, to have read thirty-one descriptions of 'Dawn in the Forest', most of which ended 'Now it will live forever in my memory'. None of these girls' mothers would ever have let them get up at dawn to prance around a forest, so they had had to use their imaginations, meaning their stock of dew-beaded, furry-nosed clichés. Saoirse Mullan had got the exercise number wrong – on purpose? I wouldn't put it past her – and written on 'The Old Person I Admire Most', which at least was a break from the phantom forests. He turned out to be dead, Saoirse's admirable grandfather; she listed his virtuous eccentricities and described his grave. She seemed to miss him. I decided not to penalize her for being in temporary thrall to the word 'bittersweet' – I found it a couple of pages back, in 'Jerusalem at Dusk on Good Friday' as well as in 'Autobiography of a Seed' – and gave her a V.G.

After I'd handed them back for the girls to whisper over their Goods and Fairs, it was time for the reading. I had this down pat. Girl in top-left seat read first paragraph – 'Thank you, Mary' – girl beside her read the next – 'Take your time, Eileen' then a switch to the opposite corner of the class just to keep them on their toes. When the paragraphs ran out I would clear my throat and say, 'Well now, line one, what do you think he means by that, Alison, in your own words?' This was the blessing of work, that without asking much of my mind it kept it humming along till half past three.

I went to meet Robbie ten minutes after the bell. The Pâtisserie was far enough from the bus stops so we wouldn't be pointed at by sun-paled children in drooping uniforms. He was late. I established myself in one of the white plastic chairs outside, so the afternoon sun could massage my shoulders. I dropped my worn satchel on the seat opposite, and pulled up a chair beside me for Robbie, its back to the light. That way he would not have to squint as he looked at me; his long rectangle of a face would not be fearful and naked in the light.

'Hello, hen.'

I peered up, and patted the back of the spare chair. 'Sit you down. Can I buy you a coffee?'

'Don't stir, I'll get it.'

As I watched Robbie rush into the café, his faded paisley shirt catching on the handle of the door for a second, I realized that he was coddling me. I supposed it was a metaphor; he really wanted to give balm to my mind, not rest to my body. He carried back two brimming cups and a plate of raspberry tarts and pains-au-chocolat.

'Now, you're not to say you don't want one,' Robbie warned me. 'Stress burns up calories, I read it in a Sunday supplement.'

'I'm really not hungry.'

Robbie's face was creased with concern. 'Try a tart,' he said, tucking his hair behind his ears with paint-stained fingers. 'The jelly is perfect.'

'In a minute maybe.'

His day had been, in a word, boggin. The carved potatoes had dried up and he had forgotten to bring in any more, so Senior Infants had had to learn the joys of fingerpainting. Big Dom was on Robbie's back about cleaning again, because some six-year-old had left a trail of blue footprints down the top corridor, unaware that she had trodden in her paint saucer. The chat drifted to pay freezes and how long it would take before we'd have earned career breaks.

'Listen, this probably isn't a good time to ask,' he said suddenly, 'but without your housemate, will you be able to keep up your mortgage? Or were you renting? If you need to find someone else right away, Sheila's got a cousin . . .'

'No, it's, it's not like that.' My heart started to thud, the familiar symptom that meant my subconscious had decided to come out to someone without informing HQ. In a curiously detached way I could feel the kite-ribbons of language jerking up to my hand. 'We were living with Cara's father, it's his house.'

'So were you like a family friend?'

'I was like a lover. I mean,' correcting myself a little hoarsely, 'a lover, not just like.'

Robbie's pale eyes bulged. 'Jesus Christ. For long?'

'Thirteen years last May. On and off.'

'But that would have made you just a wee girl when you two . . .'

I nodded, with a hint of a grin. It seemed odd that age was the variable that shocked him.

'And how did Cara feel about it?'

An odd question. How to summarize the emotional weather of so many years? 'Happy, mostly,' I hazarded. 'When she wasn't bored.'

'So she knew all along?'

I paused, the cooling coffee at my lips, and stared at him. 'What, that she was a lesbian?'

Robbie had flakes of puff pastry all around his mouth, which was jutting a little open. 'Hang on a minute. You're telling me you've been having a thirteen-year affair with your housemate's father, *and* that she's a lesbian? Was,' he corrected herself automatically, then winced.

I lifted a raspberry tart, concentrating on biting it neatly to stop myself from laughing. 'Let's take it from the top,' I mumbled. 'I'm the one who's gay.' I didn't stop to gauge his reaction, but took a mouthful of coffee and carried on. 'Cara too, though she didn't like the word. We got together when we were doing the Inter Cert, and for the past few years we've lived with her father, who's not having an affair with anyone that I know of. He's a librarian,' I explained.

Robbie's cheeks were resting on his fists. 'And this year's Moron Medal goes to Robbie Brown. Sorry. I hadn't a clue.'

'Really? You made some joke at the Christmas party last year, about marriage or something, and I thought you might have sussed me.'

'Not at all. I don't actually know any . . . at least I didn't think I . . . ach, shut up, man, you're digging yourself in deep.'

We studied our plates. I pressed my finger on to fragments of pastry and lifted them to my tongue. Robbie was the first to look up. 'That's wild. Even better than the story of you and the middle-aged librarian.'

'There's hope for that one yet,' I told him. 'He makes a great soufflé omelette.'

Robbie was blinking into the distance, as if trying to get things clear in his mind. 'Well,' he said into his coffee cup, 'aren't you the woman of mystery?'

'I never lied about it,' I told him. 'You've often heard me mention my housemate, and I didn't invent any men's names or anything. The L-word just never seems to come up at staff meetings.'

'Funny, that,' he said with a great snort. And then, nibbling on his long guitar-playing nail, 'I suppose we really don't know the first thing about each other, even though we all share a building.'

I nodded, reaching for another tart. 'These are good stuff.'

'When did you eat last?' asked Robbie.

I was surprised by my calculations. 'This time yesterday.'

'Ach, Pen, you mustn't do that.'

'I didn't mean to,' I told him, 'I just lost the knack of eating.'

'I suppose,' he said, staring at the passing traffic, 'it must be like when a husband or wife dies. Only less . . . official.'

I nodded. My throat was full of angry words, but they weren't for him.

'Thirteen years, you said. I just can't imagine what it would be like if I was with Sheila for ten more years and then she . . .' Robbie ground to a halt. 'I'd better zip my gob; I'm probably making it worse.'

'No. It's good when someone tries to understand.' Even if it takes a death to reach parity, spat the back of my brain.

He was staring across the main road again. 'Sometimes when I hear an ambulance, I wonder if it's her. But that's just paranoia. I never seriously think of it coming true.'

'Yeah, I used to do that.' How urbane I sounded.

'I don't even know anyone – not anyone our age –'

I nodded, intent on the crumbs. 'I did meet another dyke once' (as soon as it slipped out the word embarrassed me, but I carried on) 'who'd lost her lover in a motorbike smash.

Someone told me about it at a party; I hadn't the nerve to talk to the woman myself.'

Robbie nodded.

'I wish now I'd talked to her. It'd be good to know what was normal for someone in my situation.'

'Would you want to be normal?' he asked, fingering a raspberry off my plate.

My eyes widened. We both started laughing at the same time.

'Honestly, I didn't —'

I interrupted him. 'No, you're dead right, it's a bit late for normality now.'

By the time we had finished the last pastry between us, I had to be heading into town to meet my mother. Robbie gave me a lift in his little red Datsun as far as the canal, where he was turning off. I was glad to stretch my legs, after their day wound together under the chalky desk. I thought the air would be refreshing, but it was getting hotter; the ducks seemed to crawl over the sticky surface of the canal. After a minute of walking, the satchel's old leather handle slid about in my sweaty palm.

Normal or not, maybe I did need to talk to someone. That was what one did nowadays, wasn't it? Though I seemed sane enough to myself, maybe underneath I was cracking up. No one would notice till the day I drove into Immac stark naked and taught Fifth Class how to cha-cha. Then the white van would come for me, they'd make me decent in a hospital nightie and ask me about my childhood. Cara thought therapy should be available free from your G P. She insisted that everything should be shared and talked out — everything except what she didn't feel like talking about herself. She used to bring home over-photocopied flyers with headings like *An Absolute Beginner's Guide to Co-Counselling*. I was always willing to try anything once, if only to prove to her that it wouldn't work.

On a long wall on Leeson Street was stamped, over and over, *Dublins beautiful keep it clean*. I thought of adding *Language*

is beautiful; keep it punctuated, then sighed at my teacherly in-
tolerance and looked away. Dublin was undeniably beautiful
today, the sun bringing out the red of the brick terraces,
catching the fan-lights over the Georgian doors. Even the
odd burnt-out building looked rather decorative, as if left
over from a film set.

I decided to cut through Stephen's Green, something that,
being a driver, I hadn't done in years. I had forgotten that
bronze of the Three Fates placed just inside the gates; I
stopped short to look at it. A toddler bumped into the back
of my knees, then stumbled on, its mother twitching the
reins. The Fates sat holding the inch-thick rope of life, one
behind another, their black eyes gloomy but by no means
malevolent. Their hands were palms outermost, as if to ask,
what do you people expect of us anyway? Water gushed
from the rock they were sitting on. The youngest one had a
drugged smile; scissors idle in her lap, she seemed to be
absorbing memories from the frayed end of the rope which
trailed against her skirt.

Jazz was booming from the bandstand as I walked farther
into the Green. The tune was familiar to me, though I
couldn't put a name to it. The only jazz I knew was from
those afternoons Major to Minor used to play in Sachs
Hotel, and I mostly went to those to eye up the women in
sensible shoes who surrounded the piano. Here in the Green
no one was paying the trumpet solo much attention. Couples
cuddled sleepily on the bumpy lawn between beds of late
roses. I nodded to Con Markievicz as I passed; her bronze
head was almost hidden in holly and purple leaves. I had
always loved the story of her setting her citizen army to dig
trenches here in 1916 without thinking how easily they
would be gunned down from the windows of the hotels that
overlooked the Green. Or no, maybe I was underestimating
her. Maybe she knew what would happen, but wanted to
keep her men busy, like the games I made up for my Immac
girls on sleepy afternoons.

The generous fountain was spurting in three plumes,

making me thirsty. My mouth was dry from the coffee and pastries that my stomach was struggling to reconcile. At the edge of the meandering pond, a toddler stood casting strips of bread at the ducks with such vigour that I thought he might topple. Keeping one eye on him, I looked at the island in the middle where two swans were digging at the weed. There was an overgrown path up around the pond, I remembered now. Cara had dragged me up here once to kiss on the bend in the path where just for a moment you were screened from view. I strolled up that way now, to see what nostalgia would do to me. When I turned at the bend there was a couple on the grass; I doubled back immediately.

I left the Green by the gate beside the toilets. On the wall in dripping white letters it said *Abortion Information 6794700*. Cara used to wear a badge with the illegal number on it; acquaintances of her father's, meeting her at the supermarket, would bend their heads to read it, then straighten up sharply.

This walk seemed to be taking forever, partly because the heat switched the world into slow motion, and partly because my attention kept being grabbed by things. The clothes in Grafton Street windows, for instance. I was not usually a very sartorial person, comfort being my main requirement, which was just as well, since the shops only seemed to stock size 10s. But today I examined all the mannequins as I passed; a race of lean Martians come down to make us feel alien. It struck me as strange that Cara was the shape of these plastic glamour-girls, yet she was the one who had most trouble with clothes. We used to call it her Cinderella complex, because often when she had agreed to go out in the evening she would be seized by panic and announce that she had nothing to wear. Every outfit had too many associations for her: 'too Woodstock' or 'too Dynasty' or 'boring, schoolgirly, borrrrring'. I played fairy godmother, my words enchanting each garment into wearability for a couple of seconds until the magic fell out and it was dowdy again. Sometimes the wardrobe would have disgorged its entire contents across the bed by the time I found Cara something she was willing to be bullied into, or else gave up and filled her a hot-water bottle.

Life seemed to be more of a battle for Cara than for anyone I knew. What was water to the rest of us might become thick mud or paralysing ice when Cara moved her arms. When she found out that agoraphobia meant fear of the market-place, she decided it was the right word after all, because what scared her on social occasions, during her lows, was feeling judged, priced, haggled over. I used to remind her that in your average crowd, nobody would be taking a blind bit of notice of her. 'You just have to take the days one at a time,' I'd tell her. Once she had an answer: 'It's them that take me.'

Uillean pipes were throbbing from a busker crouched against a wall. Why they made me so exquisitely sad I could not tell, since all I associated them with were TV documentaries on basket-weaving or turf-cutting, snapshots of an Ireland I never knew. I ignored the impulse to stand at the mouth of the alley and listen to the pipes. I speeded up as I rounded Trinity College; at this rate I wouldn't get to my mother's shop by five and she'd be hanging round waiting.

Car roofs glittered along Dame Street. Sometimes they put a Big Dipper there for the carnival; Cara took me on it once to cheer me up as she was leaving me for . . . Ben, was it? The New Man of the old sort? Couldn't remember. She'd left so often, for such a variety of reasons. Sometimes I could feel it coming: the slow puncture, our ship riding low in the water. Other times it was a complete shock. Other times still it never quite happened; she'd tell me down the eloquent phone-line, twice a week for a few weeks, how much she loved me, how that was why she had to go, because she thought she'd treat me better as a friend . . . and then she'd come over and put her tongue in my ear.

Anyway. On this particular occasion it was night, and it seemed a time for being brave, so I said yes to the Big Dipper, even though I knew they usually made me feel sick.

I hadn't worn my jacket all week since she'd told me we were over; I wanted to let the wind blow right through me. Poised above Dame Street, persuading my stomach to keep up, I started shivering. Cara squeezed my hand in a platonic way and said, 'Look at the lights!' I glanced down at the spangled trees but could think of nothing to say about them. Then the metal scoop we were sitting in gave a buck and began to slide backwards. I peered behind but couldn't see a thing. That was the worst, not knowing what I was falling into.

But this was daytime and I was on level ground. Below the sign that said O'Connell Bridge sat a tiny girl wheezing into the tin whistle which dangled from her lips. I dumped a pocketful of small change on to her blanket and ran on before she could shame me with a blessing.

I got to the jewellery shop by ten past five, but my mother was long gone, said the smoothie young manager. I stood in the door, stiff with anger that she couldn't have waited for me, that she hadn't guessed somehow that today was more important than all the other days we had met for coffee. She just didn't have a clue about my life, and it was too late to start; all the years of not-saying had layered like dust on a window.

I was still rigid, halfway down the street. A sign for the Pro-Cathedral seemed a useful hint; I climbed its steps. It was smaller than I had remembered from the odd midnight mass my mother brought me and Gavin to when we were children, but still impressive. Banks of candles flamed on every side; ten pence for a little cup, twenty for the tall tapers, one of which (beneath Mary's hem) keeled over as I walked by. I stopped to straighten it. Others had flags or ruffs of white wax. I would have liked to light one, but I had no more change. Our Lady's head was bent under a crown of thorns with ten electric lights on it, strangely reminiscent of the European Community logo. She also had a faint blush. 'I'm No Saint Reveals Queen of Heaven', or maybe 'Only Technically a Virgin Says Lesbo Mary'.

She must rue the day she had him, I thought, watching her pained eyes. All those high hopes, and then he went and got himself killed; what an anti-climax. In the thirteenth oil picture above my head, she was sitting straightbacked on a stool someone had thoughtfully carried up Calvary for her, with her son's ungainly body sprawled across her lap. I had none of her certainty, only memory. I could almost hear us, me and Cara, sitting in the back row of the church, whispering the time away. 'Will we be allowed to have sex in heaven?' she'd ask me, or 'What kind of fish would you like to be?' She once said that the reason she kept coming back to me was that she couldn't find anyone else who'd take her questions seriously.

When two women in headscarves groaned into the pew beside me, I realized that this was a queue for confession, and moved back three rows. The women would think me a sinner who had lost her nerve. Confession was a habit I had dropped from the menu of what the newspapers called A La Carte Catholicism some years ago.

It was on a school retreat when I first went off the whole business. The priest was very busy, and the sight of this long string of adolescent girls prompted him to adopt a novel strategy: instead of waiting for admissions, he asked the questions. I was only halfway through my opening prayers when he muttered, 'Good girl now. Tell me do you smoke?'

'No, Father.'

'Do you drink?'

'No, Father.'

'Do you give cheek to your mammy and daddy?'

'No, Father.'

'Have you a boyfriend tell me now?'

'No.'

'If you had a boyfriend, would you do bad stuff with him?'

'No.'

'Aren't you the great girl. You have the conscience of a saint. Say a nice act of contrition now.'

While I was saying it he began the absolution, and he was finished before me. I sat on the window-sill outside, bewildered by the unearned compliments. It became clear to me at last that my story just didn't show up in their terms. I never much bothered after that.

As I walked down the side aisle now I passed half a dozen women doing their rosary beads, which clacked like spiritual knitting. In the porch, below ads for courses on *Billings Method Natural Family Planning* and pleas to *Support the Missions*, they were compiling November's altar list of the dead already; there was a basket in which you could put your loved one's name in an envelope for the priest to mispronounce. I could never quite work out the logic of the doctrine that if you got people to pray for your dead they would get out of purgatory faster. If it was a matter of contacts and pulling strings, then it hardly seemed fair. Sister Dominic reassured our class once that the dead who didn't have living friends and relatives were the special concern of nuns in contemplative convents.

'But Sister, Sister, if everyone gets prayed for, doesn't it all balance out then?'

'No, no, it's not a competition.'

'Well, he's hardly going to let everyone out early, is he?'

'Penelope O'Grady, you have an irreverent attitude.'

I tried to imagine Cara doing time in purgatory. If you put her in jail she would certainly not take it meekly; rather than doing a PhD, she would probably smuggle dope and get herself a big butch girlfriend.

On the steps the air hit me; it surely couldn't get much hotter without the thin Irish sky bursting? Across the road was a tacky religious goods shop and an advice centre, its window featuring pamphlets called *Think Before You Emigrate* and *Coping With London*. On O'Connell Street a pair of fiddlers were making a gallant stab at Pachelbel's Canon. The patient bars of it brought me back; Cara and I used to play it loudly on her tape recorder whenever I'd come over to the big house to 'help her with Biology homework' (oh, the salty leaves of her, magnified in my gaze). Time was I used to get turned on whenever I heard it, but my body seemed to be dried up these days.

In the shop beside the bus stop I bought a carton of grapefruit juice and a macaroon. I leaned against the rusty pole of the bus stop like a scarecrow, a knot of limbs that had forgotten how to walk. The bus looked top-heavy, leaning inwards at the corner as if it had had a couple of pints over lunch. I was sure it would be full up with school-girls three to a seat, their legs sticking together through the creased gaberdine. I crossed my arms on my ribs. A droplet trickled down my neck, hidden under my hair.

When the bus conductor opened the door a crack and held up two fingers I read it first as a flippant peace sign, and hated him. Then I realized that he had room for two of us, and leaped up, just ahead of an old man with a sunburnt scalp. I had to stay standing as far as the canal, when a worn woman lifted her four bags of groceries down and I had a third of a seat. I lowered myself so firmly that the boy in unlaced trainers had to shrink back or be sat on.

The high-pitched chatter of Continental students filled the bus; I tried to decipher the odd word on the basis of what Latin I could remember. Then I remembered the juice, and scrabbled in the bottom of my bag. After the first slug, I rested the carton against my belly; the chill of it made me shudder. Sweat was cooling under my arms. It was Cara who taught me to love the body's infinitely varied soda fountain. She used to nuzzle under my breasts after a long day's work, and sample the backs of my ears with her tongue. Her own liquors were so faint – she faded off my fingers as fast as they dried – that she envied mine. She liked to see my clothes stick to me in summer; she used to trace the patterns the salt water made as it broke through that silk vest she brought me from California.

I chewed on the coconut macaroon, alternating with sips of juice. I had enjoyed the toasted bit at the top, but it seemed to be getting bigger as I ate it down to the base. I didn't stop eating; I liked the rhythm. The sun was making a kaleidoscope of my eyelashes. My shadow on the back of the seat in front of me joggled like a cowgirl with the motion of the bus. We passed the football club where the Immac school dances used to be held before someone got half his ear chopped off and they were banned. I remembered one in particular, some rainy night in my late teens when my ankles bled down the back of my new white court shoes as I danced to three songs in a row by David Bowie, who had one eye blue and one eye green and was living proof that a perv could win fame and glory.

Four seats behind, turned away from me, I noticed a girl carrying a three-foot sunflower upside-down. The top of its stalk was swathed in a plastic bag; the yellow head hung near the floor. I wondered where she was bringing this odd gift. Maybe it was for herself, and there was a basement flat and a rinsed milk-bottle waiting for this giant flower.

I finished the macaroon and wiped my hands on the paper bag. That ache in my fingers again, as if I had been wearing them out. The engine fumes were rising; there was a window behind me, but I couldn't reach round to open it. The juice was sharp in my stomach, colliding with the coconut. I concentrated on planning tomorrow's lessons in my head – industries and exports of the main Italian cities, then more long division – as we trundled past the shopping centre. Its white-and-blue shrine was positioned beside the bus stop, as if Our Lady was waiting for a 39A. The sunflower girl turned her head to look, then stared forward again. Older than I thought, very dark lashes; her hair curved round her ear as if a hand had pushed it back. She looked like she was following a tune in her head. Freckles stood out sharply on her pale forehead. She had one of those snub noses you laugh at but want to take between your lips.

I shut my eyes. Would you just look at me: my lover one day in the grave and I was fancying others already. Roll up, roll up, blondes, brunettes, we've got the lot, all aboard on the Big Dipper of serial monogamy. They said it was healthy.

Life went on, it was only natural, mother earth's rhythms would always jog you along. Eventually I would forget: Cara, which one was that, I'd ask myself; did she have grey eyes and red hair, or was it the other way round?

And there was Cara in the window of the bus paused beside ours, her features chaste and distant behind the scratched glass. I blinked. Don't panic. It was somebody else, a total stranger. Don't panic. Hallucinations are only to be expected.

Suddenly I felt that uneasiness in my teeth that meant I was going to be sick. I bent over, hanging my head a few inches from my knees. People were looking at me. I didn't want it to go on, this cosmic cavalcade; I didn't want to hurt and heal and survive like any animal. If this love thing was to be repeated over and over, how could the words stay fresh or even halfway sincere? How could I wrench any of it back from Cara and give it to someone else, with it all still reeking of the grave? No, I couldn't wait just three more stops. Coffee, raspberry tart, pain-au-chocolat, grapefruit juice and coconut macaroon were going to splatter all over somebody's shoes. I lunged for the pole, pressed the button, kept my teeth clamped shut.

Only when the bus had chugged away in a haze of exhaust fumes did I let myself throw up over a wall. The hedge hid most of it. I picked a leaf to wipe my mouth on. A man walked by, adjusting his tinted bifocals disapprovingly. I wanted to tell him that I was not odd or mad. Then it occurred to me that maybe all the people we saw behaving oddly or madly were not a distinct type at all, they were just us on a very bad day. Still, it wasn't like me to panic like that. Maybe Cara and I were switching personalities; I was becoming a crazy lady as she sobered into death.

Any time I did lose my grip, she tended to wise up and look after me. The last time she came back, for instance. She'd spent a year vacuuming a library in Berlin, reading the spines of books, smoking so much dope that her memory was patchy afterwards. Meanwhile I was doing all right; I suspected she'd come back sooner or later. I got on with my new job at Immac, and bought myself a personal stereo; it was like a secret lover, spinning a private horizon of sound all around me. Only at Easter did I start having this recurring dream of a limitless warehouse filled with desks and chairs, through which I plodded in pursuit of Cara. At the end I'd corner her behind a desk, and she'd say, you're always shadowing me, get away from me, and then it would all go black.

My phone bill was unbelievable. 'I love you,' I would repeat, my voice abasing itself along the line.

'It doesn't help.'

'Don't you want to be loved?'

'Not this much,' growled Cara. 'Only as much as I deserve. When you walk into the room there isn't enough air for me to breathe.'

'I'm sorry.'

'Pen, what do I have to say to get you to tell me to get lost?'

She can't see my smile. 'I'll never do that,' I say. 'This is how I'm made: good at hoping.'

'Well, stop fucking well hoping.'

I didn't think either of us believed her. The phone calls were too intimate to be those of two people who will never kiss again. Sure enough, by May Cara was back in Dublin. She found me in my bedsit, watching breakfast television and unravelling a jumper every time I got the pattern wrong. We didn't discuss anything. She pulled my clothes off, starting with the socks. As she lay on my back as if on a surfboard, her breath evaporating the sweat on my nape, she whispered, 'There'll be no more leaving, you know.' And there wasn't, not in the sense she meant.

I was glad my face was turned into the pillow when she said it, so she couldn't see my expression, the odd mixture of relief and dread. Was the quest over then, was the lady won, and what would happen now? How would I recognize Cara if she was not always on the brink of leaving? How would I see her without the glint from the sword hanging over our heads? Would she relax, now, beginning to bore me at last as she thickened into some kind of wife?

I needn't have worried. Cara meant it literally: she would not leave me. But she made no guarantees about not wandering, not straying, not falling for other women. When she nipped back to Berlin for a visit the following summer – telling me, not asking me – it was brought home to me that I could never keep her in one place. She spun herself an elastic chain that allowed her any journey short of leaving me. I was not sure which way I would have preferred it, if I'd had the choice. This way she never left but often seemed beyond my reach.

The following year when the ceiling of my bedsit fell in, bruising my cheek with a lump of plaster, Cara said it was a sign. She persuaded me to stay in the big house until the ceiling was fixed, then till Christmas. The sunny front bedroom became mine, and, since her small one at the back was so full of teetering piles of paper, it was mostly in my room that we slept wrapped round each other, never raising our voices above a whisper in case Mr Wall heard us. I was the live-in long-term full-time hyphenated partner now, but Cara stayed as unwon as ever.

It amused me that it never occurred to her that I would be the leaver. We kept to our roles, like figures painted on an urn. Sometimes, yes, she would spit out some paranoid accusation, like 'I hurt you, I wear you out, you're only staying to look after me, you could just walk away and find someone nicer'. But that worked only as a rhetorical device. Both of us knew that I would never be the one to go; sometimes you just know these things.

Ever since she invited me to live with her I'd been sure that the pair of us would be together until we were ninety and as creaky as our rocking-chairs. It was not a particularly sentimental vision; I could imagine how viciously accurate our 'discussions' would be by then. But I did fancy the adventure of a lifetime's journey in this unpredictable craft.

It never occurred to me that she would slip away with the bogeyman, long before her time.

I had a suspicion that it was not purely accidental, either. Once I remembered saying to her, 'I want to grow old with you,' and she answered, 'I don't want to grow old.' Whereas I was the type who would live to be a hundred, getting bigger and bitchier and scaring small children more by the year. And if I cracked up in my thirty-first year there would be no one to save me, so I should just get a grip on myself straight away, and stop being the kind of person who vomited into public hedges. I wiped my sour mouth on the back of my hand again and started walking home. It was as hot as ever, but the sun had gone in; clouds were thickening above the city.

Crossing the bridge over the dual carriageway, I noticed a tiny plaque: 'Blithe Spirit', it said, with a set of dates that I totted up as lacking a decade of Cara's. The story suddenly came back to me: a laughing girl who'd tightroped along the handrail one night and tripped to her death in the traffic below. I traced the lettering with a fingertip. Was she drunk, or usually lucky, was that what made her try it? And what were we to do with these Achillean types, these careless losers of life, when there seemed no way of locking them up, strapping them down, forcing them to take only the risks the rest of us considered worth it?

The first drops were falling on my neck as I reached the big house. If Cara was home when I came in from school, she used to leave whatever she was doing and come to cup her mouth over my ears. It was not a big rainfall like on Monday, but a reluctant leaching of water. I went upstairs and changed out of my dusty clothes.

Pulling my shirt over my head, I heard a kind of grunt from the next room. Could Kate have been taken ill? Mouth to the wall, I said her name, but there was no answer. I pulled my shirt back on, and went and stood outside her door. It was showing a crack of light; I heard that painful sound again. When I pushed the door open, Kate's startled eyes met mine. She was lying on her back in such a contorted position that I wondered for a second if she was having a fit. Her head cradled in her hands skewed one way, her knees another; as I watched, she raised them higher and let out a careful breath. 'Just doing my exercises.'

'Right, yes. Sorry.' I backed away.

Through dinner – Mr Wall had grilled some turkey breasts into submission – the rain spattered down. I wore my black fringed shawl in an attempt to make myself feel elegant. The effect was rather like a chaperone watching the flappers do the Charleston.

The rain kept on playing on the kitchen windows as I worked my way through the paper, marking concerts and films with a leaky red biro as if this might inspire me to go to them. At five to eight I harnessed my irritation and rang my mother.

'But I finish work at four these days,' she said.

'Oh. I thought it was five. Sorry, my fault.'

'I waited till twenty-five past.'

'Ah, Mammy, I'm an eejit, sorry.' My voice was shaking so I sucked on my lips and waited.

'Are you well, anyway?'

'Oh yes,' I said, the words making a jolly arc.

'How's school?'

'Grand.'

'Is it still raining over your way?'

'Seems to be drying up a bit.'

'Getting heavier over here,' she told me.

Some evenings my mother and I had nothing to say to each other, so we talked about the weather. We should have been hired by the Met Office as a forecasting double act. As if by quantifying a thin sheet of snow, or counting the seconds between lightning and thunder, we could get through the distance between us.

Kate stood in the hall as I was saying a protracted goodnight to my mother. I stared at her, but she didn't move. When I finally put the phone down, she said, 'I don't suppose you fancy a drive?'

'In the rain?'

'It's stopped.'

'So it has,' I said, looking out the window over the stairs. 'Does it get you down?'

'The rain? It's a relief from the heat.'

'I suppose sun's not what you came to Ireland for.'

'No.' Kate stayed where she was, leaning against the coat cupboard.

'What have you been up to all day?' I asked her, suddenly guilty about my deficiencies as a hostess.

'Oh, you know. Reading reports. Watched a political documentary; I'd forgotten how much better British TV was.'

'The house closes in a bit sometimes, doesn't it?'

'Yeah.' She smiled back.

Grace ran out of the kitchen, stopped short when he saw us, and slunk back in again. 'He gets restless in the evenings,' I explained.

'Has he always been like this?'

'I've noticed it more since his operation. He probably resents us for making him a eunuch.'

'Right.'

And suddenly I couldn't bear this woman to be so brittle, so ill at ease in her own family home. 'Come on, let's go for a spin.'

Kate's face brightened. 'Unless you had something to do?'

'Not a thing.' What were any of us doing this week except killing time? I busied myself finding a raincoat and my keys. My crow-headed umbrella was missing; finally I remembered that I had lent it to Jo.

As soon as we reached the car I said, 'Damn. She wouldn't budge this morning; there must be something wrong with the starter motor.'

'Give it a try.'

Against all logic, Minnie burst into life the minute I

turned the key. As I was backing out, I paused in the gateway. 'I never thought to ask your father to join us.'

She didn't respond.

'But I think he was listening to something on Radio 4,' I invented, and wheeled on to the road.

'We could go to that pier,' suggested Kate. 'Can't think of the name. You know, the one down by the sea.'

'Not like all the other, landlocked piers,' I commented under my breath.

A good savoury laugh she had. 'Fair point. I mean the long one, where Dad always used to take us on Sunday afternoons.'

I smiled to think how little Mr Wall had changed in his ways, and turned on to the road to Dun Laoghaire. 'Do you remember the neighbourhood much?' I asked her. 'Or is it all gone?'

'Bits,' said Kate.

'Like?'

A few seconds passed; it was like prising open a tin of old paint. 'This overhead bridge, say' – she pointed through the windscreen – 'I remember Cara nicked the hood off my school gaberdine and ran up here and dropped it over.'

'The brat!'

'There were all these muddy tracks from the trucks across it by the time she picked it up. I made her wash it and dry it with Mum's hairdryer, but it was never the same.'

'Did she do it for devilment or to pay you back for something?'

'No idea,' said Kate, from a distance. A new sandstone wall went by in the window, then a private clinic surrounded by young trees, then one of a chain of pizzerias with a grinning neon face on the side. I tried to watch it all flow by through her eyes.

'So,' she said at last, in the tone of voice used for resuming a confidential conversation. 'Thirteen years, then, if you got together the year after we left. If you don't mind talking about it . . .'

'No, that's fine. Not talking wouldn't keep me from think-ing, so I might as well talk.'

'Suppose so.'

'There were plenty of gaps, though,' I told her, keeping my eye on the road. 'Cara left me for men a couple of times in the early years.'

'A couple of times?' I could hear the rebuke in Kate's voice.

'It did her good,' I added brightly. 'She always said it was her scars that had turned her into a serious feminist.'

'Real scars?'

'Well, all I remember is one little burn mark between her finger and thumb, from when Roderick bellowed at her as she was lifting a vegetarian lasagne out of the oven. I laughed at it once, and she said that if I trivialized male abuse I was complicit with the patriarchy.'

Kate hoisted herself in her seat to straighten her trench-coat. 'Did she always talk that way?'

'Nah, she put it on for special occasions.'

'I'm rather glad I never met the grown-up Cara. I'd have told her she was full of shit.'

'I didn't think corporate people used such language,' I murmured.

'I didn't think grade-school teachers were . . . a bit like you.'

I took my eyes off the road for a moment, amused by the euphemism, but she was looking away. 'And what would Cara have said if she'd met the grown-up Kate?'

'No idea,' she said uncomfortably. 'Possibly she'd have thought I was full of . . . a different kind of shit. We were never exactly bosom buddies.'

'Ah, you never know how well you might have got on, once you were past the adolescent hormones.'

'Yeah, well, never know is right.'

That put a lid on the conversation for a good half-mile. Kate stared out the window at the footpath going by, its wet patches lightening as they dried. What I really wanted to ask was, if she couldn't care less about her sister, what was she doing back in Dublin? But I supposed the fact that she was here meant that she had to care, on some subterranean level.

Just as we were locking the car doors, the wind changed, making my eyes water. We made it along the pier as far as the first set of slippery steps down to the boats before it started to rain again. Two girls hurried past in sleeveless T-shirts, their shoulders striped with sun. 'Yeah, but no matter how happy . . .' I heard one of them say, before their conversation was out of earshot. I fought back the impulse to run after them and ask who was so happy, and what negative was to follow?

Kate's brown eyes turned to me; she huddled in her jacket. 'So when did Cara come back to you for good?'

For better, for worse, in sickness and in health . . . 'Eighty-seven, I think it was. I moved in the next year.'

She absorbed this for a minute. The last splinter of sunlight was digging into the sea; the lighthouse was starting its periodic wink. The drops were getting bigger, so we turned back by silent consensus. A dog went by with its rain-hatted owner, straining at the leash and scrabbling on the wet granite. We climbed back into Minnie and sat looking out through the windshield.

Then, as I turned on the wipers, some perversity made me add, 'Of course we still had our ups and downs. For a while, when she was seeing this girl in Kilkenny . . .'

'Seeing?' asked Kate, as if the word was new to her.

'Sleeping with.'

'What, you mean while she was – while you and her –'

'I gather Boston is the last bastion of absolute monogamy,' I put into the strangulated silence.

'No, but – just, if my sister was cheating on you –'

'Oh, stop it,' I spat, staring into the rain. 'Why do hets always call it cheating? A relationship that's negotiated in a civilized and honest way to allow for the occasional other sexual partner is hardly the same as one of your grubby little

200

bits on the side.' I choked myself off at that point, before I could say anything worse. Three slow breaths. 'Sorry,' I added, turning off the windscreen wipers. 'That was totally out of order.'

'No,' said Kate, 'I was tactless.'

'No,' I told her, 'I'm taking things out on you that are nothing to do with you.' The rain brimmed freely on the glass now. I cleared my throat with a roar that seemed to fill the car. 'As you may have gathered, you got me on a sore point.'

'Yeah, well, it's a sore point for everybody,' she said.

After a long minute, wondering if she had a story to tell, I went on, 'Cara and I were honest, at least, but I can't claim it was always civilized.'

She nodded.

'So if you're wondering how I put up with it, well, it was still a lot better than anything else around. I like a challenge,' I went on rather frantically, 'and I liked Cara, and I liked who she was when she came back from travelling. You know what I mean?'

'Not really,' said Kate.

I sighed. 'She wasn't somebody you'd want to restrict to just one of their selves.'

'Right,' she said flatly.

'And I figured I'd just have to get used to the fact that people don't stay still. You left and never came back, didn't you? At least Cara kept coming back.'

'Do you think Cara minded that I stayed away?' said Kate, her voice going off on a tangent.

'Sometimes,' I said wearily. If it hadn't occurred to her that anyone else minded, I wasn't going to be the one to tell her.

'When I'd been in Ohio a year, I really wasn't the same person any more,' she went on. 'All I really remembered about Cara was that horribly clean podgy look of hers.' She was staring out the window, as if making out her sister's features on the rain-blotted tarmac of the car park.

'But she's a skinnymalinks.'

'She had lots of puppyfat before puberty stretched her out. I remember when she was small we tried to teach her to use the phone, because she was scared of it. Mom wrapped Cara's pudgy fingers round the receiver and gave her a nudge, and you know what she said?'

'Hi?' I suggested.

Kate's voice sounded caged in her throat. 'She said, "Hello, is this me?" That sums Cara up; always had to be different. I get, I used to get so irritated with her.'

'You still do,' I pointed out after a second.

She was staring down at her hands. 'It doesn't seem decent now.' After a minute, 'It's normal to be like that when you're kids. Cara had a face like, like a balloon, you know?'

'Red and round?'

'Bright. Easily deflated. I used to long to prick it, but I was always sorry when I did.'

'I know what that's like,' I told her.

'Yeah?' Kate's eyes met mine, amused. 'I suppose if you knew her for nearly as many years as I did, you must have got to know her weak spots.'

'A few,' I admitted. 'Though Cara was much quicker with the needle.'

'Only if you let her. What really bugged me was when she'd get all mushy and go on about loving things,' said Kate. Her voice rose to a whine of imitation: '"I love Mammy and I love Daddy and I love Cáit and I love God." "Get into bed this minute," I used to say, "or the rug'll eat you."'

'So you're the one who told her the rug came alive at night?'

Kate looked slightly sheepish. 'She wasn't meant to believe it.'

'Took her years of therapy to get over that one,' I said with a theatrical sigh.

The whine began again: '"I love rhubarb and I love jam and I love when the leaves go red . . ."'

'Yeah, well, love was a bit of a hobby of hers.'

Neither of us could think of anything to say after that. I started the wipers again, and turned on the engine. By the time we got home, the sky seemed to have drained itself. I listened to Minnie's engine cool, suddenly too lethargic to undo my seat-belt. 'The house must strike you as awful shabby,' I commented. 'We haven't done much with it for the last few years.'

'No, it's pretty much how I remember it,' said Kate, staring through the windscreen at the garden wall. 'It's a losing battle, keeping a house up. I used to have to paint that lumpy wall every few summers.'

'It soaks up gallons of paint, doesn't it?'

'It's a monster. One year I tried to liven the job up by turning up Pink Floyd on the radio so I could hear it out the window, but Dad said did I mind, he thought it might bring on one of his headaches.'

'He gets them bad, you know,' I said with a hint of reproach.

'It's his sedentary lifestyle. Librarian's blight.'

I was worn out myself; it seemed a year since I had set out to school this morning. I went into the house without a word, leaving the door open for Kate. It was not ten yet, but I thought if I went to bed straight away, I might be able to catch sleep before it sidled away.

Clothes were strewn around the bedroom, and the curtains had been half-closed for days now. Cara would laugh at me for becoming a bigger slob than she ever was. The horrible possibility occurred to me that I had to be both of us now: my own messer and tidier, rebel and nag, a little bit of everything.

Please, Lord, let me sleep tonight. I knew I had to grow and change and expand, but I was so tired I couldn't face it. Grant me spiritual enlightenment through pain, sure, Lord, grand, you're on, but not tonight.

I decided to put my clothes away at least; I felt ugly enough these days without going round as crumpled as a bag-lady. I stooped to pick up the black silk shirt I had worn to the funeral. How many handwashes before it would be cleaned of that association? How faded would it have to be before I would think of it merely as my black silk shirt, or that old thing, rather than as the shirt I wore to Cara's funeral? I was checking the pockets when I remembered the hair I found yesterday, down by the gear-stick. It was still there, curled on my fingers when I lifted them out of the silk. In this light it looked brown; it took sun to bring out the sparkle of ruby. I held on to it, pulling gently. So strong for such a thin thing. Where could I put it so I wouldn't lose it? If I laid it on the bedside table it was sure to get swept away by an elbow. I had no locket, and besides, I needed to touch it, not just to know it was there.

I pulled it over my lips; it was an invisible finger, calling the nerves to life. The reading lamp over the bed, that would do; I tied the hair around its narrow metal base. Clean and springy, it tried to slide out of the loop. I tied it in a double knot, then a triple, and secured it with a triangle of tape. Last thing before turning off the light, I reached up and the hair tickled the pad of my finger. For a second I tugged on it like some kind of bell-cord.

I dream of a tower, a cascade of red hair which I am climbing, clinging to the delicate strands which break off in my hands as my feet struggle to find a purchase on such slipperiness. I am about a third of the way up, and can see no face at the window. Is she there at all, or is this just a wig tied to a bar? I hear voices, one deeper than the other. I keep climbing.

And then the sound of a horse and harness jingling, and a rider comes by, pausing at the foot of the tower where the long mane of hair heaves like a dying snake. Face upturned, disdainful in the moonlight, the rider who is Kate puts back her hood and spits at me.

I woke gradually, my stomach tight with tension. It was still dark; I hadn't made it to dawn, then. I watched the clock's green fluorescent fingertips resolve themselves into ten to twelve. All at once I couldn't bear to lie there, a prisoner thirsting for the royal reprieve of sleep. I got up; my foot landed on the cool surface of a book before I kicked it away. I supposed I could always sit downstairs in my dressing-gown and drink cocoa; that was what they did in the TV movies, and it seemed to help. But mostly, it occurred to me, because on TV small children came in and climbed on your knee and offered unknowing words of comfort. I could not imagine Mr Wall coming in and sitting on my knee.

Walking back from the bathroom, rubbing the dust from my eyes, I caught sight of the half-moon out the window. It was irregular and translucent, like a slice of some newly discovered fruit. My mouth imagined how cool and crisp it would be to bite.

I hauled on layers of clothing and my anorak over it all. I was startled to find Mr Wall in the kitchen. He peered up: 'Oh good lord, I thought you were a burglar, in that coat.'

'Just fancied a bit of air.'

He was looking down again at the stiff page of the photo album held between his finger and thumb. I waited a few seconds, rather stifled in all my gear. I was just shifting my weight towards the door when Mr Wall said, without looking up, 'This is a good one.'

I went and looked over his shoulder. His index finger – knobbly, the skin dry beside the white nail – pointed to a sixties snapshot of two girls in an inflatable paddling pool. The darker had to be Kate; the smaller had her pale face turned up to the sun. Mr Wall turned a few heavily encrusted pages – past the gap with four tape-marks from the photo I stole – and gestured at another one of Cara, longlegged in bell-bottoms, slouching against the garden wall. 'I had no idea what to do with a growing girl like her after the separation.'

I couldn't think what to say, so made a little sound of interest.

'I fear I am a dull person to live with,' said Mr Wall. I could tell he was not fishing for a compliment. 'Then you came along,' he went on, 'and made her much happier.'

I kept my eyes on the picture, tracing the pattern of ivy along the wall that needed repainting. 'Not sure I did, not all the time.'

'Oh, Cara was her mother's daughter. She could never have been happy all the time.'

He didn't know, I was sure of it. I'd been eating off his table for four years now, and the poor sucker thought I was a good influence. 'I'm off out,' I said, too loudly, the words booming round the shadowy kitchen.

'What, at this time of night?'

'I'll be fine.'

My voice must have been sharper than I meant, because he nodded fearfully and bent his head over the albums again. I paused at the door but could think of nothing nice to say. Maybe I should have asked him to come with me, but I didn't want to.

I let myself out, pulling the front door behind me very softly in case it woke Kate. The clouds had cleared, the air was drying. I meant to stick to the well-lit roads around the woods, but the streetlights dazzled my eyes. When I came to the side entrance I slipped in around the steel stile. As the last orange bulb disappeared behind a great trunk, the stars spread themselves above me. I had never seen them so clear before, a huge join-the-dots puzzle for the eyes. Why had I never come up here at night before? What timid creatures we were with our baths and cocoa and bedside books.

Below me a row of houses underlined the glittering skyline of the Dublin suburbs. A telephone wire, curved like a gondola, seemed to carry a floating load of dark yellow lights. I kept to the path at first; if any of those blotches of darkness resolved themselves into an attacker I supposed I could always run for it and scream until the people in the nearest house heard me. I pulled my anorak hood down on my shoulders so I wouldn't be surprised from behind. These were all habits; I did not seriously believe that anyone else was up here at half past midnight, nor that anything they could do to me could make my life much worse.

A stunted silver birch caught my eye; I strayed from the path to the tree's muddy outskirts, and stroked its side. I wandered to the next, and the next, unnamed grey ones with slow muscles and knotted joints. It was almost bright here; I could see the difference between mud and grass. The street-lights had all disappeared behind the clump of rocks, so it had to be moonlight I was seeing by. Three stars hung in a row with a long line below them; I could never remember if this was Orion or the Plough. I wondered whether Cara had ever come up here at night and seen the stars. It would have been nice to have shown them to her, but I suspected she would have insisted on talking about them. The ideal companion would be silent.

I would have liked to meet someone up here, just by chance. I would be standing with my neck uncomfortably craned to see the Pleiades – I had no notion what those ones looked like, but I adored the name – when I would become gradually aware of a figure to one side of me. We would look across the small clearing, nervous at first, then, having decided that we were both women, exchange a small smile. Our faces would seem to float in the moonlight. We would stay looking upwards, our feet shifting us from one tree to the next. The two of us might end up crouched at the foot of the same tree, looking different ways. Not a word would be exchanged. There would be nothing domestic about such romance.

Cara comes back from an extramural course on French feminism one evening, full of metaphorical sites of otherness and the topos of phallogocentrism, at which point I laugh until she has to cover my mouth with hers to shut me up. She has a quote on a card, she reads it aloud in a careful accent. 'Tout sera changé lorsque la femme donnera la femme à l'autre femme.'

'What the hell is that supposed to mean?' I ask, kneeling over the fire to poke it up a little.

'Everything will change when woman gives woman to the other woman.'

'I know what the words mean,' I tell her scathingly, 'I just don't understand it. Who is this other woman?'

'Any of us,' says Cara, with a yawn, settling back into the cushions.

'I might find it easier to give woman to the other woman if I knew either of their names.'

'You're taking it too literally, you're missing the point.'

'No I'm not. What is the point, then?'

'If you're going to be . . .'

'Come on, Cara, just tell me what you think it means.'

'All right.' She glances down at the card again, to check. 'The point is the giving.'

'Ah, sure I know that much.' The smell of coal clings to my fingers.

'Look, maybe it's like one of those riddles: what is it, that the more you give away the more you have?'

'So I'm supposed to say "love", am I?'

Cara turns her face away. 'There's no one answer.'

'It's not true, you know,' I tell her, throwing another knob of coal on the flames. 'The more you give away, the more you've given away.'

I found myself holding on to a tree, my hand gripping its corrugated bark. How long was I going to put myself through these rehashed re-runs of old arguments? I should just accept the fact that Cara and I had not always agreed, had not always understood each other, had not always liked what we did understand. Though we probably understood each other better in the fourteenth year than in the first, though we had both grown up somewhat, though we had made more of the necessary adjustments and were therefore officially happier, I was far from sure that it was a success story. Sometimes I suspected that what had really happened was that we became more resigned, more cynical, raised our pain thresholds as we lowered our expectations. All in all, settled for less.

We shouldn't have talked so much, it occurred to me now; we should just have fucked our brains out. Because the memories left over from that were simple: no narrative, few details, just a blur of bliss across the brain.

Why didn't we ever come up here at night and make love under the stars? All those wasted opportunities. If we'd known she was going to die young we'd have got around to everything. Once, in the twilight, we nearly did it. We were lying together behind the rocks in our long coats, beginning to feel the internal music. I was leaning up on one elbow, angled over Cara, my mouth hovering above her eyelids, when a straight couple walked by. We kept our faces together and didn't move. 'We'll be all right if one of us looks like a boy,' whispered Cara. 'But not both,' she added as an afterthought, 'we're buggered if we both do.' And then at that word we got the giggles, of course, and lay there shaking until the couple were out of sight.

But that was early evening, and this was night, and the woods were not safe territory. I felt in my coat pocket and realized that I wasn't even carrying my steel-handled comb, I'd left it in my bag. I turned and strode off across the muddy grass, trying to send out signals of confidence and bulk. My heels kept slipping on the spongy ground. I put my thumb and finger to either side of my little gold galleon and held on, the chain sharp along my sunburnt neck.

As soon as I got on to the road, the streetlight's glare dimmed the stars. I felt the familiar anger at being driven out. A breeze was picking up, raising goose-bumps on the back of my wrists. I set off down the hill through the church car park, pacing out one giant C on the tarmac to finish off the night.

FRIDAY

I need it to happen soon, yet I want this feeling to last. If it doesn't happen now I may weep with exhaustion, but I want to give up every volt of energy I have. I want it, I need it, I can't think of anything else, but I have to wait till she gives it to me. I want it to end, but not till the very last possible minute.

I heave once, like a dying animal. My forehead smashes against the headboard. My mouth opens wide. I pull Cara's hand away, holding her soaked fingers still. Our bodies are stuck together like the pages of a book left out in the rain.

After a little while, she says, 'That was yum. Can we watch *Northern Exposure* now?'

The trick was to get up quickly. I shook the dream from my head, swung back the duvet and planted my feet on the floor. The first thing that struck me was the cold; no sunshine today. Exhausting as it had been, I found I missed it; I wasn't ready for winter yet.

Only when I had brushed my teeth and splashed cold water on my face did I look at my watch and interpret the hands as a quarter to seven; I didn't need to be up for another hour. I got back into bed and pulled the quilt over my head. The sheets had cooled already, enclosing me in a cocoon of chilly air.

Let's be honest: I didn't like being in bed on my own. Nearly all the times I was, I was waiting for Cara. Sometimes if she was far away being political or sociable, I used to wrap up in myself like a whale in deep waters, enjoying the respite. Other times it was hell frozen over. The jealousy that choked me on occasion wasn't really about sex; I couldn't imagine her having a better time in bed with anyone else than we had. Nor was it about possession exactly; Cara could never be owned by anyone, the way (though it's against the rules to say so nowadays) some people can. No, it was more like a fear that whoever Cara was with on a particular night would turn out to be so interesting that she'd never come home.

Having fallen for Cara in the context of her infatuation with someone else, I could hardly have expected this to be a conventional relationship. Mrs Mew (a woman with too much mascara who, though I never admitted it to Cara, I had never liked) was the key, the catalyst, the flagpole on which we hung out our days. And after Mrs Mew there were the others, one at a time, all in a row, a sort of emotional orienteering course. Once when she was doing a play at college, Cara met me for cherry buns and said glumly, 'I think I may be falling for Jenny.'

'Which one's Jenny?'

'You know, the one who plays the waitress. I suppose we're going to have to break up again.'

Suddenly I felt like changing the script. 'Nah, let's not bother.'

'Huh?'

'You can fall for who you like but it doesn't change what we have.'

Cara said I was unutterably wonderful. She said that no matter how her heart hurtled towards someone she always knew deep down that it was a loop away from the central point, the Pen thing.

And in fact she never really fell for Jenny; it blew over in a few weeks. Her unrequited loves were easy enough to handle. And when she left me for men, the issue was not jealousy so much as loss. What were harder to deal with later on, when I was living with her, were the times when she got lucky and slept with a woman who requited her lust.

It wasn't so much the sex Cara needed as the sense of freedom, of unconstrained possibilities. Her rhetoric could always convince me that having a wee fling now and then was the best way to keep a long-term relationship alive. 'Even when I'm with other women,' she told me once, 'I belong to you.'

'You're too flighty to belong to anyone,' I answered, chewing on her earlobe.

'Well, but if I was anybody's I'd be yours.'

I believed her. I let her stand on my broad feet and lick my eyebrows. I was happy most of the time.

There were bad nights. I remembered the first time, the night I lay awake knowing she was in Kilkenny. It wasn't that I imagined their lovemaking inch by inch or anything; I just felt so completely alone. But Cara got the train back early the next afternoon and came home on the bus with her pockets full of Cape gooseberries from an exotic fruiterer in town. We pulled their webs off one by one, popping the yellow balls into each other's mouths. When we were lying in a bathful of dark water, with our breathing synchronized, I knew no jealousy.

Another time, Cara ran up to me with a paperback, and pointed. I read out loud: 'It's possible to see where Melanie used to live . . .'

'No, higher up.' She grabbed the book. 'By betrayal,' she recited, 'I mean promising to be on your side, then being on somebody else's.' Cara paused for a reaction. 'Well, I don't do that,' she explained. 'I'm always on your side, I'm just not always in your bed.' Put that way, it sounded fair enough.

But sometimes when I was alone in the big house at night and the wind made the panes rattle, I forgot the explanations, and I was three years old. My mother once said the worst thing about having children was that when she went into the cubicle of a public toilet, we would begin to snivel, and while she was struggling with her zip she would see these little hands come under the door, and would get an overpowering urge to stamp on them. I could understand that, but I could also understand the kind of abased neediness that motivated Gavin and me to put our hands under the door.

In the early days of our negotiations, Cara used to want to share every detail. 'Half the fun would be running back to tell you about it,' she'd say wistfully. But I knew my limits, and I knew that if she told me all about what she did with whom, my ears would burst. I could handle hearing who she'd slept with in another town far away, and that it was 'nice' or 'OKish', but any more vivid details tended to form themselves into a video that played itself through my head at top speed on the nights I couldn't sleep. And of late I had stopped asking her exactly who, either. I found it was easier to hear her enthuse about various people and make my own deductions. I adopted this policy the day Cara responded to some strained question with 'Do you honestly want to know, love?' and I realized that I didn't.

I developed a taste for discretion – an outmoded concept, I knew, but maybe I was Mr Wall's true daughter, and Cara and I had been switched at birth. This way I had more of a sense of privacy and control than some blaringly 'open' relationship would have given me. This way I was the girlfriend, the lover, the partner. It was important to me not to feel upstaged, if we all bumped into each other in the street. And to be fair to her, Cara kept to other unwritten rules as well, such as: don't bring anyone else to the big house, don't make me beg for your time, don't bring me to a party and go home with somebody else. She never fell madly in love with these women, and if they ever began falling madly in love with her, she wriggled away. I remembered overhearing a snatch of a final fraught call from the woman in Kilkenny. It surprised me how well my clumsy beloved learned this balancing act, keeping her dalliances (as I called them in my head) well in the background.

So much so that I had never got around to finding out which of the women in the Attic she was sleeping with this summer, the odd night when she stayed over there after 'missing the last bus'. I hadn't thought there was much to choose between them, with their torn woolly jumpers and home-grown yoghurt; it hadn't seemed too important as long as she was alive. Cara always came home to me by lunchtime. Wasn't that the important thing?

Sometimes it got to the point where it didn't feel like love. No liking or bliss to it, some days, just a feeling of connection so sinewy and enduring that I could not consider doing without it.

Twenty to eight; I swung my legs out of bed again. This whole day had a feeling of déjà vu. My 'To Do' list hung on the cork board, mocking my inertia. I picked up a pencil to add 'laundry', and the sharp tip tore into the paper; I let it rip right through.

More mass cards had arrived. Mr Wall (who seemed to be getting up earlier and earlier, since the smooth sides of the kettle were only barely warm after him now) had arranged them on the mantelpiece like Christmas cards. He probably didn't mean to be macabre. Listening to the radio distracted me from the toast I was grinding through. The forecast said it would heat up again later; I went to look for my swimsuit. I bumped into Kate on the stairs. She looked at the crumpled green togs in my hand. 'I'm going swimming after school,' I said almost guiltily. 'D'you fancy coming?'

She was looking pale again, behind her tan. 'I'd love to, but I've no suit.'

'Oh, I'll find you one of Cara's. Unless . . .'

'No, that's fine,' said Kate hastily.

I couldn't discover the swimsuit in any of the overstuffed drawers in Cara's room, then I remembered that she would have brought it to Greece. I pulled the suitcase out from under the bed and zipped it open for the first time. Luckily the togs were on top, angel-blue in a tangle. When I held them to my face they smelt not of Cara but of salt. I had an impulse to keep them in my pocket, a slice of the Aegean for when I needed it. I didn't want to give them to Kate to stretch out of shape and stink up with chlorine. But she called from downstairs, so I inhaled again briefly and carried them down.

Grace was on the table, nosing at the milk left in Kate's

bowl of cereal. I pushed him gently, twice in a row, then picked him up to lift him away. He lunged at me, claws catching my throat. I dropped him and swore. Mr Wall came into the kitchen just then; I felt ashamed and contented myself with hissing as I rubbed the skin. He fetched me some antiseptic from the first aid box in the cupboard under the stairs. Grace sat by the cat-flap, scowling as if to blackmail us with his imminent departure.

On the way to Immac my abdomen felt leaden, with the occasional spasm; I wondered whether it was grief, or something I'd eaten. It was calming down by the time I got into the classroom. Ten minutes early. I wandered round reading all the tired posters for the nth time: The Proclamation of the Republic in 1916 offering to 'cherish all the children of the nation equally', the Road Safety Bureau's informational cartoon strip, and a chart of common woodland flowers.

I had just enough time to comb my hair in the staff toilet. In the mirror I looked just the same as ever; my mouth curled pleasantly at the corners. No one could tell at a glance that there was anything wrong with me. The wolf had eaten me up and was walking the corridors in my cardigan and lace-up shoes, burping softly so no one would notice.

I passed Robbie on the stairs; he held on to my sleeve with one hand and started scrabbling in his tartan satchel with the other. 'Got something for you.'

I waited. What kind of present do you give on such occasions? Not a mass card, surely, not from a Glaswegian agnostic.

He pulled out a smartly striped paper bag. There was a book in it; he scraped at the price label with his long guitar nail. 'Sorry, just a sec. I picked this up in town yesterday.'

The cover featured a woman in a lavender dress, her hands sunk deep into the pockets, strolling along a mountain path. *Finding Yourself on Your Own*, it proclaimed. Who else is going to help you to find yourself, I thought, then registered the subtitle in pale letters: *A Guide for the Widowed*. Robbie rushed to reassure me: 'It's not an Irish book. It covers all sorts of . . . partnerships. There's a section on' – before I could clap a hand across his mouth his eyes had swivelled to Sister Luke, descending the steps one at a time above us like a well-fed angel – 'your line of business.'

I could not keep a slight smile off my mouth.

'Sorry,' whispered Robbie. 'I don't mean to sound patronizing.'

'Thanks very much. I'll definitely give it a read,' I promised him, putting it back in the bag as Sister Luke passed us. Then a queue of little girls in tracksuits began to back up behind us, so I let him go.

My class were brats this morning. Lucy Parkes had got a paperclip caught in her fringe and couldn't get it out, and no fewer than three of them claimed to have done their Irish grammar but left it at home. No one could remember the past continuous. Saoirse Mullan kept mixing up *againn* and *agaibh* like a four-year-old. I hauled them through the exercises till ten past ten, my patience fraying away strand by strand like a rope in an Alpine thriller.

'Please, Miss O'Grady, can I go –'

'*As Gaeilge*, Deirdre.'

'*An bhfuil cead agam dul go dtí an leithreas?*' And before I'd given permission off skipped Deirdre Summers to the bathroom, where she'd probably spend ten minutes at the mirror admiring her hives. Brona Tyrrel claimed to be 'bursting' too, but they were pals, so I made her sit still till Deirdre dawdled back. So this was what my four years of educational psychology had trained me for: the distribution of toilet privileges.

The clock hand seemed to stop moving round twenty to eleven. Several times I was convinced it had broken, but then it would make another minuscule shift, as if twitching in its sleep. My eyes refocused to find Deirdre Summers with her hand on the door. 'Where, may I ask –' (It was funny how primary teaching brought the Mrs Thatcher out in all of us.)

'Cut myself, Miss, I'm bleeding, can I go and wash it,' she gabbled, holding up a finger so deeply gashed with red that I thought she must have driven a compass right in. Then I beckoned her over.

'Ah please, Miss, it hurts . . .'

My chair made a screech on the parquet as I pushed it back and walked over. Up close it was red biro, leaked all over Deirdre's fingers twisting in mine. The girls nearest us were giggling nervously. I looked into Deirdre's eyes, and opened my mouth.

'Get to fuck out of my sight you stupid little bastard, if you ever do lose a finger it'll be better than you deserve. How dare you waste my time with your amateur theatrics when the woman I love is rotting in Glasnevin?'

I hadn't said it. My throat had knotted to throttle the words as they emerged. I hadn't said a thing. Deirdre's gaze had wandered to her mates; she was starting to snigger. I let her fingers slip out of my hand. My whole body ached for the satisfying sound of hand smacking cheek.

'Go back to your seat, please,' I told her.

The class seemed unnerved by my politeness. They stayed hushed as I sat back down behind the fortress of the teacher's desk and told them to read the story of Fionn and his dog quietly to themselves.

'Would you do something for me?' Cara's voice is almost lost in the pillow. We are making spoons on the bed in late winter, my body's wool and denim shadowing hers as far as her calves, where my legs run out.

'Sure. Probably.'

'Would you slap me?'

I stare at the back of her neck. It is too close to focus on but with my nose I can feel each tiny hair at the nape. Cara turns her head, to check whether I heard her. 'No way,' I whisper.

'Please.'

I shut my eyes and burrow my face into the cavern between her neck and the sheet.

'Ah, go on. All I need is one sharp slap to knock me out of this low.'

I wish my ears had a way of shutting.

Cara twists like a flounder, until her nose is against my eye. 'PenPal? Please? Bet you've wanted to, sometimes.'

'Never. You've been watching too many old movies,' I say lightly. 'Slapping doesn't bring anyone to their senses.'

'It might. Ah, come on, just once, as a favour.'

'No,' I say into the pillow. 'Go hit your head off a wall if you want to.'

An upheaval of wool, and she is sitting against the head-board. 'Fine then, retreat to your high moral ground as per bloody usual.'

'It's not that.' Cara's back is curved like a boulder. 'I just don't want to hurt you,' I plead, leaning up on one elbow.

'Physically, you mean.'

I ignore that. 'I'll do anything else to cheer you up . . .'

'But you won't give me what I want.'

'Ah pet, you can't really want to be hit.'

'I asked for one wee slap to break this mood, that's all,' her voice rising to a squeak, 'we're not talking major maso-chism here. But god forbid I should know what I want. God forbid you should have to treat me like an adult once in a while.'

'Then act like one,' I say, rolling upright.

'You're just afraid of doing anything that might sting your conscience.' Cara spits the words over her shoulder.

'Well, yes, if you mean I'm not going to behave like a shite just to keep you company.' Then I falter. 'Ah sweetheart, let's not be like this.'

Her eyes turn on me, cold as gravel. 'You know,' she drawls, 'we'd get on so much better if you had the guts to hate me a little.'

I lean my eyelids on my knees.

'Your love is so relentless.'

I'm making stars.

'I don't have to work for it or earn it,' Cara goes on. Her

voice lifts as an idea strikes her: 'I know what it's like, it's like the free milk cartons we used to get at school. Sometimes I want it and sometimes I don't want it but it's just sitting there every morning, so sometimes I stamp on it.'

What saves me is a tear, leaked from the corner of my eye. She sees it and bends to absorb it into her lips. 'Ah, PenUmbra, don't cry. The milk is the best thing for me. And when I get around to drinking it, it does taste lovely.'

I hope more tears will come but they don't. Cara cradles me anyway, rocking my tight frame back and forward. I say nothing, for fear of provoking her. She kisses her way from my crow's feet to the hollow of my ear. Then she disengages to sit upright and yawn. 'Sometimes,' she says, 'I walk around college and pretend I'm free.'

'Free?' I ask.

'Of you.'

I press my wet face back into my knees before she can see it.

'Ah would you stop wincing at everything I say. You know not to take me seriously when I'm in a low.'

'Yes,' I say hoarsely, 'but telling me not to take you seriously might be just part of the low. Where does the mood end and the you begin? How do I know which Caras are real?'

'None of us,' she jokes, planting on my ear a kiss so loud it deafens me.

We lace up our shoes.

I lied when I told Cara I never wanted to slap her. Sometimes when I was making love to her I did. When her face was all distraught with pleasure, her throat bent back gaping for breath, I would occasionally be overtaken by rage. For a fraction of a second I would find myself wanting to slap her eyes shut, press a pillow over her face, throw her off the bed. But most of all I wanted to stop what I was doing, to simply withdraw my hand and see how Cara would react. Because what she was panting for was mine to refuse. What she needed I needn't give.

I never did stop, of course; the tenderness always came back and kept me moving. But what if it was the thought that counted?

'Miss O'Grady?'

I stared down at Saoirse Mullan, at the apple and buttered cracker held to her chest.

'It's breaktime now, Miss. The bell went ages ago.'

'Thank you.' I didn't stir till she was gone.

I sat in the staff-room, as far as possible from the Geography teacher's dangled cigarette. *Finding Yourself on Your Own* was poking out of my satchel. The British price was clearly printed below the sticker he had scraped off; what a dote Robbie was, shelling out well over a tenner for a guide-book to see me through this. I took it out for a quick flick, keeping it angled down so no one would read the cover. I decided I could not bear the sympathetic address of the preface, so I skipped straight on to a cross-cultural survey of funeral practices. Orthodox Jews, I learned, sit on low stools for seven days without washing, eating only boiled eggs and salt fish. It sounded like a recipe for depression, but I supposed it was surreal enough to be appropriate; what was really absurd was any attempt to carry on life as normal.

Stages of mourning, offered the next chapter; I'd heard about these. Numbness, anger, regret, loss, taking up to three years, it said. What, nine months each, a full swelling and birthing of each, or did they overlap? Or was numbness just the opener, before a three-year storm of the others? I didn't see how on earth you could time such things. Maybe after three years the participants in the study just got sick of reporting the same old symptoms. Maybe they didn't even notice them any more, having forgotten they ever felt other than numb, angry, regretful and lost.

Let's see how far I'd got: was I a good girl, as bereaved people went? I seemed to have run through numbness rather quickly. You couldn't spend many days not feeling the grief at all, unless you were skilled at living on another planet or had some very powerful plants in the garden. Maybe I had a partial numbness, a bandage to slow the bleeding. Then anger; well, my anger with the driver of the car that crashed into the taxi was limited by the fact that he was dead now. I supposed I was angry with Cara for having a rackety lifestyle so full of travel that the odds of getting killed in a road accident were high. But then again, I was often angry with her when she was alive, so that couldn't be a symptom of mourning. How about regret, then? Perhaps I had leapt straight to stage three in my first week. No, regret was nothing new either. This was ludicrous, I was getting the stages all wrong. Loss, yes, that was a good simple word for it. If I was doing numbness and loss together, with a bit of denial (that was another one to fit in), that explained why I was still able to go about my daily life and get some pleasure from watching telly. And what about terror, which I felt every time I woke? Damn the experts and their stages and their emotional clocks; this thing was such a mess, no one could impose order on it.

Loyal to the bell, I heaved myself out of the armchair and walked back to my class. Line by stumbled, mispronounced line we read our way through an extract from a novel about a boy fleeing Cromwell. I amused myself by guessing the questions that would be asked at the end of the text on the next page: definites included 'Where and when does this story take place?' and 'Which adjectives are used to show how evil the Lord Protector is?' I moved quickly on from Lorna Mulcahy, who never had a word out of place, to Sinéad Green, who had to learn to stop taking a breath in the middle of a clause. I turned over the page, and there it was in faint pencil between two lines of print: *I love you, big thing.*

Panic grabbed me by the throat and squeezed tight. I was on my feet before I realized it. 'Read the rest quietly to yourselves, girls, and then you can be looking at the questions, I'll be back in two ticks.' They must have thought I had wet my knickers.

I stood just outside the classroom door, leaning against the knobbled paintwork. The cool came right through my shirt, raising goose-bumps all down my arms. I ignored the swell of conversation from the other side of the door. My pulse was booming in my throat; I thought I was going to sick up my heart. She must have written those words in the book months ago, guessing that my class wouldn't get to that exercise till September. She was not writing me notes from the other side. Ghosts couldn't use pencils.

I knew I probably looked stark staring mad, so I walked down the corridor and slipped into the children's toilet. I held my hands under the tap until they hurt, and held them to my cheeks. I met my eyes for a second, then shut them.

On the way back I passed the Senior Infants. Their mantric chant put the stress on every second syllable.

> What makes the lamb love Mary so?
> the eager children cry
> Why Mary loves the lamb you know
> and that's the reason why

I turned the corner and stumbled over Sister Luke. Lurching backwards, I broke into 'Sorry, Sister, I'm so sorry, so clumsy of me, are you all right?'

She adjusted her habit, which I was sure I had trodden on. 'I'm not made of bone china, Pen; it'll take more than a bump to finish me off.'

'Yes, Sister,' I said, grinning back at her.

'I heard,' she mentioned, 'there was a death in your house.'

My face slipped. 'There was,' I said.

'Is it your first, by any chance?'

I blinked at her.

'Your first brush with the whole business?'

Strictly speaking, my father was my first, but I said, 'It is, Sister.'

'Ah,' she said, her breath trailing away. After a second she said, 'You'll get better at it.'

'What, does each one get easier?'

225

'No, no,' she said, tucking her hands under her habit, 'but you'll have more know-how next time.'

I walked on to my class. There was a loud hum rising from the room that fell to nothing as I opened the door. I didn't bother lecturing them. I launched straight into question one: 'What do the following words mean: Papist, Roundhead, Puritan, plantation?'

Later, while we were working out how many jugs of milk a chef would need to make a pancake ten feet wide, I spotted Saoirse Mullan's French-plaited head bent over her notebook, her shield-arm curved round it. I stepped down the aisle and held out my hand. She said nothing, simply handed it over with a look of injured guilt. The class went on with their sums as I looked at Saoirse's drawing. It was not the rude or satiric sketch I might have expected. My outline took up two whole pages of her notebook.

My head was sagging over my book, there were curtains of dark hair which Saoirse had busily darkened with her pencil, and a long shaky curve of arm and breast. Is this what I looked like to them – a voluptuous giant? I noticed a little curve of smile pencilled in behind the hair.

I put it back on the girl's desk without a word. I could hardly reproach her for finding a sketch more interesting than the ingredients of a giant pancake. Doodling was how I had distracted myself from the boredom of my own schooldays, before I had Cara to talk to. Only I never had the skill to sketch real people; instead, I drew ballerinas, or elephants, or blank faces to which I added false eyelashes and chignons. When I couldn't think of anything new to doodle I used to put a penny under the paper and rub on it with my pencil till the delicate lines of the harp showed through. In science I used to make necklaces of staples and paperclips. Such restlessness, before my hands found out what they were for.

From my desk, I glanced down at Saoirse's head, her mouth silently totting up figures now. She might make a good wee dyke one of these years. So might Eilish McGrath, or Joan Durcan, or any of them really; even the very femmy ones, you never knew. I never would get to know, myself; they would have long passed out of my orbit by the time they were sure of anything. This job gave me no chance to be a role model as anything but a confident fat spinster. I hoped one or two of these girls would look back, and guess, and not despise me for my compromises.

The bell for lunch went, then; I was pleased with myself for not having watched the clock. I was afraid Robbie might come and find me in the staff-room, so I walked down to the deli on the corner. They had three minuscule tables tucked between the glass counter and the dresser full of different jars of olives. I pushed a table out from the wall to make room for myself, ignoring the expression of the waitress, and ordered onion tart.

As I launched into Chapter Three of Robbie's book, I realized that I was treating it as homework, almost as if, by working through a description of each aspect of bereavement, I was getting past the thing itself. I browsed through 'Everybody has a Different Worst Time of Day' and 'Know Your Weak Points'. What a menu of delights this book was, whetting your appetite for each misery. I took a huge bite of onion tart.

I was beginning to feel guilty about not doing so much 'sharing' as the book recommended. I scored one point for the heart-to-heart with Robbie yesterday, surely? It just wasn't in my nature to go round emoting at people. Whenever Cara had left me before, I had kept extremely quiet about it, partly for dignity, partly to keep the break from being official and therefore real. Whereas now was probably the time to start clutching at new straws. Come on, PenTimento, Cara seemed to whisper in my ear, it'd be such a waste of good flesh if you pined away. Better talk to anyone who'll listen; make some connections that might keep you attached to the surface of this spinning planet.

'Even if you do not feel like seeing your friends,' the paragraph concluded in earnest italics, 'it is best to make an effort.' I kept chewing on the mouthful of tart, but it didn't seem to be reducing. I tried to visualize my friends, lined up like a choir. The benches looked almost empty. If I couldn't see them in my head, how on earth was I supposed to see them socially? There was Robbie sitting at the back, passing the newspaper to Mr Wall. Jo was leaning against the side of the benches, chatting to a cluster of passing women I only knew to see. Schoolfriends whose faces I half-remembered, college friends whose wedding receptions I had not much enjoyed, they drifted by in twos and threes, leaving the occasional Christmas card on the bottom bench. There had to be some more, surely? I remembered that lovely girl from primary school whose family had moved to Australia, but I could not visualize her beyond the age of nine; I put her on the bottom bench anyway, her plump calves dangling. And there was Cara crosslegged beside her, asking her something; she was always good with children, being more like them than I ever was. Cara, what the hell are you doing here?

I'm your friend, she said. Always have been, always will.

Ghosts don't count, I told her. Shift that skinny ass out of there.

She stuck out her tongue. It was as pink as ever.

The waitress was staring at me. I must have looked as if I'd fallen into an onion tart-induced trance. I gathered up my accoutrements, giving her a *grande dame* smile and leaving an excessive tip on the saucer.

When I walked into my classroom, I found Fiona James and Mary O'Hanlon staging a kiss, with Mary lying back in a faint over Fiona's knee, her head cradled in Fiona's elbow, Fiona's hand a safety barrier between their goldfish mouths. They leaped apart as soon as the general hiss alerted them to my presence. I had to repress my smile as I made my way to the desk. Take your hand away, Fiona, I would have liked to say if it wouldn't have lost me my job. Go for it, a kiss won't kill you.

They were always up to high do on a Friday afternoon. The weekend hovered like sun behind a cloud, promising them untold freedom and excitement, though by the time

Monday came round again it might have granted them only a game of solo tennis against the wall of the garage and a Sunday afternoon black-and-white weepie.

To calm the girls down I led them through half an hour of Italian cities, then let them take out their knitting. It was while I was unravelling the mutant toe of Angela Gainey's mohair slipper that it occurred to me: I didn't particularly want to be a teacher any more. The whole point of my good secure job was to provide a solid base for Cara to rush out from and change the world. But now she had changed her world for another, what was I doing this for? No one actually needed me. Immac could offer my job to one of those eager little subs who would be much better at licking up to Big Dom. Mr Wall could move into a bachelor flat and have fellow librarians over for tea to help him with the crossword. My own family might hardly notice the difference; sad, but true.

I could run away in the morning. I could visit all the places I used to leave to Cara. I didn't have to be anybody's rock any more.

I let my class put their half-crafted slippers away three minutes before the bell, so they could run for their buses. I liked the sound of their thudding heels and farewell calls; it was like loosing a herd of antelopes. I sat in the classroom for a few minutes after they had gone, listening to the silence. Wiping the Geography notes from the board sent chalk powder floating through the air; I banged the duster against the board, for the hell of it.

As I was passing the assembly hall, the draught sliding through the convent opened the swing door slightly. The choir were staying behind for an extra practice, poor kids. All I remembered of choir was hysterical, stifled laughter at the *double entendres* we managed to hear in any lyrics. The very best was 'Jesus had appeared on the mountain', which, I remembered Kate Wall had interpreted as 'Jesus had a period on the mountain', and repeated in a piercing whisper. Somehow the thought of Jesus having to struggle with tampons was the funniest thing ever. So crammed together on the benches were we, the whole block of us shook. I remembered Kate on the bench below me, her sharp shoulder-blades not six inches from my knees.

I glanced in the swing-doors now. Lines of red jumpers swayed in obedience to the new music teacher's urgent hand. But the songs hadn't changed since my day. 'Sweet vale of Avoca how calm would I rest' . . . I remembered the words still. Had we sung them as earnestly as these children? Theirs was meant to be a flippant generation, raised on Australian soap operas, but they sang the end of the verse as if they had little time left to live.

> Where the storms that we feel
> in this cold world should cease
> And our hearts like thy waters
> be mingled in peace

I hoped no one ever took them to Avoca on a school trip; I didn't want them to discover what a disappointment the Vale was. Better let them keep imagining.

I walked out the main door and down the steps, switching my bag to my other hand. I could not free myself of the illusion that I was never coming back. The afternoon was warmer, but still cloudy. Weekend. Though that gave me nothing to look forward to, the word still triggered an automatic rise in my spirits. I leaned against Minnie's side, rummaging for my keys. My possibilities were limitless. So why was it that all at once all I wanted was to be face down on a sheet with somebody fucking my brains out?

A good hard swim would be the best thing for me; besides, I had promised to meet Kate at the pool. I wheeled Minnie out between the gateposts, not looking at the ivy-covered stone where after the occasional jaded Friday afternoon I used to find Cara waiting for me with a choc-ice.

No Reversing Under Any Circumstances said a sign at the mouth of a small cul-de-sac. I had never noticed it before I stared at it, wondering if it had a cosmic meaning or was I just losing my grip.

I hadn't been to the swimming pool in months. I turned sharply down the old road where the tarmac was sprouting emerald and copper moss. When I saw Kate leaning against the outside wall, the broad shoulders of her tangerine jacket sharp against the pebbledash, I faltered. But I couldn't turn back now, she might have recognized the dark green car already. Why hadn't I thought to tell her to meet me in the pool itself? I loathed undressing in front of strangers, especially strangers I had fallen for at the age of fifteen.

It occurred to me now that I had never been in love since, at least in the falling sense. Cara was something I stepped down into, an inch at a time. And as far as I was aware, no one had ever fallen in love with me. It wasn't something I seemed to need.

I waved briefly at Kate's upturned sunglasses to show that I had noticed her, and parked the car. At least there were individual cubicles with plastic curtains, not like the shared benches in that health club I went to once, with unknown women talcing their behinds and showing each other their Caesarian scars. Kate lent me a fifty-pee coin for the locker. 'Am I remembering right?' she asked. 'In our day you could just leave your stuff in your cubicle, if you covered anything pricey-looking with your towel.'

'That's right.'

In our day: what a funny phrase, as if each generation had only one day in which they truly lived. Though in the case of Kate Wall and myself, there really was only one day we had shared, because apart from the time we bumped into each other at this pool and she asked me home for tea, I couldn't remember her having paid me any particular attention.

Our feet were trying to remember how to walk without shoes now; our hands were tugging the edges of our togs down in the traditional gesture of modest discomfort. I caught just the briefest glimpse of us in the mirror as we picked our way towards the shower: Kate narrow but muscular in her sister's blue, beside me in my comfy old green. Our bodies had changed in the doubling of years since we met here in the water. How our fourteen-year-old selves would have been frightened to see us; how carved and lined and over-ripe we would have seemed to them.

Mostly I liked the way I was, my to-hell-with-you-all shape. But now as we passed another merciless slab of mirror, its background full of teenagers whose heads lifted to gawk, I could not see myself as anything but Nessie, all lime-green billows. Kate stalked on, but I hung back in the disinfectant shower for a minute. You're not ugly, I told myself in the habitual formula, you're a grand girl. (Hey, I was doing 'affirmations' long before they called them that.) But just for a moment I wanted to be a blank and underfed child again, with no choices made, no deposits laid down, no unhideable flesh. A knot of adolescents shivered by and I was alone in the shower again. I cupped one breast in my hand. Cara called them the Many-Splendoured Things. Used to. Don't think about her now, push her back into the changing-room, she can curl up in the cubicle and take a nap while you're swimming.

I had always found a refuge in water. Most times I came here I climbed in at the steps and only gradually worked up to diving, but today I felt like showing off how much I had learnt over the years. I walked straight to the deep end, found a clear space, bounced on my toes a little, my eyes scanning for her dark head. Always that moment of terror, when I thought I had forgotten how. Then the entry, fairly clean today, but with a good crash of water just for fun.

I came up gasping thirty feet away, near where the dark head had been, but was no longer. My throat stung; Grace's claws had left their mark this morning. I began swimming lengths in my usual breast-stroke, my head held up like a meditative turtle.

Alongside me, going a little slower, were two women, their hair still dry on top, chatting between kicks. Probably wife-and-mothers, sharing a babysitter for the afternoon. I glanced back; they were looking straight forward, their mouths wide with the amusement of whatever they were talking about. I imagined their fingertips touching for a second, under the skin of water. Kate, doing a speedy crawl, emerged on my left and pulled ahead of me. She turned on her back for a few strokes, and I caught a glimpse of her chin, jutting up towards the glass roof.

After a few conscientious lengths I let my face sink into the silky water. I hung there for a while, limp as a suicide, my shoulders sloughing off the weight of the week. My thighs drifted in the wash of a passing swimmer. My breasts floated free of gravity. Then someone grabbed my shoulder, and I came up spitting.

'Are you OK?' Kate's face was twisted in concern.

'Of course.' Treading water uncomfortably, I spoke more sharply than I meant.

'Sorry. I wasn't sure.'

'I just like to hang there sometimes,' I told her.

'Sure. Race you to the end?' she suggested, her voice suddenly fifteen.

I was taken off guard, so I let her get a head-start, but I soon caught up, with the overarm crawl I hardly ever used. It felt good to be pounding up the pool with no room for anything in my head except how to keep my body going. Our hands slapped the bar in a flurry of water; we couldn't tell who won. I dangled monkey-style, squeezing water out of my eyes. My legs drifted towards hers, and one of my feet brushed against one of hers, cold and light. I doubled over, sending my legs out behind me.

Kate slid off again. I stayed by the bar, stretching my back and watching her do another six purposeful lengths. Letting air out in tiny bubbles, I sank down towards the blue floor of the pool and stayed there, absorbing the silence. The water pressed gently on my eyes but I kept them open. In this pale green light there was nothing binding my body. Nothing could follow me down here.

When I kicked my way to the surface, lungs bursting, Kate was beside me. I gasped for a breath. My flailing arm struck her hand; for a moment she held me up, till I got my balance. 'You're pretty fit. How do you stay so fit?' I gabbled.

'Swim every morning at six in a health club. We have corporate membership.'

'Before breakfast? God help us. For me the best bit of swimming is this,' and I showed her how I liked to spin like a dolphin, round and round till I was dizzy.

Kate looked bemused. 'You know swimming has little or no aerobic value unless you keep it up without stopping for fifteen minutes?'

'Yup,' I said, queenly, and kicked off down the pool. She wouldn't have said that when she was fifteen. Something scathing, maybe, or at least sarky, but nothing as pompous as that. What had they done to her in Boston?

I put my face in the water and made my legs do all the work, letting my arms float out behind me like seaweed. When I raised my dripping face Kate was at the shallow end of the lane, standing against the wall, adjusting her goggles. I swam straight towards her but her eyes, dipped in concentration, didn't register me. I had never kissed this woman and never would. But it still gave me some obscure pleasure that the same water was on both our lips.

After the showers, Kate slung a towel around my shoulders and complained that she still reeked of chlorine. She peered at the grazes on my throat: 'You should get those seen to. Is he often vicious?'

'Ah, Grace is just a bit unhinged at the moment,' I protested, 'probably picking up the house vibes.'

On the way home in the car, I looked across at her dark curls a few times, as they gradually sprang back from their weight of damp. When I held the hairdryer for her, that day she invited me to tea after swimming, her hair had copper highlights in it, but she seemed to have grown out of them.

As we were coming up to the cluster of shops, she asked, 'Could we get some chips?'

'You mean your chips like crisps or our chips like french fries?' I asked, smiling at the language gap.

'Irish chips aren't like ordinary fries. I know it sounds stupid, but I'm starving.'

'No problem,' I told her, making a quick left into a parking space.

'Dad always used to buy us chips after swimming,' said Kate while we were waiting at the counter, 'even though Mom hated the smell of vinegar in the car.'

'Minnie loves the smell of vinegar,' I reassured her.

The Italians always gave huge portions, so we asked for a bag between us. The big-eyed daughter offered salt and vinegar with a tremendous smile. We watched her pour them on and didn't say stop. In the car, I popped in the first chip and shifted it around with my tongue, puffing out so it wouldn't burn me. Kate made an incoherent sound of pleasure. 'God, this brings me back,' she said at last. 'How have I survived without these for fourteen years?'

'Lord knows.'

'They taste like they've been cut from real potatoes.'

'No!' I said in theatrical disbelief.

'And the little crispy bits are totally soaked in vinegar,' she added to the litany.

We put our hands into the translucent bag at the same time. I grabbed the big one Kate was picking; it broke and released a wisp of steam. Laughing, she raised her torn half to her mouth. 'Just as well these aren't available in Boston; I can't imagine the calorie count.'

'Yum. Just as well I'm fat already.'

The chip paused, halfway to her mouth. 'Do you have to knock yourself like that?'

'I wasn't.'

Kate was shifting in her seat. 'Well, the word does tend to get used as a – a disparagement.'

'That's not how I was using it,' I told her silkily. 'For me it's a positive description of the shape I happen to be.'

Her head bent as she finished her chip.

'Ah well,' I said, relenting, 'I may be no supermodel but at least I'd live longer than you if a plane dropped us into the freezing Atlantic.'

Kate looked up, dog-eyed. 'I'm not getting at you, honestly. I think, you know, in that fringed shawl of yours, you look magnificent.'

I had no idea what to say, so I said 'Thank you' like my mother taught me. I kept my eyes on the wall in front of the car, feeling pink. 'Free Nicky Kelly,' said the splatter of paint, a Republican graffito from years back. We talked about the likelihood of more rain. The last few chips were stuck to the bottom of the bag when Kate surrendered it to me; I had to dig into its slick recesses. I licked the grains of salt off my fingers, one by one, then wiped my hands on a tissue and started up the car. Seeing a truck come towards me, I realized that I was well over the white line. Kate said nothing when I swerved to the left.

When I turned into the drive and shut off the engine, the car ticked softly. Kate stared out her window. 'I love my apartment, but I miss having a yard to sit in,' she said.

'What would you want to sit in the yard for? It's full of dustbins.'

She looked confused, then said, 'Sorry, you'd call it a garden. The green bit.'

'Ah, right.' I added, 'It looked wonderful a couple of years back when there was snow.'

'What, a whole inch?' Kate mocked.

'Several.'

'Hey,' she said, turning towards me so her seat-belt twisted, 'there was quite a big snowfall my last year at school, I don't suppose you remember?'

'Don't think so,' I said, recalling the white crystals hanging in her fringe.

'We couldn't believe it. As soon as the bell rang we all ran out and pelted each other. And Sister whatshername, the one in charge of fourth year –'

'Dominic.'

'– when we trooped back in after breaktime, she was announcing over the intercom, "Will any girl who threw a snowball please report to my office immediately." Just imagine if we all had.'

I put back my head and laughed. 'A queue of six hundred miscreants, dripping up the stairs all the way to her door.'

'She didn't really expect us to turn ourselves in, did she?'

'Not at all. Dom's the head of the Junior School now, you know; she's my boss.'

'No!'

'That thing about the snowballs is typical; not a real order, just a way to make us feel doubly guilty.'

'Well, it worked.' Kate sighed. 'The odd night when insomnia hits, I compose postcards to her in my head "Dear Sister, as you probably knew I did throw a snowball, but I was not the only one . . ."'

'"Dear Sister, it was not exactly a ball of snow, more like a wet handful,"' I contributed.

'"Dear Sister, it's not like I crammed it down the back of some small child's shirt."'

'"Dear Sister, what's the harm in a wee snowfight anyway?"'

'"Dear Sister, I'm not even a Catholic any more, get off my case."' We were laughing so hard it bent us double. Kate was leaning on her seat-belt, gasping for breath. Her head hung a few inches from mine. Below her curls I could see the curve of her open mouth.

And then Jo's face appeared at the window. I snapped open my seat-belt and got out. 'Hi,' I said, over the car.

'Hey.' Jo was wearing a fawn business suit; she looked like somebody's mother. 'Just thought I'd drop in as I was passing, to make sure you were coming to the wake.'

Kate was opening her door; Jo stepped back out of the way and gave her a friendly nod. 'So,' she resumed, 'can you two make it tomorrow afternoon?'

'I'm afraid I'm flying out in the morning,' said Kate.

'Actually, you know, Jo, I don't think it'll be my kind of

thing.' My eyes were flicking to follow Kate across the lawn to the doorstep, her suit and towel swinging.

'Really?' she asked

'Well, songs and rituals and stuff, I think to be perfectly honest it'd stick in my craw.'

'You went to the funeral,' she said, hands on tailored hips.

'That was different,' I snapped. 'Besides two in one week . . .'

Jo leaned her elbows on Minnie. Her pale blue eyes had creases round them in this thin sunlight. 'Look,' she said, 'it wasn't my idea, but actually I think it'd be good for all of us.'

'Go ahead, I'm not stopping you.'

'But it might do you some good too. And it'll be all wrong if you're not there.'

'I thought Sherry was organizing it. Doesn't the most recent lay get to be principal mourner?' I couldn't believe such bile was spewing out of my mouth.

Jo straightened up and looked at the yellow roses for a second. 'All I'm going to say right now is that you've got the whole thing arseways.'

'If you say so.' Then, guiltily: 'You coming in for a cuppa?'

'Thought you'd never ask.' Her grin caught the sun as we turned towards the front door.

'I'm really tired,' I told her, filling up the kettle. 'I've been swimming for the first time in ages.'

Jo yawned as she sat down, loosening the tangle of jewellery in the neck of her blouse. I counted two gold double-headed axes, a triple women's symbol (meaning sisterhood or threesomes, I wondered?), and a star of David with a lambda sign in the middle. 'I never knew you were Jewish,' I said, bending closer to see.

'I'm not, actually; I got it from my last girlfriend. I just like confusing people. Not that the crowd I work with would have any clue what all my metalwork means.'

I took down the mugs.

'So,' Jo went on, 'you seem to be hitting it off with the sister all right.'

'We're civil enough,' I said lightly.

'What's she like?'

'Hard to tell. She's only been around a couple of days, and most of the time she's upstairs reading reports.'

'Has she sussed about you two?'

'Oh yes.'

'Well, is she like Cara at all?'

'Not a bit.' I scattered Bourbon Creams across a plate. 'Cara looked most herself when she was naked, right?'

'Did she?' asked Jo, adjusting her white collar.

'I mean, when she didn't have to decide what to wear, when she could sit on the grass all crosslegged and unself-conscious, reading the paper.'

'Mmm.'

'Whereas Kate . . . I can't imagine her naked.'

'Have you been trying to?' asked Jo lewdly, bending to scratch Grace under the chin.

I ignored that. 'See, Kate might not say anything very interesting, but she does give the impression that interesting things remain to be said.'

'Like she's saving a few for the last minute?'

'Yeah.'

'I know the type. It's an illusion.'

'No, there's definitely something there.'

'Trust me, I'm an expert,' said Jo heavily. 'I used to specialize in really fucked-up girls who had nothing to say but gave the impression they had.'

I wetted the tea. Somewhere in the depths of my memory I found the information that Jo took milk and two sugars. Grace was poised in a gingerly fashion on her knee. After I handed over the mug I said, looking away, 'Nice having you around this week.'

She took a loud swallow and uncrossed her legs. 'I'd have liked to be more of a friend before, you know, but you never seemed to need one.'

'Didn't I?' I stared at Jo. 'But I don't really have any.'

'Well, you always seemed self-sufficient. Kind of imperme-able, what with your busy job, and you and Cara.'

I mulled over this for a minute. 'When I ring my mother she asks after my job first of all, as if that's Who I Am.'

'That makes Who I Am a part-time market research analyst,' complained Jo.

'You're not, are you? I assumed you were a full-time Amazon.'

'Afraid not,' she said, burying her nose in Grace's marma-lade fur. 'Hence the drag.'

'I wasn't going to mention it,' I said.

Jo met my grin, then asked, 'So have you talked to your mother yet?'

'Yeah, rang her the other day . . . Oh, you mean, talked talked. Not yet.' After a few seconds I added, 'Haven't had a chance.'

Steam from her mug was sidling along Jo's cheek. 'Why not?' she asked.

'Ah, give us a break. I can't face losing them both in one week.'

'What's there to lose, with your mother?'

'Look . . .' I strained for an image. 'Imagine a clearing in a wood that you come across when you're about seven.'

'Those of us who grew up on Charlemont Street . . .'

'Ah, it doesn't have to be a literal wood. Just somewhere private and safe.' I rushed on: 'You haven't been back in years, but when you shut your eyes you can see it perfectly.'

A slow nod from Jo.

'If you went back now you might find a fox carcass, or they might have chopped down the trees. Whereas if you stay away it can't be spoiled.'

'Can't be enjoyed either.'

'But I know it's there.'

'You don't, not really; it's rotting away in the back of your mind.'

'Ah, don't give me that philosopher's bullshit about the

cat that doesn't exist until you open the box and look at it.'
As if on cue, Grace crashed through his flap and out into the
yard. I added, 'Grace always exists.'

'So have you come out to him yet, or are you just assuming
he knows –'

I let out a laugh, and then in a split second was shaking.
'Why are you pushing me so hard on this, right now?'

'Is there a better time?' she asked.

'I'd have thought you'd have noticed that I've more than
enough to deal with this week. Look, I'm sorry if I'm not
politically correct enough to win the Amazon Attic seal of
approval, but that's the way it is.' I took a sip of tea and
waited till my voice was steady before going on. 'I suppose
you came out to your mother at the age of twelve.'

Jo rubbed the crook of her elbow where the pushed-up
sleeve of her blouse seemed to be pinching it. 'No, actually, I
never got around to it.'

I shut my mouth.

'I always figured Mum sort of knew but didn't want to
know for sure. And then she got cancer. Died nine years ago,
and I've been coming out to her in my head ever since, but I
don't know if she can hear.'

'I'm sorry,' I said weakly.

Jo put her throat back and finished her tea in one long
swallow. 'Don't waste your time being sorry. Just get around
to things, all right? We have damn-all time.' She stood up
and stretched. 'Tomorrow afternoon then, at the Attic?'

'I really don't . . .'

'If you change your mind.'

'I won't.' We smiled at each other.

After I had shut the front door I leaned back against the
cold radiator and wondered why I was being so ratty. I felt
that tightly pleated sensation in my lower belly again. Ah,
surely my libido would have the decency to stay away for a
few months?

The clouds over the hammock were still dark blue. I went
upstairs, shut my bedroom door tightly and lay down on my

back on the rug. The floor was satisfyingly hard, lengthening my spine. I felt as if there was a rubber band around my middle; what I needed was a big O. Or even a little O, seeing as I hadn't long before dinner.

I let my legs fall open. I was lacking in enthusiasm, partly because I was afraid to make myself any more vulnerable, and mostly because to lay a hand on myself felt disloyal to a woman not two days . . . no, don't think about it, Pen, you've simply got to be a practical Taurean, think about your greedy body instead. The door of the middle bedroom squealed, and Kate's steps went past and downstairs.

This was no time for experiment. I focused on the blank wall six feet in front of me, the gentle ripple of woodchip. Then I shut my eyes and called up that reliable fantasy of the woman in the black leather jacket who says nothing but looks everything, whose only script is in stares and touches. What I ran was an edited version of this story, leaving out the initial eye-contact across a crowded nightclub and all the minor characters. It was all proceeding satisfactorily – my breathing had harshened, my body had shifted a few inches across the floor, my wrist was tired but steely – when Kate barged in.

Or rather, her shade. The thirty-year-old face looking over the upturned leather collar was hers, altered only by the addition of a wet-lipped smile. I stopped. No good hostess steals her guest's image and rubs herself against it. I could hear the woman vacuuming downstairs, for god's sake, quite unaware.

But the Kate looking into my head was not unaware of anything. She began what she was doing again, moving faster, pushing me farther. I tried to convert the image into Cara, but couldn't visualize the face clearly; all I could do was add a tangled sheet of red hair, and you could still see the dark roots under it. She shook it back and looked at me, then her breath was against my ear, murmuring honeyed insults. You know who I am, she whispered. I was the first, a year before my little sister. I was the very first to make you wet.

Her hair kept changing colour, as I squeezed my eyes tighter shut. The red slipped away, darkened to black, curls flashing yellow and grey and purple, then reverting to brown. Damn her for doing this to me without even knowing it. The dark phantom hair irritated my eyelids, stuck to my cheeks, tangled in my mouth. I went faster. I knew I should stop, but I wanted this to be over, and stopping now would mean not coming to an end, quite an interesting philosophical point there, Pen, don't you think. I went faster. I didn't care who I was fantasizing about at this point. I'd have used anyone or anything to get that feeling of release, lift-off like a jet plane dipping upwards, breaking the skin of cloud.

I couldn't do it. My flesh was shrinking, getting sore now. My clumsy arm was losing circulation. My mind was wandering, chasing two sisters. I sat up. I tried again, pressing harder.

A gentle knock on the door. Fuck her, fuck her, what did she want now? 'Just a minute,' I called, shrill. I leaped up, straightened my shirt, and grabbed a towel to wrap around my damp hand. With the other I opened the door. It wasn't Kate at all, but her father, wearing a red and black diamond tie. 'I'm off so,' he said almost gaily.

'Sorry?'

'I'm dining with a colleague from the Wotherby; I believe I mentioned it?'

'Oh. Yes.'

'I won't be late.'

Why did he have to reassure me about his movements? I didn't care if the man stayed out all night. My body was cold and flat now. I crossed the landing and washed my hands. I could hear Mr Wall in the hall below, fussing with his raincoat. I had no right to be angry with him, he hadn't done a thing. It wasn't even as if I had plans for dinner; I was full of chips, my tongue still harsh with vinegar. He had a perfect right to escape from the house for the evening. I could hear him whistling a line from some symphony I faintly remembered; it trailed off halfway.

When I heard the door ease shut I went downstairs and almost walked right into Kate. 'Was that you vacuuming?' I asked stupidly.

'Yeah, I had walked some mud into the carpet.'

'That was nice of you. To clean it up, I mean.'

'It was a bit dusty, so I opened the windows.' The tension in the atmosphere was suddenly tangible; it filled the hall like tear-gas. Kate looked down and adjusted her watch-strap. 'So Dad's out for dinner, yeah?'

'That's right.'

'I thought we'd eat late, when the chips wear off. I'm cooking.'

'Something impressive?'

'Wait and see. Tell you this much,' she added teasingly, 'dessert is a gâteau. I won't steal the last slice this time.'

'A chocolate one?'

'Would I fob you off with anything less?'

I grinned back at her. Then I asked, 'What time's your plane tomorrow?'

'Eight a.m.'

'That's early.'

She looked up and our eyes met for a second then fell away.

'Have you done your packing?'

'Almost. Better finish it now.'

Ten minutes later, I was watering a rubber plant on the windowsill when Kate came back into the kitchen with something folded and blue under her arm.

'All done?'

'Nearly. Where's that box of yours?' she went on, a little hoarsely.

'Which box?'

'Old clothes. For Oxfam.' On the last word, her face caved in. I watched two creases crack her forehead, her eyes narrow to knife-cuts, her lower lip be tugged down on one side. I had never seen this face lose control before; I was fascinated. It was only when I saw the first tear on the tip of her nose that I recognized this seizure for what it was. I took two steps towards her. A tear fell on the dusty parquet. I could think of no words that would get through the air between us. 'What? What is it? What's the matter?' I said stupidly, hoping some of the syllables would reach her.

The first sound came then, a great wail like a baby's. Kate began to cough her way through some incomprehensible sentence. I shushed her, told her to take her time. When I reached to relieve her of the blue bundle, she clutched it to her chest and sobbed faster.

'OK, it's all right, it's all right.'

'It's not all right,' she roared, and shook out the folds.

Gradually I recognized them from the rollerskating photo. 'Are they your dungarees?' I asked carefully. There was a Rolling Stones tongue badge on one of the straps.

Kate gulped till her voice made some sense. 'I grew out of them years before I left.'

I waited, then said 'Yeah?' There had to be more to it than this.

A huge sniff. 'I kept telling Cara that they fitted me just fine, I just didn't happen to wear them very often.'

'It doesn't . . .'

'I told her she was too short and too fat,' said Kate, her lips punishing the syllables one by one, 'and the legs would never fit her. She got Dad to ask me to lend them to her just once, for a youth club disco, but I said no, and when he asked why, I said because they're mine.'

I kept nodding.

'I forgot all about them,' she said, her voice wavering like the flight of some erratic bird. 'They were folded up in the wardrobe. She never even touched them. She could have had them, if she'd asked me again.'

I took a breath. 'Cara was probably too big for them by then; she really shot up after you went to America.'

245

'I know.'

'I really wouldn't worry about it,' I said gently. 'Anyway, she had a pair quite like them she got in a sale.'

At this, Kate's eyes flooded.

'Oh, I'm sorry, I didn't . . .' I stepped close, and her head fell on to my shoulder. I let my arms wrap around her, careful as ribbon, and I held her, ready for any sign of resistance. But she sank all her weight into the hug and began to sob again. I couldn't tell how many minutes passed like this, our bodies balanced in a sort of steeple, before she quietened down. 'I'm afraid I've snivelled all over your blouse,' she said.

'That's all right.'

We stepped apart with blurred smiles. My shoulder was wet; I rubbed at it. There was an awkward pause. Through the kitchen window came a very faint whimper.

'Grace doesn't sound very happy,' said Kate, too loudly.

I leaned out the window. 'That's not Grace.' I couldn't see anything, but the whine came again.

'Some stray, then?' Her voice was still uneven.

'I've never heard a cat make a noise like that.' The warped kitchen door yielded to my third tug. Kate followed me into the garden, wiping her eyes with her cuff. We stood around looking everywhere but at each other for a few seconds, until the sound came again. It took me a while to pull away enough of the purple-leaved bush to see it. The hedgehog was on its side, motionless, with one leg splayed backwards. It looked flat, not like the plump bristling ones in the cartoons. I could see the loop of blue netting holding its tiny paw in the mud.

Kate's breath was loud. 'D'you think it's dead?'

'It's still making that noise, listen.'

'Wonder how long it's been lying there.'

Under our gaze the animal began to twitch slightly.

'Is it having a fit?'

'I think it's just panting,' I told her. 'I can't see anything wrong with it apart from the leg.'

246

'How do you think you feed a hedgehog? Milk in a dropper?'

I met Kate's red eyes, appalled. However good for me Hollywood would no doubt think it to rediscover inner peace by nursing a wounded animal back to life, that was the last thing I wanted to take on. 'I'm bringing it to the vet,' I said.

A furious rummage through the kitchen drawer produced the secateurs. The plastic netting proved obstinate, and the hedgehog winced, but at last it was cut free. Using the thick gardening gloves, I scooped it up and into the cardboard box Kate was holding open. She had padded it with torn-up newspaper. Swaddled in headlines, the hedgehog was barely visible. When I had rung around five vets to find one with Friday evening surgery hours, she carried the box to the back seat of the car like a precious relic. 'Should I come with you?'

I hesitated, unable to think of a single reasonable reason for saying yes. 'I think I can carry it on my own.'

'Of course.'

I hadn't meant it as a rebuff. I searched for a way to change my mind, but all I could come up with was, 'We'll eat later, when I get back?'

'Great.' The red around Kate's eyes was beginning to fade. She stood on the drive for a minute, watching me go, or maybe looking at a bird in the garden, I couldn't tell. By the time I'd straightened up the car she had gone back into the house.

The teatime streets were empty; scraps of paper speckled the grass verges. At one point I got rather lost, because a road name was so swathed in yellow St John's Wort that I couldn't read it. Turning the final corner, the road opened out and I caught sight of a most peculiar sunset; dark grey clouds ganged up in a white sky, their undersides burnished by the aftermath of the sun, which seemed to have gone down the chimney of the vet's house.

Sitting in the waiting-room, which was crowded with

everything from dogs and budgies to a lethargic goldfish in a bowl on a little girl's lap, I resigned myself to a long wait. By the time I got home my stomach would be rumbling. Kate and I could open that last bottle of Rioja and grill a couple of steaks from the freezer. Maybe if the evening was chilly she would have lit a small fire. We could share a disproportionate slice of chocolate gâteau by firelight.

After five minutes I was bored of playing Blink with a senile labrador. The hedgehog hadn't stirred. The only book I had in my bag was *Finding Yourself*, so I ploughed into Chapter Five. I skimmed through 'Using Pills as a Prop' and didn't feel the need for the pro-masturbatory section called 'Self Help, Not Self Abuse'. Oh look, there was the section Robbie had promised me: 'Homosexuals mourning their partners often carry a burden exacerbated by invisibility and prejudice', and several other sensible statements I didn't need to read. Somehow, what galled me most was that if it had been a husband, Sister Dominic would have given me two weeks off. On the other hand, it occurred to me now, watching the widow-type opposite with the fretful tabby grinding hairs into her black wool lap, losing a husband would have been horribly public. I couldn't have it both ways, I supposed, couldn't have my closet and bitch about it. The small girl was bent over her goldfish bowl now, peering in the side. I hoped she would not spill its water; I couldn't take seeing it gasp on the carpet.

After I had resorted to reading the book's bibliography – it was the least depressing section – it was my turn at last. The vet was a tired man in his sixties. He lifted the animal's leg very gently, and removed the rest of the netting. Yes, he could drop it round to a shelter tonight after the surgery closed. As a wild animal handled by humans, it was under extreme stress, but they had been known to survive this kind of trauma.

'Will it get better, then?'

'No way of telling, Miss O'Grady.'

I didn't bother saying 'Ms'. I thanked him and cast a last glance at the quivering spiky ball before I went.

Stopped at the traffic lights, I sniffed my wrist for the tang of chlorine. Tiredness weighed down my arms. I had done my good deed for the day; surely I had earned a warm bath, a fluffy towel, and dinner for two by the fire? As I drove down past the woods towards the big house, a detail I'd forgotten from that first day after swimming floated into my mind. At dinner with the Walls, I'd managed to swap our forks: when Kate put hers down beside mine, I rested my palm over them both, and raised hers to my mouth. Nobody noticed. It gave me such bliss to close my teeth over the stainless steel that had just come from between her lips. Of course I got a cold the next day, and suffered agonies of guilt over the germs, but Kate turned out to be fine. What outrageous gall my young self once had.

The dark pink honeysuckle was making a cloud of sweetness around the front door; I stood and breathed it in till I was reeling. A bird in the long grass was making a sound like the clicking of spoons. 'I'm back,' I called as I stepped on to the mat. No sign of dinner yet, but I was only just getting hungry.

Preparing my bath, I was ridiculously gay. The taps roared as I lined up a new apple soap, sea sponge and loofah. I shut off the taps when the bath was half-full. 'Kate?' I shouted, leaning round the door of the bathroom. 'I'm just having a bath before dinner.' I turned on the hot tap again. Then I thought she might need help finding utensils, so I wrapped the biggest towel round me and walked down the stairs, a little shyly.

The windows were too wide; it had got dark without my noticing. Kate wasn't watching telly in the living-room. Night was settling over the curves of the sofa; a street-lamp glared in the bay window. Nor was she sitting in the kitchen, where the light spilled out the window, yellowing the rough wall of the yard. Nor in the back garden, nor in Mr Wall's room, nor upstairs in the middle bedroom, which was just as it had been a week ago, except that the bed had been stripped. I stared at it stupidly.

Eventually I found the folded note in the middle of the kitchen table. It was the pivot of this house, which was suddenly obviously empty, even sounded empty; why hadn't I heard it before?

Pen, it began, this disembodied voice in blue ballpoint, *you must excuse my leaving without saying goodbye, but really all things considered I have decided I can't bear to haul myself up as early tomorrow as I would need to in order to get to the airport by taxi by six thirty, so I thought it might be best if I went out to the airport hotel now and overnighted so I need only get up two hours before my plane. I should have thought of this before but it only just occurred to me.*

Many thanks for looking after me during my stay. It is not a visit I will forget. Give my best wishes to my father and I hope to see either or both of you again if you're ever passing through Boston.
All the best,
Kate Wall.
P.S. Good luck with the hedgehog.

I re-read the note. The wind was a black cat outside, rattling the chimney and spitting at the windows. Fingertip tracing the lines, I counted: it had taken her a hundred and forty panic-stricken words to say nothing at all.

I was sitting wrapped in a towel at the centre of an empty house on a Friday night, getting colder by the minute. Soon my legs would be numb and I would forget I had them. My lips would go blue. I would put my head down on my marbled arms and future explorers might find me there: 'Almost magically preserved by trace elements of chlorine,' they would announce, 'the skin of the Female Colossus is still glossy.'

I scanned the note again. *Good luck with the hedgehog*, for god's sake. Standing up with a shiver, I rubbed my arms, but that only brought up more goose-bumps. Wandering into the living-room, I reached to turn on the telly, but then

I realized that by the law of chance there would be nothing good on, and that the demented flicker of images would make the room even darker around the edges. I turned on the light, but that was a waste, because there was nothing to look at; I turned it off again as I left the room. No sign of Grace. A rummage in the larder produced nothing worth eating. Must shop tomorrow, I instructed myself automatically. Maybe it wasn't appetite that kept us living, only habit. I found a slab of cooking chocolate and nibbled at the corner, but (as with every such attempt since childhood) it was mild and disappointing. The smell of chlorine on my fingers reminded me of the bath, and I pounded upstairs.

Water was gurgling down the overflow. I turned off the taps and dipped my hand through the scorching water down to the plug to let some more out, then held it under the cold tap to reduce the pain. As I bent over, the towel came undone. I threw it over the radiator. Waiting for the water level to sink, I stared at myself in the steamy mirror. Such a blank page, this body; the years had left no signature marks so far. Once, my hand down Cara's jeans, I didn't notice my knuckle was grinding against the denim till afterwards, when it was bleeding. When my mother asked about it, I said I'd grazed it off a wall. The scar faded, much too soon.

I sat on the edge of the bath. The colder and more miserable I got, the better the water was going to feel. In my mind I was chasing to the airport hotel in a taxi, pounding on the door of room number seven, where Kate would be nervous in a white towelling robe, and I would be the sure one, and I would be the free spirit, and I would have my way.

Best to get all the puerile fantasies over with now, so they wouldn't keep me awake later. I put the plug back in and poured a little lavender oil on to the water, as a soporific. It broke into little gleaming circles. Such a stupid fantasy, anyway, a sick joke. What had I to go on? All I knew was that Kate Wall had flirted a little, that she had seemed to like me more than could have been expected, and that several times today I had had the outrageous notion of trying to keep her up all night so she'd miss her plane. As for my motives, it was probably best not to pry too deeply into them.

It wasn't true, I realized now, shivering on the edge of the bath, what I had once told Cara about not having room in my head for more than one woman. Yes, I meant that I wouldn't actually sleep with more than one, would cling to my technical fidelity, because it made me feel better. (Better meaning better than Cara, I supposed, but most importantly, better than the Pen I would have been if I'd degraded the whole business by going to bed with other women just so I could say I had.) But it would be nearer the truth to say that there were always two women in my head. And that there was more than one kind of infidelity.

How many times over the years had Cara, teasing or serious, asked me who I'd been in love with at school? First I tried to play it down, by saying oh, she didn't know her, wouldn't remember her face, and it didn't matter anyway – but Cara remained tantalized. Only when I finally said that I couldn't tell her, that I was protecting someone, did she give up. But the only someone I was protecting was me. I used to tell myself that if Cara knew what I had felt for Kate, what I still felt in occasional dreams and on restless afternoons in traffic jams, she would go mad with jealousy, but in fact she was much more likely to turn it into a giggly anecdote. Cara and I discussed so much, scattered so many words over so many subjects, that I had to keep something safe from her tickling fingers. Something, anything, my longest, most untouched fantasy, spun out of air, wound round the blurred image of a haughty schoolgirl. Something that had little or no real connection with the thirty-year-old American who was in a taxi halfway to the airport right now. How on earth had I considered trying to take fourteen years of idle fancy and make them flesh?

Let it go, Pen, I told myself, almost aloud. Kate's not here, she's not a dyke, and she's not what you need. None of these things are her fault. You went to school with her for a year, back when bell-bottoms were the coolest thing to wear. You once put her fork in your mouth. You've shared a house with her for five of the worst days of your life, maybe of hers too. Now shut the book. Let the woman go home.

When I stood up, there was red on the white rim of the bath. It couldn't be, it was only two weeks . . . well, but stress was known to mess up the hormones. '"The curse has come upon me," cried the Lady of Shalott,' as Cara used to groan into her pillow. That explained some of the rattiness and even the unreasonable lust. PMT always acted on me like the flower from *A Midsummer Night's Dream*, making me pine for the next person I laid eyes on. I should be sane by morning, I thought.

The blood was trickling down the edge of the bath now, so I climbed in and let out my breath in a long gasp as the heat took hold of my muscles, layer by layer, and my breasts began to float. One of my earliest childhood fantasies was of being Cleopatra, bathed by her attendants; the plain white soap became a rare unguent brought at great risk from the island of High Brazil. I liked to squeeze my stomach muscles until my belly-button was emptied of water; I would pause a second, then dip my back and flood the whole landscape again.

Baths on my own would take less getting used to than bed on my own. Baths offered reliable bliss, no matter who was in them. I was briefly troubled by a memory of a picnic bath I'd shared with Cara a summer or two ago; a peach had fallen in and bobbed along beside us, cooking slowly, until I'd wiped it on the towel and bit in, spilling the hot juice, and Cara had leaned over to lick the drops from my throat. Well, never mind. There would be peaches next summer. They would still taste like peaches, or almost the same.

I could feel my stomach begin to tighten in a cramp. My fingers throbbed in unison; I let them sink into the water, resting my wrists on my hips, willing myself to relax.

Stupid, stupid, stupid woman; a Saturday night crash

wasn't even an original way to go. I could see no sense in this early walkout. Surely we would have got the hang of it, if we'd had a few years longer; our relationship was like a picture hung on a wall that needed to be adjusted a little every time you walked by. There were lots of things I was intending to have my say on eventually; so many issues I put to one side, assuming we'd have time to work them out. I had known well that I shouldn't nanny Cara or smother her or try to run her life for her, and any year now I was planning to really put this wisdom into practice. Or the whole GogMagogamy business, as she used to call it in moments of flippancy; yes, I'd accepted the fact that she went to bed with somebody else the odd time, but secretly I had thought of it as a short-term compromise. Any year now, when Cara trailed back and laid her eyes on my shoulder till the wool was soaked through, I would say, enough of this nonsense. (Perhaps I would wear a tails suit, every inch the Victorian patriarch.) Enough of this wandering and bruising yourself and me and god knows who else, I would boom. Haven't you had enough freedom yet? Doesn't it go stale in your mouth, tire your jaw, coat your tongue? And haven't I earned a bit of settling down? Haven't I proved my love with truly troubadour patience?

And Cara would murmur yes, oh yes. Here I am now, she'd say. It's all so clear and simple. You're the only one. I'm yours. We were meant to be together. And other such preciously anticipated clichés.

I lay in a daze of heat, my heart thumping irregularly. If I stayed in the bath too long, I might fall asleep, slipping below the skin of the water and breathing in a lungful. No, stupid thought. Shut up, Pen. How bored I was already with these self-generated, self-pitying conversations. Cara, come back, all is forgiven.

No, scrap that, nothing is forgiven.

My hand reached down through the skin of water to comb out my curls and open me up to the water. A clot, silky between finger and thumb. It looked like a baked raspberry, leaking two or three little jewels which fell and went floating on separate eddies. I leaned my elbow on my padded ribs and held the cluster of blood up to the light. Women who slept with men, it occurred to me, felt enormous gratitude or grief when the blood came down, depending on what they were wanting. Kate took a pill every day of her life to make sure the cycles kept spinning safely. I opened my fingers, the chips of ruby clinging to their tips. For me this month, it was a proof of something similar, of life surviving in this separate, single body of mine, whether or not I asked it to.

So this was my first bleeding with Cara not in the world. I waited to register the thought, trying the pain on for size. This blood was the sound of a body clock ticking in my ear, not telling me the shortness of life, like the magazines say it does for childless women, but tolling its length. Life in this unnatural century being generally longer than any one passion or journey, so that even when the story for which you seem to have been born is told, the body clicks on, telling you that you're alive, you're alone, you're alive, you're alone, and you cannot have one without the other. The choice of dead and together not being available to you, because if you ran after the one you love into death, like a squalling child, she might easily be angry and say, you're always following me, give me space to miss you in, back off a bit, all right? If I stayed here, not in this bath but in this rapidly cooling life, if I stayed here and lived out however many years were allotted to me, then surely by the time I got to heaven Cara would be impatient to sweep me off my feet?

I climbed out of the bath with a crash of water and dried myself carefully to avoid bloodying the towel. To bed quickly now, before the emptiness of the house had a chance to suck me down. I lined up the resources on my shelf; a glass of water, a small packet of aspirin, a packet of lemon puffs, my walkman with Bach already loaded and extra batteries. I pulled back the duvet and studied the markings of the sheets. I speculated on which faint tracks were Cara's, which were mine, which were the most recent, and how we'd made that V-shaped tear in the bottom of the sheet. I hoped I wouldn't leak tonight; it would seem disloyal to lay down a fresh mark, as if sealing a new document that superseded the old.

I settled on my back and shut my eyes. The ache below my waist was just beginning. The only thing that ever really helped it was not a tablet but Cara's sure hand, lapping at the red, eager to heal. 'Strictly for medicinal motives,' she'd murmur in my ear. That was not a painkiller I'd ever have again, I told myself, and then I told myself to shut up, because my self was too tired for reality tonight, it would rather take any bit of oblivion going.

What Cara liked best was the taste of me bleeding. She got her red wings – don't ask me where she picked up the phrase, very Air Force – when we were seventeen or so. In her vegetarian phase, I figured it was her primary source of iron.

Blood could be dangerous. About two years ago we started reading those articles on safe sex seriously rather than skimming over them; the first I remembered was a piece in Cara's newsletter, about how little the scientists had bothered to discover about woman-to-woman transmission. We had decided that, rather than having Cara take a test, we'd make our practices safe from now on. (I suggested this because I didn't want to hear exactly what risks she had taken, or was planning to take, with which people.) In fact the biggest change we made was to stop sharing a toothbrush.

Cara came home with a free dental dam from a club once; it was made of such thick latex that we got the giggles and ripped eye-holes in it for a Zorba mask. Instead of barrier methods – the phrase always sounded to me like strategic nuclear defence – we agreed to give up the taste of blood. For a while Cara sulked, like a vampire denied her prey. We felt fearful and ignorant, like schoolgirls all over again, only this time there was no book of secrets to borrow from our mothers' shelves. We were a little angry with each other, and very angry with whoever was failing to tell us just what we were risking. Thinking about it now, I suspected that avoiding blood was more of a token sacrifice in this long Lent. It was as if we were saying, we're not so arrogant that we think we're absolutely safe, so in the meantime, death, here is something we will leave to you, a small thing, but the most intimate.

When I shut my eyes now, I was hovering over Cara, an inch from her cherry-red clitoris.

The hood of the clitoris was not a hood to take off, only to push back In fact the whole thing was a series of folds and layers, a magical Pass the Parcel in which the gift was not inside the wrappings, but was the wrappings. If you touched the glans directly it would be too sharp, like a blow. It was touching it indirectly, through and with the hood, that felt so astonishing. Like an endearment in a mundane sentence, or a cherry on a rockbun, the combination was all. It was not the bald revelation that thrilled me, but the moment of revealing; not the veil or the bare body, but the movement of unveiling.

I rolled over until my forehead was pressed into a cool part of the pillow. The quilt was heavy on my back.

Even if I had had any basis for comparison, I think Cara's clitoris would have seemed to me to be the most beautiful thing. I remembered one time when not licking her turned me on even more than licking her could. Perverse and Catholic, no doubt, but just calling up the memory of it softened and hardened me.

I slide on to my back. She reaches over in exhaustion for a throatful of water; the glass lurches in her hand, sloshing water over the bedside table. I wait till she has put it down in the puddle, then pull her to sit over my face, without asking. There are berry-black tide marks on the tops of her thighs, and a clear droplet suspended in her rusty fuzz. She arches her back, holds herself away from my face. 'Gimme,' I say gently. 'I'm thirsty for it.'

I cannot see Cara's expression, but her voice is rough. 'I'm still bleeding.'

'I know,' I tell her, 'I can smell it.' I let out a sigh; it blows back her coppery curls, tickling her, so she laughs under her breath and leans forward, her spine curled. Hair falls round her face, obscuring it. Her legs spread wider, for balance, and as I strain to focus my eyes I can see a drop of blood blossom between them. I remember the risk, but right now I want to be so close that anything carried in her veins will be carried in mine too. I am so tempted; I suspect that if I did, she wouldn't have the heart to stop me. The drop glints in her curls like a hidden ruby. I breathe in loudly so she can hear me smell her. Ginger and mackerel and chocolate cake and the ring of metal, that's what she smells like. I laugh out loud because she smells so damn good. I want to arch my neck and take the drop between my lips like nectar. I want to find her out with the tip of my tongue, going straight to where, though she might expect it, the sensation will startle her most. The reliable surprise of the body saying, oh, that, oh yes that indeed, please that, I had forgotten quite how sweet that was. She will hurl her head back, and only my arms will anchor her to the bed. The delicate folds will spread wide as I shut my eyes and burrow into the red; they will keep my whole face warm. I want to take Cara into my mouth so that no danger can find her, no monster can terrorize her, where there is no lack or draught or hollow, nothing but heat and pressure and the safety of knowing every drop of you is wanted.

And because she knows right well that I want all that, the wanting is enough. I contract inside with a slow shudder. I hover below her, murmuring breath into her as if I am praying. At last Cara growls like a big cat and leans back to sit on my chest. She rubs herself up and down, skidding and slipping, her wrists in my fists, her growl rising. The breath is almost knocked out of my lungs as she grinds on my ribs, daubs me like a furious painter, marks me for her own.

Keeping time with my own memory, I came to meet myself.

In the blessed lull that always followed, I brought my fingers to my mouth and tasted – my body no danger to itself – the mixture of blood and excitement, iron and silver. I wiped my fingers on the edge of the sheet; laundry tomorrow. I could see their stain in the arc of light as a car went by.

My other hand closed over the boat resting in the hollow of my throat. It was no ocean-crossing caravel tonight, but a mutinous hulk riding low in the waves, its great wheel spinning unattended, its long ropes twitching like scars. Still, I held on.

How many months and years did I have to bleed on my own now? How many spoonfuls of blood could the body lose before the river of it would sweep me up to Cara, before I felt her mouth on me again?

I shut my eyes tight, heaved on to my side and composed myself for sleep. I was throbbing; it shook the bed. I was more alive than I could bear.

SATURDAY

I woke in the night, to find myself flat on my back, limbs stretched to the four corners of the bed like Leonardo's diagram. I was stiff but I didn't move. I was taking up the whole bed. Hard to breathe, spreadeagled on this raft, bucking on the waves of memories. I lay there until everything calmed and the morning started coming in under the blind. My cramps were gone. I was wrapped round, anaesthetized by light.

The clock said five to eight. I rolled up the blind; the yellow light was raw silk puckered in the tree-tops. Kate's plane would be taxiing on to the runway now. As it took off, with the low sun behind it, it would cast a plane-shaped shadow on the nearby fields, a shadow which would shrink and slow and fade as the plane rose. Her eye would let slip the tiny arrow of darkness for a minute, then finally lose it in the dark blue of a winding road.

It's not every day you get the chance to win £20,000 but today's the day, Miss O'Grady! I tore the prize draw leaflet in quarters and poured milk on a small bowl of oatmeal. The cat stretched hugely, his claws scraping the wicker chair, and jumped on to the table. Grace, I thought, do you need me? Does it have to be me who feeds you and scratches you behind the ears?

He looks at me dubiously.

Ah, go on, Grace, you do sort of like me, I can tell.

I put a little lump of milky oatmeal on the table; he bent to sniff it, then jumped down on to the lino. Need, no, that was not it. I suspected that anyone would serve his purposes. But the fact was that he was still here.

I peered down at his clawmarks on my chest. They were

healing up already, so miraculous were the regenerative powers of skin. Of course, it never really healed the old, it just grew more to fill the gaps. I tried to remember how many months they said it took for the entire surface of the body to renew itself. When would I have shed the skin that touched Cara, that Cara touched? When would I have wriggled away like a snake and become something new?

Having worked my way through half the bowl – not bad at all – I emptied and washed it. The light was sharp in the kitchen window; I could see blue sky stretched over the sycamore tree. A walk would be the best thing for my body, which was starting to cramp again. When I stepped out the front door, I caught the whiff of autumn for the first time.

Halfway up the road, a sudden cacophony at my feet made me leap sideways on to the grass verge. That little bastard of a Jack Russell, I could hear him panting in triumph at the bottom of his garden door. I found a fallen branch in the long grass, and, stepping quietly up, shoved it under the door. A yelp of shock came from the other side. I dragged the branch from side to side twice, then left it there, as a warning.

It must have been earlier than I thought, because the woods were empty. There were red berries coming on a bush near the entrance, but fuchsia still hung their scented finger-tips nearby. I cupped one in my hand. Around the long stamen clustered five or six shorter ones, dusted in pollen; I brushed them against my lips. I nipped the flower off where it met the stem. When I put my tongue to the cut it only tasted like plants usually do. Cara taught me to do this: 'Taste the nectar,' she'd exclaim. I'd lick the fuchsia, say 'Mmm,' and meet her smile. I didn't want to disappoint her. Whether or not that counted as a lie depended on what level of satisfaction was implied by 'Mmm'. Besides, maybe I wasn't missing anything; maybe that thin plant taste was all nectar was.

The sky was absolutely clear over the tree-tops as I made

my way upwards. My steel comb was in my coat pocket but I hardly felt the need of it today.

I knew a girl at school who liked to go hitchhiking in the summers. She had made her way round Ireland with no trouble, because everywhere she went she carried a bag of apples. If she accepted a lift from a man, she sat in the front seat, exchanged a few pleasantries, and then took out her knife and began peeling one of her apples. She would make that apple last the length of the journey, slicing it into transparent crescents against her thumb, peeling off the skin and eating it separately, tangy between her teeth. None of the drivers ever laid a hand on her. Now, I'm not sure how good she would have been with that small knife if she'd had to defend herself – worse than useless, I suspect – but on a symbolic level she had them cowed from the start.

All the women I knew carried some kind of blade, though they were not all metal, or even visible. Whether something had happened to them, or whether they had only anticipated it, it kept them awake the occasional night. I found it interesting that some who had only imagined the man in the woods were more haunted by him than some who had looked him in the eye. Not that women often actually put words to such things, not in this country anyway, but if you listened carefully you could hear the gaps in the conversation.

Such fear was very far away now. The air was clear. I walked on, tracing figure eights around the trees. If I shut my eyes for a second and concentrated hard, I could feel Cara's cold hand in mine.

We are up in the woods once, whiling away our teens. Cara has just been on an expensive drama course – we suspect her father is trying to make sure she doesn't pine for her mother and sister – and can remember nothing but the trust exercises. She is fascinated by the idea of putting yourself in someone else's hands. 'But that happens every time we go to bed,' I point out.

'Yes,' she answers, 'but we have to do exercises as well.'

She blindfolds me with my school tie. The nylon is heavy, chafing my cheek-bones. I can open my eyes slightly but the lashes scrunch against the material, so I close them again. When the tie begins to slip, I reach up and knot it so tightly that I see stars behind my eyelids.

At first Cara leads me along, that's easy. I hold on to the frayed cuff of her red jumper, and step only where she has stepped. Then we try it with her behind, pushing me on; that is scary but still safe. Finally she makes me try it with no hands. Her voice directs me away from the woods into the big field, with only the occasional 'right a bit' to interrupt the calm. She tells me that there are no trees for a hundred yards in every direction. I have no reason not to believe her.

'Go where you like,' says Cara now. 'I'll only say something if there's an obstacle.' I walk on, but I can feel my shoulders hunching to protect me and my face furrowing into a helmet. 'Run,' she calls.

'I'll go out of earshot.'

'No you won't, I'll keep up with you,' she promises.

I begin to jog, but my bones are frightened stiff. I hear an occasional laugh to one side, behind me, in front; I change direction to follow it. Then there is no voice, no birdcall, nothing but the sound of the wind picking up. I try to loose myself like a kite and run right into the wind. I run as fast as I can for a couple of seconds then am brought up short, convinced there is a wall just in front of me. I can almost feel the rough bricks against my nose. I throw up my hands and can feel nothing, but I know the wall is there.

I hear Cara's feet thumping to my side. I try to explain about the wall. 'There isn't any wall,' she says. 'Don't you trust me?'

I can still feel the wall but I don't take off the tie. I trot on cautiously. Hesitation removes the balance from my run, and so when my foot hits an awkward hummock it does not have enough speed to carry it over, but turns, and throws me on to damp grass.

I sit up, dizzy, and wrench off the bandage. Cara is stuttering with apology. Do I still trust her, will I try it again?

'Later,' I say.

As soon as I got back to the big house, I hit a rush of energy. I corrected my class's mediocre Maths homework, then put Grace into a frenzy by moving the feather duster like a bird for him to chase. I went into all three bedrooms to fetch the sheets. Kate had left hers in a neat pile. In the bin was a broken comb, some papers torn in half, and an apple core. On the wall over the bed I noticed a sticking plaster. Was it covering a rip in the wallpaper? I pulled it back to see, but the only rip in the paper was the one I had just made.

In my room I stripped off all the bedding, then put Cara's crumpled knickers back under the pillow. I carried the sheets downstairs and pushed them into the washing machine, then went into Mr Wall's room because the door was slightly open. He was still in bed, curled up with the blanket over his head. When he heard me he leaped, like a rock splitting. His pale face turned towards me, eyes shut against the light. I had never seen him unshaven before.

'Are you all right?'

His voice came out in a whisper. 'Fine. Had one of my headaches last night, I'm just sleeping it off.'

'Not another migraine?'

'Just at the front of the head. The worst of it's over now.'

'They say if stress builds up it can –'

'Cheese,' he interrupted, 'I was unwise enough to have Wensleydale with the port last night.'

'Chocolate does that to my mother,' I said after a second.

Mr Wall nodded, then lifted his hand to his head as if holding it together.

I softened my voice. 'I'll be going shopping later; was there anything particular you wanted?'

'No. Whatever you like.' One eye opened. 'Perhaps you could pick up the paper? I don't quite feel up to it.'

'Sure.'

As I poured the liquid into the plastic ball for the washing machine, I was troubled by a vision of Mr Wall after I moved out. He might 'feel up to' less and less, start living off dry toast, sit watching a blank TV screen and finally be found three weeks dead by the electricity meterman. Then I turned on the washing machine and told myself to stop being ridiculous; the man was just taking a morning off.

While I was feeling so extraordinarily capable, I emptied Cara's luggage on to her bed. The small plastic bag from the hospital included her passport and ID cards. I put each in an envelope addressed to its issuer – an easy enough task, since none of the horrible inch-wide photos looked a bit like her – and sealed them up.

The car started first time. I found myself humming along to the radio as I turned the corner; how bizarre. Maybe this was the day I would lose my mind.

The local supermarket was clogged with matrons in cashmere cardigans hesitating over smoked salmon. I walked round the five aisles as fast as possible, throwing into the basket whatever took my fancy. I dropped in a tin of tuna, then put it back on the shelf, because it was Cara who liked tuna.

When I got home, the plastic bags of groceries sagged on the counter. I stood still, and heard one of the bags whistle under its breath then settle down. There wasn't enough room in the fridge for all I had bought; I had to tug out a white box which turned out to contain a chocolate gâteau. It was nice of Kate to remember; she had done her best, really. I cut myself a narrow slice; it tasted of nothing in particular, but I finished it anyway. There was no room in the fridge, so I left the rest of the gâteau in the larder in case Mr Wall wanted any.

As I was putting the spaghetti away, I found the last two tins of Cara's tuna, and put them into the box the video came in. Then I noticed the half-empty jar of capers, and added that. After a complete editing of the shelves, the box was jammed with everything from pimento olives to coarse-cut marmalade. I could decide what to do with it later.

Under a Sunday supplement from last week I found this morning's post. An invitation to a teacher-training college reunion, an offer of cheap window-cleaning, and a postcard of a black cat basking on a whitewashed wall. Oddly enough it took me a second or two to recognize the tiny handwriting.

My Fountain Pen, how's it go? Hope you two are taking care of each other and not pining more than is strictly necessary.

This is a good island I'm on. Oranges that fill the fist, and more sunlight than a girl knows what to do with. Keep having profound thoughts then forgetting what they were. Slept last night on warm black gritty sand, here is some. Below the words was the mark of some tape or sticking plaster that had fallen off; one grain of black still adhered to the cardboard.

Yesterday I found an old nunnery built over a ravine. It's run by goats now, one black and one white. Never been anywhere so beautiful. I wanted to jump out into the blue but don't worry I didn't. We're going to the beach bonfire now, I have to go. The wimmminyn send their love. My legs are getting so strong now (though no tan only freckled knees) are you proud of me? Do you miss me? See you sooner.

The smell of beeswax came into the room before Mr Wall did. He smiled at me, and started on the cabinet with his soft cloth. When he had moved on to the arms of the big chair, I said, 'Lovely, aren't they?'

'What, these old things?' He stared down. 'I've always thought so.' Halfway down the back of the chair, he murmured, 'My wife used to stumble into them and swear. Under her breath, so the children wouldn't pick up bad language.'

I let out a chuckle.

'If she'd ever actually asked me to move them, I expect I would have.' His jaw looked immovable.

'How long was it before . . .' I got embarrassed halfway, and ended gruffly, 'You know, it went wrong. Between the two of you. If you don't mind my asking.'

Mr Wall put down his cloth and rested his knuckles on his hips. 'Do you know, Pen, I'm not sure it was ever right.'

'Yeah, but when –'

'Well, I remember by the time we went to the Outer Hebrides for our fifth anniversary, we were no longer charmed by the contrasts between us.'

I waited for more. Was Winnie irked by the way he used to fold his socks over the chair? Did her rudeness to waitresses jar his nerves? Then I realized that he was of a more tactful generation than mine, and unlikely to offer any details. 'So did you stay together for the children?'

'No,' he said pleasantly, 'we hadn't had them at that point.'

'So why on earth –'

'One did.' He blinked up at me. 'That's what one did, in those days.'

'Oh.' On impulse, as I looked down at the scrawled card in my fingers, I asked him, 'Have you read this?'

'It was addressed to you,' said Mr Wall with a hint of rebuke.

'But didn't you recognize the writing?'

'Oh yes.'

I wouldn't believe it from anybody else, but I was sure he hadn't read past the first words. Not that it mattered, because Cara hadn't said anything indiscreet. I handed the postcard over. While Mr Wall read it – slowly, as if memorizing the sentences – I busied myself with washing a few dishes. When he spoke I had to turn the taps off to hear him.

'She seems to be having quite a nice time,' he repeated.

I stared at him, then looked down at the postcard as he handed it back. My fingers were wet, they smeared the ink at the side. I put the card down on the counter and dried my hands on the stiff tea-towel hanging over the radiator.

Mr Wall went back to his beeswaxing. My cramps seemed to have disappeared. I climbed upstairs and began on the bedrooms.

It's not that I'm trying to wipe you off the surface of the

earth, I told Cara; I'm just clearing myself a bit of room, and if I don't do it today I may never get around to it.

Fallen down the back of her stuffed bookshelf, I found my Inter Cert English poetry book. I let the pages fly by between my fingers. How scarred these innocent lyrics had been by the time my bossy pen was finished with them; loops connected every death image or alliterative *s*. Stern vertical lines of *abab ccdd efe* reminded the verse of its rhyme scheme. Yellow fluorescent marker, faded to pale orange, determined the lines to be learned 'off by heart' – such a euphemism for rote learning, as if the heart had anything to do with it. And how pompously sure I had been in my interpretations at sixteen: *theme: man seeks immortality*, I had informed my future self, or *sad images but triumphant conclusion*. Only one wobbling *perhaps entire sonnet ironic?* suggested that I had left any room for doubt. I watched the round squiggling handwriting of the girl who had never had a woman come in her hand.

Most of our private notes, Cara's and mine, had been hastily rubbed out – there were crumbs of rubber in the cracks – but the occasional word was still legible. On the bottom right-hand corner of 'Kubla Khan', faint letters spelled out 'Hello PenUltimate'. I browsed on, the titles stirring my memories. The daffodils were still jocund, gallant Bess was still tied to the bed with the gun to her breast, and the traveller kept on knocking at the moonlit door and asking over and over, 'Is there anybody there?'

I tucked the book into the shelf, and opened Cara's wardrobe. Her house-painting smock with the blue and yellow handprints all over it: I held it in my hands for a minute, and felt loss like a knife between the ribs, but pushed it away. I'd keep the smock. Everything else was too small for me. Thank god we never had a chance to be one of those clone couples who shared each other's clothes. Except, the odd time, Cara would fold herself up in one of my ever-growing cardigans, and prance about with the wool hanging like bat's wings, crowing, 'I'm you, look, I'm you now.'

I worked on. I found it helped to be objective, as if I was

going through a rack of costumes for a play. The wardrobe's rainbow of fabrics reflected Cara's uneasy shifts in taste and self-assessment, ranging from an opera cloak to black denim dungarees, from a short red gypsy shirt to a home-dyed combat jacket. (And then there was her anti-objectification phase in the early eighties, when, if anyone remarked that her trousers looked nice, she'd take them off and put on a plainer pair.) The range of T-shirt slogans was bewildering; apart from the ones in German that I couldn't understand, the prize for oddity went to a hand-painted 'IF THE TRUTH COULD BE TOLD ...' As I folded them all into a couple of black binliners, I wondered what the Oxfam customers were going to make of this motley collection. I hauled the sacks downstairs, and looked for the blue dungarees to add in, but they were gone from the window-sill; Kate must have taken them home with her.

I shook open another big bag for Cara's collection of Agatha Christies and back issues of *Spare Rib*. Then a sack for the bin: boxes of manifestos, address lists, flyers for marches and fund-raising pub quizzes. Badly typed draft letters for Amnesty International prisoners that all seemed to begin, 'Dear Most Honourable Grand Minister for Internal Matters, I know how busy you must be'. Stacks of yellow and green T-shirts that never sold, from her year in the printing co-op.

It was when I was glancing through the choked drawers of the tiny desk that I found her cache of letters. Old paper, softened at the folds like lines on a face. I had no wish to read them, but I couldn't bear the idea that words she had prized enough to keep should simply be thrown in the bin. I decided that any with addresses on the back of the envelope could be sent back with a note, and if the addresses had changed, well, they would be forwarded. Any with a name on the last line that I recognized could be sent back too. The ones with names that made no sense to me would have to go in the bin. As I sorted through the letters, my eyes could not help catching the occasional line, like snatches of passing conversations as you walked down a street. 'I think the root of the problem', I read, and 'what makes me laugh' and 'don't you sometimes find', and one rather pathetic 'we are all well here'. Luckily my eye never caught my own name. I didn't know what I would have done if it had. My morality had never been tested under circumstances like these.

When I got tired I sat on the bed, shifting back until the curve of my spine was against the wall. All these people, all these letters, the complex relations of a truncated lifetime. What gave me the right to dispose of them? Only the number of times I had woken beside Cara, before the post brought the day's letters.

I wake up with touch lust, some summer morning. We are in her room at the back of the house, to avoid the sun. My arms are stuck to my sides, my fingers are aching. I smile at Cara's sleeping eyelids. I rest my forehead lightly against hers, and reach around her to trace with one thumbnail from the crown of her head, through the damp hair, down the path of her spine. I'll do this over and over, sometimes sending sharp fingers down the back of her arms, sometimes veering round her ribs or ski-jumping her hip, till she floats to the surface of consciousness. I can tell I'm turning her on already because her nose is itching; she scratches the pointed tip of it confusedly.

I know where she was last night – here, in the bed we shared – but not the night before. She came home from the Attic with dark bags under her eyes, and I had to tell myself for the thousandth time that if it was anything important, anything that threatened or rivalled what we have, she would tell me. None the less, as her breathing starts to quicken and her shoulder-blades to writhe under the rasp of my nails, I realize that I always have something to prove. Not to Cara so much as to myself. If I am not to be her only lover, then I need to be convinced that I'm the best.

She twists around, all at once, and wriggles backwards into the bow my body makes, murmuring sounds that are not words in any language I know. Her surfaces cleave to mine. I move her legs to where I want them to be and hold them down. Her surprised breath is punched out once a second, now, as if making room for me in her narrow body. At this point I always question my motives, my greed for power over the ins and outs of her. Is it still love if I am speeding this rhythm not so much for her pleasure as for mine? Cara would laugh at the question, if she could hear it. I move her wider till she starts to make a sound like a sob. I whisper in her ear, 'No noise. Your dad mightn't be gone to work yet.'

It occurs to me now that maybe it is the occasional bloodletting of Cara's infidelities that has kept us pulling each other's clothes off, on and off, for thirteen years, when according to so many of her books, lesbians are meant to hit bed death after two. She has told me that no one else could know her body and her body's mind the way I do, and I believe her. But always, in fear and delight, I have something to prove.

She is hyperventilating now; I hope she doesn't faint like she did once. Her whisper when it emerges is salty as old rope. 'I believe in God.'

'No, you don't.'

'Right now,' she pants. 'Right this minute I do.'

After the waves throw her, she lies placid as seaweed. Her two tears taste of harbours. Her eyebrows huddle like gulls.

I shook the memories out of my head and got up, grabbing the pile of envelopes. I'd have to do the rest another day. I simply had to get out of this room or I would be sucked back in time till there was nothing of me left here.

While the vacuum was on was the only time I liked singing. I moved from the landing into my bedroom now, keening into the roar of the machine:

> but her ghost wheels her barrow
> through streets broad and narrow
> crying cockles and mussels, alive alive-o

The traditional songs were best for housework. Their rhythms kept my arms moving, like the women doing roughly this kind of work (only longer and sorer) in all the other centuries.

> with their drums and guns and guns and drums
> the enemy nearly slew you
> my darling dear you look so queer
> och Johnny I hardly knew you

Why were the death songs the catchiest? The lyrics were cruel, but somehow satisfying.

> you haven't an arm and you haven't a leg
> you're an eyeless noseless chickenless egg
> you'll have to be put in a bowl to beg
> och Johnny I hardly knew you

Cara would have laughed at that. It was as well that she hit the frame of the car head-on; she would not have wanted to survive as an eyeless noseless chickenless egg. She found the juggling balls of life hard enough to keep in the air, with all her limbs intact.

When I came downstairs, slapping the dust off my palms, Mr Wall was bent over the newspaper. 'I hope the noise didn't bother you?' I asked him. 'I forgot about your head.'

His reading glasses glinted as he turned his face up. 'Oh no, all better now.'

I made myself a cup of coffee so that I could offer him one without it seeming any trouble. He passed over the Weekend section of the paper; I sat at the opposite end of the table, my eyes meandering through the articles. When I glanced up, the lines in his forehead seemed a centimetre deep. 'I've,' and I paused to clear my throat, 'I've been reading this book on bereavement my friend Robbie gave me.'

'Oh yes?'

There was no way to say this without sounding rude. 'It said that if you don't talk to someone it can sort of fester.'

'Really?'

'You might think you're doing all right, but it builds up, and then you get backache and migraines and things.' Mr Wall was staring into his coffee cup; I ploughed on. 'I know friends can be hard to talk to, so I thought maybe someone professional . . .'

'You want me to see a psychiatrist?' His tone was odd. I had never seen him angry, so I was not sure I would recognize the symptoms.

'Or a priest,' I added. 'They're meant to be able to give . . . some comfort.'

Mr Wall nodded. 'But I would be taking it under false pretences.'

I stared at him.

'I don't believe,' he explained. 'Heaven and hell and all that.'

'God.'

'Afraid not,' said Mr Wall with polite regret. 'Not since . . . 1977. Yes, that was the year I lost it.'

'Was that –' I swallowed. 'Mrs Wall went that year, didn't she? And Kate.'

'No, that was the year after.'

I sat in silence, my teeth closed over the edge of the coffee cup. I took a long slug of it, then remembered something. 'But I've never known you to miss mass, even.'

'Well, in the early days, you see, I wanted to set an example for Cara. And even when she stopped coming along, I had the habit of it. Sense of community, I suppose. Kept an open mind, you know, in case I was wrong.'

'You don't go to confession?'

'Oh no.' He cleared his throat in amusement. 'I've no wish to argue morality through a grille with the Monsignor. I do take the host at communion, but it's really just bread to me.'

'Bread,' I repeated. 'So. If you don't believe any of it . .

276

you don't think you'll meet Cara again?' As soon as I had said it, I wished I hadn't.

'Well, you never know,' said Mr Wall tactfully. 'But no, I imagine we are snuffed out like candles. Little candles,' he repeated.

My coffee was lukewarm but I drank it down. I couldn't meet his eyes, so I traced the pattern of knots on the table.

'Now, Pen,' he said more briskly, 'I understand you may have somewhere you want to go.'

'I've been shopping already,' I told him. 'Did you want a lift somewhere?'

'No.' He took out a cotton handkerchief and blew his nose. 'I mean in the more long-term sense. I suppose you will be wanting to move in with friends, or perhaps back to your mother's house?'

He wasn't wasting much time before chasing the wolf from the hearth, was he? My head swung heavily. 'I suppose.'

'I was wondering if you could delay your departure for a little while.' He coughed softly. 'Quite a comfort having you here.'

'It is?'

'Of course.' His eyes were owlish. 'I would hardly have thought that needed saying. And if there were any arrangement we could come to that would persuade you to stay –'

'But I'd love to.'

'If you didn't have other plans.'

'I don't have any other plans,' I told him.

'But you said . . .'

'Well, I thought you were kicking me out.' My voice was high with embarrassment and relief.

'Quite the opposite.' Mr Wall took his glasses off and rubbed at them with a fold of his cardigan. 'I'm afraid I just presumed there would be other places you would prefer to live. If you have the slightest interest in staying here, you would be most welcome.'

The air was breathable again. 'You're sure I wouldn't be in the way? My salary does me fine, I could afford somewhere else,' I gabbled. 'It's not like I'm a relative or anything, you've no obligation to house and shelter me.'

'You've been more than ... Like a daughter,' he concluded, so low I could hardly hear.

'Well.' I took a long draw of air. 'That would be great. What rent should I pay?'

Mr Wall seemed to remember something. 'I was wondering if we might come to some terms. Just a second.'

I leaned my forehead on my crossed arms for a minute while he was gone.

He returned with a coverless pamphlet in his hand. 'I came across this a while back,' he said, 'and it was most convincing. These women argue about the economic value of all work, you see.'

I took it from his eager hand. It was an early seventies publication of the Wages for Housework Campaign; Cara and I had got it in with a job-lot of trashy lezzie novels when the Alternative Bookshop had a clear-out. I wanted to laugh but held it back.

'It strikes me,' he rushed on, 'that you do all these jobs that family members often do for each other; you cook almost all the meals, do more than your share of the cleaning, you drive me around in your car and ... well, generally contribute to the quality of domestic life. So really you are earning your rent already.'

'That seems far too generous,' I told him.

'Well, leave the details for now. You could tot it all up yourself later and see what's fair.' He buttoned up his cardigan. 'I should be getting on with things,' he muttered, and went off to his room.

I stared around me, at the white walls, the curve of grass held in the window, back at the long sweep of table. No goodbyes, then. Did Cara's father have any idea what kind of woman he was giving the keys to the castle? I felt a stab of guilt at the prospect of taking free lodging from a man whose daughter I had seduced in just about every room of this house while he was out at the library. But I supposed he liked my company. Like a daughter, he said.

There were a dozen chores left to do, but instead I was going to make biscuits. I shoved *Reward Women's Work Now* and various books and papers out of the way, to clear a circle on the kitchen table. The sleeves of my baggy flannel shirt wouldn't stay above my elbows, so I found a couple of elastic bands in the back of the drawer. I remembered another occasion on which I had countered depression with biscuit-making and left the sugar out by mistake, creating what Cara, returning from another lengthy weekend in Bruges, had christened Chocolate Charcoal. But this time I would get it right. I'd use honey instead of sugar; honey was less forgettable.

The flour fell through the sieve into the shape of a sand dune. Resting a slab of butter on my palm – I had never held with measurements – I cut it in chunks that fell noise-lessly into the flour. Rubbing in was irksome, but once I had overcome my resistance to getting my fingernails full of glue, and found a rhythm for my fingers it was satisfying. It took just enough thought – where to rub hardest, when to swirl the loose flour round – to keep the bogeys from my mind. Grace leaped up on the table with his curious look on, but I gently slid him off with my elbow.

The strangest thing about this week was how little I had cooked. The few meals I'd pulled together had been done on autopilot. Not that grief had cut my appetite much, but it did seem to make me consume in a more mechanical way. Eating a packet of cheap biscuits demanded nothing of me, whereas baking my own made me live in the here and now.

When I was a child my mother only let me bake on special occasions, because of the expense of ingredients. But as soon as I paired up with Cara, who despaired of ever being able to grow a decent curve anywhere, I invented and ate all the desserts I wanted. It fascinated her, how heat metamorphosed such staples as flour and eggs into something quite different, and how my figure blossomed over the years into this extravagant shape.

Mr Wall walked by; I could see him through the glass panels of the door into the hall, as he paused with his fingers on the handle, then seemed to remember something and sloped off again. Funny man.

I remembered the honey this time. I also remembered the ground almonds, scoop of semolina for crunchiness, sprinkle of salt, baking powder, spice. I pounded the dough into a wide sausage and sliced it into rounds, laying them on a blackened tray greased with the butter paper. I did everything Mammy taught me, with the speed that had always characterized her culinary movements at ten to six on a weekday. Then, looking at their dull leavened surfaces, I decided to jazz them up. To the first I added two raisins for eyes, and half a roasted cashew nut for a smile. (It occurred to me to use a sliver of glace cherry instead, but that would be just too femme.) The biscuit looked rather like Cara when she was smirking at something. I did the next one with the cashew turned down in a groan, then continued round the tray, giving each a slightly different expression. Amazing how anthropomorphic was the human eye, that it needed only two raisins and half a cashew nut to conjure up a human face, so desperate were we for company in this wide world.

When I was putting the spices back in the larder I found an old bottle of food colouring, left over from a Red Velvet Cake I made Cara a couple of Valentine's Days ago. I swirled it against the light; plenty left. When I had diluted it in a little water, I brushed it on with my finger, dabbing round the edges of the biscuit faces, making a Jackie Kennedy bob on one, a lone quiff on another.

For ten minutes I sat over the crossword, letting the smell of the biscuits begin to circle round the kitchen. Mr Wall came in just as I was taking the first tray from the oven. He didn't speak until I had put it down; he was probably afraid to make me jump and burn myself. I glanced up at him as I shovelled them on to a wire rack to cool.

'Might I have one of those?' he asked. I made him a cup of Earl Grey to wash it down. He made no comment on my portraiture, just pronounced the biscuit 'very tasty'. Perhaps he thought the red colouring was essential to the flavour. 'Kate,' he said suddenly, 'has invited me to visit Boston next summer.'

'Really?'

'I could drop in on my uncle in Chicago as well. And of course there would be Win.'

'Would you want to see her?' It came out rudely.

'I don't think *want* is the right word,' said Mr Wall. 'It would seem appropriate.'

'I think it would have been more bloody appropriate for her to come to her daughter's funeral.'

He blinked at me.

'It's probably not my place to judge,' I jerked on, 'but to miss it for a speech at a conference –'

'But my dear girl,' he interrupted, 'the conference was neither here nor there.'

'Kate said –'

'Sometimes Win just can't face things, you see. She used to run away from things that were much easier than . . . this occasion.'

'Oh.'

Mr Wall put his biscuit down. 'She said in her letter, you know,' he confided, 'that she'd always been intending to invite Cara on holiday with her. To catch up. Become close again, you see, as two adults rather than mother and daughter.'

'It wouldn't have worked.'

'Probably not.'

After a long minute I said, 'It'll be horribly hot in Boston. You'll have to go without a vest.'

Mr Wall gave a small grin and finished his biscuit.

'I didn't think you were into jetsetting.'

'No, but at times like this they say it's advisable to embrace change.' He patted the crumbs on his plate into a little pile, then pressed his finger into it and raised it to his mouth. Sucking it clean, he rose to go.

'Feel free to change your mind about – sharing the house and all.' My voice came out as a bray.

Mr Wall raised his thick eyebrows.

'I mean it's far too nice of you – no one would expect it – it's not like I'm family.'

He looked at the floor as I flustered, then up at my face. 'But you are my daughter's friend,' he observed in a tone of slight reproof. His gaze shifted to the biscuits again. 'Might I be a glutton and take another up with me?'

I rushed to put two on his saucer, but he put one back on the rack again. 'Delicious.'

I watched his slippers disappear up the stairs. I could not work out why I was so shaken. Only when I had washed up the bowl, knife, spoons, pastry board, and was pushing the brush at an obstinate lump of flour in the sieve, did my mind clear. Mr Wall's words pranced across it, sparkling. *My daughter's friend.* He had practically capitalized it. He didn't mean palsy-walsy friend, schoolfriend, housemate. He meant friend – in the way his generation used it, as a polite euphemism for all the subtle non-marital relationships they didn't want to pry into. He knew. The little bastard knew all along!

I grinned into the orange suds. The sieve was clean enough; nod's as good as a wink to a galloping horse, as my mother liked to say. I laid it on top of the dripping pile of crockery and wiped my hands on a damp dish-cloth. The phone had rung several times before I really registered it.

'What you up to?' Robbie's tone was an uneasy compromise between compassion and cheer.

'Nothing much,' I said automatically, then decided not to bother lying. 'Actually, I've been going through her stuff.'

This was a good phone-line; I could hear the little intake

of breath before Robbie stopped himself from asking what I meant.

I went on. 'Working out what to chuck, what to give to charity, that sort of thing.'

'Are you sure that's a good idea?' he asked.

'No. I'm not sure any of my ideas are good.'

'They say you should leave all that for a couple of months, till you're feeling stronger,' Robbie confided. 'It was in that book I gave you, I saw it when I was glancing through.'

'Well, I'm sorry I'm not doing this bereavement according to the manufacturer's instructions.' The sharp words were out before I had licensed them.

Silence on the line.

'Sorry. I just hate being treated like an invalid.'

'No, I wasn't taking offence, actually,' said Robbie, 'I was just trying to think of something useful to say.' After another gap he went on, 'If you really feel ready to, you know, look through her things, then go for it.'

'I'm not likely to be feeling any stronger in a couple of months,' I told him, 'so I might as well do it while everything's still a blur.'

'Right.'

'Besides, if I don't do it now, I'll spend the next year tripping over Cara's socks and magazines and pickle jars.'

Robbie got halfway into a breath of laughter. 'So, you staying where you are, then?'

'Looks like it.'

'What's keeping you there? Nostalgia?'

'No,' I said, nettled. 'I just like it. Mr Wall has asked me to stay.'

'He the father?'

'Not any more. He's just him now.'

'Suppose so.'

'And I love the man.' The words spilled out of my mouth, surprising me.

'Yeah?'

'He's earned it,' I tried to explain. 'We're not related, I don't owe him a thing.'

'That's nice,' said Robbie warily. 'Didn't think there was much room for men in your life.'

'Ah, come on, don't do the predictable male paranoia thing.'

'How d'ya mean?'

'I'm still the same woman as I was before I spilled the beans on Thursday; you don't have to develop a castration complex all of a sudden.'

He let out a great hoot. 'Fair enough.' After a minute he added, 'You seem to be coping surprisingly well, by the way.'

'I'm sticking out,' I told him.

'Which accent was that meant to be?'

'Belfast. But it didn't work.'

'Listen, hen, I'm just remembering,' said Robbie. 'The book said not to throw everything away, because you might regret not having things to remember her by later on.'

I was living in Cara's house, with her father and cat, under the pictures and fluorescent stars we'd stuck up together, wearing the shirt she'd unbuttoned with her teeth. She was soaked into the walls, stained on the sheets, scratched on the bedpost. 'I don't think I'll be short on memories,' I told Robbie.

''Course not.'

I could tell this call was putting him under some strain, as it was me. I was used to sparring with Robbie always at arm's length; it was unnerving to stand in the hallway of the big house with his voice in my ear. So I pretended I had a cake in the oven. He asked me to come walking in the mountains.

'Next weekend would be better for that. We're . . . sorry, I mean I.' I took a breath. 'I wish I could get used to not saying we.'

'I think the word should be banned.'

'Sorry?'

'We is a myth; how can you possibly speak for anyone but yourself? Sheila says it all the time, it drives me nuts.'

'I suppose you're right.'

'Actually, now,' said Robbie, 'I remember once in the staff-room you said "We thought" about some film, and I wondered who you were time-sharing a brain with.'

I laughed. 'I didn't! Shame on me.'

'You probably didn't even hear yourself say it.'

'But Cara and I never ever thought the same thing about a film.' Then I remembered the excuse about the oven; I hadn't followed it through. 'I'd better be having a look at that sponge, I suppose.'

'See you Monday, then. Take care of yourself.'

I stood at the counter and ate one of the biscuits. Not quite spicy enough, but not bad. I carried the binliners out to the boot, two at a time; they were as heavy as treasure sacks. I went back for my handbag, and then, feeling its accustomed weight on my wrist, felt a surge of impatience. I emptied it out on the kitchen counter: what on earth had I been toting round all these years?

Purse and keys, fair enough. Steel-handled comb. Aspirin, antacid tablets, and sticking plasters, in case anybody needed them. A hairbrush, two combs. A big box of tampons. A spare asthma inhaler for Cara's panics (bin it, go on, do it now before you think about it), half a tube of lozenges stuck together, two half-full packets of tissues (bin them all, you never get colds before Christmas). A worn-down 'Raspberry Risk' lipstick (whose?), a bus timetable, an out-of-date voucher for two pizzas for the price of one. Four biros of assorted colours; I began to test them on the corner of the newspaper, then told myself not to be so anal. I put my purse, keys, and one tampon in my pocket, then opened the top drawer, and swept everything else in. I was going to leave my handbag on the counter where it lay, but I thought Mr Wall might think I had forgotten it and worry, so I squashed it into the drawer too.

My hands felt weirdly light as I went out the door.

Passing the yard, I caught a glimpse of Mr Wall standing at the top of the garden. I joined him, with a mutter of 'Nice day.'

'It is.'

The yellow cushion was still underneath the hammock; perhaps it would rot away slowly this winter, grass embroidering itself through the old brocade. The birdbath had dried up; while I was thinking of it, I went for the watering can and filled the stone bowl up. Mr Wall was staring past me to the bottom of the garden. 'Must do a final mowing one of these weekends,' I said.

'And we should get one of those tree surgeons in to take a look at the sycamore.'

'Do you happen to know,' I asked him, 'which of them planted it? Kate or Cara?'

He looked over his glasses in slight bewilderment. 'Oh, the girls were always grubbing about in the garden, burying all sorts of things.'

'Were they?'

'To tell you the truth, I think sycamores just plant themselves.'

I absorbed that. Then I asked, 'Do you really think it could fall on the house?'

'There's always some danger with trees of that height. But I suppose,' his eyes crinkling at the corners, 'we could give it the benefit of the doubt for another year.'

The traffic was slow, but I rolled my window down halfway and concentrated on the breeze. Town was crawling with shoppers buying summer clothes for next year in the sales. I took a chance and left Minnie on a double yellow line on Stephen's Green, since I'd only be a minute. I found a shop that sold stamps, and posted my handful of ID cards and returned letters. On my way to Oxfam with the first binliner bouncing and slipping on my shoulder, I thought I must look like Dick Whittington's mother chasing after him to London with his clean socks. I swung the door open. Stooping women circled round the navy-blue section, and a boy kept trying to whip open the cubicle curtain to reveal his friend in a Victorian tails suit. I let my sack down beside the desk, and cast an apologetic smile at the woman reaching for her glasses. 'Shoes and raincoats?'

'Lovely,' she said resignedly.

At the top of Grafton Street I paused, feeling the blood well out between my legs. Behind me a pair of horses shifted in their jangling traces as another tittering couple climbed into the carriage. The Jesus man didn't seem to be here today, but one of his 'The Way, the Truth, and the Life' boards was resting against a lamp-post. Up and down the street poured the Saturday afternoon crowd; mothers bent on finding perfect autumn overcoats, old men in greasy tweed hats, bored suburban girls bringing £9.99 bargains to show off to friends over tea and Millionaires' Shortbread. From here I could hear the familiar queasy mix of at least three buskers; that interminable 'Annie's Song' on flute, I thought, and the man with the African drums, and a brass band. I watched the ground; the reddish bricks disappeared and reappeared as the feet and coats rushed over them.

Minnie would definitely get a ticket now. I realized that I didn't care if she got three tickets and was towed away. The sound of the flute lifted for a bar or two above the clang of the brass band, and I was happy. Perversely, incredulously, momentarily happy.

When it was gone and the wave had dropped my feet down hard against the pavement, the crowd looked different to me. The shoppers were no more likeable, but they did have faces. It came into my head that everyone on this street had either gone through a loss more or less equivalent to mine, or would do by the end of their life. Some would have it easier, some worse, some over and over.

Imagine if a giant hand in the sky gestured us to stop, this minute, figures frozen halfway through a stride or a sentence, all along Grafton Street. If the hand gestured for us to tell what was really preoccupying us, then death would be on every second mouth: 'My mam's gone for more tests', one would admit, and the next, 'Well, my uncle and my teacher went last year', and another, 'Our first was stillborn', and another, 'I've a feeling this Christmas might be my last'. I wanted to make everyone sit down on the sun-warmed pavement, arranging their bags and bundles round them, and turn to their neighbour to talk of this huge headline hanging over us. Who have you lost to death, they would ask each other, who are you afraid of losing, who were you glad to see taken, and when do you think death might come for you? The brass band should be playing a triumphant funeral march, and the sun should be making skeleton shadows of our bodies on the gaps of pavement between the groups. The signs behind the polished glass fronts should say 'How many shopping days left?' It made no sense for us to be talking about anything else. And why did we pretend to be strangers when we were all webbed together by the people we had lost and the short future we had in common?

Through the crowd I saw a girl running down the street. Only the back of her; all I could make out was a rusty head of hair, catching the light whenever she emerged from a building's shadow. Probably running for a bus, or twenty-five minutes late to meet a friend at Bewley's. She had almost disappeared into the wide mouth of the crowd; I saw something moving but wasn't sure if it was her. I would never know who or what she was running from or to. My eyes let her slip.

The crowd was swirling, no longer frozen in my vision. It was Saturday afternoon, and there were coats to be tried on and teacups to drain.

When I reached Minnie she was miraculously unticketed. On the hoarding twenty feet away, I noticed, someone had sprayed a huge pair of interlocked women's symbols with smiley faces in the circles. I wouldn't put it past Jo to go out spray-painting at night, once she'd changed out of her work drag. I glanced in the car window at the bulging binliners. It occurred to me now that it would make much more sense to bring them round to the Attic and see who wanted what.

And if that wasn't too awkward, I would consider staying for their wake thing. I was not going to have some crowd of dykes mourning Cara Wall in my absence.

I stopped off at the big house to collect the biscuits. When I was halfway to the car, I remembered Sherry's toothbrush. I found it upstairs in the side pocket of Cara's tote, in the middle of a coverless paperback called *Murder Under Aegean Skies*.

When I got to the Attic there seemed to be no one there. Only after my third set of knocks did Sherry open the door in a crumpled black shirt. 'Sorry, Pen, we're all out the back garden trying to get the barbecue lit.'

I let her glide her lips across my cheek, and handed her the toothbrush without a word. 'Thanks,' she said, staring at it. I walked past her into the hall, which was as shabby as ever; posters of art exhibitions taped up slightly askew, and a catnip mouse at the top of the stairs. Then I remembered the bags, and had to ask Sherry to help me bring them in. Her fine-boned wrists were surprisingly strong. 'What is all this stuff?'

'Cara's clothes and magazines and so on,' I said crisply. 'I thought people might, you know –'

'That's a lovely idea.' Sherry's eyes were very green. 'That's so big of you.'

I ignored her and went back to the car for the basket of biscuits.

Fiona was in the basement kitchen, chopping up apples for the punch. She made me tea in a huge mug with a crescent moon on it, and introduced me to a friend from the History department called Ruth. Jo was not there; she had gone into town to look for nut cutlets for her fellow-vegetarians. The others were skewering sausages and watching the charcoal smoulder on the old bin lid they were using as a barbecue. I was introduced to five or six of them in a row, and instantly forgot their names, except for the fact that at least two of them were called Mary. Since the black bags were attracting some curious glances, I up-ended them on the lawn and told everyone to help themselves. Putting together a plateful of salad, out the corner of my eye I watched a couple of strangers poking through Cara's clothes. Their movements were tentative. I felt for them, as they were clearly afraid to seem greedy, or, on the other hand, lacking in enthusiasm. One tiny woman tried on the 'IF THE TRUTH COULD BE TOLD . . .' T-shirt. When she saw me looking she started to pull it off, but I smiled at her and called out, 'It suits you,' so she kept it on.

Whatever Cara wore looked borrowed. In all her phases, from the theatrical to the sporty, she had seemed to me to be trying someone else's image on for size. So as these women picked their way gingerly through the pile, it was as if they were reclaiming the skins she had stolen. Whereas Cara was naked now and travelling light at last; no tote to fill up with things she thought she might need or presents to lug home. I could imagine her grinning as she watched her clothes being passed out, spread all over Dublin, shared with exes in Cork, given to friends emigrating to America, slowly wriggling their way across the lesbian web. God only knew where that particular dress, for example – a red sleeveless one in scrunched silk that Sherry was tugging over her head – would end up.

Fiona's friend – Ruth, that was the name – was leaning over a lavender bush, its purple heads faded to grey. She rolled one between her fingers, and inhaled, then she rubbed the scent on her temples, under the rim of her black velvet cap. Catching me watching her, she smiled a little sheepishly. 'Good for headaches,' she explained.

'Do you want an aspirin?' Too late, I remembered having left my handbag at home.

'No, no, I'm fine, it's just preventive because of the sun.' She held out the crumbled flower, and I opened my palm for it. 'Hope you don't mind my asking –' she began, her face sobering.

'Mmm?'

'Well, Fiona said you were together for a really long time.

You and Cara. I only met her a few times, over here,' Ruth stumbled on, 'but I remember her talking about you.'

'It was thirteen years this May,' I said rather grandly. It was already beginning to sound unreal, a figure arrived at by adding together your age, weight, and phone number, then dividing by the number you first thought of.

'Wow,' said Ruth, her voice hushed. She hesitated, combing the grass with the toe of her boot. 'This is a kind of crass question, but if she hadn't – if –'

'If she was still here,' I suggested, to save her embarrassment.

'Yeah. Would you, do you think you two would have managed the long haul?'

'Depends how long the haul would have been,' I said.

'You mean, like, for life?'

Ruth nodded, her fingers knotted in the curls at the nape of her neck.

'I've no idea,' I told her. 'I certainly expected we would. But right now I don't have much faith in my ability to predict the future.'

Her nods were deepening. I thought the conversation was over, and was starting to move away, when she said, 'That's what I want.' Her pointed chin was set firm.

'You think so?' I asked, with only a hint of condescension.

'Getting more sure by the year,' said Ruth. Just then Fiona called her over for advice on barbecue sauce.

'Good luck,' I said after her, suddenly, but I wasn't sure if she'd heard.

I held the crumbs of lavender to my nose, lulled by the sweetness as I talked to another primary teacher about class sizes, then to a part-time waitress about tax evasion. From behind us came a squeal of 'Look at all the Agatha Christies, my sister will be in ecstasy.'

Jo turned up at last, windblown and sticky from her bike ride, with no nut cutlets. 'Fuck it,' she said, 'I'll have a sausage.' She put her arms around me lightly then led me inside, the char-black sausage between her teeth. 'Listen,' she said, 'the ritual thingy's not till about seven, and if we all start talking about Cara this early we'll get depressed, so I thought it would be best to watch my French and Saunders videos and eat popcorn.'

It was good to have someone else make the decisions. I sat through the comedy sketches in a state of utter passivity, eating a handful of popcorn every time the bowl passed on to my lap, but never reaching for it. It was strange to be so squashed on a sofa; I was used to empty space around me. Rather funnier than the sketches was listening to Mairéad take the piss out of the ads in between; she had the screamed jingle from the sanitary towel ad almost perfect.

Jo went over to a long-haired woman I didn't know to bum a cigarette, then settled herself back on the sofa. Fiona ruffled Jo's layers of hair as she went by with a bowl of salad. 'There'll be no smoking in our Old Dykes Home, you know,' she said, 'not even at parties.'

'Ah, don't worry your head about me,' Jo called back. 'If I live long enough to have to think about any of that, I won't still be sharing with hardliners like you.'

Fiona blew an absentminded kiss.

Towards the end of the video I must have been looking rather glazed, because Ruth peered up at me from the rug and said, 'Are you OK?'

'Just cramps.'

'Here,' said Sherry, 'let me do your pressure points.'

Engrossed in the next sketch, Mairéad shushed us.

Sherry sat up on the arm of the sofa and, as I was searching for a polite yet barbed rebuff, picked up my right hand. She took my palm between her finger and thumb, and pressed deeply. It hurt for a second, and then I felt something inside me relax. By the time she was finished, in fact, I was gushing so fast that I feared I might leave a permanent memorial on their sofa. I staggered off to their tiny toilet, and read my way through all twelve months of the *Dykes to Watch Out For* calendar on the back of the door. The cartoons didn't make me laugh out loud today; I made a mental note to read them again under different circumstances.

When I came back, they were all carrying cushions out into the garden. 'Jo,' I whispered, tugging at the sleeve of her T-shirt, 'I think I'll be heading off, this isn't my kind of thing.'

She raised her eyebrows as she interlocked her brown arm with my pale one. 'Barely thirty, and already she knows exactly what her kind of thing is.'

I let her lead me out into the back garden. The barbecue had been built up into a real bonfire; it made the garden seem much darker. The rest of Cara's things had been put back in a binliner and propped against the wall.

A woman with hundreds of beads in her hair got us to make a big ring. I sat as far back as I could without breaking the circle, between Jo and Ruth. I listened with one ear as the bead woman called on the elements; I passed the candle, the water, the stone and the feather as each came round to me. As I handed the bowl of water to Ruth, it slopped a little over the knee of her jeans, and we both let out a nervous giggle. No one seemed to mind; it wasn't like being at mass.

With the rest of my brain I was wondering what to teach my class next week. After some stuff about the four quarters, a teenager in lycra running shorts knelt up and sang something in Irish. It sounded sad, but so did most Irish songs; it could have been about donkeys for all I could tell. Then Sinéad read an Adrienne Rich poem, rather gruffly; she kept her dark head low. I thought I recognized it; probably Cara had read it to me once while I was chopping onions. I didn't really listen to the words this time. I thought they might either irritate me – since a cheapo hike around the Greek isles was hardly comparable to the death-defying climbing expedition described in the poem – or move me. I didn't want to be moved in front of all these strangers. I knew that if I cried they would not even have the decency to ignore me.

None of that was too bad. There was no compulsory bursting into spontaneous dance or shedding of clothes. The bad bit was where the hippy with the beads (who was trying to act like she wasn't the leader and it was all just happening under its own steam) threw the floor open, as it were, to individual testimonies about Cara. During a few of them I had to button my lip so as not to mutter 'Ah, come on, she was *not* a wonderful cook', or 'Psychically sensitive, in my eyeball'. Others described Cara in terms that were too pedestrian, as a 'really nice person', or someone who 'gave so much to the women's community'. None of them seemed to catch the colour of her. And what really enraged me, as I sat listening to them praise a woman I barely recognized, was that I didn't figure. I had thought of us for so long as a partnership, but now I was forced to see us as individuals.

There was a silence, then, and when I glanced up from the cooling grass I saw several faces turned towards me. I realized that they were silently conspiring to offer me, as official partner, the last word. I was grateful, but suddenly could think of no speech that would not be facile. The silence was growing; I might miss my chance. 'I'm Pen,' I said at last, staring at the clover and counting its leaves. 'Cara's' – the usual list of possibilities tickertaped through my head – 'lover,' I added in explanation, before the words petered out.

It was getting dark, and colder as the bonfire died down. The beaded woman encouraged us all to inch inwards on our knees and join up. My hands were held by Ruth and Jo; theirs were much warmer than mine. The hippy began a chant. Shy voices all round me began to take it up on the third round.

> hoof and horn
> hoof and horn
> all that dies will be reborn

Sherry came in away to the left with a descant of surprising sweetness, and then the words changed to

corn and grain
corn and grain
all that falls will rise again

Eventually my need to be a part of it floated me over the barriers, and I cleared my throat and joined in, singing very quietly. I don't know how long we kept it up, alternating the two verses; the effect was hypnotic.

When we went back inside, the light from the fire and the lamp was bewilderingly bright. Someone with a pierced eyebrow was rolling some homegrown, and Mairéad was up-ending liqueur bottles for the last eggcupfuls. The punch was a puddle of apple chunks, so Jo passed me a bottle of wine. I would have liked to get absolutely out of my face, but I was driving, so I poured a small glass.

'That was kinda nice,' said Jo doubtfully.

'Could have been much worse.'

'What were you expecting? Babies on pitchforks, or having to weave garlands out of bindweed?'

I gave her a shove on the shoulder.

Jo steadied her wine glass. 'You were brave to come.'

'Hadn't anything much else to do, had I?'

That bottle was soon empty, so another was opened. Sinéad passed round a birthday card from her mother in Wales which said on the inside. *In case you think the passage of time is softening my attitude to your lifestyle, well, it's not.* We groaned in chorus. 'At least she's referring to it,' said Ruth, her chin wedged on the heel of her hand. 'When I finally came out to my mother, she dropped her best sherry decanter in the sink. She hasn't said a word about the subject since, except to beg me not to tell my great-aunt with the dicky heart.'

This line of conversation was depressing us all – except the teenager in the running shorts who claimed her mother was 'totally cool about it' – so I started telling Jo a story about Cara. Just a silly thing about once when she was collecting for the Rape Crisis Centre on Grafton Street and it kept coming out as 'Please support the Ripe Grape Centre'. Halfway through I realized that I had the attention of the whole group, and wished it was a rather more significant anecdote. When they had laughed obediently, I remembered the biscuits and passed them round. The teenager lifted a curly-haired one to the light. 'Hey, they've got faces,' she said.

Jo gave her a slow hand-clap of congratulation. 'Are they meant to be Cara?' she whispered in my ear.

'They're just biscuits, Jo,' I told her. 'Take. Eat.'

Sherry had managed a bite but seemed unable to swallow it; tears ran down and collected in her dimples. I wanted to smash the biscuit into her face. Someone moved to put an arm around her. I looked away.

The bottles of cheap wine were being drained like water. I could hear tail ends of maudlin conversations all round the lounge. 'Did you bring photos?' someone asked me.

'What, of Cara? No, sorry, I didn't think to.'

Jo passed round her copies of the Greek ones. Such casual snapshots, now converted into holy relics, as women craned over each other's shoulders to see Cara in the back row of a group, Cara out of focus on a volcano, Cara sharing a plate of squid. A quick glance round told me that the weeping total was up to five or six. Soon I might be the only stony-faced one. Well, I was damned if I was going to cry just because they expected it of me.

I rested my head on the edge of the sofa and let my ears pick up snatches of conversation. Two strangers, in Cara's 'Greenham Common '87' and '"Free Women Now" – Can *I* Have One?' T-shirts respectively, seemed to be quarrelling over who had known her best. 'It's not that she was unmateri-alistic,' one was insisting, 'that wasn't it at all.' The other said something about projecting your own ideals on to our friends. In the other corner of the room, two old friends had wandered off the topic of Cara and seemed to be arguing over which of them had been celibate the longest. I gave up my attempt to hear through the fog of voices, and finished my wine.

Jo was lying back on the sofa cushions, taking a long draw from a bulging joint. I leaned over on my elbow and asked her if she thought Cara would have liked this party.

'Well, she came to a sort of wake here last year for Mairéad's first girlfriend, and she seemed to enjoy that.'

'Oh yeah, I remember.' That was one of the Attic invitations I had refused. 'Still, I suppose it's different if it's your own.'

Jo let out a giggle and passed me the joint. I told her that I was driving, and held it towards the group on the rug; a hand came up to relieve me of it.

All the women crying, except Sherry, were ones I'd never met before. Maybe tears were in inverse proportion to how well you knew the person the wake was for. Maybe these were volunteers who did the rounds of women's parties, keening or cheering or laughing, depending on what was appropriate. The woman with the beads heaved herself up and staggered towards the kitchen; Fiona climbed into her place on the sofa, tucking her feet under Sinéad's thigh to keep warm. She offered me more wine, and said if I wasn't fit to drive I could always crash there.

'Thanks, but I don't think I'd sleep. Too much emotion floating around,' I told her.

'Tell me about it. I live here,' she said wryly.

'And then there's the nights Mairéad practises her drums . . .' Sinéad chipped in, briefly distracted from her conversation with the social worker.

I covered my yawn with my hand. 'So are you all "on the team", as they say across the water?'

Fiona took off her glasses and rubbed at the bridge of her nose. 'Well, yeah, but I don't think we agree on the words.'

'Mairéad was "ambi" when I looked last,' said Jo, glancing round to find her, 'but she seems to be more serious about this woman in Rome than about any of the boytoys she brings home from gigs.'

'Sherry's "simply a sexual being", then me and Sinéad are

boring old dykes,' contributed Fiona, 'and Jo's the last of the political lesbians.'

'I am not,' protested Jo. 'I'm a lesbian who votes in elections, that's all. Now, hand over that wine with all speed.'

'But the important thing,' Fiona continued in my ear, 'is that we all watch *Roseanne* and *Coronation Street*. Televisual compatibility, that's the secret of housesharing.'

I smiled abstractedly, passing the bottle to Jo. 'You know, back when we were in school Cara insisted she wasn't a lesbian, she just happened to be going out with a human being who happened to be female.'

'Yep, I've used that one myself,' said Fiona reminiscently, accepting the joint passed up from the rug. 'Kept telling Sinéad that the whole first year we were together; d'you remember, love?' But Sinéad was deep in a discussion of Satanic abuse with the social worker.

'When Cara left me for Sean –' I began.

'Who's Sean?' asked Jo.

'Oh, the worst of the batch. He managed to convince Cara she was frigid because, according to his calculations, she wasn't as aroused as she should have been, considering what he was doing to her.'

'Bastard!'

'Then when she came back to me the last time, she said she'd made a political decision to devote her energies to women. I asked did that translate as she had decided to accept the fact that she kept falling for women?'

'What did she say to that?' asked Fiona, stretching over the back of the sofa to give Ruth the joint as she passed by.

'She said I knew her too well.'

They nodded. A sort of gloom seemed to settle over us. Sinéad's head was lying in the crook of Fiona's elbow now. 'I still can't quite believe – oh, forget it,' said Sinéad.

'No, I know what you mean,' murmured Fiona, combing back her lover's hair with her fingers. 'Cara was so bloody young.'

Ruth's head joined us, her chin nodding on the burst arm of the sofa.

'She always seemed like she had so much life ahead of her,' contributed Jo, slurring the consonants slightly. 'She didn't deserve this.'

Sinéad's comment was lost in Fiona's sleeve. 'What you say, love?'

'Who does?' repeated Sinéad grimly.

'Who does what?' Fiona's pupils were dilated, her voice confused.

I decided I was probably the only sober person in the house by now. 'Who deserves to go this young, she was asking,' I explained impatiently. 'But if you look at it the other way round, we're not entitled to a damn thing. It's all luck or fate or God or whatever you call it.'

'Yeah,' said Ruth. 'I suppose Cara got to live about a thousand times longer than most babies born in Africa.'

In the thickening gloom, Jo gave a giggle. 'That has to be the ultimate politically correct conversation-stopper.'

'Sorry,' said Ruth, burying her nose in the sofa.

'I think I need a cup of coffee,' I said, hauling myself up and giving Ruth a small pat on the back of the head.

'Try my cupboard – the one with the Frida Kahlo postcard on it,' yawned Fiona.

In the kitchen, Sherry and the woman with the pierced eyebrow were stooped over the open fridge. 'I just thought it should have been Jo who read out the poem,' Sherry was saying rather drunkenly, 'seeing as she was the last one involved with her.'

I got as far as the kettle before the words sank home. I turned on my heel. They didn't look up. When I reached the living-room, the couch was empty; everyone was clustered round some new photo in the corner. I was suddenly so tired that my cheeks sank and my jaw opened and I leaned to one side, against the burst upholstery of the sofa arm.

Jo's voice in my ear brought me back. 'Why don't you have a lie-down?'

I struggled up, protesting.

'Ah, go on, you could do with one.'

She took me by the elbow and led me up several flights of dark stairs, telling me when to duck my head. I was a hostage with a bag over my head, Jo's hand in the small of my back like a gun. It was quiet in her small room, lined with imitation wood paper to look like a ship's cabin. As soon as the door was shut my strength returned to me. 'Very cosy. Is this where you used to fuck my girlfriend?'

Jo stared at me. Her lashes were faint and sandy against her cheeks.

'You could have told me yourself,' I spat, 'rather than letting me hear it from that twit downstairs.'

'I was waiting for the right opportunity,' she said.

'How long were you going to wait?' The last of my fury leaked out through the words, and I sat down on the edge of the bed, drained.

After a minute, Jo sat down beside me. We both stared at the wall. It had a huge picture of Jodie Foster on it. 'We were just . . . pillowfriends is the best word for it,' she said very low. 'We went to bed a couple of times in total. It wasn't a big deal.'

I said nothing.

'Till I talked to you this week I thought you'd known. Cara gave me the impression . . .'

'I did in general. I didn't want to know the particulars, like who.'

Jo leaned her head on her knuckles. 'What you two had was so, so permanent, I honestly didn't think you cared about little casual . . .'

'I mightn't have cared if she was still alive.'

She nodded.

I breathed out, and couldn't find any more anger. 'I've never quite understood,' I said, 'how anyone could sleep with Cara and keep it casual. I mean, I've always found her the most extraordinary person. Didn't you?'

After a moment's reflection, Jo said, 'I thought she was a bit of a dipstick, actually.'

I was first to laugh, then after a few seconds she joined in. 'Didn't you find her mystical?' I asked through my coughs of merriment. 'Irresistible? Enduringly, erotically fascinating?'

'Nope.'

'Oh well, I must be the only one then.'

'Afraid so.' After a minute, Jo turned sideways on the bed and leaned her hair against a painted knot in the wallpaper. 'You know, I never felt guilty about the casualness of it before. But now it seems a shame that Cara and I didn't share some grand passion. We basically just had a bit of fun with playfights and foot massages.'

'So if you'd known she was going to die young you'd have done the decent thing and fallen in love with her?'

'Nah, I doubt I'd have managed that. With all due respect, Pen, the woman was a nutcase.'

'I suppose so.' A yawn came from nowhere and opened my throat.

'Have a wee nap now,' said Jo, standing up and lifting my feet on to the bed. I slid down until my head was half-buried under the pillow. I could feel Jo loosening my shoelaces and tugging on the shoes until they came off. I could have helped her by bracing my feet, but I was too tired. She took down another duvet and laid it over me. Then the light went off and the door shut. I decided I was probably too tired to sleep, but would have a little rest before going home and correcting some more copybooks. Then the dark came down and ironed me flat.

In my dream I am leaning over her sleeping ear, wide awake.

Cara, my fairly faithful flooze, now is the time I could be really jealous, and now is the time that jealousy floats out of my grasp. How can I make a fuss about not being the last to see you, when you were coming straight home to me? How can I fret about who kissed or didn't kiss you, when you are lying in a box in the mud with all our kisses falling off you like shed skins?

I am only thirty, I will not spend the rest of my life mourning you. There was nothing special about you; I could make up other stories. Don't kiss me until I'm asleep. Get your claws out of my hair.

Then I am back in the dream of the hole in the hedge and the garden with its pale summer-house. But the scene is warmer, the trimmed hedge is sprouting, there are buttercups along the edge of the lawn. I catch sight of Cara in the maze, all brocade breeches and flying ribbons. I run after her, but get distracted by a huge hooped dress disappearing round a corner. Does death wear a dress, then, and is there any give in her flesh?

I run and run till my lungs are burning up, and finally corner her. She turns, her gauzy hood falling back. Was I expecting decay behind a mask of powder, or the grin of bone? She has my face. It is my own face that looks back at me, almost understandingly. Then she turns and runs on, after Cara. I can hear their laughter in the distance.

I woke slowly. It was still dark. My eyes flickered open but the rest of my muscles stayed flat. This had to be what a kite felt like as it was tugged into the sky.

The door opened, and a cup of tea came through, with Jo behind it. She was still wearing the same cotton jumper. 'Is it morning yet?' I whispered.

She looked confused. 'It's only about half nine; I didn't think you should sleep too long or you won't be able to tonight.'

I sat up and, dizzy, leaned against the wall. Jo tucked the duvet round me and gave me the cup of tea. 'How you doing?' she asked, sitting on the edge of the bed.

'I'm all right. Sorry to be so pathetic.'

'You're not.'

'Well, ranting and raving and having to be put to bed . . .'

'Ah, don't be so scared of showing a bit of human need.'

'Yeah, but you shouldn't have to look after me, it's not like we're old friends.'

'So where's the queue of your old friends?' asked Jo, resting one ankle on the other knee.

I turned my head away.

'I'm not being a bitch, I just think you need a few more. I'm here, and god knows I'm old enough.'

I took a long swallow of tea, though it scorched my throat. 'I hate being weak,' I said between my teeth.

'Look, you're not weak just because you're not a bloody monolith.'

I blinked up at her.

'Besides,' said Jo, 'I wouldn't mind building up some credit by looking after you a bit. Any week now I'm likely to hit the winter blues, and it'll be me doing the leaning, and I need someone a bit older and wiser than the babelettes I share a house with.'

'I'm only thirty, you know,' I told her.

'Yeah, but you've always seemed more solid than the others.'

'That's just my size. People have always treated me a year older for every pound I put on. At fifty I'm going to start fasting and the years will slide from my hips.'

Jo grinned, and took a mouthful from my mug.

I let my head loll back against the wallpaper. I ran my hand over it. That was how automatic love became; the dry ripple under fingertips. 'I talk to her, you know,' I said.

After a tiny pause Jo said, 'Cara?'

'But it's like talking to God. You have to sort of guess the answers. Pick up the mood.'

A tiny snort. 'I gave all that prayer business up decades ago,' said Jo. 'Decided it was all in my head.'

'Well, of course. Everything's in our heads.'

'No, but I mean it wasn't real.'

My jaw cracked wide in a yawn. 'None of this is real. All that's real so far is that my girlfriend's not back from holiday yet and I miss her,' I said with my eyes shut. 'I'm going to be so bloody lonely this winter.'

'No,' said Jo sternly. 'One or the other, take your pick, but not both.'

I stared at her.

'Ah, come on, you know that real loneliness is having no one to miss. Think yourself lucky you've known something worth missing.'

I said nothing for a long time.

'You took it better than I thought you would,' Jo resumed more brightly. 'About me and Cara. A couple of days ago you had me really scared.'

I gave her a small smile.

'It really wasn't that big a deal,' she repeated. 'Like, I've been to bed with most of the women at this party at one time or another.'

'Seriously?'

'Fiona calls me Fat Slag.'

'You let her?'

'She's got ex's privilege. Anyway, ever since their tenth anniversary party I've been calling her and Sinéad the Role Model Couple, which really pisses them off.'

'I never guessed you had such a reputation,' I teased her.

'Ah, I blame my irresistible bosoms.'

'Not a patch on mine,' I murmured, breathing in to inflate them.

Jo let out a little wisp of laughter. 'So,' she asked after a minute, 'is the sister still around?'

'No, she went off . . . just last night actually. It seems longer.'

'Did you make up your mind about her?'

'What about her?' I asked.

'Just, what she's like?'

'She's all right. Not how I remembered, much more ordinary. I don't think we live on the same planet,' I added after some reflection. 'Like, I told her this story about a friend of a friend who went down the country one December and said, "Mam, I'm a lesbian." Her mother stiffened and asked, "Does that mean you won't be having turkey for Christmas?"'

304

Jo gave a chuckle.

'But Kate didn't get it. She asked whether it was generally thought that all lesbians were also vegetarians. I said it was worse than that, that the mother didn't even recognize the word. She said, "Oh."'

'Mmm. I've never figured out what to do with people who just say "Oh."' After a minute Jo added, 'You know, the exact same thing happened to a friend of a friend of a friend of mine too. Maybe it's a rural myth.'

'More likely it's the same woman. That friend of a friend of a friend of yours is probably friends with my friend's friend.'

'If you're going to get delirious I'll have to fetch the restraints . . .'

'No, nurse, please, I'll be good.'

Jo stood up and yawned. The desk lamp cast her huge shadow across the walls. 'We were thinking of going to the pub about half an hour ago.'

'I'm going over to my mother's,' I said, and realized that it was true.

We all stood around in the hall like bomb survivors. I collected my basket and jacket. On the doorstep, Jo turned and said, 'By the way, there's a place coming up here when Sherry goes to Thailand, if you'd any interest in applying . . .'

'Thanks,' I said. 'But I'm staying where I am for the moment.'

'Well, you can always drop by for toast parties.'

'Will do.'

She wrapped her arms around me for a minute. Unseen hands patted me as they went by. Jo found me my umbrella, and then I was away, unlocking my car.

On the way through the barely lit suburban streets, I had to steer carefully. Every tree seemed to call to me; crashing seemed so inevitable. I concentrated on getting through to the northside without entangling myself in the one-way system.

At one point I realized that this was the road towards Glasnevin. I wondered did they lock the graveyard at night? Were they troubled by Heathcliff types refusing to leave at the end of the day, stretching themselves on the fresh graves of their split-aparts? The last thing I wanted was to become melodramatic, an embarrassment to my friends. Yet I could see the appeal of scrabbling down through loose earth until you felt the wood against your nails. Rossetti buried his poems with Lizzie, then regretted the extravagance, and had them dug up; they said her scalding hair had grown to fill the coffin. I wondered whether the poems read differently, after he had tugged them free of her posthumous tangles.

I hadn't told Mammy I was coming over. I rarely did. Wasn't it awful how we assumed that our mothers, unlike our friends, were always in? We said things like 'You should get out more,' but if we turned up and they weren't there, how approving would we be?

I parked on the kerb, blocking half of the pavement outside my grandmother's two-up-two-down. This was the narrow house I had started from; how far I had come from it, and how far back. Minnie's engine sighed to a halt. The panoply of pollution tinged the sky. Down the end of the street was an indigo skyline of chimneys against the orange night; it was jagged, like the graph of a heartbeat in the last minutes before it smooths out.

I thought I was coming empty-handed, but the basket turned out to have two biscuits still in it, hidden under the napkin; I wrapped them up and put them in the pocket of my cardigan. The light was on in the kitchen where my mother stuffed and addressed envelopes till late into the night. She was good at this second job; she had reduced it to the fewest possible movements. I was often on at her to take a cut of my salary as some repayment for the years I spent as a mewling child taking a cut of hers. But she always said that debts didn't work that way, and each generation should be glad to raise and pay for the next. 'But Mammy,' I told her, 'I don't have children, so why can't I help you out instead?'

'Ah, your brother pays me rent.'

'And borrows it back the next night,' I reminded her.

Through the net curtain I could see the warm light and a figure at the table. (Cara loathed net curtains, until I explained to her that it was the only way of getting privacy in a house that opened directly on to the road.) My mother's bird-shape was unmistakable; I took after my father instead, a solid man with spade-worn hands.

I had a key, but I preferred to ring when my mother was downstairs, so that she would feel like the mistress of her own house at last. Also I liked the moment when I stood on the mat that said 'WELCOME' in worn letters and she opened the door. We never hugged, since I'd pushed her away in sullen puberty, but her eyes were just as good.

Mammy took a while to answer the chime tonight. Her face wrinkled gladly when she saw who it was. She had her red glass beads on. I didn't know how many times they had been burst by a baby's clutch, how many times she had restrung them herself on invisible thread, each time missing a couple that had rolled under the skirting-board, so the circle gradually narrowed around her throat.

'All on your own tonight?' I asked her.

'Peace and quiet. Gavin will be in later, though.'

My mother led me into the dining-room, where a pool of light covered the scarred table. No envelopes nor reading glasses tonight, just a large mug of tea.

'Will you have a cup?'

'If it's in the pot.' This was a ritual answer. We both knew that she made tea with a bag in each mug.

All these familiar lines made it so difficult to begin anything new. I wondered whether I would tell the tale logically and chronologically, by starting with my realization of my true nature (play the genetic card), then mentioning my relationship with Cara, then tempering my mother's outrage with sympathy by blurting out something about the accident.

Or maybe I should begin with my loss of a housemate, getting my mother on my side, then reveal the lovers business and hope that she would be unable to bring herself to reject me at such a time. Or tell her about the death now and the thirteen years of life together some other time? Or vice versa. Or I could always tell her nothing at all except for school, weather, supermarket bargains. If I chose I could let my mother slide farther and farther away from me down a white tunnel.

I rested my fists on the table. There were crumbs caught in some of the wider cracks. I used to sit here for hours when I was small, with the tin of Plasticine to keep me out of my mother's hair. Other children modelled their doggies and baskets and faces, then mashed them together, but I kept all my colours wrapped separately. What I liked best was to plait worms of three different shades, then smear them together, roll and twist and repeat, and keep slicing the ball open with my penknife to check for unevenness of texture or colour. Eventually the work always smoothed the Plasticine into a perfect dull brown.

A short cough from my mother made me look through to the kitchen. She was leaning over the sink. Lying was too easy; this particular closet door came prefabricated, with smooth edges and a sealed diamond window. I almost wished my secret was visible: a brand on the forehead, say, from Cara's last kiss as she struggled out of sleep to kiss me goodbye the morning she was going to the airport. But no, nothing showed at all, as I sat down in the chair still warm from my mother's thighs.

I had never been this tired in all my life. I tugged the sailboat out from under my collar. I leaned my elbows on the table and let my fingers drag on the crisp gold. I wanted to shut my eyes and float away on it, past the neck of the woods, down the estuary, out to sea.

'That's pretty. Is it a leaf?' My mother had come back in with that awful *Beloved Daughter* mug. Her hands had light brown blotches on them.

'A boat.' How had she never seen it before? Had I always buttoned up my clothes to the neck?

'New?'

All at once I couldn't stomach another lie. 'No.'

'Where d'you get it?'

She was only making conversation. I could easily gloss over it, and in a couple of decades she would be dead and need never know.

'It's a very long story.' The words glided out of my mouth, surprising me. 'I'll tell you when the tea's made.'

This birth is long overdue, mother. It'll be a tight squeeze. You'd better open your arms to this screaming red bundle, because it's the only one I'll ever bring you.

'Grand,' she said. 'I'll open a packet of biscuits.'

'I've a couple of home-made ones left over,' I said, extricating them from my pocket in their napkin.

'Forgot the milk,' murmured my mother, going back into the kitchen for the jug with its beaded veil.

All of a sudden I couldn't see; my mother slid into a fish shape, the table melted into a pool. It had been so long, I'd forgotten what tears felt like. The first drop touched the skin under my eye as the sky opened and sent down the rain.